The scrape of leather on the floor interrupted Drake's thoughts

In the mirror behind the bar, he observed a young woman sitting next to him. Even in this dim lighting, her hair gleamed like metal. Dye job or a wig. She wore so much eye makeup he couldn't tell the color of her eyes.

His gaze dropped to her top—what little there was of it. A flicker of heat leaped in his chest as he caught the outline of her breasts straining the red, white and blue material.

She looked like a Fourth of July celebration about to pop.

"Like my top?" she asked in a Southern drawl.

He picked up her signals more clearly than if she'd banged a gong in his ear. Just because he picked them up didn't mean he had to respond. Nope. He'd mind his own business and ignore her.

"It goes with my skirt," she continued as though it were a two-way conversation.

He knew better than to look, but it was like telling Bambi to stay out of the forest. The skirt was thigh high and red. Below it, shapely legs in fishnet stockings ended in a pair of black stiletto heels with some kind of symbol on the side.

"It's a fleur de lis," she explained, pointing at her shoe with a frosty-pink fingernail, "for my boys, the Saints." She grinned so wide, he saw she had a slightly crooked front tooth, which almost gave her a sweet, naive quality.

Clunk.

He looked stupidly at his phone lying on the floor and wondered when he'd let go.

Dear Reader,

I had so much fun writing *Sleepless in Las Vegas,* which follows up on the story of Val LeRoy, the best friend of Cammie Copello, the heroine in *The Next Right Thing* (Harlequin Superromance, March 2013).

I relate to Val, who has her heart set on being a private investigator. Nearly ten years ago, I had that same goal, and like Val, I had only a general idea what P.I.'s did when I started my internship. It's one thing to watch Jessica Fletcher, the female sleuth in the old TV series *Murder, She Wrote,* or Nora Charles, the other half of the Nick and Nora private-eye team in *The Thin Man* film series. But it's a *whole other reality* when you're working a case undercover, trying to blend into your surroundings, hoping you don't blow it! An experience Val and I share, by the way.

One reason I so enjoy writing for the Harlequin Superromance line is that the stories, like life, thrive on romance, family and love. The hero in this story, Las Vegas private investigator Drake Morgan, has given up on finding love, but Val hasn't...for the most part, anyway. Although they share a passion for their profession, they seem to have nothing in common in their personal worlds. Their story is about two very different people, a case of opposites attracting, who struggle with giving and receiving, contentment and heartbreak. What they gradually learn is their hearts have more in common than they realize.

I love to hear from readers, so I invite you to drop by my website, colleencollinsbooks.com, and let me know how you liked Val and Drake's story!

Happy reading,

Colleen Collins

COLLEEN
COLLINS

—

Sleepless in Las Vegas

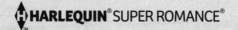
HARLEQUIN® SUPER ROMANCE®

Recycling programs
for this product may
not exist in your area.

ISBN-13: 978-0-373-60817-1

SLEEPLESS IN LAS VEGAS

Copyright © 2013 by Colleen Collins

Printed in U.S.A.

ABOUT THE AUTHOR

Colleen Collins has written several dozen novels and two nonfiction books. She has also written articles for various writing organizations, including the Private Eye Writers of America and Romance Writers of America, and for periodicals such as *USA TODAY* and *PI Magazine*. Similar to the P.I.-intern Val LeRoy in *Sleepless in Las Vegas,* Colleen began her P.I. career being mentored by a man who drove her crazy at times—and vice versa—but they're still together over a decade later.

Books by Colleen Collins

HARLEQUIN SUPERROMANCE

HARLEQUIN BLAZE

Other titles by this author available in ebook format.

To Elle Kaufman, with love

CHAPTER ONE

THE PHONE RANG, giving Val LeRoy a start. If it rang more than once or twice a day at Diamond Investigations, maybe she'd get used to its high-pitched jangle.

She swallowed the last bite of her lunchtime tuna-with-chutney sandwich while checking the caller ID. No name, but a 219 area code. She had been trying to memorize different area codes—after all, a phone was a private investigator's most powerful tool. She wasn't a P.I. yet, but when the day came, she wanted to be a knowledge bank in stilettos.

This incoming call was from…Michigan? No, Indiana. As she reached for the receiver, she noticed a glob of papaya chutney on her fingers.

Another jangling ring.

She didn't want to sticky up the phone with her gooey fingers, but Jayne Diamond, her boss, insisted Val always answer using the handset, never putting the phone on speaker, to maintain the confidentiality of conversations. Rules, rules, rules. That woman had more than a reform school. Val had to remind herself constantly that being mentored by one of the best investigators in Las Vegas was worth all the restrictions.

Keeping in mind the confidentiality of the call, she

glanced through the picture window next to the agency's front door, which offered a view of their business parking lot and the sidewalk beyond. Their office was a renovated corner bungalow on a street with other similar bungalows. Not a high-traffic area. Although they sometimes had walk-ins, nobody was headed toward the agency on foot, and the only car in the lot was Jayne's shiny Mazda Miata.

She glanced at Jayne's office door. Closed.

Val rapped the speaker button with her knuckle.

"Diamond Investigations," she answered softly, plucking a tissue from the box on her desk.

"Uh, are you a private investigator?" The man's voice was low, hesitant.

"Yes." Technically an apprentice, but Jayne didn't want her saying that to potential clients. So Val could answer yes to such a question, but the truth was she'd done little else other than screen calls these first few months of her internship.

"I…think my wife's…having an affair."

Have mercy, a brokenhearted tale was on its way. She wiped her fingers with the tissue. "I'm sorry to hear that. What's your name, sir?"

"George. My wife's name is…Sandy." He cleared his throat. "She started acting different about four months ago…in April, around our anniversary…doing things like walking into the other room to answer her cell, losing weight, buying new clothes. I suppose I coulda justified some of that, but when she started working later and later…"

Val watched a bright orange angelfish dart around rocks in the aquarium against the far wall, guessing what was coming next—Sandy was traveling to Las Vegas for A, a business trip; B, to visit family; C, to see old friends....

"Anyhoo..." He blew out a puff of breath. "Sandy is flying to Las Vegas later next week—on Friday, August sixteen—for a reunion...some kind of hookup with her cheerleader buddies from high school..."

Or another kind of hookup.

"And..." His voice grew thin. "I was wondering if..."

A P.I. could follow Sandy while she's in Sin City.

"You could follow her?"

"We offer such services," she affirmed. Val couldn't wait for the day when she could just say yes and take on a case. But for now, she only passed on callers' information to Jayne, who would make the final decision.

"I know the hotel my wife will be at...she mentioned renting a Dodge Charger..."

Ever since meeting her best pal, Cammie, a real-life P.I., a year ago, and hearing her stories about sitting on stakeouts, digging through trash to find evidence, interviewing witnesses to crimes, Val wanted nothing more than to be a private eye, too. But first, she needed to earn a Nevada license, which required logging ten thousand hours of investigative experience. After that, the plan had been for Val to become a student Watson to Cammie's Sherlock in their own kick-ass, all-girl Las Vegas agency.

Val had to make adjustments to the plan when Cammie found true love and moved to Denver, but she hadn't given up.

Jayne's door creaked open, followed by the tap-tap of her sensible heels across the hardwood floor.

Which stopped abruptly at Val's desk.

"…I could describe what clothes she'll be bringing, jewelry, too, although…" George sniffed loudly. "I guess she might not be wearing her wedding ring…"

Val looked up at her boss, a trim sixtysomething with cut-glass cheekbones and gray-blue eyes that always seemed to carry within them a withering understanding of the human condition.

Jayne shot one of those withering looks at the phone, back to Val.

Who shrugged apologetically. She could almost hear another "you can't always do things your way" lecture.

"I had that ring made special for her…" George stifled a sob.

Jayne mouthed a silent "no" while plucking a ballpoint pen from the breast pocket of her linen blazer, the same bloodless color as her short, bobbed hair. The blazer used to fit her better before she started losing weight recently.

Jayne jotted something on a notepad on the desk and held it up for Val to read: no infidelity cases.

Val nodded, waiting for George to calm down.

"Unfortunately," she said gently, "we're currently not accepting infidelity cases."

After a moment of uncomfortable silence, during which the hum of the aquarium pump filled the room, Val added, "Let me give you the number of another P.I. who might be able to help you."

After looking up the information on her computer, she gave him the number and ended the call.

Then she rolled her gaze up to Jayne's.

"You cannot always do things your way," the older woman began, arching a pale eyebrow. "Although I admire your strength of will and creativity—" she glanced at Val's purple-streaked black hair, which today she'd knotted into a loose chignon "—you have a habit of forgetting that investigations are not always about autonomy. Often you must work closely with people. Even if you disagree with them or believe you have a more advantageous idea, it would behoove you to treat others' suggestions with respect."

Sometimes she wondered why Jayne always made it sound as though Val were interacting unbehoovingly with some nameless third party and not Jayne herself. But then, her boss had a way of distancing herself, as though she was always observing the world rather than living in it.

"Yes, indeed," Val agreed, "I knew better than to put that call on speaker. Although, if you don't mind my adding a side note, nobody was in the room with me, so it wasn't like I was broadcasting the poor man's broken heart to strangers."

A look that might pass for amusement flittered across the older woman's face. "Sometimes I wonder if we should post my rules alongside your side notes."

The older woman reminded Val of the English actress Helen Mirren—formidable, sophisticated, articulate. But whereas the actress had played her share of industrial-strength women in the movies, Jayne was the real deal. In a *Las Vegas Sun* interview three months ago, a reporter had referred to her as "one of the best sleuths in Sin City," and that "a new P.I. earning Jayne's Diamond Grade designation is like a restaurant earning a Michelin star rating."

After reading that *Sun* article, there was only one P.I. Val wanted to be her mentor—Jayne Diamond.

Who now stood in front of her, lips pursed in thought. "What else is on your mind?"

"Well, these landline phones are—" *older than dirt* "—quite antiquated. Plus, cradling a jumbo-size receiver under my chin while taking notes, looking up information on the computer and talking is like juggling pancakes—hard to keep a grip on everything. It would make *so* much more sense if we used cell phones."

"Cell phones have speakers, too. The point is not landline versus mobile, it is about confidentiality."

"Yes, ma'am."

"Jayne."

"Yes, Jayne."

"Also…" She smiled, but it looked more like a grimace. "I've reached the conclusion that Diamond

Investigations needs to reduce the number of cases it accepts. Starting today, we no longer accept infidelity cases, except if they are part of an investigation that we are already conducting for a law firm."

"But…I thought infidelity investigations were steady business for a P.I. agency. Although, of course, we don't accept honey traps."

When she realized she wanted to be a private eye, Val started religiously watching the reality TV show *Honey Catchers* to learn about the business. It featured hot-looking private eyes, male and female, whom people hired to set "honey traps" to test their lovers' fidelity. The P.I., dressed in some sexy outfit rigged with a covert camera, would "accidentally" run into the lover, usually at a bar, and strike up a conversation. Eventually, the P.I. asked for a phone number, a date or even got a little frisky on the spot.

Afterward, the P.I. would show the video to the client. *Honey Catchers* never showed lovers turning down phone numbers or sexual advances. Which made for a lot of high drama at the end of the shows as the cheated upon confronted the cheater.

"Infidelity investigations can be lucrative, certainly, but we have *never* conducted honey traps."

"I know…it's just that I don't see the harm in accepting those cases as long as we keep them legal…" Something in Jayne's face—exhaustion? Distress?—gave Val pause. "We don't need to do a mentoring session right now if you're tired."

Jayne eased into one of the high-back wooden

guest chairs that faced Val's desk. Through the window blinds, hazy sunlight striped the side of her face, highlighting fine lines around her mouth and eyes. "These moments always count, dear."

She couldn't think of a single time that Jayne had uttered an endearment, for Val or anyone else.

"Legal," Jayne repeated. She reflected on that for a moment. "Some agencies seem to believe that *inducing* the behavior a P.I. should be attempting to *objectively* document is acceptable. It is not. If a law enforcement officer behaved in such a manner, it would be called entrapment."

"On some reality cop shows, I've seen female cops dress like hookers and lure men, who are then arrested for soliciting prostitution."

"But those men, when they withdraw their billfolds to pay, exhibit *prior* predispositions. Honey traps are not telling of the subject's predisposition. A lawyer could easily attack such frivolous evidence in court."

As Jayne pushed a wisp of hair off her forehead, Val noticed her hand shook slightly. But she knew not to ask questions because Jayne didn't like to talk about herself.

Val had learned that well in June, the first time she walked into Diamond Investigations. She had barely shut the door before Jayne made it clear that Val had already broken a rule—clearly stated on the agency website—that people seeking internships were to *mail* their résumés, not show up in person. Besides, she had curtly added, she was on her way out.

When she swung her purse over her shoulder, the bag knocked a figurine off a side table. Val dived, catching it before it smashed into pieces on the floor.

As she'd stared at the miniature crystal figure—two birds perched side by side on a watering bowl—she swore she felt something faint, like a light passing through her. Although maybe what she experienced had more to do with the tender, yet sad, look on her future boss's face. For a moment, she and Jayne had shared concern and relief that the crystal birds hadn't hit the floor and shattered.

After Jayne gently placed the figurine on the top shelf of the bookcase—where it remained to this day—she asked Val why she wanted to be a private investigator. She had answered that she worked well alone, liked solving puzzles and wanted to help people.

Jayne had actually laughed. "If you can accept that this business is often driven by greed, revenge and self-preservation," she said, "you will be better off. Shall we start your internship next Monday?"

And here they were, two months later, having yet another of their question-and-answer sessions.

Jayne stood, picked up her purse. "I will be gone the remainder of the afternoon." After a moment of deliberation, she added, "I have changed my mind. For the time being, we are not accepting *any* new cases until I finalize some…cases I'm working on. Are you still commuting by bus?"

"Yes." Ever since the brakes and fuel pump went

south on Val's fifteen-year-old Toyota, she had been relying on mass transit. "Mornings are okay, but after five those buses are slower than a bread wagon with biscuit wheels."

Jayne blinked. "I have never heard that expression."

"Means they're slow."

That pained smile again. "Feel free to close at four. See you tomorrow."

She watched the older woman leave, not believing that line about finalizing other cases. When Val first started here, the agency carried ten to twelve cases, easy. Currently there were three open cases, two of which were on hold while lawyers decided whether to go to trial. The third involved pulling court records, which took an hour or two. If anything, the agency needed more cases.

No, Jayne was hiding something. From the recent tiredness in her face and the weight loss, Val wondered what her boss was going through. A death in the family? A financial setback?

She glanced at the crystal figurine. This small object had always seemed too fragile in an office furnished with a heavy wooden desk, bookcases, a grandfather clock and scuffed hardwood floors. The birds obviously held deep meaning. Shame Jayne didn't take it home with her, both for its safekeeping and her own comfort.

Val looked at the picture of her nanny on the corner of the desk. Her grandmother—smiling, her white hair freshly curled, wearing her favorite blue dress—

stood in front of her tiny antiques shop, Back in Time Antiques, on Chartres Street in the French Quarter. When Val was growing up, she had commuted with Nanny to the shop from their house in the Ninth Ward, the only home Val had ever known before Katrina.

She had brought the photo to work maybe for the same reason Jayne kept the figurine here. Some objects carried too many memories to keep at home, where your mind could easily wander to the past, to what was lost and never found again.

THE GRANDFATHER CLOCK chimed four o'clock. As the last metallic note faded, the front door opened and a woman walked in, her perfume smelling faintly like strawberries.

She wore a red halter dress, cut too low, and matching lipstick. Her chestnut hair hung sleek with straight-cut bangs that hovered over almond-shaped eyes. Most walk-ins looked embarrassed, nervous or dubious, but this woman looked determined or surprised, which could just be the unfavorable effect of those over-arched Cruella eyebrows.

Without a word, she sat in one of the guest chairs and crossed her slim legs. Val took note of strappy Badgley Mischka sandals, which she guessed were the real deal based on the monster-size bling on the woman's ring finger.

"My name Marta," she said, rolling the *r* in her name. "My fiancé, I think he cheats. I want you to find out."

Val tried to place the thick accent. Romanian? "I'm sorry," she said, "but we're currently not accepting any new cases."

Under a veil of thick black lashes, a pair of hazel eyes coolly assessed Val. After a beat, she reached into her purse and extracted a wad of bills bound with a rubber band.

"I pay thousand dollars." Which sounded like *I pay zouzand dolarz.* She set it on the edge of the desk.

"I'm sorry, but—"

"Tonight," Marta interrupted, "I know where he goes. I give address, you see if he cheats."

This woman did not want to take no for an answer.

Val recalled the name of the P.I. she'd looked up earlier. "Bert Warner, just a few blocks away, handles infidelity cases. I can get you his number—"

"No man investigator. Want you to dress up, see if he flirts with you."

"Sorry, that's a honey trap, and we never do those." She was being good reciting the party line, but dang, this kind of work could be profitable.

"Honey trap," Marta repeated slowly, then smiled, as though liking how the word tasted. She pulled out *another* wad of bills and set it on the desk. "Two thousand."

This is how it would be someday when Val ran her own agency. A client would walk in, discuss their problem and Val could say yes, I'll take your case. And she'd do one helluva good job, too.

She stared at the two grand, cash.

What was so wrong with honey traps anyway? Jayne talked about lawyers attacking the evidence, but wasn't that what lawyers did in courtrooms for any type of case? Didn't mean honey trapping was *illegal*. Cops did it, other P.I.s did it.

Jayne was also an older woman. Obviously she couldn't conduct a honey trap herself. But Val was young, could pull it off. She had learned a lot watching all those hours of *Honey Catchers*.

No. She had to stop thinking this way. She had to abide by agency policy. Rules were rules. Even if she disagreed with some of them.

She stared at the wads of bills. Two grand, *cash*.

Enough to cover a new fuel pump, brakes, with plenty left over to toss into the kitty for the day when she moved out of her cousin's place into her own.

Marta leaned forward, emotion shining in her eyes. "I come to United States from Russia. I clean houses, make better my English. Now I work in dress store, want to have own business someday. Did not want to fall in love, but…" She shrugged. "He ask me to marry. I say yes, then I hear about other women…" Her chin trembled.

Val nudged the tissue box toward her. "Maybe," she said gently, "you should talk to him. Tell him what others have told you."

Marta took a tissue, dabbed the corner of her eye. "*Da*. Yes. I do. He say no, people lie." A tear spilled down her cheek. "I must know. Please. Help me."

Boy, oh, boy, could Val relate to starting over. After

Katrina, starting over became the story of her life. After a short stay in the Superdome, Val had relocated to Houston, where FEMA paid her rent for a studio apartment while she looked for work. Maybe if she had felt connected to the city, or at least *known* somebody, it might have worked out. But there were days she hadn't even been able to get out of bed, much less tackle job hunting. When she moved to Las Vegas, at least she had family, but it was still tough learning her way around a new city, finding a job, making friends.

If she had also been forced to learn a new culture and language, she would have lost her marbles.

"I'm sorry. It must have been very difficult."

"I don't want person…persons…to know I hire private eye." Marta leaned forward and whispered, "Only you and me to know."

Val blew out a pent-up breath. It'd be sweet to drive her air-conditioned car again. No more walking in summer triple-digit heat, fighting for seats on crowded buses. She stared at the money. The beauty of cash was nobody could trace it, and this being a one-time gig…she felt a stab of guilt at what she was thinking, but…Jayne would never know.

Besides, one day Val would own her own agency, and maybe she would accept the occasional honeytrap case. This was her chance to gain experience, something she'd never get while interning with Jayne.

"Just you and me to ever know," Marta repeated.

Val glanced at the photo of Nanny. By the time she was fifteen, she and her grandmother had swapped their parent-child roles. Val grew accustomed to making decisions for the two of them, often on the fly. Sometimes it was like walking into mist—she might not be sure what her next step would be, but she would learn. Over time, when faced with a choice, she discovered she gained more by forging ahead than standing, undecided, at the crossroads.

She picked up a pen, shoving aside her niggling conscience. "I need to get some information, like where he's going tonight, the type of car he drives…"

AT NINE O'CLOCK that night, Drake Morgan stepped from the air-conditioned strip club, Topaz, into the outdoor sauna called summer. In his thirty-two years born and raised in Las Vegas, he'd never grown accustomed to these mind-frying temps. But then, there was a lot he'd never been able to accept.

Like why his brother Brax—the manager of Topaz—kept associating with known criminals. Drake had checked the corporate papers for Topaz and discovered the club was owned by a corporation named Dusha, the same corporate entity that owned Braxton's luxury condo. Drake ran the word *Dusha* through an online translator and learned it meant "soul" in Russian.

Yeah, real soulful. His brother was tight with the Russian mob.

Tugging off his suit jacket, he looked past the stream of traffic on Las Vegas Boulevard at Dino's Lounge, a watering hole his dad had frequented. Back before lines got drawn and doors were closed, Drake and Braxton would join him there to watch a game, shoot some pool. He and his brother had been tight then. *Thick as thieves,* their dad would say.

Today, the third anniversary of their old man's death, Drake had thought a lot about things his father used to say. Sometimes he had to dig deep in his memories, because his dad hadn't been comfortable expressing himself. Oh, he liked to kid around, jaw about some news item or what sports figure had hit a milestone, but when it came to divulging how he felt about something, or even saying a simple "I love you," he had struggled with the words.

On his deathbed, he had asked for three promises from Drake. The first was for Drake to stop gambling. He had, that very day. The second was for Drake to learn how to swim—he had carried the name "Aqua Man" since high school after jumping into a pool to save a bikini-clad damsel in distress. She'd gotten out fine on her own. Took two lifeguards to haul Drake out of the water.

Just like his dad to throw humor into life's darker situations. Aqua Man took a few swimming lessons.

The third promise was to take care of his grandmother, his mother and especially his brother. His mom and Grams were easy, his brother was a pain in the ass. Drake had asked Brax to dump his gangster chums and build his own business, but he'd refused. Seemed to think being under the thumb of that no-good scum Yuri Glazkov was the path to success.

Yuri, what a slick bastard. Brax had done things for him that should have put him behind bars, but Yuri's high-profile lawyers made sure the charges against Braxton didn't stick. It sickened Drake that his brother thought he was better than the law.

If he had his way, he'd do what their mother had done—close the door on Brax—but he had made that promise to their father.

So here he was tonight, hunting down his brother to check up on him, try to talk sense to him again about living his own, law-abiding life.

Drake had another reason, a personal one, to quiz his brother. Yuri, recently back in Vegas after an extended stay in Russia, was up to something. Drake could smell it. He wanted facts about the thug's life, the kind his brother could supply, because he had a score to settle.

But so far, all Drake had gotten was the runaround from his brother's employees at the strip club.

Have no idea where Brax is at, man.

Mr. Morgan is unavailable. If you would like to leave your name and number, I'll be sure he gets the message.

Yuri? Never heard of 'im.

Tossing his jacket over his shoulder, Drake glanced across the street at the green neon sign. Last Neighborhood Bar in Las Vegas. Lots of businesses had closed during the recession, but Dino's Lounge had stayed open, just as it had for five decades.

He decided to walk over, leave his pickup parked in

its secluded spot. Later, he would head back to Topaz, and if he didn't find his brother's car in the lot, he'd do the question routine again. Try different employees, see if one of them might get hit with a pang of conscience and tell the truth. He'd help that pang along with a bill or two.

Because in a town like Vegas, everything had a price. Especially an honest answer.

VAL SAT IN the rental car, a Honda Civic, in the Topaz lot, watching the guy standing outside the strip club. He fit the description Marta had given her earlier: a little over six foot. Buzz cut. Wearing a suit. Before he removed the jacket, the gray two-button number had looked like something Don Draper might have worn on that TV series *Mad Men*. From the way this guy walked—carrying himself like he owned his space and some of everybody else's, too—he had more than his share of mettle.

Marta said his name was Drake, but didn't want to divulge his last name. Even after Val recited the confidentiality spiel she'd heard Jayne give to new clients, Marta refused. Said she had her pride. No last names. Besides, couldn't Val do the honey trap without knowing that?

Val had agreed, partially because she wasn't sure what else to do…and then there was the money.

Drake headed toward the street.

Time to report in. Val reached for her cell phone and punched in a number.

"What news?" Marta answered. No hello. "I am anxious."

Join the club, Val felt like saying. Wearing this skimpy outfit and blond wig, which she had used at her last job as a card-dealing Christina Aguilera look-alike, and sitting on her first surveillance in a rough Vegas neighborhood outside a strip joint, was nerve-racking.

But she couldn't let on she was tense. Had to act cool, knowledgeable, as though this were her hundredth surveillance gig. After all, Marta thought she'd hired a professional, not an amateur.

"He left Topaz," Val said, "and he's walking toward Las Vegas Boulevard."

"Where he park?"

"At Baker's Service, one street over." A guy in a retro suit driving a '79 Ford pickup didn't fit Marta's sleek designer style. Val guessed they were one of those opposites-attract relationships.

"Baker's," Marta repeated.

"It's an appliance store."

After she observed him walking into Topaz, Val had circled the block and found the pickup parked in front of the store. The business was closed, its lot dark, and he'd taken the extra precaution to position it behind some palm trees.

After parking a short way down the block, she had walked back to the truck, a faded brown-and-gold two-tone with rusted chrome strips, and pointed her miniature flashlight into the bed, where she spied a toolbox, tarp, several chew toys and a small doggie bed. Next, she perched herself on the metal step below the driver's door—not easy in high heels—and pointed the light at the front seat. A closed notebook and coffee-stained foam cup were on the ripped vinyl seat. A video camera lay on the floorboard.

"How long he at club?" Marta asked.

"Forty minutes. Now he's crossing the street... there's only one bar over there, so that must be where he's going."

"You go to this bar."

Val looked at her outfit. The skimpy top and skirt could pass for a sexy summertime outfit, but fishnet stockings? They had seemed like a great addition when she thought she'd be conducting a honey trap outside a strip club, but they'd look sleazy, over the top, in a regular bar.

Even Vegas had its limits, didn't it?

Screw it. Sitting at the crossroads would get her nowhere. "I'll go."

She reminded herself that this was Sin City, the unconventional capital of the world. On a scale of one to ten on the weird scale, fishnet stockings were probably a five.

She slipped the cell into the pocket of her skirt and turned the ignition.

CHAPTER TWO

DRAKE SNAGGED A stool at the bar. Behind the lighted displays of bottles, the smudged wall mirror reflected hazy red pool table lights and the words Dino's: Getting Vegas Drunk Since 1962 in large white letters on a back wall.

His old man had groused when they had first painted that sign. "Makes the place sound like a bunch of blottos." By then in his seventies, he hung out most afternoons at Dino's with a group of fellow retirees who called themselves the Falstaff Boys, in honor of the "late, great" beer. But after the painting of the sign, they changed their name to "the Blottos."

"Well, look what the Mojave winds blew in." Sally, a thirtyish female bartender, stood behind the bar wiping dry a glass. She had small blue eyes set in a narrow face that could use some sun. She and Drake had a history that made him a bit uncomfortable.

The muscles in her arms flexed as she reached to set the glass in the overhead rack. Her black T-shirt crept up, exposing a faded tattoo on her side, a skull adorned with a crown of roses. She'd once told Drake it was from her Deadhead youth, but now that she was clean and sober she no longer listened to jam-band hogwash.

"Hasn't been too windy lately," Drake said.

"Yeah, just hot. Monsoon season is late this year. City could use a downpour or three. Fortunately, the air conditioner in this place is built like a tank." She tossed the towel over her shoulder. "Bud?"

He nodded, wondering when she'd cut her hair. These short, spiky styles on women confused him. He liked long hair on women. Long and straight, the simpler the better.

"Hey, Aqua Man."

He turned, recognized a buddy from high school. Still slim, but his face showed wear. He wore a gray shirt with "Easterman's Plumbing" on a pocket.

"Hey, Jackson," Drake said, "how's it going?"

"Got divorced." He shrugged. "You?"

"Never been married."

"Smart. How's your brother?"

"Fine."

"Married?"

"No."

"Smart." Jackson nodded. "Well, take it easy."

As he left the bar, Sally slid a bottle toward Drake. "Poor guy. Just got divorced."

"Figured it was still fresh. Thanks, Sally." He took a swig. The frothy chill soothed his mood a bit.

"Work keeping you busy?" She focused intently on washing another glass.

"Some."

"See Viva Las Arepas moved?"

The Venezuelan fast-food place had operated out of the kiosk in Dino's parking lot for several years. When he'd walked past, the place had been dark, its windows boarded, although a few stools remained outside. "Thought it had closed."

"No, moved to a bigger place in that strip mall down the street. Mr. Arellano's been driving a shiny new Hyundai, so they must be doing good."

"They survived."

"Yeah. Recession didn't kick their butt. Didn't kick Dino's, either."

He raised his beer. "To Dino's."

She picked up her tip glass and clinked it against his bottle. As he took a sip, she pointed to the framed photo over the cash register. "Some TV producer was in here the other day, saw the photo. Told her it was Dino and Benny."

"Benedict." Drake bristled at his father's nickname being tossed around by people who didn't know him.

"Kristin calls him Benny."

"Good friends, Benny. Everybody else, Benedict."

"Anyway, this TV producer was here 'cause they're thinking of filming a reality TV show at Dino's." She read his look. "I know, just what this place needs—more reality. Speaking of which, didja hear the story about one of our regulars…"

Her voice floated over his head as he stared at the faded color photo. Taken in '85, when Dino still had most of his hair. He stood next to a pool table with

Drake's dad, their arms slung around each other's shoulders, the two of them grinning at the camera. Guys from different generations, but they had a lot in common. Family men who believed in working hard and watching out for the little guy. Both veterans—Dino in World War II, his father in 'Nam—although neither had talked about those days.

Drake had followed the family tradition and joined the military, a career he'd thought would be for life, until 2006, when he'd returned home to help with his dad, who had been diagnosed with ALS. He worked in hotel security for a few years before opening his own one-man P.I. agency.

"...to this day, the wife still doesn't believe the girl accidentally fell asleep on her husband's car hood." Sally pulled in a long breath. "Now *that* would've made a good reality TV show."

He nodded as though he had been listening.

She offered a small, tight smile. "Good to see you again. Summer must bring in a lot of cases, huh?"

"The usual." He paused. "Sorry I didn't call."

With a nod, she turned her attention to washing.

After a few moments of awkward silence, filled with the pinging of video games and murmured conversations, she straightened and said, "That was a dumb stunt I pulled."

"No, Sally—"

"Yeah, it was. I mean, how juvenile can a lady get to write her phone number inside a matchbook and hand it to a guy, claiming he dropped it. I mean, a *bartender* pulling that old trick."

When she had passed him that matchbook, he had been busy texting a client, had paid little attention. Hadn't known the phone number was inside until days later, when he'd pulled the matchbook from his pocket. After running a reverse on the number and learning it was Sally's, he'd been surprised. Both at her feelings about him, and that he hadn't read the signals.

He blamed his surprise on being preoccupied with other issues. Had a lot of those weighing on his mind these days.

"No need to apologize. I was actually flattered."

One pencil-thin eyebrow arched. "Yeah?"

"Really. It's just...I'm not..."

"S'okay. No explanation necessary." She tugged the towel off her shoulder and began rubbing the same glass she'd just finished drying. Realizing it, she stopped and smiled a little sheepishly. "Gee, hard to guess I'm nervous."

"Glass still had a spot on it."

She smiled, a real one this time. "Friends?"

"Friends."

She placed the glass in the overhead rack. "How's that brother of yours?"

"Wish I knew." He took another swig.

She leaned forward and lowered her voice. "He gets a lot of business at Topaz. Nights when I close, that lot over there is packed. Limos lined up with tourists from all over the Strip. Guess that's why you're here tonight. Looking for him."

He nodded.

That's how they'd met eight months ago, when he'd wandered into Dino's one night for a beer. He'd learned she had recently been laid off from her floor supervisor job at the Riviera Casino, none too thrilled with her new job slinging drinks.

Because he had asked so many questions about the strip club across the street, it had only seemed fair to explain why. Otherwise, he didn't like to talk about Braxton.

"For a while, I didn't see that yellow Porsche of his," Sally continued, glancing at a young couple entering the bar, "but lately it's been parked in that same spot near Topaz's front entrance."

"What time?"

"Sometimes when I first get to work, around seven. More often when I close."

"About three a.m.?"

She nodded. "Sometimes four."

"Ever see a black four-door Mercedes?"

She thought for a moment. "Yeah, in the past week. Don't remember seeing it before that." The couple sat at the far end of the bar. "Gotta go. Customers."

Taking another swig, he weighed this new piece of information. He'd been tracking Yuri's black Mercedes for a little over a month now, whenever he had some down time. Had videotaped several hours of Yuri's comings and goings, hoping to capture clues of any illegal projects in the works, but so far, nothing pointed to anything. Had some footage of Yuri unloading tables at a warehouse, but he owned the tables *and* the warehouse, so nothing strange there.

Based on past experience, he wondered if Yuri might be planning a heist. He was good at those, just like the one he had set up years ago that had cost Drake his career, his reputation and a fiancée who'd grown skittish. Couldn't blame her. Hard to lean on someone who's standing in quicksand.

If he thought about it too long, he could still get pissed that his brother had played a role in that heist. Of course, Brax had said that he'd had no choice, that Yuri had threatened his life. Afterward, he had promised, over and over, he would have nothing more to do with the Russian.

They obviously placed different values on their promises.

Drake rolled the bottle between his palms, wishing Brax's deceit was the only problem weighing on him. When he had dropped by his mom's house this afternoon, he and his grandmother had talked about his dad, which led to stories of the family, which led to the family heirloom ring—a constellation of diamonds representing family marriages going back a hundred and fifty years. The ring was gone, and Grams missed it more than she liked to admit.

Drake blamed himself. It had been only a few weeks ago that Grams had finally told him the whole story of what had happened in 2009 when Drake's gambling debts had gotten him into trouble with a loan shark. Until then, he'd thought his dad had pulled money from a trust to help pay off the obligation— he'd had no idea the ring had been collateral.

In 2009, he had been a secret gambler, burying himself in debts. Desperate, he had borrowed money from Yuri. By the time the Russian had tacked on his extortionist interest rates, Drake's debt was hitting fifty grand. His father—who'd never said how he learned about Drake's troubles, although Drake guessed that Brax had told him—had insisted on helping. Said he could pay Yuri twenty grand, and a family friend could loan Drake the rest. His only condition was that he and Drake would keep Yuri's name between them. *Your mother's heart has already been broken by Braxton's dealings with that Russian.*

Since then, Drake had paid off the thirty grand to his dad's friend. He'd made payments to his dad, too, who'd secretly had his wife deposit every penny into a savings account in Drake's name. A few weeks ago, when Drake made the final payment to his mom, he'd been shocked when she handed over the savings account. His dad had asked his mom to do this, in memory of Benny, upon Drake's final payment. By honoring his debt, he'd earned it.

But his satisfaction had soured after Grams confided that she, his mom and his dad had given the ring to pay that twenty grand.

As soon as Drake had found out, he had gone to Yuri with the intention of buying back the family ring. The Russian had refused to take his money. Said Drake owed him even more in interest.

It shamed Drake that he'd caused his family to lose a cherished piece of their history. He would get the ring from Yuri, no matter what it took. That score had to be settled.

Picking up his smartphone, he tapped the alarm app and set it for two a.m., which would give him time to get to Topaz by three. If Brax's Porsche was there, he would go inside. But if he found Yuri's Benz at Topaz, he would wait and follow the Russian to wherever he went next. Sooner or later, he'd find some dirt on Yuri. With leverage, he could bargain for the ring.

The scrape of stool legs against the floor interrupted his thoughts.

In the mirror behind the bar, he observed a young woman taking the seat next to him. Even in this dim lighting, her hair gleamed like metal. Dye job or a wig. She wore so much eye makeup he couldn't tell if her eyes were brown, black or gray.

His gaze dropped to her top, two triangles of material that sheathed round, pert breasts. A flicker of heat leaped in his chest as he caught the outline of taut nipples, one straining a triangle decorated with white stars on blue, the other overworking a triangle with red-and-white stripes.

She looked like a Fourth of July celebration about to pop.

"Like my top?" she asked in a southern drawl.

With Sally, he'd been rusty at interpreting female

signals, but he picked up this woman's more clearly than if she'd banged a gong in his ear. Just the kind of wake-up call to get outside of his funk, get back to the present.

"It goes with my skirt," she continued as though it was a two-way conversation.

He knew better than to look, but it was like telling Bambi to stay out of the forest. The skirt was thigh high and red. Below it, shapely legs in fishnet stockings ended in a pair of black stiletto heels with some kind of symbol on the side.

"It's a fleur-de-lis," she explained, pointing down at her shoe with a frosty-pink fingernail, "for my boys, the Saints."

Took him a moment. "The New Orleans Saints?"

"Who dat!" She grinned so wide, he saw she had a slightly crooked front tooth, which almost gave her a sweet, naive quality.

The operative word being *almost*. Sweet, naive types didn't wear fishnet stockings, stiletto heels and small, tight triangles into dive bars.

Clunk.

He looked stupidly at his phone lying on the floor.

"I'll get it," she said cheerfully.

"No—"

But she'd already scooted off her stool, a mass of red, fleshy curves and stars and stripes…and it was all he could to sit there and stare.

She straightened slowly, a funny look on her face.

He held out his hand for the phone.

But she didn't return it. Instead, she shifted closer, so close he could see that her eyes were brown. A rich, warm color, like melting caramel. He inhaled a slow breath, caught her scent. Fresh and soapy, as though she'd just stepped out of a shower. Surprising. These girls usually poured on the perfume.

"I'm getting a pulsation," she whispered.

Took him a moment to realize it was an incoming call. "I don't like ringtones," he said. "Keep it on vibrate. Give it to me."

"It's not a call. It's a pulsation..." She waggled her fingers in the air. "From out there."

"Through my phone."

She nodded. "I'm getting a message."

Message. He glanced at her outfit. Was she a stripper from Brax's club? Someone sent over to deliver a message to him?

"From Braxton?"

"Who?"

"Yuri?"

"I...don't know a Yuri."

This was starting to feel like another damn twenty questions and no answers from one of Brax's employees.

"Are you going to tell me?" he snapped.

"I think it's from...your father."

Drake felt numb, frozen. Couldn't move, couldn't think. Finally, something inside thawed enough for him to speak.

"Impossible." His heart banged so hard and fast, his chest ached.

But she was off someplace else. She swiveled slowly on her stool, her head tipped as though listening to a faraway tune.

"He says he loves you very much." She smiled at Drake.

Enough! As though jolted to life by an electric prod, he bolted upright and blew out a lungful of air.

"Give me the damn phone." He snatched it from her hand. He didn't need this. Not from some whacked, high-woo-woo *messenger*. Was this Yuri's idea of a sick joke?

Those big brown eyes implored him. "I didn't mean to—"

"How much?"

"How much what?"

"How much money did they give you to play this game?"

For a girl who liked to talk, her silence was a message in itself. She was holding something back, but what? He no longer thought she worked as a stripper at Topaz—Brax liked his girls to wear sleek outfits, not castoffs from a Yankee Doodle Dandy parade. Plus, Brax liked to do his own talking. He would never send someone, especially *this* someone, to do it for him.

Yuri, on the other hand, was crafty, pathologically so, but immature. Maybe the Russian got the itch to dig at Drake, throw him off, so he'd hired this girl, maybe minutes before she walked in here, with hasty instructions to play on his father's death. Maybe she was hard up for money, feared the thug or both.

"Why don't you stick to what you're good at." He gave her a scathing once-over. "Although anybody who has to advertise to that extent probably isn't all that good. Who hired your sorry ass?"

She opened her slick red lips to say something, but nothing came out.

Sally appeared, pushed a coaster toward his neighbor. "What can I get ya?"

Miss Who Dat swerved her stricken gaze to the bartender. "I, uh…"

He set down his bottle, hard, on the bar. "Order something. We have some talking to do."

"Cherry cola?" she asked in a wispy voice.

Sally gave him a what's-up look. He flashed her a mind-your-business one back.

"Maraschino juice in a cola okay?" Sally asked.

"F'sure. Thank you, ma'am."

"Sally. And you're?"

"Uh…" Her gaze darted across the bar. "Remy."

"Nice to meet you, Remy." She pointed to Drake's bottle. "Another?"

He shook his head as an old Sinatra tune, "Luck Be a Lady," started playing in the background.

Remy tapped her fingers on the bar. "I like this song."

"Fine. Who put you up to this?"

She gave him a blank look. "Nobody."

"Sticking to that story, eh?"

The way she lowered her thick black lashes, then raised them slowly, made him think of a theater curtain. He wondered what show he would see next.

"Like I told you," she said, oozing earnestness, "I don't know a Brassell or Yuri."

"Braxton."

"What?"

"You heard me." He'd pulled that same stunt a hundred times. Mispronouncing a name to pretend he didn't know the person. Playing dumb when you actually knew everything about the person, from the city where they were born to their cat's name.

She acted like some kind of psychic nut, but he got the sense she was a lot sharper than she let on. No way was he going to get information from her. Not the truthful variety anyway.

"What you claim to have heard could not have been my father…" He paused, swallowed an ache he'd been fighting all day. "He's dead."

There was a stupefied look on her face. Then she keeled forward and hugged him. "Oh, mercy!" she murmured, her voice breaking. "I had no idea."

He set down the phone, trying to ignore the curious looks of others at the bar. Placing his hands on her trembling shoulders, he peeled her off him.

Her eyes glistened with emotion. Her chin quivered. What an actress.

"You knew."

She sucked in a loud, indignant breath. "That he's de—passed? No, of course, I didn't know—how would I have? Even if I did know, I wouldn't have shared what I heard…or sensed maybe is more like it, because to tell you the truth, I'm not all that sure I have the gift…but even if I was sure, I would never have said something like that without believing it offered some comfort."

He frowned. "What?"

She waved her hands in the air. "Never mind." She paused. "What are you pointing at?"

"That photo over the register. My dad was the original owner's best friend, and a lifetime member of the Blottos who still hang out here most afternoons. If somebody wanted to learn facts about my father, all they'd have to do was buy one of those regulars a drink."

"I don't know any facts." She looked at the photo. "He must be the gentleman on the right. The other one is too old."

He said nothing.

After several beats, she said quietly, "You're right. Those pulsations likely were your phone on vibrate. Sometimes I think I'm picking up on vibes, but…" She gave a one-shouldered shrug. "My nanny, though, she had the gift."

"I don't care if there's a radio frequency scanner embedded in your skull, you have no right pretending to know Benedict Morgan."

His brother had his issues, but Brax would never stoop so low as to fabricate a story involving their father. This evening was getting weirder by the minute. Time to go home, grab some shut-eye before his three a.m. return to Topaz.

He stood, retrieved his wallet from his pocket.

"Please, sir," she whispered, "it was just a...funny coincidence."

He turned away as he leafed through the money in his billfold. At least with his back to her, she'd get the hint their exchange was over.

"You got me wrong," she continued.

So much for that theory.

"I sat next to you because I *liked* you. I walked in here and I thought, 'Wow, that's one good-looking guy. Sharp dresser, too.' Maybe we could talk, get to know each other, but then your phone dropped..."

He turned so abruptly she jumped. "Let's end this nonsense now," he said in a low rumble. "You claim nobody sent you, fine. You call that...other part...a *funny* coincidence, okay. I halfway believe you because nobody in their right mind would hire a flake to put some mental muscle on me. But you can't fool me about the rest of your performance. I'm not buying, sister, so sell it elsewhere."

"Sell?" She actually looked affronted. "You think I'm...a *hooker*?"

"I'm giving you two pieces of advice. That ingénue act might work on out-of-towners who've never been to the big city, but don't test-drive it on the locals, baby. And the next time somebody asks your name, don't pick one off a bottle, *Remy*." He snorted a laugh. "I suppose your last name's Martin."

Another guilty look. "F'true, you got me there. But you're wrong about the rest. I'm not selling anything."

"Right," he muttered, "and I'm Mickey Mouse."

Sally appeared, set the cola in front of the girl.

He tugged loose a five and handed it to Sally. "Keep the change."

"Going home?" She slipped the bill into the tip jar.

He nodded. "Time to take my dog for a walk."

"Don't be a stranger." She pulled out her cell phone and headed down the bar.

He didn't look at "Remy" as he plucked his jacket off the high back of the stool. Folding it over his arm, he headed to the door as the music swelled and Frank warbled a long, long note that faded to nothing.

Drake stepped outside, and the heat hit him like a blast furnace. He wondered when he'd last taken a breath that didn't smell like exhaust and warm asphalt.

Looking up at the night sky, he picked out the Big Dipper. When he was a kid, the skies had been cleaner, the stars brighter. But like everything else in life, things changed.

He was tired of change. It demanded too much and left too little. Never understood why people liked to say "embrace change," as though it was fun, like wrapping your arms around the waist of some hot babe on a Harley, the two of you streaking toward some exhilarating destination. Change was more like sitting in the back of a taxi with some hard-nosed cabbie who drove recklessly, padded the fare and dumped you at the wrong address.

That was the problem with being a practical man. You knew life was no easy ride.

Sometimes, though, he envied the dreamers of the world, wondered what it was like to *hope*. To believe without the benefit of physical evidence. Staring at the stars again, he wished he could trust that something lay beyond life's closed door, because he sure as hell couldn't find the answers here.

He walked across the parking lot to the darkened kiosk, brushed off the seat of an abandoned stool and laid his jacket neatly over it. Rolling up a shirt sleeve, he watched the traffic along Las Vegas Boulevard. Cars, trucks and those life-changing taxis streamed past, filling the night with scraps of laughter, music and the occasional horn blast.

He scanned Topaz's parking lot. No yellow Porsche parked in its regular spot. No black Mercedes, either, but it could be parked in a section not visible from here. He'd walk through the lot on his way to his truck, see what was there.

Fighting a yawn, he rolled up his other sleeve. He felt drained. Time to close the lid on today's troubles, go home, walk his dog, then get some rest.

Click click click.

"Hello, sir?" called out a too-familiar female voice.

So much for closing that lid.

CHAPTER THREE

VAL SLOWED HER steps as she approached the darkened kiosk. The overhang cast a deep shadow around the building, making it difficult to see what or who was there, but from Dino's window she had seen Drake stop somewhere around here.

"Hello, you there?" She squinted into the gloom.

"If I told you I wasn't, would you go away?"

She huffed a breath. "Good thing that bad mood of yours isn't luggage or it'd be too heavy to carry."

"You came out here to tell me that?"

"No. You forgot your phone." She thrust out her hand, more than ready to give it up. Whatever pulsations she had felt, or thought she felt, were gone.

"You want me to come to you?"

"Mercy, must everything be an issue?" Silence. "Yes, I want *you* to come to *me*."

"Why? Afraid I'll bite?"

"Yes. But I have to warn you, I bite back."

She swiped a bead of sweat off her hairline. This damn wig was too tight, too hot. And these fishnet stockings made her legs itch something fierce. They never bothered her when she'd worn them at her old job, but that was indoors with plenty of air-conditioning, not outside where temps were pushing a hundred. Honestly, she could almost feel the steam rising from the pavement, even at this time of night.

She debated whether to set the damn phone on the ground and leave, but she didn't want to fail at this. F'sure, she'd told Marta there were no guarantees to the honey trap, but what if Drake, her fiancé, told her about the weird hooker who claimed she felt pulsations through his phone, channeled his father, then stalked him into the parking lot? Hardly the techniques of a seasoned, knowledgeable private eye.

Marta would demand back every cent of the retainer.

Val would *not* let that happen. She had to suck it up, figure out how to salvage this mess. She and Grumpy were here now, alone. Which meant she had one more chance to sweeten the honey trap.

"You're right, I'm a girl for sale." Technically, she sold her investigator services, so that was true. "But I played the wrong man. You're too smart, too hip to fall for this silly costume and come-on. I apologize."

Her vision had adjusted enough to the shadows so that she could see his dark silhouette. He leaned against the building, and from the angle of his head, he was watching her. She remembered that gaze at the bar. The faint lines that fanned from the corners of his eyes, their smoky color. How they shone with intensity, as though he was on the verge of asking a question or in the process of formulating one. But when he angered, their color darkened to a flat, dull shade like gunmetal.

She wondered what color they were right now.

"Let's call a truce, okay? I'll bring your phone to you, then you can thank me."

He didn't respond. She had probably taken him by surprise with her no-harm-no-foul attitude. Or maybe he was mulling over her ability to actually tell the truth. That man sure spent a lot of time in his head.

She walked almost to the edge of the shadow and stopped. "I'd walk to you, but it's not so easy to see in there, and I'd hate to fumble and drop the phone while handing it over. Of course, it might survive bouncing on the ground a few times, and you wouldn't need to replace it, so—"

"Stay put."

He stepped forward. Hazy moonlight slanted across his face, not enough to clearly see his features, but enough to see the pronounced line of his jaw, the bulk of his shoulders. He reached out with both hands and wrapped them around hers.

"Do you still feel those pulsations?" he asked, his voice husky, and unless she had lost her sense of hearing, more than a little suggestive.

"No," she whispered. His hands were big and warm, triggering pulsations that had nothing to do with the phone. In the space of a heartbeat, the edginess between them had shifted, intensified, from a mental struggle to a physical one.

"Nothing at all?"

He tightened his hold, stroking his thumb in a light, lingering path on the back of her hand. Sensations sparked within her.

"Of course I feel something," she managed to say around her heart thundering in her throat. "I'm flesh and blood, aren't I?"

A throaty chuckle. "I like it when you're honest. One moment, let me put the phone away."

She realized she was holding her hands in midair, suspended where he'd abandoned them, as though they had no purpose other than waiting for his touch. "Don't leave me hanging."

He captured them again. With a squeeze, he drew her closer, then placed her palms flat against his chest. Through his shirt, she felt his heart pumping, its beat steady and strong. *That's how he is. Steady, strong, focused.*

Raising one hand, he kissed her index finger before drawing it into his mouth. She shuddered a release of breath as he suckled it. Maybe she should admit she wasn't really a hooker.

Slowly, his mouth released its hold on her finger and moved to her wrist, which he kissed and nuzzled.

Or maybe not.

"Do you like that?" he whispered.

"Ye—" The rest of the word ended in a small, ragged moan as his talented mouth and tongue tickled, nibbled and kissed the inside of her arm.

"What's your real name?" His voice, rough and low, reverberated through her.

"V-val."

These were just caresses, and some wicked attention from his mouth, yet her insides were rocking and rolling as though they were buck naked in bed. She stifled a building moan and told herself to chill, gain some ground. She was acting as if she hadn't been touched by a man in years.

Well, she hadn't. Two years, if she didn't count that backseat fumble in Houston. A realization that was as depressing as it was embarrassing.

But when he lightly trailed the pad of his thumb across her bottom lip, then dragged it leisurely down her neck, his touch both deliciously coarse and gentle, the only thought she had was *more, more...*

"Why the wig, Val?"

"Hmm?"

"The wig. It's obvious you're wearing one. Why?"

She mentally fought her way through the haze of arousal. "Does it...look bad?"

As soon as she asked, she regretted it. Made her sound pathetically insecure about her looks, which was *so* far from the truth. If anything, she had been pathetically insecure about how she'd prepared for her *job* tonight.

"It looks—" he fingered a lock "—like strands of moonlight. Gives you an unearthly, dreamy quality."

For a man who bottled up his words, he sure knew how to pour them on sweet and thick at the right moment.

"I always wear it with this outfit." Also true.

"Interesting outfit to wear to Dino's. Who hired you, Val?"

"Nobody."

"Was it Yuri? You can tell me."

"Nobody."

Interesting, too, how he'd deftly manipulated this encounter so *he* was now in control. He'd plied her with his mouth and touch, worked her with compliments until her reserve dissolved, and she was ready to divulge whatever he wanted to know.

This man had taken over *her* honey trap!

Oh, no. Two thousand dollars, and the small but significant fact that her self-esteem needed her to succeed at her first P.I. gig, were at stake.

Time for the queen bee to regain her territory.

She had a job to do. Maybe she'd flitted here and there, floundered a little in her flight, but she would land this job, and do it right. This was *her* career, *her* future. Val Louvinia LeRoy would prove she had what it took to be a professional private eye.

"I wore an interesting outfit," she said, sliding her arms around his waist, "in the hope I'd meet an interesting man." *You drone, me queen, sugar.*

She nuzzled her face against his shirt, taking in its clean, crisp scent. Finding a gap between buttons, she slipped her tongue inside, touching the mat of hair on his chest. She probed a little farther and licked the slick, wiry strands, filling her mouth with the tangy, salty taste of his sweat. Closing her eyes, she sensed the warmth rising from his body, imagined what it'd be like to slowly undress him, piece by piece, unveiling his strong, powerful, male body…

Adrenaline surged through her veins. Ah, she felt alive, lost in the sensations. She could stay like this forever, indulging in slow, erotic play, teasing and prolonging the sweet torture until…

With great effort, she shoved down the fantasy.

There would never be an *until,* only these moments now. Of course she knew that, yet something inside of her splintered, the shards slicing, hurting.

"Val?" His voice was gruff, yet tender.

"Sorry." She opened her eyes. "Got lost in my thoughts."

"Anything I should know?"

Staring into his face, she cupped his cheek with her hand, half wishing they were indoors so she could read the look in his eyes. Those brooding, wary eyes, always watchful, always vigilant.

"You need to lighten up more." The words spilled out before she'd thought them through.

"Are we back to my carrying bags?"

"Actually, it was luggage."

"And my bad mood fitting into it."

"Actually, I said it was a good thing your bad mood *wasn't* luggage because—"

"It'd be too heavy to carry."

Listening to his amused chuckle, she smiled. Didn't completely ease the pain she felt inside, but it was good to share a moment of playfulness.

"How about I lighten up more now," he said, his

voice dropping to a rugged register that sent a thrill skittering up her spine.

"Let me help…"

Pressing closer, she wrapped her arms around his neck. Molding herself against him, she let him feel the length of her body against his, close and tight, from her breasts to her thighs. Emitting a throaty purr, she opened herself to him and gently thrust her pelvis against his. Then once more—giving him an unmistakable confirmation of her body signals.

She felt him hardening against her.

He lowered his head. "That's not what I call light."

Leaning back her head, she parted her lips, shuddering her pleasure as he nuzzled her neck, his big hands kneading her bottom. She felt the change in him, the tensing of his muscles, his labored breaths. Kissing was no longer a game. She was playing with fire, and she wanted to be scorched, consumed.

She pulled his head down to her, closer, closer, until she felt his breath warming her lips.

"Give me some sugar," she whispered.

With a low, guttural groan, his mouth barely touched hers—

A trumpet blasted a riff.

"Wha—?" He jerked back his head.

She blinked, steadying herself as a clarinet wailed, a snare drum tapped.

Drake looked around. "That sounds like…a Dixieland band."

"It is."

"'When the Saints Go Marching In?'"

"Right again. It's my ringtone." She reached into her pocket and glanced at the caller ID. Someone from home was calling. Had to be one of her cousins, probably worried as it was late and they didn't like her taking buses at night. She hadn't had a chance to tell them that she was driving a rental for the next few days, or that her car would be fixed soon, thanks to the money from this honey-trap gig.

Now wasn't the time to talk, though. She turned off the phone and stuffed it into her pocket.

"Let me guess," Drake said, his voice taut, "that was Hubby."

She barked a small laugh. Couldn't help it. Of all the secrets he'd accused her of, she hadn't expected that one. "Girls like me don't have husbands. You got a wife? Or a girlfriend? A fiancée?"

"None of the above."

His lie bothered her, even though she'd been expecting as much. She was glad the night shadowed her features, because confusion and hurt were probably stamped all over her face.

The door to Dino's swung open, and the faint strains of a Coldplay song wafted onto the street. Traffic cruised down Las Vegas Boulevard with its mix of honking horns and screeching tires. The air simmered with the never ending, relentless heat.

Everything was the same as it had been when she first got here, but she had changed, irreversibly so. Until the past few minutes, she had not realized that, deep within her, she had put up a wall that protected something fragile, yet potentially devastating. Now it had been freed, and she could never put it back.

"I need to go now," she said, fighting to keep her voice even.

"Where are you parked?"

"There." She pointed in the general direction of the Honda rental, thirty or so feet away.

"I'll watch, make sure you get into your car okay."

She didn't trust herself to speak anymore. With a wave, she walked away.

As her heels clicked across the lot, Jayne's words drifted through her mind. Diamond Investigations never did honey traps because "inducing the behavior" to "objectively document" was unacceptable. Just like Jayne to couch it in clinical, detached terms.

Val could add an important side note to her boss's rule. Honey traps were especially unacceptable because people whose hearts had been numbed might unexpectedly wake up and realize what had been missing in their lives—an impassioned connection, a sense of belonging or maybe just a person's touch. When that happened, inducements became deterrents, and all objectivity was lost. The game became real.

She reached her car and turned.

He stood where she had left him. A dark, lonely form, vigilantly watching, protecting.

A SHORT WHILE later Val sat at the intersection of Las Vegas Boulevard and East Charleston. She still felt wobbly about what had happened in Dino's parking lot. And embarrassed by telling him about the pulsations. At the time, she would have sworn they were dead-on real. She winced at her choice of words. Well, whatever, she should have kept the bulletin to herself.

Her nanny was the one who really had the "soul's eye," as she called it. Through it, she said she experienced *impressions*—images, feelings, voices—in the part of her brain where dreams lay, which resonated from objects imbued with memories of their owners' lives, anything from significant events to people they had loved. Although some people called her gift psychometry, Nanny called it "measuring people's spirits."

When Val was thirteen, she'd thought she was picking up on objects' impressions, too. Sometimes when she touched one of the antiques in their shop, especially ones with metal or stones, her fingers would tingle slightly. Immediately following that, an image or emotion would pass through her mind. Never heard a voice, though, like Nanny did. Not until tonight.

Looking back, she couldn't honestly say she really saw or felt those things. Sometimes she wondered if it had just been a way to be closer to her nanny, the two of them sharing something special. Hindsight could sure give a person twenty-twenty vision.

But still, what happened earlier in the bar had seemed like an impression. She had definitely heard an older man's voice when she held Drake's phone, but thinking back, she remembered an older couple sitting at a table behind them, and Val had overheard him expressing his love for his lady friend. And those pulsations from the phone? No-brainer. The phone was on vibrate.

A horn honked, jerking Val out of her reverie. Sheepishly, she realized the light had turned green.

Another honk.

"Hold your britches, bubba," she muttered, stepping on the gas and turning down Charleston Boulevard.

Time to call Marta with a final update. After a quick check to verify no cops were around—Nevada might have legalized prostitution and gambling, but drivers could get hefty fines for handheld cell phones—she punched in Marta's number.

"It done?" No hello.

"Yes."

"Where is he?"

"I left him in the parking lot at Dino's."

"When?"

"Ten, fifteen minutes ago."

"So that be…quarter to ten."

"Sounds about right."

"He go inside Dino's? Or to Topaz?"

Who cares where he went afterward? "I don't know," she said absently. "Listen, Marta, I have something to tell you."

This next part was going to be tough for her client to hear, even if she had been anticipating it.

"The honey trap," she said gently, "confirmed your intuitions, Marta."

Silence. No tears. No rants. Just…silence. *Poor girl. Probably numb with hurt.*

"What is this *intoshuns?*" Marta snapped.

Her tone took Val by surprise. "Intuitions…uh, they're your suspicions. Inklings. Doubts."

"Too many words. I ask for information, not words."

Like one wasn't the other. "He kissed me." Well, almost, but close enough. "He cheats. So don't marry the man." So much for the sensitive approach.

After a beat, Marta muttered. "He like that."

He like that. What was that supposed to mean? He likes fooling around with women he doesn't know?

Val felt an ugly zap of the green monster.

Oh, no. She *refused* to get jealous over the guy. This had been a job, one she had been paid well to do. Didn't matter what he liked or didn't like, he was a notch in Val's investigative career belt, nothing more.

"I'll send you a report when I get home," she said tightly.

"No report. This between you and me."

"Fine." Like she wanted to rehash all the smarmy details anyway.

"I want you go back to bar."

"When pigs fly."

"What?"

"I fulfilled the job request, Marta. The work is done. Completed. *Finis.*"

"So many words again."

"Then let me give you just one. *No.* I am not going back to that bar."

"Please, Val," she said, her mood shifting from cold to needy. "I must know if he still there."

"What does it matter? He kissed me!" Kinda. "That's what you wanted to know!"

"Yes, kiss. Good. Still…must know if he—"

"Call the bar and ask."

"No. Want you to—"

"Call his cell, then."

"I don't have— Why not you go? It *your* job! Val, please—"

"Job is *over*. Terminated. Wrapped up." She tried to think of even *more* words, but those would do. "Goodbye."

She ended the call and tossed the phone onto the seat next to her, then frowned. Why hadn't Marta cared about that kiss?

Hardly the reaction of a woman whose heart had been broken. She had been teary talking about her suspected philandering fiancé in the office this afternoon, but the only thing Marta seemed upset about tonight—besides Val's vocabulary—was her not going back to check on Drake's whereabouts.

Something else bothered Val about that conversation. Couldn't put her finger on it…something Marta had said. Or didn't finish saying. When Val told her to call Drake's cell, she had said something like *I don't have*…

She didn't have what?

The nerve to call him?

The time to make such a call?

Val's stomach growled. Spying one of her favorite fast-food pit stops, Aloha Kitchen, she decided to pull over. Time to put the crazy case behind her. Maybe she didn't understand the conclusion, maybe she never would, but some things were best left in the shadows.

DRAKE DROVE HIS pickup along Las Vegas Boulevard. Warm breezes rushed through his open driver's window, almost drying the sweat on his skin. Far off, a siren wailed, peppered with a variety of horn blasts. Ambulance and a fire engine? Maybe a police unit or two thrown in for good measure.

At a red light, he glanced at his phone, which he always set on his thigh when he drove, and checked the time. A few minutes after ten. He'd be home in twenty minutes, fifteen if traffic picked up. He'd piled plenty of food into Hearsay's bowl, so his dog wouldn't be hungry. After a short walk around the block, Drake would be in bed by eleven. If he was lucky and fell asleep right away, he'd get three hours before his early-morning surveillance.

Hadn't been that lucky lately, though. At least he put his insomnia to good use. Was halfway through Michael Connelly's *The Lincoln Lawyer,* which made him wish he had someone to drive him around while he caught up on his paperwork and made calls. Not a partner, just a grunt with a driver's license.

He hadn't seen Brax's Porsche or Yuri's Benz when he'd walked through the Topaz lot, not a big surprise as Sally said she typically saw the cars in the wee hours. He hadn't been in the mood to go inside Topaz. Same shift, same nonanswers. Nothing like wasting time trying to convince people to talk who didn't want to talk.

He passed Bonanza Gifts, its parking-lot-wide marquee advertising itself to be the world's largest gift shop. More like the world's largest tacky emporium, but it had been one of his favorite hangouts as a kid.

He remembered a long-ago birthday gift, a dice clock, he'd bought for his dad there. Each hour had glued-on dice, their dots representing that number. "Snake eyes" for two o'clock, "little Joe" for four, "six five, no jive" for eleven. Over his mom's protests, his dad had proudly hung it in the living room, over the TV. After a while, he and his dad started telling time by dice slang. "Billy's coming over at Nina from Pasadena" meant Billy would arrive at nine. "He wants you to call at puppy paws" meant call him at ten.

Years later, after the old man died, Drake asked for the clock, but his mom refused, playing on dice slang by answering, "Six five, no jive."

His dad would have gotten a kick out of that.

He blinked at the streams of red lights ahead, swallowed feelings he didn't want to recognize.

Damn it to hell. He wished he had never met Val, if that was even her name. Wished he'd never heard about those damn pulsations. Like his dad would send such a message through a total stranger, especially one dressed as though she shopped at Army Surplus for Hookers.

Whatever her scheme, he was one up on it. When she pulled out her cell, he'd memorized the caller ID. He'd run it through some proprietary databases and by the time his head hit the pillow he'd know more about Miss Who Dat than her own mama ever did.

The phone vibrated against his thigh. He checked the caller ID. Las Vegas area code, but he didn't recognize the number. Without moving the phone, he punched Answer, then Speaker.

"Morgan Investigations," he answered, raising his voice to be heard.

"Drake Morgan?" A woman's voice.

"Yes."

"Sir, I'm a dispatcher, Clark County emergency call center, and are you the Drake Morgan who resides at…"

As the dispatcher recited his address, the hairs bristled on the back of his neck. "That's correct."

"I don't want to alarm you, but I need to advise that your home is being worked on by several Clark County fire units—"

"Are you saying…my house is *on fire?*"

"Yes, sir—"

Adrenaline jacked his pulse. "I'm on my way."

"The firefighters are doing their best, and what they need most is for you to remain calm when you arrive—"

"My dog is inside!"

"Anyone else?"

"No." He gripped the wheel with shaking hands. "My dog likes to sleep under the kitchen table!"

Spring Mountain Road, the main artery to his street, was ahead. As he shifted to check traffic, the phone slipped and clattered onto the floorboard.

"Look under the kitchen table!" he yelled, flipping the turn signal. "I'm on my way there!"

Pumping the horn, he shot through an opening in traffic, straight through to the far lane. A horn blasted. He jerked the wheel left, barely missing an Audi wagon, before he wrestled a turn onto Spring Mountain.

"Check the kitchen," he shouted again, jamming his foot on the gas pedal, "under the table!"

TEN OR SO minutes later—although it felt like hours, a lifetime—he slammed the pickup to a stop across the street from his house, his stomach lurching as he saw the gray-white smoke billowing to the sky, its core pulsing orange and red. Monstrous flames shot twenty, thirty feet from the roof. The wooden structure resembled an oversize pile of kindling.

Jumping out, he jogged across the street and around one of several fire trucks. Three or four police officers stood on the periphery of the property, keeping neighbors at bay. Several firefighters handled a hose, pointing its gushing stream of water at the flames. Others worked another hose, aimed at the roof of the neighboring house.

He headed up the driveway.

"Hey, buddy, you can't go in there!"

"Chuck, stop that guy!"

A firefighter, his mask pulled off his face, blocked Drake's path.

"My dog's in there, damn it!" He tried to shove past, eyeing the crackling flames that licked at the side of the house. His office.

"Stop!" A second firefighter, his face gleaming with sweat, grabbed Drake's arm. "Calm down or I'll call those cops over to drag your butt to jail."

The heat radiating off the fire was intense. Sucking in a breath that tasted like soot, Drake glanced at the name on the firefighter's helmet. "Captain Dietrich, I'm Drake Morgan and I live here. My dog's inside."

"I know. Heard it from dispatch." He looked over his shoulder and yelled, "I said, *step on it!*" Turning to Drake, he continued, "Sorry, but I can't have you doing something stupid like trying to go inside. We got enough on our hands fighting the fire, looking for the dog. Can't be trying to save you, too."

"I won't fight you." Drake swiped at his brow. "My dog—"

"Two guys made an attempt to go inside, but I had to pull them back after a wall collapsed."

His heart jammed in his throat. "Where?"

Dietrich jabbed a thumb over his shoulder. "East side of house. Looked like an office. According to neighbors, that's where the house first exploded in flames. Did you store flammable chemicals, other petroleum distillates, there or anywhere else?"

"Absolutely not." A small relief sifted through Drake's fear. The office was the farthest from the kitchen. "I think my dog is in the kitchen."

"Where is it?"

"Back northwest corner."

Dietrich stared at the front door, smoke swirling out the opening.

"It's a clear shot," Drake said, "thirty feet diagonal, from the door. Table is against the west wall. Hearsay—that's his name—likes to lie under it."

Dietrich pointed at Chuck. "Got that? Back northwest corner? Look under kitchen table for the dog. You and Ross are going in."

Chuck pulled up his mask as Dietrich strode to a truck, gesturing and talking to several firefighters.

Drake watched Chuck and Ross, air tanks strapped to their backs, enter and disappear into the smoke.

"Hang in there, buddy," he said under his breath, "they're almost there."

When the mutt—who looked to be part whippet, part retriever—showed up at Drake's house a year ago, he'd ignored it, figuring it would meander back home. Instead it hung out in his yard like a lonesome guy in a bar who had nowhere to go after last call.

The next day, he'd grudgingly put out a bowl of water, some leftover meat loaf. It was cool enough in April that he didn't worry about the mutt hanging around outside, figuring he'd soon go back to wherever he belonged.

Within the week, Drake was lugging home dog food. Mutt sniffed it, turned away. Wanted meat loaf.

Drake's gut clenched as a front window exploded, glass shattering. Gray smoke streamed out the window, curling furiously over the roof as flames lashed through the opening.

He tried to still his thoughts, told himself that the worst of the fire was in his bedroom and office, was traveling only now into the living room…hadn't yet reached the kitchen.

"Mr. Morgan?"

He turned. An elderly woman, who he vaguely recalled lived several houses down, stood hunched in her chenille robe.

"I'm so sorry." In the flickering light of the fire, her milky blue eyes brimmed with emotion. She clutched his hand and squeezed it. "Oh, your sweet little dog…"

He couldn't deal with this.

Clamping his mouth shut, he looked at the fiery hell, grinding his teeth until his jaw ached, willing God or whoever was in charge to hear him out. *Take it all. Destroy everything I own. But please, spare one small heart…*

In the doorway, a form materialized in the whirling smoke. A firefighter emerged, cradling a limp form in his arms.

CHAPTER FOUR

As THE FIREFIGHTER laid the limp dog onto a cleared area of the yard, Dietrich ran over, carrying an oxygen tank.

Drake stumbled forward and dropped to his knees next to Hearsay. The dog lay on his side, unmoving, eyes closed.

Tugging off his own mask, Chuck knelt across from Drake. Dietrich, positioned at the dog's head, strapped a small plastic mask over the dog's muzzle.

Dietrich jabbed his chin at Chuck. "Turn it up."

Chuck adjusted the nozzle on the tank, then pressed two fingers against the dog's throat. He held it there, a studious look on his sweat-slicked face, before giving his head a small shake.

The two firefighters exchanged a look.

Which Drake caught. His insides constricted into a tight ball of hurt and rage.

He refused to believe it.

Not *his* dog. Not Hearsay.

He would find the bastard who did this, make him pay. After Drake was through with him, he would wish he had died a slow, agonizing death in this fire instead.

The crackling of the flames, movements of people

and machinery, even the fierce heat shrank into the background as Drake stroked Hearsay, still soft and warm, willing his life force to not seep away.

Please. Spare him.

"Come on, buddy," he whispered, his voice strained, "you can make it."

Dietrich, his face grim, peered intently into the dog's face.

Chuck lightly shook the dog's shoulder. "Stay with us, boy."

Drake ran his hand down the dog's side, stopping when his fingers grazed stiff, charred hair.

"Looks to be only the fur," Dietrich said, "nothing deeper. Bigger problem is how much smoke this little guy took in." He lightly brushed some soot from Hearsay's nostrils.

"I heard whimpering as I approached the kitchen," Chuck said. "He hasn't been out long."

Drake leaned closer. "Stay," he whispered hoarsely, every fiber of his being commanding it to be so. He swiped at the tears coursing down his face, not giving a damn who saw. "I need you, buddy."

A crackling crash. On the west side of the house, flames blew out the shattered kitchen window.

"Got a pulse," Chuck said.

Drake stared at the dog's chest, catching an almost imperceptible movement. "He's breathing!"

The men stared at another rise and fall of the chest...and another...

"Keep at it, boy," Dietrich coached, "you're almost there."

Three grown men on their knees cried and whooped as Hearsay's eyelids fluttered opened.

Dietrich grinned at the dog, his teeth white in a face streaked with soot. "You're one tough bastard, Hearsay."

Blinking, the dog looked around, his gaze settling on Drake.

In that moment, he met God.

"Welcome back, buddy," he murmured.

After a few minutes, Chuck slipped the oxygen mask over the dog's head. "There's an all-night emergency vet hospital near here—"

"I know where it is." Drake stroked Hearsay's head.

"Take him there right now, have him checked over. He's alert, breathing on his own, but the little guy took in a lot of smoke. He's gonna need medicine to prevent lung issues later."

"I will." He looked over at Dietrich, who had moved away and was yammering orders to several firefighters. "I never got to thank him."

"Captain lost his own dog a few months ago," Chuck said. "Saving yours helped him, you know? Helped all of us. It's an honor to save a life." He put his hands underneath the dog. "Let's get him up."

Together, they lifted the dog.

Cradling Hearsay in his arms, Drake walked down the driveway. As he passed through clusters of neighbors, people touched his back, murmured words of encouragement. He held Hearsay close, knowing there were difficult, frustrating days ahead, but at the moment, nothing mattered but the life in his arms.

At the pickup, he opened the passenger door. Cuddling Hearsay close in one arm, he lifted the jacket lying neatly on the seat with his free hand. Then paused. The vinyl seating was old, ripped. A jacket would provide some cushioning.

Carefully, he laid Hearsay on the jacket, which still carried lingering scents of his dad's Old Spice cologne and love of cigars. His old man would have approved. He liked the material things like anybody else, but nothing—not even a jacket that had cost him a month's pay—was more important than family.

"Mr. Morgan?"

He double-checked to make sure Hearsay was comfortable, then turned. A streetlight highlighted a stocky man dressed in pants and a sports shirt.

"I'm Tony Cordova, arson investigator for this district."

Drake guessed his raspy voice was from years of smoking, inhaling smoke or both.

"Like to ask you some questions," Tony said.

"Later." He carefully closed the passenger door, which shut with a solid click. "Need to take my dog to the vet hospital."

"Saw the firefighters bring him around. Glad the tyke's okay." He followed Drake as he walked to the driver's door. "You're a private investigator, correct?"

"Yes."

"Then you understand the importance of my asking questions right now."

"I understand." He yanked open the door. With any crime, the faster you gathered data, the faster you were on the trail. "But as I said, I'm on my way to the hospital."

"Was anyone else in your house when you left tonight?"

"I already told dispatch there was no one."

"Did you accidentally leave the stove on? Any faulty electrical apparatus that you were aware of?"

Drake climbed in, slammed the door and glared at him through the open window. "Tony—that's your name, right?—I promise to cooperate with your investigation, but now is not the time." He held out his hand. "Give me your card, I'll call you."

Tony handed over a card. "Are you aware of anyone who might wish to harm you?"

"No."

After checking Hearsay one more time, he shoved the key into the ignition. As Drake drove off, he heard Tony yell something about calling tomorrow.

Heading down the road, he called the vet hospital and made arrangements for Hearsay's emergency care. Afterward, one hand resting on his dog, reassured by the steady rise and fall of his pet's chest, he thought about the lie he had told to the arson investigator. No, he didn't know anyone who wished to harm him.

It wasn't so much that Yuri wanted to harm him— more like he wanted to leave his calling card, a violent, fiery one meant to intimidate. Which told him the Russian knew Drake had been tailing him.

How? He had taken extra care to park his pickup in secluded areas, always used covert and long-range cameras. In the nearly six years he'd been a P.I., only once had he been caught surveilling someone, but not because he got sloppy. In that case, his client, during a phone call yelling match with his almost ex-wife, had informed her he'd hired a P.I. to surveil her that very day. After that, Drake had never shared his investigation schedule with clients.

No, Yuri must have heard from one of the employees at Topaz that Drake was sniffing around the club, asking too many questions. If Yuri had nothing to hide, he wouldn't have cared.

But his savage reaction showed the depth of his paranoia. He was afraid Drake might have documented something incriminating. Something the police would find of interest.

Drake had a good idea what had happened tonight. Before setting the fire, Yuri, and probably one or two of his boys, had ransacked the office, snatching cameras, the laptop, recorders. Hearsay, hackles bristling, had barked at the intruders. But it hadn't taken long for the dog's street smarts to kick in, sense that retreat meant survival, so he'd withdrawn to his spot under the kitchen table.

The men hadn't bothered with the dog after that—they had work to do.

Yuri and his stupid cretins. No concept that images

could be saved in places other than physical devices. Idiots probably thought "the cloud" was something in the sky, not a remote storage option.

After gathering equipment, they'd drenched his office in gasoline. Considering how rapidly the fire spread through that part of the house, they must have also splashed gasoline down the hall and into the bedroom, too. Then torched the place.

With the dog still inside.

His fingers dug into the steering wheel. That son of a bitch would pay dearly for what he did tonight. And Drake would do it personally, not hand over the meting of justice to some arson investigator.

Sure, he could have leaked Yuri's name to Tony Cordova, who would have tracked the bastard down tonight for an interview. The Russian would have had an alibi, of course, along with a string of witnesses who'd back up his story. Plus, with Drake siccing government dogs on him, Yuri would go into hiding, and Drake's personal investigation would grind to a halt. Any hopes of digging for more dirt, or ever getting back the ring, would be crushed.

Then there was Brax.

His brother felt above the law, but arson? He wasn't that dirty. But if Drake offered up Yuri to arson investigators, trails could lead to his brother. And if they didn't, Yuri would ensure sure they did.

A form materialized in Drake's mind. That woman. Who Dat. Had she been a player in this arson? Paid to keep Drake busy, give Yuri and his goons time to do their job? His gut said yes. Just like the Mississippi River that ran through her city of New Orleans, she was twisting, swift and treacherous.

She had never been to Dino's, a dive bar in a lousy neighborhood, yet she showed up tonight, out of the blue. Made a straight line for him, too, and even after he'd shunned her, she didn't budge. Stayed perched on that stool like some kind of tufted bird of prey, waiting for an opportunity to sink in her talons.

He'd walked out of that bar knowing she was trouble, but had given in to the night, the heat.

He clenched his teeth. And for those few hot, heady minutes, his home had been destroyed. Hearsay nearly killed.

Just as Yuri would pay for what he had done tonight, so would she.

By morning, he would know her name, age, address, where she hung out, where she worked. And he would pay her a visit.

The kind of visit a person remembered for the rest of her life.

AT TEN-FORTY, Val walked through the door of her second cousins' Char and Del Jackson's home, carrying a paper bag from Aloha Kitchen.

Their home was a hodgepodge of secondhand furniture, along with some everyday objects Char, with Del's handyman help, had remade into furnishings. Stacked crates had become a bookcase in the living room, and a polished wooden wire spool now served as a small table on the patio. Val's favorite was an old trunk they had recycled into a wine rack. "It's not about what God took away," Char liked to say, "but what we do with what's left."

To Val, that said everything about their being survivors of Katrina. Char and Del had visited her and Nanny, Del's cousin, several times when Val was a child, but they had lost touch over the years. Right before Katrina, they had moved to Gulfport, Mississippi, an area also ravaged during the storm, during which they'd lost their home along with Del's job as a truck driver.

Six years and a relocation later, they owned the Gumbo Stop, which they'd grown from a concession trailer to a store that offered creole cuisine in boil-in-a-bag portions. After locating Val, they'd asked her to come to Las Vegas to live with them and their daughter, twenty-one-year-old Jasmyn.

Who was curled up on the couch in her pink capri pajamas, patterned with the word *Paris* in a flowery script along with miniature Eiffel Towers. She called them her *Je rêve*—French for "I dream"—jammies because her overriding desire was to live in Paris. Her parents accepted their daughter's dream to live in the romantic city, but weren't so thrilled about her wanting to work there as a burlesque dancer.

Jasmyn had years of training as a dancer. At ten she'd won a regional tap competition, followed by several summers working in the chorus for regional musicals. The past few years, she had been teaching tap and ballet to kids at the Dance-a-Rama Studio.

As a counteroffer to the burlesque-dancer-in-Paris dream, Char and Del offered Jasmyn full tuition to Le Cordon Bleu, which they called "a virtual Parisian experience," which just *happened* to have a college in Las Vegas. Instead of struggling as a dancer, they argued, a prestigious culinary arts degree opened doors to a lifetime career as a chef.

Jasmyn's interest in the idea was about as peaked as a collapsed soufflé.

"Hey, baby," Jasmyn called out in her soft, lazy drawl. She twittered her fingers in greeting, her eyes glued to the black-and-white movie on the TV screen.

"Weren't you watching that show last night?"

"I bought the DVD because this movie, *Double Indemnity,* defined film noir. Those old-time movie stars Fred MacMurray and Barbara Stanwyck are *hawt,* cuz."

Sometimes they called each other cuz, although in the two years since Val had moved in here, she'd come to feel more like a sister to Jasmyn. Or what she assumed a sister would be like. They sometimes argued, sometimes irritated each other, but they were also each other's sounding board and confidante.

Jasmyn played with a curl of her long raven hair. "Cuz, I'm thinkin' of dyeing my hair platinum, the brassy but trashy color of Barbara Stanwyck's page-boy wig."

Val glanced at the screen. "Looks better than my brassy but trashy wig."

Jasmyn's gaze landed on Val's hair, where it paused for a moment before darting down Val's outfit, then quickly up. "Whoa, sugar, *laissez les bons temps rouler!*"

It was French for "let the good times roll," a popular saying heard all the time in New Orleans.

"Actually, this wasn't worn for fun." She set the bag on the coffee table. "I worked my first investigation tonight."

"Investigation?" Jasmyn punched a button on the remote. The room instantly grew quiet, the movie frozen on an image of Fred MacMurray looking at Barbara Stanwyck's leg. "Isn't that outfit the one you wore at that casino where you dealt blackjack and lip-synched Christina Aguilera's songs?"

Val plopped down on the couch. "Has nothing to do with her, though. I dressed like this to…" Her heart and mind felt all jumbled up with everything that had happened tonight. She wasn't ready to talk about it yet. "Hungry? I picked up some to-go from Aloha Kitchen."

After shooting Val a knowing look, Jasmyn gestured at the bag. "I love them funny little rolls. You get some of them?"

"Lumpia Shanghai. Got extra just for you." She handed her a few of the mini egg rolls stuffed with ground pork, carrots and onions on a napkin.

They ate in silence for a while. The air conditioner

chugged quietly in the background. On the TV screen, Fred continued to stare at Barbara's ankle. The way he looked at her—startled and hungry—reminded Val of the look on Drake's face when she showed him the fleur-de-lis on her heels.

Like she cared. It was over. Dead. Gone.

She gestured to the screen with an egg roll. "What's Fred looking at?"

"Her anklet. It's a big deal in the movie."

Chewing, Val made a keep-going gesture.

"The anklet is a symbol that represents sexual fascination." Jasmyn grinned. "Read that in some film critic's review on the internet. In my own words, that little gold anklet sends a signal as big and bright as a lighthouse beacon. It flashes 'I'm a bad girl looking for trouble.' Women who wore them were thought to be loose."

Val wiped her fingers on a napkin. "This movie was made when?"

"Nineteen forty-four."

"You just turned twenty-one, what, three months ago? And you know all about anklets worn nearly seventy years ago?"

Jasmyn gave a casual shrug. "It's my thing, the forties and fifties."

"Your noir thing."

"More like my *neo*noir thing. Digging the old styles, but updating them, too." She waggled a magenta fingernail at the screen. "Like that anklet she's wearing. I'd wear one with peep-toe pumps, capri pants, a slim cardigan and Dita Von Teese's bad-red lipstick, Devil."

"You love that Dita Von Teese with her skintight dresses and corsets and elbow-length gloves."

"She's an artist, a burlesque queen."

"I see you haven't thought about this much."

"I celebrate my life through my style, what can I say? I know you understand 'cause you go a little retro yourself, cuz."

Val had a thing for simple, vintage black dresses. When she was a kid, she'd loathed *reach-me-down*— secondhand—clothes, and had sworn that when she grew up she'd always buy off-the-rack. But when that day came, she hated how stiff and scratchy new clothes felt against her skin. Missed the softness of reach-me-downs, so she'd started shopping at second-hand and vintage stores.

"Y'know," Jasmyn said, "with your black-purple hair, pale skin and those hot-cute little black dresses you wear, you'd make a great noir chick."

"I'm still not even sure what noir means."

"It refers to the type of movies being made back in the forties and fifties. Dark and bleak with people who had no morality or sense of purpose."

"Sounds like a badly lit casino in Vegas."

"F'sure!" Jasmyn peeled off a throaty laugh. "That anklet is famous, by the way," she continued, looking at the screen. "Right about here, Fred says 'That's a honey of an anklet you're wearing' and that term—

honey of an anklet—is now one of the classic lines in film noir." She paused, frowning. "Val, what's wrong?"

"That word. *Honey.*" She picked up some wadded napkins and put them into the bag. "Tonight I did what in the P.I. trade is called a honey trap. Which is where a P.I. entices some guy to see if he's unfaithful, which is a bunch of crock because enticing isn't investigating." Wouldn't Jayne be proud to know Val finally understood? And sorely disappointed if she knew how Val reached that understanding.

"From the looks of you, cuz, you overshot *enticing* by a city block."

"Thanks."

"Just sayin'."

"Got it."

Jasmyn was thoughtful for a moment. "I thought your boss wasn't going to let you do any investigations for four more months."

"Jayne doesn't know I did it." Val felt ashamed to have repaid her boss's trust with such insubordination.

"Dawlin'," Jasmyn said gently, "what happened?"

"After she left work early, this new case walked in, and…you know my bullheaded streak." She gave a halfhearted shrug. "Although that's hardly an excuse for my misbehavin'. I'm feeling mighty bad that I took a case that I had no right to take because I wanted fast cash."

"How much *fast cash?*"

"Two grand."

Jasmyn emitted a low whistle. "That's fast, all right. Now you can get your car fixed."

"Already in the shop. I'm driving a rental until it's ready."

"You bad, bullheaded girl, you. Mama will be glad to know you got wheels." She gave Val a knowing look. "Speaking of mamas, now that you're a private eye in training, have you looked for yours?"

Val felt a stab of guilt. "No."

During Katrina, when she and Nanny had been stuck on the roof of their building, her grandmother confessed she had lied about Val's parents dying in a car crash when Val was two years old. Nanny's daughter, Val's mother, had survived, but left soon after that. "She was born Agnes Monte Hickory LeRoy, after your great-grandmother Agnes Lowell and great-grandfather Elias Monte Hickory, but if she's remarried, her last name's prob'ly different. Promise me, dear girl, you'll try to find her, make my wrong right."

Val made that promise.

But since then, she had not tried to find the mother who had abandoned her. Not once.

"Truth be told, Jaz, I can't work up the desire to meet a stranger who gave birth to me, then abandoned me."

Jasmyn nodded. "Everythin' in its own time."

Left up to Val, that time would never come. But she felt wretched breaking her word to Nanny.

"Wow, two thousand!" Jasmyn exclaimed, bringing the conversation back around. "Except for the sneaky part, of course, but who am I to talk? I'm the one sneaking around taking burlesque classes."

For the past five months, Jasmyn had been taking private burlesque dancing lessons from Dottie "the Body" Osborne, a former headliner at the Pink Pussycats in Hollywood, a famous burlesque club where the dancers plied their G-string gimmicks in the 1970s. Val, sworn to secrecy about Jasmyn's clandestine studies, knew if Del and Char ever learned about this, their daughter would be grounded until she was forty.

"The problem with secrets is that they can blow up in your face," Val murmured. "I need to tell Jayne."

"No, cuz, bad idea! Don't blow this internship by gettin' all confessional. Look at the money you made in one night! Plus you tackled your first case and probably learned a lot in the process."

"No," Val said solemnly, gathering the rest of the trash, "I learned investigations are about using the mind to solve puzzles, not playing body games."

"Hey," Jasmyn said, "enough with our heavy noir talk. Let's dish about something fun. I think I got my burlesque name. Ready? *Ruby Stevens!*"

"Definitely sounds like a burlesque name."

"It was Barbara Stanwyck's real name. But they wouldn't let her use it because—guess what?—it sounded like a burlesque dancer! Y'know how burlesque dancers gotta have a gimmick? I'll be Ruby Stevens, and I'll always wear a shiny gold anklet to go with my brassy and phony blond hair. Like your wig, only curlier."

After a beat, Val said, "You know I love ya, right Jaz? Word to the wise. One of these days, you're gonna need to have a sit-down with your mama and be up front about those burlesque lessons. Doing that gives *both* of you dignity."

She wasn't just talking to her cousin. She was talking to herself, too.

Because at that moment, Val knew she was going to be up front with Jayne tomorrow morning and tell her what she had done. Nanny used to say that secrets destroyed relationships, and she was right. If Jayne threatened to end her internship, well, Val would give her one hell of a side note on why she should stay.

After she and Jaz said their good-nights, Val dumped the trash in the kitchen and headed to her room, reflecting on all kinds of things, from blond wigs to honey traps to young women who needed to keep their word.

Just because a hurricane had wiped out Val's world didn't mean it had also taken her self-worth.

CHAPTER FIVE

AT EIGHT-TWENTY the next morning, Val pulled into the parking lot at Diamond Investigations. The office didn't open for forty minutes, but she wanted a chance to talk to Jayne as soon as she arrived, which was usually a few minutes before nine.

Stepping out of the air-conditioned Honda felt as if somebody had opened an oven door in her face. When the monsoons finally rolled in, the moist winds and thunderstorms would bring lower temperatures. Meanwhile, Las Vegas baked.

After flipping on the office lights and setting a bag containing a warm cinnamon roll from Marie's Gourmet Bakery on her desk, she checked herself out in the bathroom mirror.

This morning, she'd woken Jasmyn and told her about her plan to confess the honey trap to Jayne. "Cuz," Jasmyn said sleepily, "you need to wear somethin' to say grace over."

Jaz helped her pick out what to wear, a vintage black crepe dress with a delicate white lace bow, swearing it gave Val a "demure innocence." She wouldn't go that far, but nevertheless played on the theme by pulling up her dark hair in a sleek, tasteful topknot and paring down her makeup to mascara and peach lip gloss.

After tucking a stray hair into the topknot, she went about her morning office tasks. First thing each morning, she fed the fish. Sprinkling vitamin-enriched brine shrimp into the tank, she watched a bright blue-and-yellow angelfish disappear into a dark crevice of a miniature castle. The first week Val was here, Jayne had explained how angelfish needed to hide or they stressed too much. A few fish nibbled at the fare, but as always Mr. Blue-and-Yellow lurked in the shadows of his castle.

"You always do it your way, on your terms," Val murmured.

She headed to the kitchenette nestled in an alcove next to the grandfather clock. In addition to a sink, the closet-size space housed an antique chest of drawers on which sat a coffeepot, cups and a wicker basket filled with packets of sugar, powdered creamer and spoons.

After starting the coffeemaker, she sat at her desk and checked emails. She deleted a spam message and responded to an inquiry—stating that Diamond Investigations was not accepting any new cases.

She paused, staring out the window. Any minute Jayne's Miata would pull in beside Val's rental car.

Scents of warm dough and cinnamon wafted from the pastry bag, but her stomach was like a big knot—no way could she eat. Listening to the coffeemaker burble and hiss, she busied herself by rearranging items on her desk. After stacking the notepads, making a pile of paper clips and tossing a couple of dried-out ballpoint pens, she stared at the grandfather clock.

Eight forty-six.

The front door clicked open.

Val jumped a little, knocking over the cup of pens. They clattered across her desk. She fumbled to pick them up with trembling fingers, listening to the soft click of her boss's sensible heels crossing the floor.

They stopped in front of her desk.

Val looked up, the knot in her stomach tightening. She hadn't seen the Miata pull up, but there it was, parked beside her Honda. And here Jayne was.

She wore a taupe linen blazer over an off-white shell top and...jeans? Her boss never wore jeans. Maybe that was a good thing. Meant she was relaxed, comfortable...ready to hear bad news.

"Good morning, Val."

"Mornin', ma'am—Jayne."

On second look, she realized her boss's eyes were slightly swollen. Had she been crying? Maybe this wasn't the time to spring bad news.

"No calls have come in yet this morning," Val said, doing her best to sound nonchalant, professional.

"Good. I had hoped my calendar was clear this morning because..." Jayne offered a tight smile. "I have something important to discuss with you."

Val's heart pounded like a tribal tom-tom. Did her boss already know about the honey trap? How could she? Didn't matter. Val needed to seize the moment and explain, *now*.

As she opened her mouth, a thump-heavy tune blasted from a car on Garces Avenue. The women stared at each other as a loud, gravelly male voice rapped about pimps, gangstas and blunts for breakfast.

The tune faded as the vehicle continued down the street. The hum of the fish tank and the air conditioner again filled the room.

"You were starting to say?" Jayne asked.

Val eased her shoulders back, took a deep breath… and jumped as the phone on her desk jangled.

They both looked at the caller ID.

"Local number," Jayne said. "Might be that private investigator I spoke with this morning, but I need to discuss the situation with you first. Take a message," she said, walking away, "then come to my office."

Val picked up the receiver, wondering why Jayne had met with another P.I. Was it there that she'd cried? What could have affected tough, no-nonsense Jayne so deeply?

"Diamond Investigations," she answered.

"Is this a, uh, private-investigations agency?"

No, it's a jewelry inspection plant. "Yes."

"I think my apartment is bugged. When I walk over to a certain wall, I hear this pinging sound…"

As the guy rattled on about suspecting that somebody, like maybe his landlord, was planting listening devices in his apartment, Val waited for him to pause so she could give the not-accepting-new-cases spiel.

But he was on a roll, rambling on about beeps on his phone, a funny hole next to a ceiling light where somebody might have planted a camera…

Just as she was wondering how many *a*'s were in the word *paranoia,* the front door clicked open.

She looked up and nearly dropped the receiver.

Sunlight etched the dark silhouette that blocked the doorway. She couldn't see the man's features, but she recognized the bulk of his shoulders and his slouched, wary stance.

Drake.

How did he know she worked here?

"…and sometimes at night, there's this squeaky noise in the kitchen," the guy on the phone rambled on. "It almost sounds like tiny little fingernails scratching. What should I do?"

"Call an exterminator." She watched Drake step inside and close the door, his eyes never leaving hers. He looked about as happy as a homicide detective arriving at a crime scene.

"I'm serious," the guy said, his voice rising, "this is freaking scary!"

"Tell me about it." She hung up.

As he walked toward her, her insides whirled like seagulls circling before a storm.

He wore the same crisp white shirt as last night, although it no longer looked crisp or white. Like his pants, it was wrinkled and creased with dirt. As he drew closer, she saw shadows under his eyes, a slash of grime on his chin, a ragged tear in his shirt.

He stopped, the muscles bunching in his jaw. His eyes were dull, flat. Not even a glimmer of the passion they'd shared last night. He towered over her desk like a vengeful, brooding Heathcliff, his appearance ragged and dirty as though he had walked through hell itself to get here.

Considering he reeked of smoke, maybe he had.

She swallowed almost convulsively as thoughts zigzagged through her mind. Had he followed her last night, this morning? Was he here to report that she'd played a honey trap? But the questions didn't stack up. Something else had obviously happened, some ordeal that had nothing to do with her.

Be cool. Think.

They hadn't ended on bad terms last night. In fact, they had ended on hot, excellent terms. A full-body clutch, a kiss in the works. If her phone hadn't rung, the next moment would have been one smoldering, memorable lip meltdown.

Which meant…maybe he didn't recognize her.

Compared to her sexpot look last night, today she could pass for a prison matron. Didn't explain why he was here, but life was full of crazy coincidences.

"May I help you, sir?" She tried to flatten her speech to mask her New Orleans accent.

He gave her a look that made her insides shrivel. "I'm here to see Jayne," he said in a low, rumbling tone.

"I'll check if she's available."

But he was already heading to her boss's office.

Despite her banging knees, she managed to stand. "You can't go in there—"

"Like hell."

The door shut behind him with a solid thud.

TEN MINUTES LATER, which felt like several lifetimes to Val, Jayne's office door yawned open. The older woman stepped outside, a strained look on her face.

"I don't want any walk-ins during our meeting," she said, "so please lock the door, then come directly in here." She retraced her steps.

Val stood, her heart racing, regretting last night as she had never regretted anything in her life. If only she had obeyed Jayne's rule, if only she hadn't been so greedy to take the cash, if only...

Her body felt drained of life force, yet somehow she managed to walk to the front door. She had hoped her new look had fooled him, but so much for that la-la dream. Now she seemed doubly dumb, first for conducting the honey trap, second for pretending she didn't know the subject of the honey trap.

No, there was a third dumb move. She should have confessed to Jayne the *instant* she walked in. Spilled her guts, laid it all out, talked right through the rap music, the jangling phone. Now it appeared as though Val had been trying to hide her double-dealing.

After locking the door, she walked into Jayne's inner sanctum. The room had always unnerved Val because it felt oddly remote. She had always chalked up her reaction to the cool, off-white walls and sparse decor consisting of a modern, glass-topped desk, two metal guest chairs and several silver-gray filing cabinets. The only real color was the soft jade-and-rose area rug and a painting of the San Francisco skyline, its heavens a mix of vibrant golds and blues.

Jayne sat behind her desk, fiddling with a fountain pen, turning it over and over like a slow-motion propeller blade. Drake leaned against the far wall, his arms folded imposingly across his chest, glowering at Val as though she were a bug he wanted to quash.

She stopped near a chair, but didn't sit. Seemed more respectful to stand. Overhead, a ceiling fan quietly thumped, measuring out the painful moments.

For an unguarded moment, she returned Drake's granite-hard stare. Damn, even the presidents on Mount Rushmore gave back warmer looks. Her gaze dropped to his downturned, sullen mouth and its sensuously curved bottom lip, and for a surreal instant, she remembered his large hands kneading her, his hot whispers turning her insides molten.

She jerked her gaze to the rug. Here she was, her job on the chopping block, and she was getting all romance-cover steamy over a man who looked as though he'd rather throttle her than straddle her.

"Val," Jayne said ominously. She set aside her pen and folded her hands. "I have heard some rather disturbing news. It seems that you conducted a honey trap yesterday evening. Is that true?"

"Yes." Val forced herself to stand straight.

"In doing so, you violated agency policy."

She nodded, her eyes stinging with emotion.

"You also damaged my trust in you."

That hurt the most. "I'm sorry," she said, fighting to speak above a whisper, "what I did was wrong."

Jayne's frosty eyes assessed her. "I have known Mr. Morgan for several years. He is one of the more highly respected private investigators in Las Vegas."

He was a *private investigator?*

"Drake," Jayne continued, "has other, far more serious allegations, which we will discuss later. Meanwhile, tell me in your own words what happened last night. And Val," she added, a hardness creeping into her tone, "do *not* cloud my office with useless, petty defenses."

The last words hurt, but even more upsetting was that Drake had *far more serious allegations.* When had a lousy flirting job, some inappropriate body maneuvers and a not-quite-there kiss become offenses?

"Yes, I conducted a honey trap last night. But that was all I did, Jayne, I promise you."

"And he was the subject."

"Yes."

Jayne leaned forward. "Yesterday, minutes before I exited the office, you and I discussed in detail why this agency *never* undertakes such cases. Had you accepted the case at that time?"

"No."

"When did you?"

"Yesterday around—" she recalled the metallic chimes of the grandfather clock "—four p.m."

Jayne nodded brusquely. "Call-in?"

"Walk-in."

Jayne cast a look at Drake, then returned to Val. "You are not licensed to conduct investigations, which in Nevada, at the very minimum, constitutes a misdemeanor."

"I know."

"You should," Jayne snapped, "because we have discussed it often enough." Her eyes remained glued to Val's. "Did you previously know this client?"

"No."

Jayne blew out an exasperated breath. "For God's sake, Val, why did you do this?"

"Because..." This was the hard part. Admitting her penny-grasping, self-serving reasons. "She paid in cash and I wanted to get my car fixed." She heaved a sigh. "And put some money aside for my own place. I was just plain brainless and greedy. I'm sorry, Jayne. I...would like a second chance. I will never do something dumb-ass like this again, I promise you."

That wasn't the speech she had planned, but considering a glob of sweat was rolling down her back, and trying to stand tall was giving her a bad case of tight neck, it was the best she could do.

Jayne was so quiet, Val mentally steeled herself for the termination speech.

"Oh, Val," she finally said, the angry look on her face crumbling into sadness, "sometimes you remind me..." After a small shake of her head, she lifted her chin. "Mr. Morgan was the victim of a violent crime last night, and he would like to query you."

"A violent crime?" He looked a mess, but she hadn't realized the severity of what he had gone through. "Mercy, what happened?"

He didn't answer. Just stayed leaning against the wall, watching her through slitted eyes.

"Who hired you?" he growled.

"She said her name was Marta."

"Last name?"

"Didn't give one. She said she didn't want to divulge too much personal information. That she had her pride."

"You accepted that?"

Val shifted her weight from one foot to the other. "She was embarrassed that her fiancé, who she said was you, was cheating on her, said it was painful enough to hire a stranger to find out the truth, and that someday—you know, in the future—she didn't want me to know her sad, humiliating secret if I ever were to chance upon her name or see her in public."

His dark eyebrows pressed together. "She said all that?"

"I'm paraphrasing."

"Private investigators deal in facts, not *paraphrasing.*" He looked at Jayne. "Her accent is also a detriment. She could never work undercover."

The bastard. Trashing her ability to be a private investigator!

"Not fair," she blurted. "You have no right—"

"Val," Jayne said, "please answer his questions without commentary."

Seeing the do-as-I-say look on her boss's face, Val clamped her lips shut.

Maybe he wasn't playing fair, but Jayne was trying. Val could tell she was listening, trying to understand what happened. If Jayne had blindly believed everything Drake said, she would have fired Val by now.

Take her lead. Stay grounded, don't rush forward.

"She identified *me* as her fiancé," Drake said to Val.

"Yes."

"I'm not."

She gave a noncommittal shrug.

"What's that supposed to mean?"

"The way you carried on last night, sucking my fingers, laying a track of kisses all along my inner arm...other things...I had a hard time believing you belonged to *anybody* else."

"That's enough," Drake barked.

"You asked the question," Jayne murmured, a smile playing on her lips.

His scowl deepened. "Did she tell you my name?"

"Just your first name."

"Because she had her pride?" When Val nodded, he peeled himself off the wall and took a step toward her. "And you bought that bunch of crap?"

"Didn't know it was crap at the time, but yes."

"What else did she tell you?"

Mercy, he was relentless. "That friends of hers said

you were cheating on her, and she wanted to know if that was true."

He was walking toward her, closing the space between them.

"Their names?"

"She didn't say."

"Did you see the car she drove?"

She thought back to sitting at the desk, facing Marta. "No."

"You didn't look?"

He was crowding her, intimidating her, but no way would she budge. She inched up her face, her nose nearly touching his shirt that reeked of smoke.

She inhaled a sharp breath. "No."

"I take it she paid you in cash."

"Yes."

"How much?"

She was glad he blocked her view of Jayne. "Two thousand."

He shoved his face closer. "Had you ever spoken to Marta before?"

"No."

"Ever *seen* her before? Around your home, this agency, anywhere else?"

"No, never." Val eased back a step, needing some distance from his intensity.

"She has a Russian accent?"

How did he know? "Yes, a thick one."

"Anything else unusual about her?"

"She…wore designer clothes, although they could

have been rip-offs." She wanted to sit down, but the last thing she wanted to give him was a psychological advantage. "Her perfume smelled like strawberries. And she wore a large diamond ring."

He flinched, almost imperceptibly, but this close, Val caught it.

"Where did she tell you I would be?"

"At Topaz, the strip club, probably around eight or eight-thirty."

"And you surveilled me there?"

Val nodded. "Didn't see your truck, so I drove around the block and found it parked at the appliance store."

A glimmer of something shone in his eyes. "Did she say how she knew I would be there?"

"Friend told her."

"The nameless friend," he mused darkly, his eyes searching hers. "Did you take a photo of my truck?"

"No."

"Why not?"

She hadn't thought to bring a camera last night, but she wasn't going to admit that. "Didn't want anyone to see me taking pictures. Instead, I quickly checked out what items were in the back, on the front seat."

"Why?"

"I thought if you were fooling around, I might see ladies' things. A purse, lipstick or something."

"What did you see?"

"A notebook. A dog bed, some chew toys."

Outside on the street, the old tune "Thunder Road"

blasted, Springsteen's crooning, aching voice begging the girl to make it real.

As the tune faded, Drake said in a low voice, "Last night my house burned down. I believe Marta was working with someone who set it on fire."

The silence was thick, uncomfortable as the overhead fan sliced at the air. No wonder Marta had wanted her to go back to the bar and look for him. They had probably been torching his place at that very moment, wanted to know if he was on his way home or not.

Now she understood, after she'd suggested Marta call Drake, why she'd said "I don't have...." She didn't have his cell phone number.

"Did you know what they were planning?" he asked.

"Of course not!" An ominous wave of emotion rose in her, filling her with anger and despair. This interrogation was becoming way more than just the possibility of losing a job.

She could end up in jail.

In the time it took to take a deep, calming breath, she was ready to charge ahead and fight for her future. One that didn't include time behind bars.

"I was willing to stand here and answer questions," she said to Jayne, "but if he's going to accuse me of committing a crime, I must stand up for myself." Not waiting for Jayne's agreement, she turned to Drake. "Since you don't believe me when I say I had *nothing* to do with the fire, give me a polygraph."

He smirked. "Those aren't cheap, sister, and *I'm* not shelling out the bucks for one."

"Then I will!"

He rubbed his jaw, muttering something about irrational, reactionary women.

"I call you on that," she snapped, jabbing an index finger at him, "and raise you one biased, egocentric, Neanderthal male."

Have mercy, the man actually looked taken aback.

"Jayne," he growled, "did you hear that?"

Her boss acknowledged the question with a nod. "Difficult not to."

"What are you going to do about it?" he asked.

"Nothing. She appears to be holding her own quite well."

Val felt a surge of empowerment. She had never felt anything other than respect for Jayne, but at the moment, she honest to God *loved* that woman.

She met Drake's damning gaze straight on, refusing to bow to his contempt. "What gives you the right," she said evenly, "to accuse me of a crime I didn't commit?"

His expression hardened, but he didn't say a word.

"I believe," she continued, "that in the U.S. criminal justice system, a person is presumed *innocent* until *proven* guilty. Although based on your inquisition, it seems you are so much more than just a private investigator. Why, you're also a prosecutor, a judge *and* a jailer."

She kept her gaze locked on his, unswayed by his

big, black-hearted, disapproving self. Those gray eyes predatory like a wolf's, all that dark stubble roughing up his face, the muscles bunching in that strong jaw.

Oh, he was bad all right.

But she'd faced bad before. Back in their shop in the French Quarter, Val had confronted several sticky-fingered thieves, once pulling her nanny's Saturday night special on a nasty-tempered fellow who'd stuffed a fine-cut crystal decanter underneath his jacket. He had shakily given it back, and Nanny later scolded Val that she'd rather lose a decanter than a granddaughter.

The way Val had felt during that would-be theft was how she felt now. Like Drake had tried to steal her very truth. "I already admitted my wrongdoing," she said, "to both you and Jayne. And I apologized. And I really am very sorry you lost your house."

"I almost lost something much more important."

To her utter astonishment, a flush crawled up his neck, disappearing into the underbrush of his five o'clock shadow. He shifted his gaze to some remote spot past her left ear and dropped his hands to his sides. She might have reveled in her ability to have won this round, that maybe her words made the man question *himself* for a change, but his reaction took the fight right out of her.

Because what he emoted was visceral, raw, *pained*. She swore she could feel his suffering across the room, as real as a searing blast of Mojave winds.

"I think we've all said enough on this topic," Jayne said quietly.

The cold in Drake's eyes had thawed, their stony color lightening to a smoky gray. The lines in his face were still hard and rugged, but his intensity had lost its edge.

"Drake did not sleep at all last night," Jayne continued. "He was at the vet hospital with his dog, who, thank God, survived the fire. Years ago, I spent my share of late nights at vet hospitals, too. Became a ritual for me to welcome my dog home with a big pink ball. Silly, really, but my male dog loved them."

Val's insides twisted at the thought of what he'd gone through. No wonder he was reacting more than thinking.

"I'm glad to know your dog's okay," she said.

He nodded his thanks.

Jayne was watching him with a thoughtful intensity. "Drake, I realize how upset you are, but this young woman is not an arsonist. I did a thorough background check on her before she started work at Diamond Investigations, and she has no criminal background, not even a speeding ticket. Her main fault is that she has an impetuous streak, but she is incapable of such a grievous crime."

Val had to bite back a smile. *Impetuous streak.* No one had ever said it quite like that.

"Plus," Jayne added, her tone softening, "she survived Katrina, although her home and immediate family did not. During that horrific event, this young woman was a hero. Showed the kind of courage that few in life can claim, which says more about her character than any background check. Suffice it to say, I cannot read her mind, but I know her heart. She would never wish such losses on anyone else, much less cause them."

Val blinked rapidly, astonished. Her boss had never before mentioned Katrina. Of course, she herself had never mentioned it, either. Outside of her cousins and best pal, Cammie, Val never talked about it. Sometimes she feared that if she looked too deeply into those shadows, they might swallow her whole.

She hadn't been a hero, though. Heroes succeeded at their tasks. Val had failed at hers.

"Drake, I am your friend and colleague," Jayne said, "but if you take criminal action against her, I will stand in your way."

He met her gaze. "I will not take criminal action."

Jayne nodded, shifted slightly in her seat. "I realize this isn't the time to broach the next topic, but I have no choice. Events in my life are such that..." She snatched a breath. "I...must leave tomorrow, and I do not wish to close Diamond Investigations."

"Close?" Val sank into the chair. She'd guessed right—something devastating had happened in her boss's life.

The older woman forced a smile, which quickly dissolved. "Today both of you have been honest in this room, sometimes brutally so. Now I...must be honest, too."

Jayne studied her hands for a moment. When she looked up, her features were tight, pinched.

"I have cancer," she whispered.

FOR THE NEXT few moments, the three of them were like a tableau, frozen in their spots, nobody speaking. The only sound was the metronomic whoosh of the overhead fan.

Drake stared at Jayne, the news belatedly hitting him like a slow-moving shock wave.

Cancer.

He had known Jayne Diamond since launching his own private-investigator career five-plus years ago. Had worked a few high-profile cases with her, too: an intellectual-property investigation that netted a notorious counterfeiter and an undercover sting that fingered a crafty embezzler. He respected her tough, smart, sophisticated style. Liked how she faced life ramrod straight and worked rock hard.

To see her now, her handsome face etched with worry, those blue eyes clouded with fear, gutted him.

"Jayne," he said, "what did the doctor say?"

"Hodgkin's lymphoma. Stage four." She stilled, holding her emotions in check. "Apparently, it has spread to my liver."

When Val choked back a cry, Jayne held up her hand. "Please. I cannot…"

Val pursed her lips and nodded.

The older woman gestured to the other guest chair. "Drake, please sit so I may look at both of you while we discuss a few things."

He did as told.

"I am leaving tomorrow morning for the Mayo Clinic in Scottsdale, Arizona. I will be staying with my brother and his family while I undergo chemo-therapy and radiation treatments. They also recommended steroids."

"And?" he asked.

"I declined. Although I like to work out, I do not wish to bulk up like Arnold Schwarzenegger."

Drake got her. The ship might be in rough waters, but the captain was still at the helm. And if she chose to find humor in the situation, then by damn, so would he.

"Or get into trouble like Lance Armstrong," he quipped.

Jayne's lips twitched with amusement. "I might have to give up my Tour de France medals."

"*And* go on Oprah," he added.

Jayne shrugged. "If it was her favorite things show, maybe."

"I can't believe you two are joking." Val sniffed, touched her nose with the back of her hand.

Jayne searched the young woman's face. "As trite as this may sound, sometimes humor truly is the best medicine."

Val, fighting tears, nodded. "I just…don't want…"

"Neither do I." An uneasiness crossed Jayne's face. "I will be gone for two weeks, possibly three. As we discussed earlier, Drake, I am Val's mentor in her quest to earn a Nevada private investigator's license. I have not been able to find a mentor to take my place. I met with Gary Parker this morning, but he is understaffed at his agency and does not have the time to tutor an intern."

"Put your mentoring, and your office, on hold. Pick both up after you return," Drake suggested.

She gave her head a shake. "As I said, I prefer to not close my office. Calls not being returned, emails unanswered, doors locked...only hurts future business."

Good that she was talking about the future. Although he wouldn't have expected anything less of Jayne. "You can forward calls to your cell while you're out of state. Take your laptop and answer emails, too."

"Jayne doesn't have a laptop," Val murmured, "prefers desktops."

He shot her an I-wasn't-talking-to-you look. "Then check email on your smartphone."

"No smartphone, either," Val said. "She prefers her stand-alone cell phone."

"Maybe Jayne can speak for herself," he muttered.

"Actually," Jayne said, looking amused, "I think my assistant is doing a grand job."

He was starting to feel like an interloper at a sisterhood rally.

"Jayne likes more *established* forms of communication," Val said. "For example, she likes calls to her landline being answered by a human voice because she believes it shows professionalism. People know someone is really *in* the office, not answering their cell phone while getting a manicure or something. Just goes to show landlines are *not* an antiquated system." She gave her boss a smile.

He cut a look at Sister Suck-up. "Whether something's old or not isn't the issue. We're talking about interim solutions while Jayne's away."

He looked at Val's prim black dress and its oversize lace bow and her hair—a crazy combo of black and purple—knotted into that conservative little bun on the top of her head. What was with the spinster librarian look? He expected her to put her fingers to her lips and shush him any moment.

Last night, different story. She'd worn so little there had been more flesh than cloth on display. Probably 90 percent skin, 10 percent garments. And of that ninety, he'd give a solid 30 percent to that cleavage.

He shifted in his seat and met her eyes, all big and brown and expectant.

"What?" he asked.

"Jayne just asked you a question," she said, her voice oozy like molasses.

He glanced at Jayne, who had an expression on her face that he'd seen before. The one where it seemed she had read your every single thought. She couldn't, of course, but the lady was definitely picking up on signals. Helped along by her cohort's earlier admission that he had sucked on her fingers and nibbled on her arm.

"I know you worked out of your home office," Jayne said. "Therefore, I thought it would help you—and certainly help me—if while I am gone, you worked out of the back office here at Diamond Investigations. When I started the agency, it was my living quarters.

Private entrance and parking area. Small bathroom with a shower. At one time there was a full kitchen, but I made that into a supply room after…" She made a dismissive gesture. "Anyway, I have rented out the space to other investigators, but for the past year, it has been empty." Her eyes shone with a purpose he read loud and clear.

Oh, no. Not that.

"So," she said sweetly, "I thought perhaps you could mentor her while I am gone."

Yes, that.

He tilted his chin to look at Jayne, acting as though he was listening, considering. Being polite wasn't his strong suit, but today he would be on his best behavior, not give the lady any more trouble than she was already juggling.

But *mentor* Miss Who Dat?

He'd backed off blaming her for being part of Yuri's arson, and not only because he agreed with Jayne's request. In his experience, guilty people didn't make impassioned speeches—speeches, maybe, but not with the fervor of a small-country dictator. And Jayne, never one to spoon out compliments, had ladled them on her intern.

Now he knew, too, that he and Val were survivors. Although his losses didn't stack up to hers. The fact that she didn't let her past shadow her life earned his respect.

Didn't mean he wanted to mentor her, though. She talked too much. Had a way of dressing that defied logic. Distracted him with those rosebud lips, that body, what had almost happened last night…

There had to be a way around this.

"…Val can also help you field incoming calls, file reports, conduct some basic internet research."

"I have my own phone."

"But do you have a computer?" Jayne asked.

"Probably not anymore," he muttered.

"Jayne, ma'am, I'm sorry to interrupt, but I need to say something." Val nervously licked her lips. "I think it's a super idea that Drake uses that back office, but I don't believe he and I would…"

"Get along?" Jayne prompted.

"Exactly," he said, straightening.

"You might say our *get-along* has a big ol' hitch in it," Val agreed. "But I am at fault for that." She laid her hand on that lace bow and dipped her head slightly. "Indeed I am, for doing that honey trap 'n' all. If Mr. Morgan wants to use the back office, I would make sure he had complete privacy, and if he needed assistance, I would certainly help out, but I wouldn't want him to mentor me. It's far too much to ask of him, especially now." She slipped a look at him, her eyes all dewy and full of concern.

It took everything he had to not roll his eyes. But for once he was on her side. Together they would defeat this mentoring delusion of Jayne's.

He put on his best thoughtful face. "She makes some good points. But I understand your not wanting a gap in her mentoring. A gal like her—" He caught his gaffe. "I mean, a *woman* like her deserves regular, ongoing sessions because, well, she just does. *Fortunately,* I know another P.I. who can fill in."

He'd talk Eddie into this babysitting gig. Just make it clear these mentoring sessions were to take place in the office, not at Caesars' sports book, where Eddie liked to spend every spare waking hour with the other horse-racing freaks.

"But you'll be in the adjacent office, which makes getting together convenient." Jayne picked up her fountain pen. "Plus, mentoring only takes a little time each day, maybe thirty minutes or so…" She turned the pen. "To be frank, I do not want her to be mentored by anyone else. Like that fellow Eddie Mueller. I want her to learn the art of *investigations,* not if Fancy Lady will win, place or show."

Drake blinked with surprise. Either she really could read thoughts or had heard through the grapevine that he and Eddie were buds. Whatever the reason, she was one sharp lady.

But she shouldn't have to be matching wits right now. The bad news was fresh. She had every right to be selfish and tend only to herself at a time like this. She needed people to support her, not take from her.

He pulled in a long breath and blew it out. "I'll mentor her."

Jayne gave him a grateful look. "Thank you."

"But…" Val looked at him as though he'd grown donkey ears. "You don't have the time!"

"It'll only take thirty minutes or so," he muttered, shooting her a get-with-the-program look.

She frowned, obviously confused by his signal. Oh, this was going well already.

When she started to speak, he cut her off with a wave of his hand. "First lesson is to follow my lead. I am mentoring you and that's that."

She slumped in her chair and eyed him warily.

"Excellent," Jayne said, looking relieved. "I also would like for you to be here full-time starting tomorrow, if that is acceptable."

Full time? "I, uh, have off-site meetings, surveillances, pulling records at the courthouse."

"Of course," Jayne said, "otherwise, you'll be in your office."

If that's what the lady wanted, she'd get it. "Fine."

"Are you interested in Val forwarding my client calls to your cell? I could request she forward them to another P.I. in town, but since you will be here..."

"Fine."

"Excellent." She closed her eyes for a moment, then slowly reopened them. "Thank you, both of you. It is reassuring to not have to worry about the agency while..." A look of withdrawal came over her face as she glanced away.

Drake followed the focus of her attention. It was that painting on the far wall. A city landscape. Maybe a place she'd once lived or visited or perhaps where her family came from.

His father, who had worked in hotel security for

years, had known Jayne peripherally. Drake recalled his once saying she had lived with a woman, a lawyer, somewhere downtown. He wondered if that had been in the back apartment.

Drake wasn't one to grieve openly, but after a few beers, he sometimes loosened up about his dad, his brother. He would bet Jayne never did that. She faced her ghosts alone.

And now she was facing life's harshest challenger. Death. Not that it was at her door, but it was lurking in the neighborhood. If anybody could outmaneuver the Grim Reaper, it was sure as hell Jayne.

But if not…

He thought of his father those last few weeks of his life, their talks, Drake's promises.

"Anything you need, Jayne, call me. My phone is on 24/7. Don't worry about the office or clients or…" He scratched his throat. "The mentoring. I'll be here. I promise."

CHAPTER SIX

AN HOUR LATER, Drake stood at a door marked 3B in the Willow Creek Apartments, which were nowhere near a willow or a creek. The building sat in a not-so-good Vegas neighborhood, but being on the third floor, with a picturesque view of the busy U.S. Route 95, gave it some security.

He knocked on the door.

"Who's there?" asked a peculiarly strained male voice.

"Drake. Open up."

After several clicks and the sliding grate of a latch, the door creaked open. A paunchy, barefoot guy in chinos and a T-shirt with the words I'm Calmer Than You Are stood there, his eyes pinker than some people liked their steaks. An old Aerosmith tune, "Sweet Emotion," played in the background.

"Aqua Man," he murmured around an exhale of smoke, "long time no see. Worried that Mayan apocalypse got you, my brother."

Drake wished his nickname had stayed back in high school along with pimple cream and bad cafeteria food, but it had stuck, being used by people who overheard others use it or who, like Li'l Bit, thought the name sounded groovy.

"Can I come in?"

His buddy stepped back and made a gesture as though he was welcoming a player to a game show.

Entering Li'l Bit's place was like stepping into the '70s. The furniture was a mix of wicker, chunky wood and chrome lamps. A creepy spider plant dominated a corner, seemingly thriving on stray fluorescent light aimed at a poster of Hendrix with a rainbow flowing out of his guitar.

"Shut the door," Drake said. "We gotta talk."

Li'l Bit, who claimed he got his nickname after answering "a little bit" whenever asked if he liked something, complied.

"You gotta air out this place," Drake said, waving his hand. "It reeks of weed."

"Man, you should talk. You smell like a marshmallow roast."

Drake swiped at his hairline. "My place burned down last night."

Li'l Bit pressed his palm to his forehead as though keeping the thoughts in place. "Whoa, no...you mean..."

"Arson."

A stricken look crossed his face. "Hearsay?"

"Smoke inhalation, but he's okay."

Next thing Drake knew, he was wrapped in a bear hug. The kind only a two-hundred-and-fifty-pound man, most of it heart, could give.

Ever since Drake had hired Li'l Bit four years ago to serve some legal papers, the two of them had clicked. Not because they shared interests—Drake could care less about ganja, three-day concert festivals and the film *The Big Lebowski*—but they shared a passion for their professions.

Li'l Bit, born Nathan Davidovitch to Lillian and Bernie Davidovitch of Brooklyn, had been enrolled at Brooklyn Law School five years ago. After falling in love with a massage therapist named Xela and following her to Vegas, he'd opened a process server business, Boss Services, Inc., with the motto When You Want It Done Right, Leave It With the Boss.

He probably would have returned to Brooklyn after the breakup with Xela, but by then Boss Services, Inc. was thriving, and Li'l Bit had grown attached to the aging dogs at the canine retirement ranch project where he volunteered.

"I got your back, my brother," Li'l Bit said, pulling away, his eyes filling with tears. "Wanna beer?"

Minutes later, the brew had chilled Drake's mood. Not completely, but enough that Aerosmith's rocking, rolling and screaming was starting to sound good.

"Man," his pal murmured, dragging his hand over his puffed-out curly hair, "Yuri is one sick dude. Arson investigators on it?"

"One was at the scene." Drake took another swig. "Name's Tony Cordova."

"But you didn't give Yuri up."

"He's mine."

"Aqua Man," Li'l Bit muttered, "taking on the Russian Mafia solo…" He gave his head a slow shake, as though the thought was too heavy to contemplate.

"I'm not taking on the army, just one soldier."

"This Tony dude could help you."

Drake took a swig of beer. Tony had already left a message, but he hadn't wanted to talk to him yet.

For the next few moments, as they listened to Aerosmith crooning about getting a thrill from the smell of a girl's hair, Drake flashed on Val at Dino's. Those big brown eyes. Her soapy, fresh scent. How the heat of her body fused with the heat of the night.

He imagined peeling off those little triangles of fabric, exposing her full, ripe breasts. Unzipping that red miniskirt and pulling it down, down, over her shapely legs, and helping her step out of it in those sky-high heels. He smiled, remembering her beloved Saints' emblem, the fleur-de-lis, on the shoes.

She loved that team so much, he wouldn't be surprised if she had a tat of a fleur-de-lis. On her lower back? Thigh? Nestled somewhere between those pale, plump breasts?

"…she'd eat him alive, man."

Took Drake a moment to reel his thoughts to the present. "Huh?"

Li'l Bit picked up a bag of Cheetos and tilted it toward Drake, who waved it off. "Hearsay can't stay at your mom's. That Maxine, she's one badass feline she-hulk." He popped a Cheeto into his mouth.

Maxine, a crossed-eyed Siamese cat, thought she

was put on this earth to dominate it. Li'l Bit had been with him on a day when Drake had dropped by his mom's with Hearsay. The plan had been to keep Maxine sequestered in the spare bedroom, but his grandmother accidentally opened the door, and like a deranged, heat-seeking missile with fur, Maxine found and cornered Hearsay within seconds. Poor dog shook for a solid hour after that encounter.

"My landlord's cool with pets, so I can keep Hearsay here," his pal offered, helping himself to another Cheeto. "Plus he can do my rounds with me at the canine retirement ranch. Those old dudes love youngsters' company."

"I don't want him turning into a stoner."

"For you, my brother, I'll only toke in the bathroom, with the fan on. Hearsay won't even get a whiff of secondhand smoke."

"Good. Mind if I stay, too?"

"Thought you'd crash at your mom and Glenda's."

Glenda, his grandmother, and Li'l Bit were a mutual admiration society ever since the Hearsay-Maxine encounter. Li'l Bit had stood between the cat and dog while Glenda maneuvered her wheelchair to the kitchen, returning with salmon, Maxine's favorite. While she distracted the cat, he got Hearsay to safety.

Since then, the two of them got together for occasional evenings of *Inner Sanctum Mysteries* on old Lux Radio recordings. While Glenda puffed her nightly cigarillo and sipped a martini, Li'l Bit drank beer. He said he didn't smoke weed during those visits, but knowing Glenda, she wouldn't care.

"Can't leave my dog," Drake answered. After what happened, he didn't want to leave Hearsay alone again, ever. Of course, that wasn't practical. Couldn't take the dog into courthouses, restaurants, clients' offices…but for the next few weeks, he didn't want to leave him alone at night. As much as his dog needed the reassurance that he was okay, Drake probably needed it more.

Li'l Bit held up his hand, palm out. "Gotta be there for your dog, man. Give me five."

Drake slapped his hand. "I also don't want to stay at Mom's, because I don't want Yuri following me there. Here I'm not worried about that. Dozens of apartments, people coming and going at all hours, hundreds of cars zipping down the freeway with a view of your front door…Yuri would be too visible."

Li'l Bit nodded. "Plus I got a peephole."

"Then why'd you ask who I was?"

"Forgot to look."

"Buddy," he said, motioning his head toward the baggie of ganja, "you need to ease up on that stuff."

He looked thoughtful for a moment. "Think I'm a marijuana addict?"

"Yes. No. I'm no expert."

"But you're a gambling addict."

Drake nodded.

"You go to those twelve-step meetings?"

"No, I went to a therapist."

Li'l Bit did a dramatic double-take. "*You?* I don't mean that negative, man. It's just…you talking for, like, an *hour* is like matter absorbing space and expelling it into the past."

Drake paused. "I can't believe you actually say things like that…and mean them." When Li'l Bit opened his mouth to speak, Drake cut him off with a halting gesture. "On to the next topic. I want to install an outdoor surveillance camera with motion-detection ability at Mom's."

Li'l Bit blinked. "Dude, you're overreacting. No way Yuri's going there. Anyway, your mom…" He blew out a whoosh of breath, scenting the air with Cheetos and beer. "She has a heavy antisecurity thing, man."

"I know." When his dad had insisted on putting bars on the windows, his mom had a fit. *I live in a home, Benny, not a prison.*

"Glenda, though, she gets the twenty-first century. Eighty-five and still rockin'. She'd dig a surveillance camera pointed at the porch—then she'd know if it was worthwhile to drive across the house to answer the door. That new wheelchair of hers is slick. Goes up to twelve miles an hour."

"She said five."

"Probably didn't want to worry you."

"What could worry me about her driving fast…" The truth hit him like a Mack truck. "She's taking it outside."

"You didn't hear that from me, man."

"She's *driving* that chair *outside?* She's too old to drive alone!"

"That's what she said you'd say."

"In this *heat,* too."

"She only goes out at night."

Drake took a last draw on his beer, not taking his eyes off Li'l Bit. He set the bottle on the steamer trunk. "You know more than you're letting on."

"I promised Glenda I'd keep my mouth shut."

"Yeah. Wouldn't want matter devouring space and the universe doing a backflip."

"Dude, don't be angry. It's not a bad thing I can't talk about. It's about love and life force, man."

It pissed Drake off that Li'l Bit wouldn't open up, but he couldn't begrudge his friend keeping his promise.

"Whatever's going on," Drake said, "I need to spark some common sense in Grams about driving in the dark. Especially after her nightly martini."

"She's a strong-willed lady."

"Tell me about it. Mom's just as bad."

Seemed as if every women he crossed paths with lately had a beef or an agenda. He admired Jayne, loved his mother and Grams…was mostly confounded by Miss Who Dat…but each of them had a way of being demanding and defiant. Like somebody had called a war between the sexes and forgotten to tell the men.

He was going to emerge from these entanglements either angry, frustrated or, God help him, a feminist.

"You visiting Glenda soon?"

"Was thinking about doing it now, before I pick up Hearsay. Need to talk in person about the fire."

"Yeah, man, heavy news is a drag over the phone. Do me a solid?"

"What?"

"Got a box of cigarillos for Glenda. Can't get over there for a few days, and I know she's running low."

"I'll take them to her."

A few moments later, Li'l Bit handed over the box of cigarillos. "Good Times, sweet. They're her faves."

Drake stared at the illustration of a classic convertible and palm tree on top of the box. Made him think of Yuri's Benz parked in front of palm trees outside Topaz…and an old memory of Yuri smoking those stubby, exotic French cigarettes.

"Gitanes Mais," he murmured, meeting Li'l Bit's eyes. "Those were the kind of French cigarettes Yuri used to smoke. Strong, exotic tobacco rolled in yellow *mais,* corn, paper."

"Wow, man, I almost forgot about that. Those things smelled bad."

Drake smiled knowingly. "That's the beauty of them. Distinct scent and look. Can't buy them in the U.S.—have to buy them online or on the black market."

"You're having dirty thoughts, aren't you?"

"Real dirty. I'm gonna pull a trash hit on Topaz, look for any *Gitanes Mais* in their garbage. Would be handy to run 'em for DNA, which I would bet good money matches Yuri's, then cross-reference those results to any DNA a certain arson investigator might find at my old place."

"Told you this Tony dude could help you."

"First, the trash hit. And some gumshoeing in my neighborhood. *Then,* and on *my* terms, I'll touch base with this Tony dude."

Li'l Bit grinned. "Aqua Man, you got your family's strong-willed gene and then some."

THE NEXT MORNING, Drake woke up to something wet lapping his face.

Hearsay.

He rubbed him behind his ear as the dog licked and nuzzled and wiggled his morning salutations. Drake gave him a reassuring pat. "It's good to have you back, too."

He fumbled on the floor for his phone, picked it up and squinted at the screen. Ten o'clock. Groggily, he figured out he'd slept fourteen hours, but he still felt tired. As he sat up, he winced at the black-light poster of Jimi Hendrix on the wall behind the couch. A man needed strong, black coffee before dealing with that much glowing neon paisley.

By eleven, Drake had showered and dressed. Yesterday afternoon he'd dropped by his mom's, but she had been at her bowling league, and only his grandmother was home. She had been taking a nap, Maxine curled up at her feet, and although he had the urge to wake her up and give her a scolding about carousing at night in her power chair, he had instead pulled the light throw over her, left the cigarillos on her night-stand, and tiptoed out of the room.

On his way to Li'l Bit's apartment, he'd bought some jeans, a pile of polo shirts in assorted colors, sneakers, dog food and a few other odds and ends. Then he picked up Hearsay from the vet hospital. He'd managed to feed himself and Hearsay, take the dog for a walk and watch some mindless TV before crashing.

Before dropping by his mom's again, he needed to talk to Val and explain the investigative task he wanted them to conduct over the lunch hour.

Drake rubbed the dog behind the ears and stared into his big brown eyes. "Can't take you with me today, buddy. You need to rest. It's cool in here, you got food and water, and Li'l Bit will be back from his senior-citizen dog ranch soon, and he'll spoil you rotten."

It wasn't easy leaving.

"Love you, buddy," he murmured, then stepped outside and shut the door behind him.

AFTER A HOT drive steeped in exhaust fumes, Drake hit downtown Vegas, a mix of courthouses, old-time casinos, tacky wedding chapels, restaurants and the odd retail shop. He used to see more shuttered businesses, their windows as dark as a Vegas pawnbroker's heart, but big money was pouring back into the area, creating what one politician called a "dense urban core." He hated to see vintage Las Vegas torn down, replaced by futuristic chrome-and-glass buildings that had no history, no soul.

When he reached Diamond Investigations, he pulled into a parking space in the back behind a tall wooden fence that separated the rear entrance from the street. He liked how Jayne hadn't altered the architecture of the World War II–era bungalow office.

Old, dense ironwood trees lined the fence and the other side of the parking space, making it private. One thick trunk curved over the space, its blue-green leaves providing a mottled canopy against the blistering sun. Peterson Law, an adobe home renovated into law offices, sat at the far end of the asphalt. To any passersby, the parking lot appeared to be for the law firm only.

After locking the pickup, he headed to the far side of the bungalow. There, just as Jayne had texted, sat an old doghouse. Over the doorway, he could make out the hand-painted letters P, A, T and C. Patches?

He reached inside and felt under the roof. There. The duct tape. He peeled one end and retrieved the key. Smart to hide it there. No burglar in his right mind would reach into an unknown doghouse.

Batting at a pesky mosquito, he headed to the bungalow office. Weather report claimed possible light showers this afternoon, but the sky was an endless, washed-out blue. Not a single cloud.

Inside, the cool air swept over him, stinging cold against the sweat on his brow. He flipped on the light switch. There were two windows, one with a picturesque view of his rusting pickup, the other a view of traffic along Garces Avenue.

He made a mental note to keep those blinds closed.

Turning, he let out a low whistle. In the center of the room sat a massive cherrywood desk and a high-back, tufted-leather swivel chair. Pretentious, and even though he hated to admit it, damn impressive. Not the kind of look one found in private investigators' offices, unless they had a lucrative business on the side, like neurosurgery.

He wondered if it had been Jayne's partner's former desk at her law practice.

Somebody had been in here polishing, based on the scent of lemon oil and the high gloss of the wood. A desktop computer sat on top, ready to go.

Against the wall were wooden bookcases, also polished. No books, though. Probably moved so the polish didn't stain the bindings. The scuffed hardwood floor had been vacuumed. Next to the computer were a stack of yellow legal pads, a jar of pens and a small box of paper clips.

He was mentally scolding Jayne for playing housekeeper last night, time better spent on packing and resting for her trip, when he saw what lay in the corner.

A new doggie bed. And on it, a big pink ball.

A fissure deep inside him opened up.

Since the fire, some force had kept him moving forward, through the terror, around the obstacles. Despite how much there was to do, and how much had been left undone, he kept progressing, kept advancing like some kind of android whose mechanical reflexes had taken over.

It wasn't about his being patient or accepting. He couldn't claim those traits. It was about his standing up to pain. He was good at that. Proved his strength. He could take a punch and hardly flinch. Face death and negotiate covenants.

Brush up against love and not get touched.

He walked over and picked up the pink ball. It felt soft yet firm, its color vibrant like life itself.

Until this moment, he hadn't really understood that standing up to his own pain was not about being strong, but self-indulgent. If all you saw was your suffering, your back was turned to others' hardships.

He set the ball on the doggie bed, wishing he had looked into his father's eyes and told him he loved him.

After a quick check of the rest of the bungalow, Drake headed down the narrow hallway to a wooden door, bolted, that led into Diamond Investigations. He wondered if it was bolted shut on the other side, too, but guessed not. When Jayne lived here, she would have wanted the final say on whether or not that door was open. This had been her private world, the one she protected above all else.

THE GRANDFATHER CLOCK was on its twelfth chime as Val headed into the kitchenette. She pulled a large paper bag out of the minifridge, which she had purchased on the way into work this morning with her ill-gotten honey-trap proceeds. She had hoped if she did something nice for the office maybe she wouldn't feel so bad about breaking her word to Jayne. The fridge cost eighty-nine dollars, a good deal, but it hadn't done what it was supposed to do—though it was cold inside, she still felt guilty.

Sitting at her desk, she opened the paper bag that Char had packed for her this morning. Inside was a blackened-chicken po'boy, a container of corn *maque choux,* the Cajun version of creamed corn, another container of green gumbo and a fat wedge of bread pudding.

"Made it for you, sugar," she'd said, handing Val the bag, "'cause today you need a little extra lovin'."

Char had made the thousand-hundred calorie lunch because Jasmyn told her about Jayne's cancer diagnosis, and that Val was winging it until her boss's return. All of that Val had said Jaz could share.

But no, Jasmyn, on a roll, had continued to run off at the mouth to her mama about how Val had dressed like a hooker to seduce some strange man in a sleazy parking lot, only to learn later he was a private eye who blamed her for burning his house, and that although Jayne talked him out of pressing criminal charges, he was now Val's temporary boss, and neither he nor Val was very happy about it.

After Jasmyn apologized for "maybe sharing a tad too much with Mama," she'd insisted Val wear something other than one of her little black dresses—

"Dawlin', yesterday you needed grace. Today you need a miracle"—and loaned her a vintage bluish-purple lace dress, so sheer Val had to borrow a slip to wear underneath.

She was getting ready to take her first bite of the chicken po'boy when something moved into her peripheral vision. Something large and dark and...

She emitted a raspy shriek, more air than voice.

"Sorry," Drake said, his voice rumbling from deep in his chest, "didn't mean to scare you."

Gone was the retro suit. Today he wore jeans and an orangey polo shirt, the kind of casual clothes men wore all the time, but she doubted other men filled them this well.

She peered up at his face, wondering what looked different. Ah, he'd shaved. With his stubble gone, she saw the tan on his face better. Saw his lips better, too. Wondered when they pulled back into a smile, did his teeth look startlingly white against his brown skin?

Like she'd ever see that. Smiling and Drake were like drinking alcohol and walking stairs—they didn't mix.

He gently touched her shoulder. "Your sandwich."

She looked down, surprised to see she'd squeezed it so hard, pieces of tomato and chicken were erupting out of the top.

"Lord have mercy," she muttered. She shoved the entire mess into the paper bag, then looked at him and smiled sweetly. "It's too hot to eat a blackened-chicken po'boy anyway."

"But it's cool in here."

She realized he hadn't moved his hand, which still lay on her shoulder. "Uh-huh."

"Well, maybe it's for the best, because I had something else in mind for us to do over the next hour."

In her mind's eye, she could see that large, strong hand, those long fingers with their roughened pads. Didn't need to imagine the heat of his grip because she could feel his warmth through the thin fabric of her dress, its burn penetrating her skin, searing a path down to that secret place that yearned to continue what they'd started the other night.

"Afterward, I'll buy you lunch," he continued, his voice low and gruff.

His voice seemed to enter her body, too, like ripples of heat that burned her blood, set fire to her body. Dizzily, she wondered if her dress had melted underneath his grip and his fingers now touched her bare skin.

The hardness in his eyes had faded, their color shifting from granite to silver, glistening with a sensual invitation. For a light-headed moment she swore, no, she *knew,* he was thinking exactly what she was. She felt transfixed, unsettled, hungry, with a longing so raw she ached.

Her knees shaking, she managed to stand, slowly, her gaze raking up his muscled chest, past the bulk of his shoulders, until she locked on his mouth. She yearned to kiss those firm, sensual lips…explore that mouth with hers…

Rising, she parted her lips. Ready. So ready.

She waited…but instead of a kiss, Drake started talking…about trash.

"…and since you're too dressed up to crawl into a Dumpster, I'll do it," he said, "but I'll need you on watch outside. If you see anyone checking out what we're doing, you'll alert me."

Val rocked back onto her heels. "Dumpster?"

"Right. There's one behind Topaz. Pickup is early Monday morning. As today's Friday, the heavy partying will start midafternoon, and Vegas strip clubs are notoriously packed over the weekends, so this is the best time for us to conduct the trash hit."

"Trash hit?" She didn't like how that sounded.

"Jayne ever discuss those with you?"

"No." She felt like a fool, thinking she'd clued into his steamy intentions when all along he was talking about…Dumpsters and trash?

How pathetic could she be? This topped her high school prom, when her friend Tommy had never showed. Sure, they were just pals, neither remotely interested in a girlfriend-boyfriend thing, but that hadn't lessened the sting of sitting next to the front door for two hours, wearing a prom dress her nanny had spent the past week sewing, her hair teased into a pouf, sparkling with little rhinestone butterflies that had taken her neighbor Cissy, a first-year cosmetology student, two hours to get just right.

Tommy had told her the next day he thought she had been joking when she'd suggested they be prom dates. He'd felt so bad that he made her dress up all over again, rhinestone butterflies and all, and took her out to dinner at Arnaud's, a swanky restaurant in the French Quarter.

She doubted Drake would ever feel bad about what had just happened. Hell, she doubted he even *knew* what had just happened.

"...searching garbage for evidence," he was explaining, all serious and professional, "for things like receipts, personal letters, credit card statements. Trash hits are a rich source for mining details about people's lives and assets."

"We're pulling garbage out of a bin," she said slowly, "a big, nasty, tractor-size garbage can...all those smells...all those flies..." Lord, flies were probably just the tip of the insect world festering in one of those monster trash bins.

He retrieved his phone from his pocket. "Val, sometimes you need to see the forest, not the trees. Is your smartphone charged?"

"I'd hardly compare a forest to rubbish," she mumbled, pawing through her purse. She pulled out her phone and checked its battery. "Eighty percent."

"That'll do."

"What are you hoping to find in the trash?"

"A certain type of cigarette. It'll be partially smoked, of course, but its look is distinctive. I'll describe it to you on the drive over."

"So we're looking for a cigarette butt, which could be an inch long, two if we're lucky, in a city garbage can that holds gallons and gallons of squishy, smelly, disease-infested filth."

"That pretty much sums it up." He tapped some keys on his phone, absorbed in his task.

She sucked in a breath and eased it out nice and slow, idly wondering if she should have gone to beauty school instead.

"And...why do you want this cigarette butt?"

"I think its smoker is the arsonist. I want to run it for DNA, then check the results against any DNA the arson investigator might find at my old place."

She frowned. "Why not give the cigarette to this arson investigator and let *him* run all the DNA tests?"

He zeroed his shiny gray eyes on her. "It's a long story, but in a nutshell, if I give him too much information too soon, things could backfire." He slipped his phone back into his pocket. "Know how to take photos with your phone?"

"Of course."

"Good. We'll take your car."

"What? No! It's a rental! It'll smell like a dump, and I'll have to pay an outrageous cleaning fee when I return the car."

"Val," he said, leveling her a look, "you're making a big to-do over nothing. This is an *investigation,* not a princess picnic. Anyway, *I'm* the one getting dirty—you and your pretty dress will stay in the car. We'll lay plastic bags on the backseat to protect it, although what I pull out will likely be in plastic trash bags, too. As to the smell, we'll put the AC on and open the back windows. Drive that way for a couple of days, and no one will ever know the Honda went undercover as a trash truck."

Princess picnic? You and your pretty dress? She managed to suppress a snort of derision, one she would have given full vent to if she wasn't determined to show Sam Spade she had what it took to be a private investigator, too.

She flashed him her hundred-dollar smile, full of confidence and false bravado. The one that said she was a P.I. in the making, a woman unafraid to tackle the job, even if it meant rolling in other people's filth. Although she'd only be on sentry duty today and *he'd* be jumping into the stinking muck.

A thought that gave her no small thrill of satisfaction.

"I'm in." She rolled back her shoulders. "I presume we'll be driving the trash here to look through it?"

"Right. We'll lay it on the driveway outside my office. Easier to sift through it, and the fence blocks prying eyes."

"No need to buy me lunch afterward." *Although I can't think of anything more appetizing than quaffing a to-go burger while sniffing refuse.* "I'd prefer to start digging through that trash."

Ignoring his surprised look, she grabbed her purse and headed for the door, ready for her first trash hit.

CHAPTER SEVEN

THIRTY OR SO minutes later, Val pulled the Honda over in the alley behind Topaz, leaving enough room for other cars to pass. They were about fifteen feet from the Dumpster—far enough away so they didn't appear to be parking next to it, but close enough for Drake to get there in five or six strides.

On the way, they had purchased some plastic sandwich baggies, latex gloves and a box of plastic garbage bags, several of which they'd laid across the seat.

Drake, sitting in the passenger seat, stuffed a plastic bag in one of his pockets, then looked around.

"Alley doesn't get a lot of traffic, fortunately. Remember, if you see someone watching us, tap the horn once. When the person leaves, tap it again and I'll come out."

"The Dumpster belongs to Topaz…wouldn't entering it be trespassing? Isn't that a felony?"

"Only if we kill someone in the process."

Her eyes grew huge, filled with anxiousness. Impulsively, he reached out and cupped her cheek.

"That was a joke," he whispered, trying not to think how incredibly soft her skin was.

But how he felt at the moment—protective, attracted—was anything but a joke. Of all times to feel drawn to her, this wasn't it. He never lost focus on a job, yet around Val he was constantly fighting himself to stay in control, keep his thoughts in check. Constantly trying to figure her out, too.

Her hair alone was a mystery. The first night she'd worn that silver-tinted wig, yesterday it had been a dark knot streaked with purple, but today he finally got to see her natural hair. Not that there was anything real about those dark violet streaks, but he liked how it hung sleek and loose, framing her face, complementing those warm eyes.

She smiled feebly. "Guess I momentarily lost my sense of humor."

He reluctantly dropped his hand and picked up one of the latex gloves.

"For trash hits," he said, slipping on the glove, "I prefer mitts made of a sturdier material, like leather, because broken glass can easily pierce latex, but I'd only attract attention wearing heavy gloves at high noon in August, so…"

"Be careful," she whispered.

Just a few words of care, and he felt as if he'd spent his life alone before Val—not in regards to his family, but in relationships with other women. Obviously he hadn't been alone in those liaisons, but he realized how he'd remained solitary, cut off.

He'd tried to be that way with Val, too, but he was losing ground. And he liked it.

An old car rumbled past, its engine making a chunk-a-chunk sound as it labored down the alley.

"Listen," Drake said, snapping on the other glove, "after I get out, stay put, keep the motor running. If someone approaches the car..."

"I say I got lost, stopped to check directions on my smartphone."

After a last look around, he slipped out the door, shutting it behind him with a soft click.

VAL WATCHED DRAKE in the rearview mirror as he strode to the battered green metal bin. After a non-chalant look around, as though he was out for a casual stroll, he paused in front of it, pushed back the lid and in one swift movement hoisted himself up and over into the bin.

Her heart pounding, she blew out a pent-up breath, feeling as though she was the one who had just climbed into that Dumpster in broad daylight. She darted a look around. Didn't see anyone except for a kid toward the end of the alley, riding a bicycle. To her right, a row of fence blocked people's view of the alley. To her left was Topaz's large asphalt parking lot, with only a few parked vehicles clustered around a stand of palm trees.

So far, so good.

She looked at the rearview mirror, willing Drake to find a cigarette soon. Lord, it had to be like an incubator in that metal trash can.

She thought about another heat. She could still feel

his warm fingers on her face where he'd touched her. The way he'd cradled her cheek, his touch so gentle, it had taken every ounce of her willpower not to do something dumb. Like turn her head slightly and nuzzle her cheek against his fingers.

Why couldn't she act cool and refined? Like the actress Angelina Jolie or…well, Angelina Jolie. Okay, that set the cool bar *way* too high. Forget being cool. She'd settle for being refreshingly uncomplicated, which sounded great, but she had no idea what it was.

The kid on the bike rode closer, so close she could see the blue and yellow stripes on his shirt, the superhero on his bicycle helmet. Seeing Val sitting in the car, he started riding in circles, watching her watching him.

She'd read once that most P.I.s got burned, or noticed, on surveillances by children playing around their vehicles. The kids would notice someone sitting alone in the car or van and they'd tell their parents, who would either approach the private investigator, demanding to know what he or she was doing in their neighborhood, or they'd call the cops, who'd arrive with sirens blaring and lights flashing. Either way, the P.I.'s cover was blown and the surveillance ruined.

She tapped the horn, lightly, one time.

The kid halted. Setting one foot on the ground, he kept his hands on the handlebars and stared at her.

Oh, this was going well. You'd think a kid had better things to do than stare at a lady sitting in a car in an alley. *Must be a really bored kid.* Meanwhile, Drake was broiling in that Dumpster.

She opened the driver's door and stepped outside, wincing at the blinding sunlight.

"Hey," she said, raising her voice, "I'm an undercover police officer and…some bad guys are on the loose in this alley. You must leave. Now."

"Undercover cops don't drive Hondas."

What a smart-ass. "In my top-secret division, they do. If you don't leave now…I'll call backup and they'll arrest you."

He didn't budge.

"Okay, I'm calling backup, buddy." She got in the car and made a grand show of putting her smartphone to her ear and moving her mouth as if talking to someone.

He stuck his tongue out at her and rode down the alley. After a few moments, she tapped the horn.

Drake popped out of the top of the Dumpster, tossed two white plastic bags onto the asphalt, then jumped out. Seconds later, he tossed the bags in the car, shut the door and got into the passenger seat.

"Go," he rasped, his face flushed and shiny with sweat. "By the way—" he wiped a hand across his brow "—impersonating a police officer is a gross misdemeanor."

"Well," she said, stepping on the gas, "not impersonating one could have ended up even grosser. I was trying to save you from becoming a garbage-marinated, dehydrated piece of macho jerky."

He chuckled under his breath. "Val, don't let this go to your head, but you're right."

She smiled to herself. Score one for Princess Picnic.

WITHIN THE HOUR, Val and Drake stood on the private driveway outside of Drake's temporary office. The fence blocked the view of the street, but they could hear the buzz of traffic and passing voices. The overhead leaves from the ironwood trees rattled lightly with the passing breezes, their shade providing some respite from the heat.

Val had taped a note on the front door of the agency that they were working an off-site case, and left her cell phone number to call.

Drake had moved his pickup a few feet away in the main parking lot. They had covered a portion of the concrete driveway with flattened plastic bags on which they'd laid out the trash. The smell permeated the air, but thanks to occasional gusts of wind it wasn't as horrific as Val thought it might be. They both wore latex gloves, although Drake insisted they first sift through the debris with sticks, which he'd broken off a nearby mesquite tree.

"If my cousin Char saw all these glass bottles, she'd have a conniption," Val muttered, pushing aside a beer bottle with her stick.

"What's that mean?" He swatted at a buzzing fly.

"Means she'd be angry, because she's *really* into recycling."

"You sure have a vocabulary all your own. What's

this?" He leaned down and picked up the butt of a cigarette. "Not his brand. Plus there's lipstick on it." He tossed it back.

She looked at him, his polo shirt spotted with sweat, his face flushed from the heat. Probably not the best time to ask, but this had been bothering her ever since he said it, and he'd made a reference to it, so...

"About my vocabulary... Why'd you tell Jayne my accent prevented me from doing undercover work?"

He straightened, scrubbed his hand over his hair. "I believe I said your accent was a *detriment* to your working undercover. Probably should've kept my mouth shut...but it's the truth. Especially in this town, your manner of speaking marks you. A distinct accent, or any distinct trait or style, can endanger a P.I. while working undercover."

"I can suppress my accent." She swatted at a fly.

"You've already tried that, remember? But I still heard it."

She nudged aside some crumbled paper with her stick. "Maybe I can work with a voice coach or something. Learn how to get rid of it." It might about break her heart to cut any part of New Orleans from her person, even temporarily, but the goal that kept her going now was to become a private investigator. And if that meant no more New Orleans phrases or drawl, then so be it.

DRAKE WATCHED HER, all feminine and delicate in that lacy dress, her cheeks pink from the heat, dutifully poking at trash. Val hadn't complained once about working this trash hit since they'd exchanged a few words on the topic before leaving the office earlier. Since then, she'd been a champ—not even making a single comment about the foul smell in the car as they drove here.

But learning how to get rid of her accent? Until she'd said that, Drake hadn't fully realized how much she wanted to be a P.I.—so much so she was willing to cut out parts of herself that were distinctly her own. He loved this work, too, but not enough to make a permanent identity change. If a person started letting go of pieces of themselves for anything—a job, a relationship—they could end up with nothing.

Besides, he'd miss that molasses-thick accent if it went away. That voice, its tone and cadence, were uniquely her. Both strong and soft. Thorny and charming. A woman who could infuriate him one moment and entice him the next.

"Never get rid of it," he said gently, "just don't accept undercover cases."

She tilted her head and squinted at him. "Sounds like…you think I could cut it as a P.I."

"With training, yes. In fact, a very good one."

She gave him a smile so sweet it nearly broke his heart. "I do believe, Drake Morgan, that you are the toughest, but the best, mentor an intern could ever want."

For a moment he didn't smell the rubbish, didn't hear the irritating buzz of flies, couldn't feel the sizzling summer temperatures. All he knew standing there, looking at Val, was that life was sweet. That a tender, playful glance could make his heart beat faster. That a few appreciative words made him feel like a superhero.

That he felt happy in a way he hadn't been in a long, long time.

"Thank you, Val. I—" His phone vibrated in his pocket. Making a hold-on gesture, he answered it.

"Morgan here."

"Drake," his mother said in a shaky voice, "your friend just called, told me about the fire." She choked back a sob. "Oh, my God, are you all right? And dear Hearsay…please don't tell me—"

"Hearsay and I are both fine, Mom, please don't worry. I dropped by yesterday to tell you, but you were gone. Didn't want to wake Grams. I asked Li'l Bit to not mention this until I had a chance to—"

"Li'l Bit? Oh, no, dear. It was Yuri. Said you asked him to call—"

"I'll be right there," he snapped. "Don't open your door unless you know it's me."

Shoving the phone into his pocket, he glanced at the mess laid out on the plastic.

"Gotta go," he grumbled, "but I don't want to leave this out here unattended." He glanced through the leaves at the patches of blue sky. "At least there's no incoming clouds, but with monsoon season, rains could come in unexpectedly and wash out any evidence—"

"Drake, you're worried about your mama, so go. I can finish this."

"But it's a lot of work."

"Like I won't let you forget that you owe me one?"

He tossed aside his stick and peeled off his gloves. "You're wonderful."

"I know."

STANDING AT THE edge of the strewn-out mess of garbage, catching the scents of stale booze, Clorox and something putrid she didn't *even* want to think about, Val reminded herself that when people wanted something powerfully enough in life, they had to be willing to slog through the good, the bad and the muck to earn it.

For the next fifteen or so minutes, she poked the stick at the crud, occasionally wishing she'd chosen something different to wear—like a body bag—for her first trash hit. She flipped over a dried-out, sour-smelling milk carton...and froze.

There lay a yellowish, half-smoked cigarette.

Blinking back tears of joy, she half hopped, half ran to the box of plastic sandwich bags they'd left on Drake's porch, tugged one loose, then shimmied a little dance on the way back. Heat, what heat? She was so pumped with victory, she could do the Macarena.

Stopped next to the cigarette butt, she carefully picked it up with her latex-gloved fingers, dropped it

into the bag, sealed it and placed it in her dress pocket
for safekeeping.

Then she sent Drake a text message.

Found the cig. Now you owe me two.

Grinning, she remembered Jaz's words from this
morning when she'd picked out this dress for Val to
wear. *Today you need a miracle.*

From here on out, Val would be wearing this dress
to every trash hit.

A SHORT WHILE after leaving Diamond Investigations,
Drake sat at a red light on Buffalo Drive, his elbow
resting out the open window. The heat was savage,
even in the shade.

"You bastard," he snarled toward the cell phone
resting on his thigh.

"Hello to you, too, bro," said Braxton.

"Why the hell haven't you called me back?"

"I answered this one."

"Because I spoofed your damn work number." In
the next lane sat a convertible with a thirtysomething
blonde, her hair pulled back in a clip. She tapped her
bloodred nails on the steering wheel.

"Don't spoof me again."

"Don't avoid me."

The blonde looked over. The oversize sunglasses
gave her a buglike appearance.

"So what is it?" Braxton asked.

"What else?" Bug-blonde pursed her slick red lips and blew him a kiss. "Yuri."

His brother snorted a laugh. "You think I'm the Yuri hotline or something?"

"Yes." The light flipped to green. He stepped on the gas.

"I don't keep tabs on the guy," Braxton said.

"He's your business associate."

"With a long arm. Sometimes we go for days, weeks without talking."

"Don't give me that crap. Heard from a good source that his car is in the Topaz lot most nights recently. Same time your car is. You two sit at different ends of the strip club, pretending not to know each other?"

"Drake, I'm a *manager* there, not some good-time guy stuffing bills in G-strings. I'm on the run from the second I walk in that place to the moment I leave, and between then, I'm on call."

"Not for me."

"Back to that?"

"No, back to poor you being overworked. So busy you can be in the same club with your boss yet never cross paths."

"He's not my boss, he's my *associate*. You don't seem to understand how slammed I am with work…"

The convertible was pacing him in the next lane, the blonde shooting him looks over the top of her bug sunglasses.

"…I'm there for any problem that arises," Braxton yammered on, "breaking up fights to making sure no underage bozo sneaks in and screws up our cabaret license…"

As Drake turned onto Alta Street, the blonde gave a theatrical pout and twiddled her fingers in a goodbye wave.

There was a time when he would have noted the license plate and traced it to a name and phone number. Given her a call in a day or two, suggesting they meet for a drink. But the only thought he had about Blondie was she needed to keep her eyes on the road or she'd end up in a fender bender.

"…and when I have spare time," Braxton said, "I actually might get to sit in my office and catch up on paperwork."

"Thanks for the job description. Now let's talk about Yuri."

Braxton blew out an exasperated breath. "You're as stiff-necked and hard-assed as always."

"Yeah, but I'm cute."

After a beat, Braxton snorted a laugh. "Still got that old man buzz cut?"

"Yeah, just like my buddy David Beckham. Chicks dig the geriatric look."

"On you, Drake, they'd dig the Homer Simpson look."

Drake had to smile. When they were kids, they'd liked to play who could make the other crack up first. Braxton liked to kid around a lot, but Drake usually got the winning zinger.

He missed their old camaraderie. They used to

laugh and talk, be each other's sounding board, often finish each other's sentences. He wished they could put this bullshit behind them and be close again. They'd already lost Dad, and their mom and Grams were getting older...one day, they'd be the only two left of their family.

"Still cook a lot?" Drake asked.

"Maybe once a month I get crazy in the kitchen."

Braxton had been a pudgy kid who liked comic books, Lego and cooking. Especially cooking. While Drake liked to hang in the garage when their dad tinkered with the family car, Brax would be in the kitchen crafting a recipe. Some experiments were disastrous, like the peanut-butter enchiladas, but others, like the glazed doughnut cake, became neighborhood hits. Everyone thought he'd become a chef or own a restaurant.

He had been much closer to their mom growing up, probably from all the hours he racked up in the kitchen. Which made Braxton and their mother's breach all the more uncomfortable now.

"Look," Braxton said, "I'm being square with you. I have no idea what's going on with Yuri. Those nights you see his car...he's not always inside Topaz. I know because employees mention seeing his Benz outside, so I walk around the club, looking for him, but the man isn't around."

"Why would he leave his car there?"

"How should I know? Jeez, Drake, you're like some kind of robo-cop P.I."

Drake got a gut feeling he knew part of the answer. Yuri was leaving his Benz there to throw off Drake. Which only affirmed his suspicion that Yuri was up to no good. Drake wanted to know what that was.

"Why the fixation on Yuri?"

"He torched my place."

"Shit, Drake, don't joke like that."

"I'm not joking."

"Torched as in…arson? That rental house?"

"Yes, arson. And yes, a rental. Like you own that fancy playboy pad."

"What's that supposed to mean?"

"Don't play dumb, Brax. I've checked the assessor's records. That luxury condo you call home is under the trust name Dusha. Did you know that means *soul* in Russian?"

His brother didn't say anything. Of course not. Why own up to being a lackey?

"Dusha also owns ninety-five percent of Topaz," Drake continued, "while you own five. Bet if I checked whose name is on the registration for that pretty Porsche, I'd find more Russian soul."

"For your information, what's on paper doesn't tell the whole story, so let's can the jabs and get back to you. How much of your place burned?"

Drake turned on Aragon, the street on which they grew up. Except for the repaved road and the second-floor addition to the Parkers' former house, the neighborhood was the same. Single-family ranch-style homes, gravel-rock yards, fat-trunked palm trees. In his mind's eye, he could see himself and Brax walking to school, kicking rocks, swapping items in their lunches.

He didn't want to jab anymore, either.

"Most of it. When I can get back inside, I'll know if anything's salvageable."

"Arson investigators on it?"

"Yeah."

"Didn't see it on the news, had no idea." Braxton paused. "Your dog…"

"They got him out in time."

"I'm really sorry, Drake. What can I do to help?"

"Give me information."

"You're certain Yuri did it?"

How much did his brother talk to Yuri, really? More than he was letting on, Drake guessed. He needed to watch how much he said, but at the same time feed enough to Brax so he understood the urgency of the situation.

"I believe Yuri did it, yes," he finally answered, "or instructed others to do it."

He pulled up to the curb outside their old house.

"I'm at Mom and Dad's." He cut the ignition and sat there, staring out the dirty windshield at their old home. In the front yard, the desert willow was covered with purple trumpet-shaped flowers. He and his dad had planted it a long time ago as a surprise for his mom on Mother's Day.

"Mom and Grams know about the fire?"

"Unfortunately, yes. Yuri beat me to the punch."

"*He* told them?"

"Yeah. Called Mom. Had the balls to say he was my friend, and that I *asked* him to call."

"I didn't give him Mom's number, Drake."

"I know." Brax had screwed up in a lot of ways, but he'd never put their mother or Grams in harm's way. Their dad, who had never owned a cell phone, probably gave Yuri the house number when the two of them were negotiating Drake's debt payment.

Braxton sputtered a curse. "To upset Mom and Grams like that…why?"

"It was a warning to me," Drake said solemnly. "Mom and Grams don't know who Yuri is, by the way. They know about that trouble I got into five years ago, but Dad never told them Yuri's name."

"I remember. Dad told me he took a taxi to that club to pay Yuri the twenty grand."

Their dad, who'd believed family stood by each other no matter what, had kept the lines of communication open with Braxton right up until the day he died. Benny Morgan always believed that one day his son would realize his mistakes and leave the "uncivilized" life.

Deep down, Drake wished for the same thing, but wishing was a lot like hope. It sounded pleasant and comforting, but a person couldn't count on it.

"Did Yuri tell you how Dad paid him?"

"I assumed cash. Yuri's not the kind of guy you pay with a check or credit card." Brax sounded as though he didn't know about the ring.

"I'm going inside now—"

"Hey, hold on. Need money? Place to stay?"

"Got it covered."

"Drake…does Mom ever…?"

"Yeah," he lied. He couldn't say the truth, that she never asked about Brax. For years, she'd hoped he would turn his life around, but after he'd gotten arrested on tax fraud charges two years ago, she gave up.

Drake shoved open the driver's door. "If you learn where Yuri likes to keep himself, call me. And if I call, pick up. Hey, one more thing. Does he still smoke those stinky yellow French cigarettes?"

"Like a chimney."

After ending the call, Drake walked across the front yard, pausing at the tree. He touched its rough bark, took a moment to enjoy the purple flowers, smell their sweet scent.

When he and his dad planted it, his father had talked about how tall the tree would be someday, described the color of the flowers and their fragrance. All of it had come true.

Although his father had envisioned the outcome, he'd helped it along by staking the trunk for straighter growth, pruning its branches, ensuring it received adequate water, sunlight, nutrition. But at the beginning, his father had mostly held hope for its future.

Drake continued to the door as thoughts of Braxton, his mother, Jayne, Val, Hearsay, Grams, even himself floated through his mind. Each of them faced challenging days ahead that required guidance, shaping, sustenance.

And maybe, hope.

By EARLY THAT afternoon, Val had folded up the trash in the flattened plastic bags and stacked them next to Drake's office door, figuring he could haul them in his truck somewhere, 'cause this girl had paid her trash-hitting dues for the day, thank you. Then she went inside the office, nearly dropping to her knees with gratitude upon feeling the rush of cool air.

She headed to the bathroom and dabbed herself with damp paper towels. It would take a fire hose to get the stink off her skin and clothes, but a pat here and there made her feel a bit refreshed. After unlocking the door, then grabbing her lunch from the minifridge, she sat at her desk and checked her phone.

No message or call from Drake, but he was busy handling urgent family matters.

As she took a container and plastic spoon from the bag, her thoughts drifted to Drake and his family. Didn't know anything about his mother or grandmother, but a man who would drop everything out of concern for his family got big bonus points from this girl.

She knew more about his dad. In that photo at Dino's, she had seen an approachable and gregarious man. And that the picture still hung on the wall, some twenty years later, spoke of others' abiding affection for him.

COLLEEN COLLINS   151

Approachable and *gregarious* hardly described Drake. But the way Jayne, who kept her feelings wrapped up tight, had treated him with respect and entreated him to stay in her back office said a lot about his reputation and integrity.

Drake was loyal to his family and friends, a man of character who earned people's respect. But it bothered Val how he could sometimes be so cold and forbidding. Not that she was Miss Perfect, but she liked to laugh and express herself, would rather try something silly than settle for the boringly familiar.

Were she and Drake too opposite to make a relationship work?

She opened the container and breathed in the scents of cayenne pepper and garlic in Char's homemade green gumbo. She was stirring it, admiring the chunks of okra, carrots and collards, when she heard a man's raspy voice.

"Hey, how you doin'?"

Startled, she looked up. A middle-aged guy in a red-white-and-blue plaid shirt, a packet of cigarettes sticking out of the pocket, stood in front of her desk. His hair was combed back, emphasizing his broad face, shiny with perspiration. Squint lines etched the skin around his eyes.

"I'm Tony Cordova. Drake around?"

"Sorry, no. Want me to give him a message?"

"I'll leave my card." He pulled one from behind the cigarette pack and laid it on her desk. "He knows who I am."

She glanced at the card, saw he was an arson investigator. Probably investigating the fire at Drake's home.

"Would you like his cell phone number?"

"Already have it. Didn't know he was working here, though, until Sally told me."

"Sally," she repeated.

"Bartender at Dino's."

She recalled the woman. Thirtyish, slender, pretty in a rock star kinda way with her spiky black hair and tight jeans and top. Guess Drake told her he was working here. Guess they were good friends.

"Looks good." He grinned, gesturing at the gumbo. "Could smell the cayenne in the parking lot."

"Green gumbo. My cousin made it."

"Ah, nothing like homemade. My wife was quite the cook herself. Always took the time to do it right." He paused. "People live too fast these days. Fast food. Fast internet. Slowness, my friend, is the essence of knowledge." He pointed to his card. "When you give that to Drake, tell 'im I got some news, would like to meet as soon as possible."

As he walked away, she noticed he had a slight limp. Wondered if his reference to his wife in the past tense meant they'd divorced, but she doubted it. Few men spoke fondly of their ex-wives. Plus, when he spoke about her, the look on his face had been one of bittersweet reflection.

She tasted the gumbo. Delicious, but cold after

being in the fridge all these hours. Some things were better hot.

Which made her think of Drake again. She reclosed the gumbo container, thinking she needed to put a lid on her hot Drake thoughts, too. It was good they'd eventually worked so well together today, but not so good to get all worked up over a man who played tug-of-war with her heart.

Whoa, her heart?

No. No. No.

This *thing* between her and Drake had to do with another part of her body, the part that made her palms itch and her insides sweat, and had absolutely nothing to do with her heart.

Picking up her lunch bag, she headed to the kitchenette. The problem with absolutes was they usually weren't. If she were totally honest with herself, what had started the other night between them was not just about achy hormones.

Somehow, the man really had touched her heart.

After stashing the food in the fridge, she began rearranging the coffee cups as her mind muddled with how a man like Drake, who wore so much heavy, full-body emotional armor that he damn near clanked when he walked, had gotten through her defenses, which had hardened, too, over the years. And she knew exactly when it began.

Katrina.

She remembered those days huddled with Nanny on their roof, the two of them exposed to the rain-whipped winds, with nothing to hold on to but each other. By the second day they were so hungry, Val had fished dog snacks out of the water for them to eat. By the third day, when help hadn't arrived, she'd kissed Nanny's cheek, slid into the stagnant, swirling floodwaters and started swimming to their neighbor's who had a rowboat. She still dreamed of those black, filthy waters, terrified of alligators lurking below the surface, and how she'd bumped into that corpse...

She made it their neighbor's home, only to find it, and their boat, gone.

Too exhausted to swim, she had clung to a tree as night fell, listening to a distant woman's voice sing "Amazing Grace" in the dark. Hours later, a FEMA search and rescue boat picked her up. Shivering from the cold and wet, she'd begged them to go to her Nanny, but when they arrived, she was gone.

Later, she learned a Coast Guard helicopter had rescued her grandmother, who'd died a few hours later. Dehydration and heatstroke, they said.

Holding a coffee cup, Val looked at the perfect box formation she had made with the other cups, wondering where to put this last one. She started to set it on top, but halted in midair.

I should never have left her alone on the roof.

She clutched the cup to her chest. The storm broke her city, and it broke her heart. She lost her innocence about life, grew tougher about the world.

Since then, some people—like Jasmyn, Char, Del and Cammie—had gotten through her defenses, but until the other night, no one had found a way to her heart. Not the part that loved her new family or was grateful to be alive. Nor the part that put faith in things unseen, like magic and mystery. Until the other evening, she hadn't been aware of what she was missing. She had not been open to the kind of love that could heal or hurt.

That part of her heart was not only worth fighting for, it was worth risking everything for.

CHAPTER EIGHT

"No." DRAKE'S MOTHER stood in the center of the living room, surrounded by the Swedish modern furniture she and Drake's dad had picked out twenty years ago. "I absolutely refuse to have surveillance cameras mounted outside this house."

She patted her hair, a style that hadn't changed in years—cropped close to her head, wisps of auburn framing her face. The haircut was like her, sensible yet feminine. In October she had turned sixty-five, but she looked a lot younger, probably because she stayed out of the sun, had never smoked and never drank except for a glass of wine on special occasions. She still wore her yellow bowling shirt, with "Dot" stitched in red over the pocket, from her Friday lunchtime league. That, and her water workouts at the senior center down the street, kept her trim.

Right now the center played into their argument.

"So your grandmother likes to occasionally visit the center," she continued. "It's not far. I don't need to watch her every minute. And I don't want guests knocking at the door and knowing they're being spied on." She fidgeted with the collar of her shirt. "Just like Orwell's book *1984,* governments are already oversurveilling people. Next they'll be watching us in our homes."

"I'm not talking spying, Ma, I'm talking about Grams's safety. Plus, face it, it's a pain to walk all the way to the door just to find some college kid selling overpriced magazine subscriptions."

"Which reminds me," she muttered, "I still need to cancel one of those subscriptions."

Drake glanced at the dice clock over the TV. It was way past snake eyes, or two o'clock. Almost two-forty. Since arriving nearly an hour ago, he had been talking nonstop to his mom and grandmother about the fire and answering a lot of questions. His mom had been walking him to the door when he'd casually mentioned mounting several surveillance cameras outside. One with a long-range view of the sidewalk, to ensure Grams traveled safely up and down the block, and the other positioned on the front porch to see visitors.

Bad move. Now he and his mom were embroiled in another discussion.

"Anyway, the senior citizen center is at the end of the block," he continued, "which *is* far for an eighty-five-year-old woman. Especially one who's driving a wheelchair in the dark after her nightly martini."

"Have you seen her martini glasses? They hold three ounces, barely." She crossed her arms, giving him the look that said she was in charge. The look he had seen ever since he was a kid. Back then, it was like a steel wall. No way to get over it, ram through it or dig under it. So you backed off. "No cameras."

But as a man, he better understood that look. It wasn't a barricade. More like a line in the sand.

Over the years he had guarded his own lines, fought hard for them, too, sometimes long after they had disappeared. But when you're standing alone, the lines nowhere to be seen, you start to get the message that being victorious doesn't mean you won the battle. That defending a position has more to do with one's fears than any real threat.

He didn't know why cameras scared his mother, and maybe he didn't need to know. What mattered was to not fight the line, but encourage her to step over it.

"You're right. Three ounces isn't much. Mostly it's her age that concerns me. She's eighty-five."

"Goodness, I hope you don't broadcast my age as often as you do hers. But since you're stuck on it, keep in mind she's a vigorous, healthy eighty-five," she said under her breath, "with a new hearing aid that makes her part bionic woman."

"Good to know, because that means she can hear people and scooters and skateboards. Problem is, in the dark, they might not see *her*."

She released a weary sigh. "These cameras have night vision?"

He nodded.

"How big are they?"

"Size of a golf ball. I could fit one into a bird feeder."

"I don't like bird feeders. I'll be cleaning up poop all the time."

"A fake owl, then. Lots of people have those."

She thought about that for a moment, then nodded. "What about the front porch?"

"I could put it in a...door object."

She frowned. "What kind of door object?"

"One of those..." He made a circling gesture. "Leaf things."

"A wreath?"

"Yeah, a wreath."

"It's August. Why would I want a Christmas decoration on my door?"

"A welcome sign, then."

"What I've always wanted," she grumbled, "a picture-taking welcome sign. Isn't that an oxymoron?"

She sounded put off, but he could tell she was considering it. His comment about Grams driving in the dark postmartini—even at three ounces—had gotten to her. "If Dad were here, he'd say 'Dorothy, I'm not askin' ya to give up a kidney.'"

Her features softened. "My Benny," she murmured. "Musta heard that line a thousand times."

She turned away, but not before he caught the quiver in her chin. His mother had always been a formidable person, the one people turned to with their problems, but she hadn't dealt well with her husband's passing. Maybe they hadn't always seen eye to eye, and neither backed down from a good argument, but they'd loved each other deeply, fiercely.

In that last year of his dad's illness, she had turned the couch around so it faced the living room window. They would sit there for hours, listening to his favorite jazz albums, especially Tony Bennett and Sarah Vaughan, holding hands while gazing at the desert willow.

She walked to that window now and frowned at the bright afternoon. "I'm not ready to lose Mom," she whispered. As she turned to Drake, the sunlight sparked off one of her large gold loop earrings. "Or you." Her eyes turned moist. "That fire..."

"Ma—"

"I know you said it was caused by a gas burner you accidentally left on, and I wanted to go along with that story because...well, you wanted me to, but I read an article in the paper this morning. Quoted a neighbor who said she heard an explosion, and when she looked out her window, the east side of your house was on fire." She pursed her lips. "Your kitchen is on the west side."

He inhaled a breath, let it out. If he had learned anything in life, it was that when the gig's up, don't pretend otherwise. Especially when faced with logic and facts and a mother's love.

"The fire started in my office."

"Arson," she whispered.

"Yes."

Somewhere in the rear of the house, he heard the faint beep of his grandmother's electric wheelchair starting up.

"It's the private-investigations work, isn't it? This person didn't like something you found out."

"Something like that."

"You and your father…"

She had never liked their lines of work. Didn't understand why they didn't sell tires or paint houses or anything that didn't involve dealing with bad people doing bad things.

"Son, I know you can't stay here because Maxine would terrorize that sweet dog of yours." She choked back a laugh. "Sometimes that crazy cat terrorizes me, too, but Maxine adores your grandmother." Turning serious, her eyes searched his face. "You also don't want…whoever set that fire…to follow you here."

He didn't respond. Didn't need to. She knew how his mind worked.

"Which I think is nonsense." She turned to the wall mirror and checked her face. "Remember the old Gorman house two doors down?"

"Mrs. Gorman always looked tired."

"You'd be, too, if you had five kids. Anyway, the house sold to a police officer and his wife. Nobody wants to mess with people who have cops for neighbors."

The news offered some relief.

Her eyes met his in the mirror. "Go ahead and put the camera in a welcome sign. Or a basket of dried flowers. Just no Christmas ornaments." She fluttered her fingers over her hair. "It won't be so bad. I'm tired of dealing with those college kids hawking overpriced wares to work their way through school."

"Hate to break this to you, but they might not be students."

"I've thought about that," she muttered, adjusting an earring. "And put up that camera owl with a view of the sidewalk," she added. "I need to keep an eye on your grandmother. She thinks she's the race car driver Danica Patrick."

"That new chair goes up to twelve miles an hour."

She turned to him. "Mother told me five."

"Actually, it can go sixteen." Glenda rolled into the living room in her electric wheelchair, Maxine curled in her lap. She pressed the joystick and came to a stop. "But I never go over ten."

The wheelchair nearly swallowed her diminutive figure, adorned in one of her numerous caftans, this one a silky purple-orange-paisley number that could glow under a black light. Her hair, an unruly puff of white she'd "given up taming" years ago, sat on her head like a cloud. Her slim face, the color of parchment, was tinted with pink on her cheeks and bright crimson on her lips. The latter a protest against an online women's magazine that recently admonished women "of a certain age" for wearing red lipstick.

Her jade-green eyes sparkled with interest. "Those surveillance cameras you two are talking about. Can I get a feed on my smartphone? They must have apps for that."

"You were eavesdropping," he teased.

She smiled sweetly. "I happen to live in this house, so if you don't want your conversations to be overheard, I suggest *you* step outside."

Speaking of smartphones, he had heard his beep earlier, alerting him he had a text message. He didn't want to interrupt his mom and Grams asking questions about the fire, so he hadn't checked it.

"One moment," he said, pulling out his phone. He opened the message.

Found the cig. Now you owe me two.

He gave his head a slow, admiring shake. Val had done it. Found the needle in the rubbish stack. He was relieved and pleased, but most of all damn grateful for Val's get-it-done attitude.

It felt as if they'd crossed a barrier, cleared the way to work better together.

"Drake?" his grandmother asked.

He refocused his attention on her face, crinkled with thought. "This person who set the fire...I'm wondering if it might be Yuri."

Drake stared at her, stupidly wondering how she put that together.

"The Yuri," his mother said, her voice rising, "who called here?"

His grandmother nodded. "I think he's also the one Benny gave the ring to. Is that right, Drake?"

He and his dad had never revealed Yuri's name, had only referred to him as a loan shark, but obviously he had underestimated his grandmother's ability to sleuth things out. Danica Patrick, meet Sherlock Holmes.

The gig was up.

"Yes," he answered. "How did you know?"

She pawed in a pink saddlebag draped over a chair arm and extracted a tissue. "The night Benny called the taxi—to deliver the money to the loan shark— I heard him say he was going to Tverskaya Russian restaurant. Didn't think of it much since then...but when Yuri called the other day, he had a Russian accent, and only an idiot wouldn't have connected those dots." She blew her nose.

With a craggy meow, Maxine jumped off her lap and bustled toward the kitchen, her claws scrabbling when she hit the linoleum.

"Is this true?" his mother asked, turning to Drake. "Was Yuri the loan shark?"

"Yes."

Her eyes flared. "Why am I the last to know?"

"Hey," he said, wagging a finger at the women, "the two of you have fibbed for years, not telling me you used the ring to pay the debt."

"You and Benny fibbed, too," the elderly woman retorted, stuffing the tissue into the bag. "Your mother and I had a right to know Yuri's name."

The three of them were quiet for a moment, their gazes darting from one to the other.

The silence was finally broken with an indignant huff from his mother. "Everybody keeping secrets! Hard to believe we're a family!"

"No, dear," his grandmother said gently, "it's not about keeping secrets…it's about wanting to protect the ones we love."

"From the truth?" Dorothy snapped.

Glenda tilted her head and looked at her daughter as though she were still a petulant child. "No, dear," she finally said, "from being hurt."

From the kitchen came another demanding, scratchy meow.

"Now there's a family member who never keeps a secret," Grams said. "If she feels it, thinks it or wants it, it's shared with the world." She touched the joystick and the electric wheelchair beeped to life. "Drake, sweetheart, one more question. Did Yuri burn your place because you asked for the ring back?"

"No."

"Didn't make sense to me, either." She drove toward the kitchen, then stopped, pressed a button and the chair pivoted. "He views you as a threat, though."

He debated answering, but decided if he was in this deep, it would be harder to dig his way out than come clean. "Yes."

"Because…?" She stared at him intently, her eyes shading a darker green.

"I've been surveilling him."

"Good Lord," his mother murmured.

"Does this have to do with the ring?" Grams asked.

"Partially." He could tell by the look on his grandmother's face that she wasn't going to accept that as an answer. "I want dirt on him, the kind that will put him behind bars."

After a beat, the elderly woman raised her fists and gave them a shake. "Go get 'im, tiger."

His mother snorted in disgust. "I can't believe you're encouraging him."

"Your son, my grandson," Grams said, "has a background in military intelligence, hotel security and private investigations. He knows what he's doing."

She blew him a kiss, then pressed a button. The chair pivoted toward the kitchen. "Don't forget the app, sweetheart."

"Will do."

She disappeared into the other room. "And by the way," she called out, "it maxes out at seventeen miles an hour."

"She's incorrigible," Drake murmured.

"Probably maxes out at twenty," his mother muttered.

"I can hear you!" Grams called out.

Drake and his mother shared a smile. It was better like this, the three of them grumping and teasing each other, rather than earlier when the women had sat so quietly, their faces etched with apprehension as he answered their questions about the fire.

"I'm hurt, you know," his mother said. "I like to be the tower of strength, the one in the know."

"And you are, Ma. Problem is, in this family, everybody's a tower."

Barely suppressing a smile, she held out her hand.

"Let your mother walk you to the door, the way we did when you were little."

That's how she'd sent him and Braxton off to school every morning when they were kids. She'd stand in the center of the living room, holding both hands out to her sides. Brax would take one, Drake the other, and the three of them would walk to the door.

As he took her hand, he could feel the missing person. From the shadow that flitted across his mother's face, he knew she felt it, too.

"Want to come over tomorrow night to set up the cameras?" she asked.

"Sounds good."

"Six o'clock. I'm making meat loaf for dinner." She gave him a sideways look. "Is there really an app for your grandmother's smartphone?"

"Several, actually, that will let her view the feeds." He gave his head a shake. "She's like a teenager with her whiz-bang gadgets."

"It's brought the world to her. Books, movies, friends. Doesn't make her feel stuck in a chair. Did you know she has almost seven hundred followers on Twipper?"

"Twitter."

"Ha!" They reached the door and stopped. "Guess you can tell I'm not an adventurer in the electronic frontier." She gazed into her son's face. "Nice of that woman to offer her office. Do you have it to yourself?"

"There's…an intern."

"Must be tough with the owner getting ill. Is the intern managing the business by himself?"

He was a *she,* but Drake decided to skip that part. "For the most part."

"Bring him, too."

He'd caused Val to lose her sandwich earlier, and she'd passed on his invitation to lunch. And after being a heroine and finding Yuri's cigarette, at the very least he owed her a nice meal.

But bringing her to dinner at his mother's house? That could be a recipe for disaster.

After his engagement to Liz ended, his mother and Grams took it hard. Not because they'd liked her. His mother thought Liz was shallow, and his grandmother didn't give a reason, just said she preferred spending time with Maxine. What upset them was that Liz had walked out on him when he was at the lowest point in his life.

He had brought home one woman since then. An event planner, Laura, whom he'd met while working a case. His mother and Grams went all mama bear and grilled the poor girl as if it was a witness interview, not a family dinner. Soon after, Laura gave him the it's-not-you-it's-me speech, which was okay because he was ready to give it, too, so their parting had been a relief for both of them.

He just wasn't up for another mama bear encounter. Although there was also the remote chance they might like Val, he wasn't up for that, either. The women in his family were strong-willed and determined—the last thing he needed was that kind of rabid energy channeled into matchmaking.

Which meant either way he couldn't win.

"He, uh, probably has plans."

"Oh. Married?"

"No."

"From around here?"

"New Orleans."

"Now you *must* bring him! You know how your grandmother loves to talk about that trip she took to the French Quarter. It would make her night. Plus he would probably appreciate a home-cooked meal."

"He likes to cook, so that's not an issue."

"Just like…"

He caught a glint of hurt in her eyes. He hadn't wanted to bring up Brax, even accidentally. Although his mom refused to talk about her other son, her ache was never far from the surface. Grams didn't like acting as though Braxton didn't exist, talked about him freely when she and Drake were alone, but also understood her daughter's tough-love decision. As she told Drake, "She loves her son, but can't condone the criminal."

"Bring that intern anyway," his mom continued. "Everybody loves a night off from cooking." She smiled. "Plus he's never tasted Dorothy Morgan's world-famous meat loaf."

"I…think he's a vegetarian." He was running out of excuses.

"No problem! I'll make a big salad, and we have

fixings for cheese enchiladas." She clapped her hands. "I have an idea. Since he enjoys cooking so much, maybe he'd like to help me in the kitchen!" When Drake didn't respond, she waved off the idea. "Silly idea. Forget it."

He didn't like taking the light out of someone's face. Made him feel like a jerk. She wasn't asking for much. Never did, actually. Since Grams only ventured into the kitchen to feed Maxine or make a martini, his mom cooked alone most of the time. Was it really such a big deal to bring Val?

He could deal with it. But he'd keep the element of her being a woman until they arrived. Less time for the two of them to work up any interview questions.

"He'd probably like helping you," Drake said, wondering if Val even knew how to cook. Well, learning new skills on the fly was an attribute for a private investigator.

His mom turned serious. "Have him drive."

Another reason to bring Val. He liked the idea of his pickup not being seen here for a while.

After they hugged, he walked across the yard, thinking his mom had a look on her face he hadn't seen in a long time. Happy, yes, but something else. Eager, certainly, to be bustling around her favorite room, the kitchen, with a sous chef again.

He reached the pickup and paused to look at the desert willow.

Suddenly, he realized what that look had been. She had looked hopeful.

CHAPTER NINE

SHORTLY AFTER THREE that afternoon, Val was checking her email when Jasmyn's parents, Char and Del, strolled into Diamond Investigations. Char wore a denim skirt and sandals; Del had on khaki cutoffs and Birkenstocks. Both wore matching purple T-shirts with the name of their business, the Gumbo Stop, in bright yellow letters.

"Hey, dawlin'," Char called out. "Where y'at?"

"What it is," Val answered.

Back home, people often greeted each other with this exchange, but it was more than an idle word swap. The person asking was genuinely inquiring about the other person.

Which aptly summed up Char and Del. They genuinely cared about their family, which was as much about actions as feelings. Char once said that the biggest lesson she learned from Katrina was how survival depended more on connecting, giving and trusting people than having a fistful of money.

"I swear, it's hotter than a two-dollar pistol outside." Char sank into one of the guest chairs and daintily touched the back of her hand to her brow. "That or menopause is finally kicking in."

Val smiled. "You're only what, thirty-five?"

"Bless your heart for knocking ten years off my age. Did I mention I'm leavin' you the Alps vacation home in my will?"

"Thought you were leaving me the Rolls-Royce."

"Make it fifteen years, and I'll throw that in, too, dawlin'."

Her second cousin's dark gold hair looked almost glittery under the overhead lights. She carried extra weight, which she tried to shed every now and then, but the pounds inevitably returned. "I just can't resist my own cooking," she'd say, a line her customers at the Gumbo Stop loved.

"Jasmyn's watchin' the store while we pick up some supplies," Char continued. "Diamond Investigations is on the way, so we decided to drop by." She glanced at her husband, who was peering into the fish tank. "Wha'cha lookin' at, Delbert?"

"Had one of these as a kid," he said in his smooth baritone, which always reminded Val of a jazz radio personality. "Had me some angelfish in it, too."

Pushing fifty, he was as lean as Char was round, and was probably the most honest person Val had ever met. He spoke his mind, good or bad, which sometimes gave Char fits, especially when he riled a customer at their gumbo store. He and his wife had finally reached an agreement—he'd tone it down at work, but elsewhere all bets were off.

"That blue-yellow one sure likes to squirrel away

in that baby castle." He glanced over his shoulder at Val. "Know why they like to hide?"

"So they don't get stressed."

"More likely when they're ready to breed."

Well, Jayne never said anything about *that*.

"He around?" Char whispered, looking inquisitively at the closed office door to Val's right.

"No. His office is down that hallway..." Val gestured over her left shoulder.

Del straightened to his full six foot two. "That boy treatin' you right?"

"We're working together fine, Del."

Char leaned forward, giving Val a conspiratorial look. "Delbert isn't happy about that boy threatening to file criminal charges. He'd like to have a word with him, and this time he's promised to not let things get out of hand."

The last time Del had decided to "have a word" with somebody, it had ended with his fist in the guy's face. Although the young man had deserved it after the disrespectful things he had said to Jasmyn, Del had also broken two knuckles and spent the evening in the emergency room.

"Really, everything's fine now." Lord, was she glad Drake wasn't here. With everything he was handling, he didn't need the Val family protection squad coming to her defense.

In New Orleans, Val had had to be the strong one for her and Nanny. If there was a conflict or problem, she'd handled it. Although she appreciated her new family watching her back, ready to charge to her defense, she didn't want to scare off Drake. He was still her mentor, and then there were those sizzling moments between them that neither handled so well, but which they would only handle worse, if at all, if Cousin Del put the fear of God *and* Val into Drake.

She was debating how to say that without offending them when the phone started jangling.

"I need to get this," she said, picking up the receiver. "Diamond Investigations."

"Hello," said the caller, "this is Suzanne Doyle, manager of the Riviera Casino and Hotel. May I speak to Drake Morgan, please?"

The Riviera was legendary in Las Vegas for its colorful history of mobsters, famous movie stars and the superstars who'd performed there, like Elvis Presley and Frank Sinatra.

"He's not here right now. Would you like me to take a message?"

"I left one with Sally already."

Sally again. Dang, that girl was a one-woman information distribution center. How come everybody was talking to Sally about Drake? Was there more going on between them than Val was aware of?

She experienced another zap of the green-eyed monster. Which made a lot of non-sense considering minutes ago she was fretting if she and Drake were too opposite to make a relationship work...hadn't crossed her mind that he might already be in one.

That either said a lot about her sense of can-do, or that she had a problem dealing with reality.

"Sally? She seems to be mighty good friends with Drake." *Is she dating him or what?*

"I suppose. Sally and I worked together at the Riviera for years before the company restructure. Anyway, are you a P.I.?"

"Yes." What did "I suppose" mean?

"Good. And you are…?"

"Val LeRoy. Drake and I work together. *Very well,* I might add."

Char's eyebrows raised slightly in surprise.

"Miss LeRoy, I have a special investigative request. Have you ever seen the reality TV show *Ghost Adventures?*"

"A few times."

It featured a group of paranormal investigators, called the Ghost Team, who visited places supposedly haunted by ghostly spirits. Using equipment like digital recorders, video cameras and electromagnetic devices, they tried to substantiate the existence of ghosts in each show by taking the ghosts' photos or recording their spooky wailings.

"Ever see the show where the Ghost Team stayed overnight in our Frank Sinatra suite?"

"No."

"Their recording instruments picked up the sounds of a cocktail party with Frank Sinatra singing in the background," she said enthusiastically, "which makes *perfect* sense, because he and the Rat Pack loved to throw parties in that suite. Because we received a substantial boost in business after that showed aired, we are seriously considering starting weekly ghost tours. Do you know what those are, Miss LeRoy?"

"Yes, there were a lot of ghost tours in New Orleans, where I'm from."

Char's eyes glistened with interest. Before Katrina, she had considered starting a ghost tour, which were extremely popular with New Orleans tourists.

"Unfortunately," Miss Doyle said, turning serious, "one of the Ghost Team members recently confided to a reporter that their ghost-chasing investigations were a scam. That the pictures they took of phantoms had been doctored by superimposing images of ghosts on them. They didn't mention the Riviera, but obviously, people assume they faked the ghost evidence here, as well. Therefore, we decided to hire a *reputable, experienced* private investigator to conduct a *legitimate* investigation in the haunted suite. We plan to use your qualified evidence—pictures and recordings of ghosts—to lay to rest any questions about fakery."

"Miss Doyle, I must say you're assuming we could find such evidence. To be fair, neither Mr. Morgan nor Diamond Investigations has ever conducted paranormal investigations." Although Val thought it was a kick-ass, fun idea, she knew Drake would flat-out refuse.

"Forget the ghosts. Think of it as an everyday surveillance. We're interested in what you can document with your own equipment. How about I give you the terms of our offer, then you and Mr. Morgan can discuss it?"

No new cases were coming in for either him or Diamond Investigations, so the money would be sweet. And from what Val understood, paranormal investigators were viewed as hobbyists and didn't need a license. Maybe he'd be okay with Val taking on this task by herself.

"One moment." She grabbed her notepad and a pen. It was next to impossible to talk, scribble notes *and* hold the phone receiver in the crook of her neck. Looking at Char, she held a keep-quiet finger to her lips, then pressed the speaker button and set down the receiver. Jayne didn't like Val doing this, but it was only the three of them in the room, and she trusted her cousins to never repeat anything.

"Go ahead." Val poised her pen over the paper.

"We're offering twenty-five hundred to spend one night in the Frank Sinatra penthouse suite, all expenses paid. Multiple guests have claimed they hear Frank crooning one of his songs, 'Too Marvelous for Words,' so we're especially interested in your recording that. If you hear it, of course."

That got Del's attention. A longtime Sinatra fan, he wandered over and stood behind Char's chair.

"The cocktail parties apparently occur in the living room area around nine, ten at night. Guests have taken photos, which are covered with orbs…"

Val's grandmother had believed orbs—or specks of light in photos—to be spirits or angels who stayed earthbound to be near people they loved or places that held significance to them.

Val, however, wasn't so sure. "Something to keep in mind is that specks of dust on a camera lens, or the flash reflecting off something, can appear as orbs in photographs."

"Wonderful! This is *exactly* why we wish to hire you! If two pragmatic, skeptical investigators nail evidence of ghosts, we'll be turning people away. Fantastic PR for the hotel *and* your detective agency. Of course, if you find no evidence of ghosts—" she turned serious again "—the Riviera will not discuss your investigation, which I'm sure you understand."

Del frowned. Probably dying to have a word or two with Miss Doyle about that.

"Last, to show the Riviera's good faith to retain your services, I have sent a retainer, one thousand dollars, to your agency PayPal account. Unfortunately, I must cut this short as I'm late for a meeting, but I look forward to hearing back from you and Mr. Morgan within the next few days."

Val ended the call, thinking about the PayPal button on the Diamond Investigations website. She knew how to use PayPal, but only Jayne had the password for the agency account.

"No way Frank would choose that dump to hang out in the afterlife," Del groused, "when he could haunt the Venetian or Bellagio."

"But he *lived* in the penthouse suite, honey," Char said. "It was like a second home to him."

He cocked a bushy eyebrow. "Frank liked things nice, baby, and that place looks like it hasn't been vacuumed since Carter was president." He shifted his gaze to Val. "Take the deal. Two thousand, five hundred clams, and if you find Frank really has the bad taste to haunt there, you'll get a shitload of free publicity."

"I need to discuss this with Drake."

She thought she heard the connecting door to Drake's office click open, expected to hear his footsteps in the hall to Diamond Investigations' office. But...nothing. Maybe he'd heard their voices and decided to not interrupt. Or forgot something in his office?

Whatever the reason, she needed to get Char and Del out of here, *now,* in case Drake did join them and Del grabbed the opportunity to "have a word."

"You must leave now," she said, her voice rising to a strange, wobbly pitch. "I have important work to do."

While Del flashed her a what-the-hell look, Char remained cool.

"Certainly, dawlin'," she murmured, standing. "But first I'd like to say something."

Sometimes in life there are people who move your world with just a look, a touch, a comforting remark. Val's grandmother had definitely had that affect on Val, and so did Char. Maybe because they came from a place, deep inside, that was simple and honest. Or maybe because their hearts were a little larger than everybody else's.

Didn't mean they were saints, but they knew that better than anybody else. Val thought it meant they somehow got it about life. That it wasn't a competition, or a search for its meaning or even trying to arrange for one's happiness. It had more to do with accepting the joys and sorrows of life. So when Char wanted to say something, Val listened.

"Just because you can't touch, see or hear something doesn't mean it's not real, dawlin'."

And that was it.

Char smiled at her husband. "Let's take our leave, Delbert. We told Jasmyn we'd be right back after checking up on Val."

"Thought you two were out buying supplies," she said.

Del wrapped his arm around his wife's shoulders. "We lied."

After exchanging goodbyes, Val watched them walk away, their arms around each other, their footsteps in sync.

Two people who were about as real as they came.

After they left, Val headed down the hall to the connecting door to Drake's back office. Reaching it, she turned the knob.

Locked.

She knocked on the door.

No response.

Pressing her ear to the door, she listened. No sounds.

Had she imagined the door clicking open? Walking to her desk, she wondered if she had *wanted* to hear it because she was anxious to see Drake, talk about finding the cigarette, hear how things went at his mama's…

Hearing him when he wasn't there. Imagining conversations with him. She couldn't touch, see or hear him, yet she still felt a very real connection to Drake. An invisible link. Dare she think it, *a bond*.

Her heart contracted, and giddy happiness surged through her. Sitting, she decided to contact Jayne, ask for the PayPal password. She could write her boss an email, but it wasn't a good idea to send confidential data like passwords through email. Better to call. If she didn't want to talk, which was likely the case as she was probably tired from the chemotherapy and radiation treatments, she could let it roll over to voice mail and call Val back later.

It surprised her when her boss actually answered.

"This is Jayne." She sounded worn out.

It broke Val's heart to realize the toll the treatments and illness were taking on her.

"Jayne," she said, fighting a swell of emotion, "it's me, Val."

"How are you, dear?"

"Fine," she squeaked. Oh, Lord, she was losing it. She plucked a tissue and dabbed at her eyes.

"Really?"

"I miss you." The words spilled out. She couldn't have stopped them if she'd tried.

"I miss you, too, dear."

Val sniffled back a sob. This wasn't how it was

supposed to go. Val was supposed to make the call, sounding cheery and professional, offering words of comfort and support. She would discuss business rationally, get the password, wrap up with decorum. Leave Jayne feeling that Diamond Investigations was in good hands with P.I. intern Val LeRoy.

Instead she was on the verge of being a blubbering, emotional mess who needed Jayne's virtual shoulder to lean on.

"Shall we start at the top again?" her boss said softly. "How are you?"

"You know me," Val said, struggling to keep her voice level, "I'm a challenge."

A soft laugh. "Everybody, at some time, is a challenge." A moment of silence. "Are you and Drake getting along?"

"Yes. Actually, I'm calling because…a potential client paid a retainer, without my knowledge, to the business PayPal account and I don't know how to access it."

"The password…" She coughed. "Margaret1978."

Val spelled it out to ensure she got it right.

"Val, I agree with…whatever decision Drake makes…about this case."

Jayne was sounding breathy, as though it was an effort to finish her sentences. Val knew she should sign off, but it was hard to let go. She wanted to ask so many things—how were the treatments going? What were her doctors saying? When might she return… *Jayne, please return. Please don't go away.*

Instead she said, "Thank you, Jayne, for giving me a chance."

"I thank you…for the same."

After ending the call, Val let the tears fall.

LATER THAT AFTERNOON, Drake and Hearsay walked in the front door of Diamond Investigations.

Val sat upright at her desk, her hands folded in front of her, looking like a stalk of lilac in that lacy purple dress, which was pretty miraculous considering she'd worn it while picking her way through piles of garbage.

Her welcoming smile was like a shot of life. Rejuvenating, encouraging. Damn, his heart was pumping like a teenage boy's. He couldn't think when he'd ever been filled with this much anticipation and eagerness to see a lady.

He stopped at her desk, and Hearsay plopped down next to him.

She stood and peered over the desk at Hearsay. "So this is your dog! What's your name, sweet thang?"

"Hearsay," Drake answered, watching the dog's tail thump double time. He brought his hand from behind his back and held out a vase filled with miniature lavender roses. "These are for you."

For a moment their gazes held. Her brown eyes darkened with emotion as a smile curved her lips.

"They're beautiful," she murmured, accepting the flowers.

"The color reminded me of your dress."

She let out a short laugh. "I've decided I'm always going to wear it on our trash hits. It's my miracle dress."

He didn't know what to say, so he nodded as though he understood. "I bought them to thank you for your stellar work as an investigator."

Her smile blossomed and her eyes twinkled, but she didn't say anything, which made him all the more nervous.

He pointed to the vase. "It's crystal."

She turned the vase in her hands, admiring it. "We used to have lead crystal vases in our antiques shop—haven't had one since then. My nanny also had collections of crystals and stones. She used to say that they could never be owned, but they always found a path to a person if it was meant to be with them."

Dipping her head toward the roses, she closed her eyes and took a deep breath, releasing it on a long, breathy, appreciative groan of pleasure.

It was all he could do to remain standing.

He'd never met anyone like her before. A fighter, an imp and a temptress all in one woman's body. She made his blood burn, his head pound and sometimes so damn mad he wanted to throttle her. And then she could do something so sweetly hot and teasing it took every fiber of his being to not give in and satisfy every base, primal urge he'd had since the moment he'd laid eyes on her.

She set the vase of flowers on her desk.

"Their scent is like heaven." Her plump breasts

strained against the lacy purple dress as she took in another deep breath. He hoped to God she didn't release it in another one of those elongated, admiring groans, because somebody would have to revive him.

"Want to see it?" she said, a sly look in her eyes.

He nodded stupidly.

She opened her desk drawer and carefully lifted a plastic baggie. Inside was a half-smoked, yellowish cigarette. Beaming a smile, she handed it to him.

He looked at it, impressed all over again that she'd found it, and equally impressed that he'd been so caught up in her, he'd momentarily forgotten all about it.

"Great job." He slipped it carefully into his pants pocket. "Thank you."

Hearsay yapped.

"Hey, there, sweet thang, you feeling left out?" She leaned over her desk and petted the dog's head.

Drake had a straight view down the neckline of her dress. Past the soft edge of her collarbone, creamy swells threatened to overwhelm a peachy-pink satin slip bodice. He felt a tightening between his legs and forced himself to shift his gaze to Hearsay, who was staring up at Val with a big, goofy doggie smile.

"I wish I had a treat to give you, sweet thang."

Her breathy, soft voice was like warm fingers caressing his face, teasing his senses, firing his needs...

He scrubbed his hand over his brush of hair, sweaty from the hot drive over, more so from the blasts of heat he felt being around a certain P.I. intern. He needed to reel it in, focus on work.

Blowing out a gust of breath, he checked out the wall, the floor, anything but her. His gaze finally settled on the notepad, where Val had scribbled a series of words—Ghosts, Riviera, Miss Doyle, Sinatra, Too Marvelous for Words, cocktail party in living room—as well as $2,500 and $1,000.

"What's that about?"

She straightened, her hands at her sides, and gave him a funny look. "Manager from the Riviera called. Wants to hire you for a case."

He didn't like the word *ghosts* on the paper, but decided to not attack that issue. Yet. "How'd this manager know I was here?"

"Sally told her."

"Sally?"

"The bartender at Din—"

"I know who Sally is," he snapped, "just didn't know she knew I was here." He thought for a moment. "She used to work at the Riviera...they must be friends."

"She also told Tony you worked here." Val handed him a business card. "He left this for you. Said he has some news, wants to meet with you ASAP."

Whatever steam they'd felt before had evaporated. Val was acting like some kind of übersecretary, standing there all straight backed, giving him curt, professional answers. He was annoyed that he was having to *ask* what the hell was going on, trying to string together random words like pieces of a jigsaw puzzle to form the big picture.

Whatever barrier he'd thought they'd crossed was back up, stronger than ever.

He tossed Tony's card into the trash can. He already had one. "Why did you write the word *ghosts?*"

"Seems people have been seeing ghosts at a cocktail party in the Frank Sinatra suite."

"What's 'Too Marvelous for Words'?"

"Frank—well, his ghost—has been heard singing that song."

"At these ghostly cocktail parties."

She nodded, her eyes wide.

"Let me guess…they want *me* to investigate these *ghosts?*"

Val nodded again, fidgeting with a sash on her dress. "But it's not a *paranormal* investigation. The Riviera wants a legitimate investigator to try and capture images, voices of…ghosts. They will pay two thousand, five hundred dollars for one night's work, plus expenses."

"And you *believe* this garbage?" When she opened her mouth, he cut her off. "Of course you believed it. After all, spirits pulse messages to you through cell phones."

Her annoyed sigh was a work of art, starting with a deep, diaphragm-bursting inhale all the way through a prolonged, labored exhale.

"Pardon my language," she said tightly, "but sometimes you're meaner than chicken shit."

"That doesn't even make sense."

"Where I come from it does. I'm only relaying to you what *your* potential client said. As to ghosts and pulsations—"

He snorted his disgust. "I don't give a fu—"

"Excuse me," she said, her voice rising, "but I would be ever so obliged if I could finish what I was saying. When I was a teenager, I thought I had the gift of psychometry—reading impressions from objects—but I now believe I just wanted to share something special with my nanny, who really had the gift."

Drake waved her off and started heading down the hallway. Hearsay trotted behind him.

She followed both of them. "As to hearing your father the other night, I'm sorry, that was my mistake. There was an older couple sitting behind us, and I must've overheard him telling his wife he loved her. I'm also sorry I listened to Miss Doyle, but I didn't want to hang up on her as she sounded like a very nice, sincere lady. I'll call her back, turn down the case and return her retainer, okay?"

He halted. *"Retainer?"*

"Yes," she said, her voice a thin whisper.

He turned, furious. *"You* accepted a retainer from a prospective client?"

"No, I…well, yes, but…" She wrapped her arms around herself, her chin trembling. "She sent it electronically through Diamond Investigations' PayPal account."

"I don't give a damn how she sent it. We've been

down this road before, just a few days ago, when you accepted investigative work without a license, and were told, in *very* clear terms, that by doing so you broke the law. Today, by accepting a retainer, you formed a contract with a client, which is *again* acting as a private investigator without a license. You're trouble, Val. You can't be trusted."

"How dare you."

Something inside of him cracked. It seemed that life had become a roller coaster of issues and problems and people with attitudes. He liked his world to be contained, not bleeding out into everyone else's.

But the problem was his world had lost its structure. Nothing could be contained because there were no walls, no roof, just doors and more doors, all of them opening, none of them closing, letting in a cast of characters who'd make the film *One Flew Over the Cuckoo's Nest* look downright boring.

He had no choice but to be part of everyone else's world because his had gone up in smoke. Which meant his turf became wherever he stood, and right now it was here.

"Well," he snarled, moving so close he could see the gold flecks buried in her wide brown eyes, "*How dare you* play games at that desk? You're an *intern* who needs to *learn* the job, not be some wannabe Charlie's Angel playacting a role. I had hoped you learned your lesson after that honey-trap fiasco, but no. Two days later, you're negotiating retainers for *sleuthing spooks.*"

"I didn't nego—"

"Is that what you think this profession is about? Playing hooker to prove infidelity and chasing ghosts to determine the afterlife?" He gave her a twisted smile. "You picked the wrong career, sister. Go after a job that's all show, no substance. Vegas offers plenty of those. If I were Jayne, I'd have fired your ass long ago."

Her eyes glistened with tears.

"Don't tell me you're going to cry now."

Blinking rapidly, she shook her head vigorously. "No," she said in a strained voice, "because it would give you too much satisfaction. I'm going to my desk to sit down."

She turned and left, and damn if Hearsay didn't follow her.

VAL SMOOTHED THE back of her dress and sat. As she reached for the tissue box, she felt something wet and cool against her arm.

She looked down. Hearsay, sitting on the floor next to her, nuzzled her. Dabbing at her eyes with a tissue, she petted his head with her other hand.

"The loss of civility in our society is downright alarming." She tossed the tissue into the trash.

Drake rounded the corner like a big, dark cloud and halted, glaring at her.

Hearsay's tail thumped against the floor, but he didn't move. Stayed right by her side. A true gentleman.

Drake glanced at Hearsay, then met Val's eyes. She put on her best stoic face, even as she felt a last stray tear slide down her cheek.

"I don't get off on making women cry," he growled.

"I am *not* crying." She turned away slightly to swipe that traitor off her cheek.

"I said those things because you need to learn your boundaries."

"Well," she said, scratching Hearsay behind the ear, "if anybody can teach others how to do that, it's certainly you."

He stared at her so long she figured he was finally ready to hear her side. And if he wasn't, too bad. "That manager—Miss Doyle—sent the retainer by PayPal without my knowledge."

The day caught up with her, weighed her down emotionally and physically. She was too tired to get indignant about his accusations, or care much about anything else for that matter.

"She paid one *thousand* dollars. I haven't been to the PayPal account, so I can't verify the amount, although who cares—the point is I need to refund it. I called Jayne for the password, so I'll take care of that now, then I'll leave a message for Miss Doyle that we're not accepting the case."

"I'm sorry for saying I would have fired you."

"That Charlie's Angel crack was also pretty low."

"I apologize for that, too."

She almost felt sympathy for him. But there was too much hurt in the way.

"If you didn't think I was crying, would you have said you were sorry? Because if that's what it takes to get your attention, there's no reason for us to continue mentoring. You can stay in your man-cave office, or if that's too close for comfort, stay at Sally's or wherever you're living these days."

He gave her a puzzled look. "I'm not living with Sally."

Relief rippled through her, which irked. This wasn't the time to get all distracted about his living arrangements, or notice how, when he got that puzzled expression, he looked a little shy and sweet. This was about standing up for herself, not putting up with jerks.

He pressed a finger against his mouth, dragged it to his chin. "Whether or not you were crying, I would not have fired you," he finally said, "and I'm still your mentor. If you want me to be."

She closed her eyes and caught the sweet scent of the roses, thought about the approving, happy look on his face when he had handed them to her. This man was making her crazier than a loon. One minute he exhilarated her, challenged her to do things like trash hits, the next it was all she could do to refrain from smacking some sense into him.

And when she wasn't wrestling with those feelings, she wanted to touch him, kiss him, crawl all over him....

"Yes," she murmured, "I want you to be my mentor."

He crossed his arms, turning serious. "Now that that's settled, we need to cover an important point."

She liked it better when he was puzzled and apologetic.

"As an intern, you should not be negotiating payments with clients or accepting payments. I know you did neither with Miss Doyle, but I'm your mentor and you need to understand this. In the eyes of the law, your seeming acceptance of money from a client, such as a PayPal transaction, creates a *contract* for those services. As an unlicensed P.I., you have no authority from your agency, or from me, to accept new business and funds. If Miss Doyle's retainer, based on her telephone conversation with you, was reported to the state private-investigations commission, they could bar you from *ever* receiving your license. Next time a client pressures you to take a retainer, call me."

"I will. And while we're getting along like wet on water, I would like to offer a perspective."

He looked at her for a moment, then nodded his go-ahead.

"Diamond Investigations has no new cases, which means no money coming in. It appears to be the same for you. Jayne has backup resources, but still, wouldn't it be handy to accept this case—not to *chase ghosts,* but to *gather evidence*—and put some money in the bank? I figure Drake Morgan and Diamond Investigations could split the payment fifty-fifty."

He stared at her for a long, drawn-out minute. "Some new cases coming in would be helpful."

"Indeed they would be." She stroked Hearsay's head and smiled pleasantly at Drake, who gave her one of those soft looks that made it difficult for her to remember how to breathe.

"I need to leave the office," he finally said, "pick up a few things. Jayne left a doggie bed in my office, so I'll leave Hearsay there." He lightly snapped his fingers. "C'mon, buddy, let's go check out your new bed."

Hearsay's ear lifted slightly, but otherwise he didn't budge.

"Hearsay," Drake commanded, "let's go."

The dog stared at him as though to say, "Hey, what's the rush? It's nice here."

"Want to drag that bed out here?" Val offered. "We can lay it right here next to me, and I promise I will take real good care of him."

Drake looked at his dog, back to Val. "He'd probably like the company."

"That makes two of us. When I leave, I'll open the connecting door so he can go back and forth."

He stared at her intently, scrubbing a knuckle lazily across his chin. "Would you like to go to dinner at my family's tomorrow night?"

Well, fry me in butter and call me a catfish. She hadn't expected that invitation out of the blue. "Just 'cause I'm babysitting your dog, you don't need to pay me back."

"My mother invited you."

"You talked about me with your mama?"

"No." He gave his chin another knuckle scrub. "She

asked if I was here alone, and I said there was an intern." He shrugged as though the rest was understood. "She's making meat loaf. Her specialty."

"Well, now, I don't want to disappoint your mama, so yes, I'd be pleased to have dinner with your family."

"I, uh, told her you were a vegetarian, so she'll also be making cheese enchiladas."

She had no idea how to respond to that, so she let it go. They were getting along, his mama apparently wanted to get to know her, and cheese enchiladas were nice.

He scratched his eyebrow. "I also told her…actually she assumed…that you're a man."

Val wasn't sure what surprised her more at this point—her conversion to vegetarianism, her new gender or the color creeping up his tan throat.

"Not that it matters…of course, she'll see you're not a man."

"Have mercy," she whispered, "I hope so."

"That didn't sound good. It's not that you look anything like a man—or that I even think of you that way—in fact, you look…"

That color creeping up his neck was darn near rushing now, flooding his face with red. Plus, the way he was pacing and flicking awkward, heated looks her way, she'd say the man was hotter than a goat's butt in a pepper patch.

"Mind driving?"

"We might smell like the city dump when we get to your house."

"Val," he said chidingly, "keep the AC on when you drive, roll down the windows and the trash smell will be gone by then, I promise you. Told her we'd be there by six, so let's leave here around five-thirty."

Here. "You want me to drive to Diamond Investigations to pick you up tomorrow?"

"Yeah. Thought I'd come in, take care of some insurance paperwork."

"F'sure, I'll be here."

A few minutes later, Val watched Drake as he walked toward the parking lot, her gaze slipping down those broad shoulders, over his brawny back, down to the snug fit of those jeans around his buns. The man was built like a machine. All steel, no flab.

Her gaze traveled up to his bristly head. She had his body figured out, but whatever went on in that brain was a mystery.

Through the far window, she watched him hop into his pickup and a second later cruise out of the parking lot.

Take out the part about his mama thinking she was a man, and the fact Val was doing all the picking up and dropping off tomorrow, a girl might almost think she'd just been asked out.

CHAPTER TEN

THE NEXT DAY, Saturday, Val started getting ready for that night's supper at noon. After she tried on half a dozen dresses and modeled them for Jaz and Char, the group consensus was the vintage black-and-white polka-dot dress with a white satin sash.

Afterward, she joined Jaz to watch *Chinatown,* a '70s film noir about a private eye investigating an adultery case who stumbles upon a murder, gets his nose sliced open and discovers the dark, sordid family secret that forever ruined the love of his life.

After that, Val decided to head in to work, where private eyes led much calmer lives. For the most part.

As she walked into Diamond Investigations, the grandfather clock was chiming four. To her surprise, Hearsay ran up to greet her, his tail wagging.

"Hey, there, sweet thang, is your daddy home?"

She headed down the hallway with Hearsay trotting next to her. The connecting door was open, but no lights were on in his office.

She liked the open door, but it didn't seem like Drake to leave it this way. Did he forget to close it—or could it be possible the man was starting to let down his guard and let her inside? His office, of course.

"Drake, you there?" she called.

Silence.

She craned her neck and peered through the window that offered a view of his parking space. No pickup.

"Well, sugar," she said to Hearsay, "looks like we're on our own."

A few minutes later, he had settled on the bed, still next to her desk, where he gnawed on a chicken squeaky toy, which from the bright color and lack of missing parts appeared to be new.

Val watered the plant in Jayne's office, checked the fish, then called the repair shop and learned her Toyota would be ready by Wednesday. The incessant squeak-squeak-squeak of Hearsay's toy was a bit unnerving, but she figured either she'd grow used to it, the dog would fall asleep, or she'd bribe it away from him.

After that, she was sliding several manuals on private investigations into the bookcase when she accidentally bumped against the case. The figurine of two birds toppled from the top shelf, bounced off her shoulder and would have smashed onto the floor if she hadn't miraculously caught it.

Her heart pounding, she held the crystal object in her trembling hands while catching her breath. Hearsay, alerted to the near emergency, abandoned the rubber chicken and stood next to her, his ears perked.

"This needs to be in a safer place," she said to him.

After carefully setting it on her desk next to the fragrant roses, which smelled even sweeter than yesterday, Val watched Hearsay return to his bed and the chicken. She then focused her attention on the crystal birds and thought about Jayne. After getting all emotional on yesterday's call, maybe it would reassure her boss if Val dropped her an email, told her everything was going well.

Moments later, she was tapping on the keyboard.

Hi, Jayne,
It was great talking to you yesterday. Wanted you to know everything's going well at Diamond Investigations.

She hesitated, wondering if she should share her first investigative victory about finding the cigarette butt. No, Jayne needed to think about happy, positive things, not her P.I. intern wading through filth.

Drake likes the back office, and we've already had several mentoring sessions.

That sounded good.

I hope you're doing well. I think about you often, and look forward to your being back at Diamond Investigations.

She felt a stab of sadness. Last night, Val had looked up the life expectancy for liver cancer, as Jayne had said the cancer had spread to that organ. In advanced stages, the prognosis was several months, but Jayne's cancer wasn't that severe. Plus, it gave Val hope when she read how surgery could sometimes remove the cancer altogether from the liver. Of course, there was also the Hodgkin's disease, but from everything Val had researched, its survival rate could be years, sometimes decades.

If you need anything, please don't hesitate to call.

Side note: I'm working on slowing down that impetuous streak.

Sincerely yours, Val

She stared at her message for a moment, then went back and hit the backspace over her sign-off, and instead typed,

Love, Val

After that, she played with a new motion-detector video app on her smartphone, which was pretty cool. Whenever it perceived movement, the video-audio recorder turned on, continuing until the motion stopped.

The squeaks had grown few and far between as Hearsay grew sleepy. Last she looked over, he'd nodded off, the chicken in his mouth.

She was adjusting a setting on the app when Hearsay suddenly sat up and woofed. Looking up, she saw a familiar form heading her way.

Marta.

Val's nerves started working overtime. The woman was linked to the arson. Did she know Drake had the back office? Didn't make sense, and yet, why was she here?

Val leaned her smartphone against her nanny's picture, the lens pointed at the guest chairs, then moved the cup of pens so it partially blocked the camera.

"Hello, Val," Marta said as she entered and sat in a guest chair, as though they were two gal pals getting ready for a chat.

She wore a short pink summer dress with matching pink sling-back sandals. Her chestnut hair was pulled back on one side with a rhinestone-encrusted clip. As before, she had a determined look on her face, and smelled like strawberries.

"Hello, Marta." Val made sure she said the woman's name clearly.

Hearsay had crossed around the desk and stood next to the guest chair, his eyes glued on Marta's face, as though daring her to make a wrong move.

"I see you have dog," Marta said, looking uncomfortable. "He friendly?"

"No." A lie, but Val wanted her visitor to stay on her best behavior. "I'm trying to teach him not to bite strangers."

Marta shrank away from the dog. "His name?"

"Sweet Thang." Probably a good idea to not give his real name, in case Marta or somebody made a link between the dog and Drake.

"Funny name."

"Funny dog." Val put on her best concerned face. "So, Marta, why are you here today?"

Still leaning away from the dog, Marta looked at Val. "I am so sad."

"I'm sorry to hear that," Val murmured.

"Oh, yes, very sad." She sniffed, pointed a red nail at the tissue box. "Please, my dear Val, I need."

Val pushed it toward Marta, who smiled bravely as she plucked a tissue. She pressed it to her nose and gave her head a series of sorrowful, slow shakes, as though too overwhelmed to speak.

Which gave Val a few moments to think about this situation. Call it a gut sense, but she didn't think Marta knew Drake worked in the back office. If she did, there would be no reason to play this game.

"It is my fiancé," Val said, plucking another tissue. "He is missing."

"Oh, no," Val said, leaning forward, oozing concern, "what happened?"

Hearsay, either bored or sleepy, trotted to his bed and lay down.

Marta settled into a more comfortable position. "He go away. No note." She set her purse on the desk, pulled out a fat wad of bills and set it in front of Val. "I need your help, please." She stressed the *please* with an energetic jerk of her head.

The purse blocked the camera lens.

"Absolutely, let me take some notes." She made a sweeping gesture to pick up her notepad, knocking the purse, which toppled over the edge of her desk, its contents clattering onto the floor.

Hearsay barked, but wasn't interested enough to leave his bed.

"Oh, how clumsy of me!" Val said, getting up and crossing around the desk.

Crouching next to Marta, she picked up a lipstick while eyeing what else fell out. A red leather wallet. Sequined makeup bag. Keys. Cell phone. Ballpoint pen. Bottle of aspirin. Girlfriend kept a clean purse. Shame it didn't contain items seen in private eye movies, like a matchbook with the name of a bar, a personally monogrammed lighter, a pay stub. Something to tell her Marta's last name, address, places she frequented.

"Love your purse," Val said, heading back to her seat. "Louis Vuitton, *very* nice."

Marta smiled, pleased. "I get at outlet mall. Thirty percent discount." Her purse put back together, she set it on the floor next to her chair, then returned to the grieving girlfriend act. "I last see him yesterday."

Val picked up a pen and poised it over her notepad. "What time?"

"Two."

"In the afternoon?"

Marta blinked. "Yes."

"So he's been missing—" She glanced at the grandfather clock. Four forty-five. "—almost twenty-eight hours. Have you filed a missing-person report with the police?"

"*Da.* Yes."

That took Val by surprise, but she played it cool. "Good. Which department? I'll call, get a copy of their report."

"No." Marta paused. "They say we have lovers' spat and he be back, so no report."

"Is that right? You had a spat?"

Marta's eyes filled with emotion. "Yes, little one, but he always come back."

"Where were you when you had this misunderstanding?"

"Mis…?"

"Spat."

"We were…" She made a flourish of her hand. "Outside. In park. Forget name."

Val noticed Marta wasn't wearing the megasize bling she'd had on the other day, and that Drake had seemed interested in.

"You're not wearing your engagement ring. Did you and your fiancé break up during that spat?"

Marta glanced at her hand, back to Val. "No, we not break up. I leave it at jeweler's to check its worth. If I learn he ditch me, I sell it."

"He being Drake, your fiancé."

"Of course."

She casually glanced out the window, next to the door. There sat Marta's black Lexus. Too far to read the license plate.

"So," Val said nonchalantly, "do you have any idea where he might be? Favorite bar? Casino?"

"No. He's, what you say, home person."

"Homebody."

"Yes."

"You didn't want to tell me the kind of work he did before, but as he's missing, it would be helpful to know where he's employed."

"He out of place."

"Out of work?"

"Yes. I think you go back to Dino's. He there a lot. People know him, maybe he tell them…"

She caught a movement out the front. Drake strode up to Marta's Lexus, held his smartphone close to the license plate. She quickly looked at Marta, who was pushing the wad of bills toward her.

"There will be more when you find him," she said. "You have my number. Call me. No text. I go now."

Val glanced out the window again. No Drake. She eased out a pent-up breath.

After the Lexus pulled out of the lot, the grand-father clock chimed five times. Val sat in the guest chair and peered at her smartphone. The video ran as long as it detected motion, so she was, as they said on TV news, *live.*

"My name is Val LeRoy, and I am an intern P.I. at Diamond Investigations. Today is Saturday, August 10, 2013, five p.m. The interview began approximately seventeen minutes ago. The woman in this video is Marta, and she has refused to give her last name. My mentor, Las Vegas private investigator Drake Morgan, believes Marta may be linked to a recent arson, although I do not have that address."

She reflected on the kinds of information Jayne stated on her recorded interviews, such as the time, date, location, names of people present. In legal cases, interview tapes like this were reviewed by lawyers, judges, juries, so Val had to do this right. And cover her behind.

She moved the wad of bills so it could be seen. "I do not consent to investigating this case as it is illegal for interns to do so." Sounded good, even if she said so herself. "I accepted this money on behalf of Drake Morgan."

She picked up the camera, turned off the app, then jumped a little when she saw Drake.

He slouched against the wall, his shirt partially untucked, lazily blinking those gray eyes. A white plastic bag lay next to his feet.

"I didn't want to make you nervous, so I stayed in the hall until you were finished."

She waited. He hadn't seen her conduct an investigative task yet on her own. Oh, she'd dug through the trash for a short while with him yesterday, but he hadn't been there when she found the cigarette. Otherwise he only seemed to catch her bloopers, most of which had revolved around her badly—as in illegally—handling client transactions.

But this interview was different. It had been Val flying on her own, solo, relying on her memory of Jayne's interviews, and she knew it wasn't illegal because she had referenced that her role had been as an intern only, under the mentorship of a licensed P.I. She felt no small amount of pride that at the last minute she'd relied on her quick thinking and creativity to rig a camera on Marta and record a damning interview.

If the mountain doesn't go to you, go to the mountain. "Did I do well with my first interview?"

Squeak, squeak.

He grinned at Hearsay on the doggie bed. "Hearsay, buddy, you like your new toy?"

She waited a few moments, listening to more squeaking and doggie-love talk. Okay, she got it. He dug Hearsay. So did she.

When he finally glanced up, she managed a smile. Maybe not the hundred-dollar variety, but at least a seventy-five.

"Hey," she said softly.

Men, even the densest ones, could pick up on a woman's signals as though they'd been zapped by a cattle prod. Didn't mean they *understood* what was going on, but they definitely picked up that something was wrong, and the problem had to do with them.

He scowled. "What?"

She refused to let his coolness dampen her spirits. "Did I do well with my first interview?" she asked again.

He gave her a look as though she'd just landed in an alien spacecraft. "You want a report…on your report?"

She could argue this, get defensive, make a joke or pretend it didn't matter, then spend the next few minutes listening to the incessant squeaking that was starting to get on her nerves, big-time.

Or she could ask for her due.

"Yes, I'd like a report."

He made a disgruntled sound, as though he were being called on by the teacher to give a book report on a story he didn't like.

"Probably not a problem recording her in the office, although a sharp defense attorney will claim invasion of privacy, which could throw the interview out the window, especially as you recorded without her permission. What else…you didn't ask her pertinent questions, such as her address or last name—"

"Last time I talked to her, she refused to give those!"

"Yeah, yeah, I know, but it would have been helpful to have asked again during this interview. Let's see… knocking her purse off the desk…let's see, a savvy defense lawyer can easily claim trespass, because you knocked over her purse and then inventoried its contents, as well as violated her privacy."

"But…I didn't find anything."

He shrugged. "It isn't about what you didn't find, Val, it's about how you *tried* to find it, which reflects badly on you. Oh, and there were some problems with your wrap-up, which we can go over later." He straightened, glanced at the time on the grandfather clock. "Ready to go? Said we'd be there by six."

She fiddled with things on her desk, not wanting

him to see her embarrassment. How pathetic, scrounging for a pat on the head.

"Did you take Hearsay out for a break this afternoon?" he asked.

"No."

"Should've. Take it you've never owned a dog."

"Just cats."

"I'll take him outside through the back—not a good idea for me to be seen coming or going from Diamond Investigations' main entrance anymore. He'll stay in my office while we're at dinner. I'll put out food and water."

"Hearsay was such a good boy during the interview." She would show Drake how to give a *real* compliment. "Watched Marta for a moment or two, then went back to his doggie bed. Didn't even chew on his squeaky toy. A real team player."

"Yeah," he said, warmth infusing his voice, "he's a champ. I'll be back to pick him up as soon as we're done with dinner."

Which meant she'd be driving Drake back here. Val LeRoy, Beck and Call Taxi Service.

He gestured to the white plastic bag at his feet. "Mind putting that bag in your car? It's not heavy, just a few small cameras I'm taking to my mom's."

Make that Taxi and Moving Service.

"Pick me up in the parking lot behind Al's Bail Bonds down the street. Be there in ten." He gave a low whistle to Hearsay. "C'mon, buddy, time to do your business."

As the dog got up and yawned, Drake picked up the doggie bed. The two of them disappeared down the hallway. A moment later, she heard the connecting door close with a click, followed by the grating of a bolt lock sliding into place.

Good grief. What did he think she was going to do? Tear after him, throw open his door and violate his privacy?

She put the wad of bills into her desk drawer and locked it. Then picked up her purse and the plastic bag, turned off the lights and exited Diamond Investigations.

Small pools of heat shimmered on the asphalt. Air was so thick, it took extra energy just to breathe. After setting the bag in the backseat, she started the engine, cranked up the air-conditioning and put her face in front of it, entertaining the fantasy of breezing right past Al's Bail Bonds with a little toodle-loo wave to Drake I'm-the-Man Morgan.

Let him see what it feels like to hit your mark, or try to anyway, and have someone blow right past it.

DRAKE STOOD IN the parking lot behind Al's Bail Bonds, a square of cracked, buckling asphalt with scrawny cholla cactus around the perimeter. There was no Al, a fact he'd learned after the real owner, a hefty, far-side-of-sixty woman named Mallory, had hired him to run several locates. Her pool of clients mostly came from jails, which provided phone books to inmates but no computers, and A came before M, hence the Al in the business name.

There were no cars in the lot, but then, Mallory was rarely at the office anymore. *Time for me to retire while I can still smell the roses,* she'd told him, puffing on one of her nonstop cigarettes.

He checked the time on his smartphone for the third time. Five thirty-seven. He told Val to be here in ten minutes, which would have been five-thirty, and she was late. Diamond Investigations was less than a block away—what was taking her so long?

He mopped his brow and closed the app he'd been monitoring on his phone. Thumbing through the saved phone numbers on his phone, he found Val's and punched it. As it started to ring, her rental Honda sped into the lot, lurched over a warped section of asphalt and pitched to a stop thirty feet away.

The entire lot was empty and she couldn't park closer? With a disgruntled shake of his head, he walked to the passenger door and tugged on the hot metal handle.

Locked.

He glowered at her through the window.

She gave a sorry-about-that shrug and perused the dashboard, tapping a finger against her bottom lip.

Great. She had no idea how to unlock the effing doors. She'd been driving the car for four days, and she hadn't figured that out yet? Strands of her hair fluttered, so the air-conditioning had to be on full blast. Sure, she could take her sweet time looking for the magic button because she was nice and cool. Meanwhile, he was stuck outside, the sun grilling him to medium well.

He peered inside the car, spied a series of buttons on the driver's door panel. He rapped on the window.

She turned and smiled at him.

"Look at the driver's panel." He jabbed a finger toward her door.

She frowned, shook her head. "What?" she mouthed.

Drops of sweat stung his eyes. Blinking them back, he walked around the car and stopped at her window. He pointed at the driver's panel and its buttons.

She looked down, then back up with a look of wonder as though she'd discovered a small pot of gold. Nodding eagerly, she punched a button on the panel. The back passenger window rolled down. With an oh-can-you-believe-I-did-that look on her face, she punched it again and it closed. Making a give-me-a-moment gesture, she scanned the buttons again, then pressed another one.

The door locks clicked open.

He walked back around the car, smelling the stink of melting asphalt, thinking how he'd once heard that crimes tapered off after temperatures hit seventy-five degrees. Seemed when people got overheated, their urge to do wrong diminished. At ninety or a hundred degrees, especially during the day, people apparently lost the drive altogether to commit any misdeeds.

Those stats didn't apply to him. At the moment he wanted nothing more than to throttle a certain someone.

"You storing meat in here?" he muttered, climbing in and strapping on the seat belt. When she gave him a funny look, he explained, "It's so cold in here, it feels like a meat locker."

"It's hot outside."

"You don't say," he muttered, swiping a drip of sweat off his chin. "Why were you late?"

"You said ten minutes."

"Which in your time zone apparently means seventeen minutes."

"I wasn't *that* late."

A conversation that could only go in one direction—nowhere—so he addressed the next issue that pissed him off.

"Why did you park thirty feet away from where I stood?"

"My, aren't you the number man," she said, all huffy. "*Seven* minutes late. *Thirty* feet away."

"You didn't answer my question."

"I'm not the best parker in the world."

He bit the inside of his cheek, wondering if this was worth pursuing. It was. "You didn't *park*. You *braked*."

She scoffed, gave him a look. "Like there's a difference."

"Do you park at a red light?"

"Of course not!" She gave him a look as though he'd lost it. "What I meant was, when you're pulling up to pick up someone, it's like parking."

This discussion was headed in the same direction as the other one. He'd stop talking altogether, which a wise man would do, but at the moment, his bad mood trumped wisdom.

"You've driven this car for four days and you don't know how to unlock the doors?"

"Back to the number game, are we?" Her thick black lashes fluttered. "I've never unlocked the doors for anybody else because I've been the only person in this car. Hard to know how to do something if you've never done it before."

He sucked in his aggravation and blew it out. Did he bother correcting her about being the only person in the vehicle by bringing up their trash run? "Let's go," he said between his teeth, "we're late."

She muttered something about men and moods while stepping on the gas and spinning a one-eighty, the tires kicking up dust and rocks. After gunning it for fifteen feet—a number that would not pass his lips—she jerked to an abrupt stop at the street crossing.

"Okay," she said brightly, "which way?"

"What's with the NASCAR moves?"

"I'm sorry," she said, all sweetness and light, "you said we're late, so…"

"Left," he growled.

She punched the gas pedal so hard his head jerked

back. He was about to yell at her to slow down when she sidled past a stop sign into the middle of a four-way, scaring the bejesus out of the driver in an Acura crossing the intersection. He hit his horn, she hit hers and the Honda sailed through.

Drake looked at her. "You need to—"

She waved him off. "No more."

"No more what?" He jabbed his index finger at an upcoming cross street. "Turn right up there."

"No more correcting me. We're not at work."

"When did I correct you?"

"Oh, please." She jerked the wheel, executing a right turn that could make an atheist believe in a higher being. "You disapproved of my spiel at the end of the Marta interview."

"*Disapproved?* Because I offered *feedback?*"

"Yes."

"It's called *constructive criticism,* Val, not disapproval. You seem to forget that I'm *mentoring* you."

She emitted a self-righteous exhale. "Do you realize how nerve-racking that was for me when she came in and I knew she was possibly part of the arson that occurred? That I kept my cool even though I was scared as a cat at the dog pound? And yet I managed to record her—at close range—without her knowing. Okay, so I trespassed and violated her privacy when I caused her purse to topple, but what if I'd seen a pay stub with her *real* name, or the name of a bar she hangs out at? *You're* the one dragging your feet to talk to the arson investigator because you want more evidence before you do—I might have found some for you! What about them beans?"

He was trying to focus on what Val was saying, but he could barely focus on his own thoughts. Being in the car with Val driving was like sitting shotgun in some cheesy TV show car chase scene. Any moment he expected to hear the swell of guitar-grinding, piston-pumping background music.

"...and I was pretty cool when I saw you sneaking around her Lexus," she continued, swerving around a car that appeared out of nowhere. "Somebody else might have acted surprised or nervous, alerting Marta that something weird was going on, but I kept it together. And last, I'm sorry I didn't take your dog outside, but he seemed quite happy lying on his doggie bed and squeaking and sleeping. What was I supposed to do—wake him up and insist he do his duty?"

She brought the car to a jerky halt at a stop sign.

The beauty of this part of downtown was these small two-lane streets, which mostly catered to local traffic and got cars off the congested main roads. The constant stop signs were annoying, though, especially if someone named Val LeRoy was driving.

"After you get through this intersection," he said, peering out the windshield, "pull over."

"Why?"

"Because I'm driving."

"Correcting me again?"

"Only because I'd like to live long enough to see my mother and grandmother one more time."

After a beat, a laugh escaped her. "You shouldn't hide that sense of humor, Drake. It softens your macho edge."

"I'll do that. Now, pull over."

She did.

Unsnapping her seat belt, she gave him a sly look. "Got a confession. Took me six tries to get my driver's license. But I promise you, Drake, I'll be a better P.I. one day than I'll ever be a driver."

He didn't want to bring up that she'd have to put rolling surveillances, those conducted while driving a vehicle, onto her never-do list, along with undercover work, because they appeared to be on somewhat civil terms again. No need to muck things up by opening his big mouth and shoving both his feet in it.

They got out of the car and swapped places. After Drake slid behind the wheel, he pulled out his phone and set it on his thigh. Seeing her looking at it, he explained, "So I can answer without being seen talking and driving."

"Good idea."

After he started driving, and his nervous system downshifted from red alert, he said, "You did a good job with that interview."

"Would've been nice to have said that, once, before bombarding me with all the ways smart and savvy defense lawyers could rip it apart."

He shot her a look, one filled with more irritation than sympathy. "No one is expected to know these things without training. Which is the whole point of mentoring."

As he turned onto North Fourth, he caught a glimpse of Val's polka-dotted dress. Vintage, he guessed, but like his dad's suits, it also had a timeless quality. He recalled something he'd once read that claimed people who wore polka dots sought others' approval. Maybe he shouldn't have been so tough on her, but she was entering a tough profession.

He also liked how the dress conformed to her body—didn't look sprayed on the way some girls in Vegas wore their clothes, as though a little mystery was a bad thing. He thought back to that black dress she'd worn with its oversize, frothy bow. Little too librarian for his taste, but it had that timeless look about it, too. She didn't mess with what worked in the past. He respected that.

"Let's talk business," he said. "To be honest, I couldn't hear parts of the interview. What did Marta want this time?"

"To hire me to find you."

"Retainer?"

"Thousand dollars. Cash. I know I'm not supposed to accept cases, but if I had refused it, it would have alerted her that something was up, don't you think?"

"Absolutely. Where is the money?"

"Locked it up in my desk before I left."

"That's why you were late?"

"No, I drove around the block a few times. I was mad at you."

He pulled to a stop at a red light. "Over it?"

"For the most part."

He glanced at her, waiting for her to tell him exactly what stood in the way of his being absolved, but she wasn't telling. Just sat there, pretty in her polka dots, her hands folded primly in her lap as she stared out the window. One minute a road warrior, the next a sedate schoolgirl. One minute making him so nuts he swore he could turn criminal like his brother, the next intriguing him with a quiet reserve and a timeless style that left him a bit in awe.

He had the sense he would never understand her. And if he tried to, she'd inevitably surprise him with a quirk of her mind, a deeper layer of her personality or another facet of her beauty.

Val turned her head and their gazes met and held. Her eyes glistened with light, their color a swirl of brown, gold and green. His heartbeat accelerated, and his skin burned as though he was standing under the blistering sun again.

A warning bell clanged in his head. This was too much, and at the same time, it wasn't enough. He was in the grip of something he couldn't suppress, a fight he couldn't win...but was he ready to lose?

"The light's green," she whispered.

He snapped his head forward and stepped on the gas.

CHAPTER ELEVEN

VAL HAD BEEN staring out the window at the traffic on U.S. Route 95 for the past several minutes. Not that the view of cars, concrete and exhaust was all that interesting, but she wanted to give Drake some space— dang, she needed some breathing room herself—after that sizzling stare-down at the red light.

As they drove in silence, she thought about what had transpired between them in those moments. When their gazes locked, she could almost sense something shift, deepen between them.

It wasn't an awareness of sexual desire. She already knew he did things to her libido that were downright unholy, and she'd already accepted that he touched her heart in a place that made her want to believe in things she hadn't dreamed about or wished for in a long time.

It finally dawned on her that it didn't have to do with her, but him.

He had let down his guard.

Of course, one look at his stern profile, those big hands darn near squeezing the life out of that poor steering wheel, and she knew he'd tried to resurrect the wall. But if he had been successful, he wouldn't be glowering at the highway as though it were a mortal enemy he would conquer and destroy.

My, oh, my. Had she gotten under the dark prince's skin?

She still didn't know what the total story was between him and Sally, but at least she knew they weren't living together. And he sure hadn't looked at Sally the other night the way he had just looked at Val. And as bizarre as his invitation had been to this family dinner, he'd asked Val, not Sally. Plus, she'd caught him checking out her dress twice today. The second time, when they'd been stopped at the light, right before that mesmerizing eye lock, he had stared at her dress with a look of pleasure on his face, a secret smile playing on his lips.

She'd never thought she'd go for an alpha male like Drake. That type had always seemed laughable, with their leader-of-the-wolf-pack mentality. She'd pegged alphas as being pigheaded, cold and overmuscled. But that was like saying all Southern girls were gossipy, lazy and had big hair. The truth was people were more complex than their labels.

The Drake she was getting to know could be pigheaded and then some, but he could also be flexible. Like the way he accommodated Jayne's requests. And although he had that cold, unfeeling act down pat, Val was learning that's what it was—an act. Anybody who saw him with his dog knew Drake had a soft heart. And overmuscled, well, she hadn't had a chance to peel off that label yet.

"You're awfully quiet," he growled.

Oh, if he only knew how unquiet her thoughts had been.

"Figured I'd show you I can be from time to time," she teased. "Sometimes my mouth tends to overload my tail."

He quirked a questioning eyebrow.

"Which means I can talk too much."

She caught one side of his mouth lifting a little, threatening to smile, then the scowl returned.

"After I took a picture of Marta's license plate in the lot, I forwarded it to a buddy who ran it. It's registered to a bogus business."

Talking business, being brusque—she got it now. He'd retreated to his safe zone. *Well, move over, Drake, 'cause I'm joining you there.*

"How about we run a reverse on her cell phone number," she suggested, "like you did on mine, to get her real name and address?"

"Already did. Registered to the same bogus company."

She thought about that for a moment. "How did you get her cell phone number?"

"Took it off your phone."

He'd obviously checked it at some point while she was away from her desk. Made her feel a bit intruded on, but she didn't exactly have a spotless record when it came to deception.

"Mind asking next time? I have nothing to hide." She laughed softly. "Anymore, anyway."

He gave a brusque nod. "View it as a lesson to never leave your phone unattended. By the way, your Saints LISTSERV was open on your computer. Good idea to kill it. Companies can legally monitor everything employees do on work-issued devices. Jayne doesn't, but many employers do. At my hotel security job, I saw people fired on the spot and walked out of the building for accessing porn sites."

She stiffened. "I do *not* watch porn at work."

He gave her a look that made her heart beat faster.

After readjusting her seat belt, which didn't need readjusting, but fidgeting with it gave her a moment to settle her thoughts, she switched topics.

"Why does Marta want to find you?"

"I believe she's working with a man named Yuri. He thinks I have something he wants."

"What is that?"

"Evidence."

"Do you have it?"

He shrugged. "There might be some in the surveillance footage I took of him, but only he knows what is actually incriminating. The cigarette butt you found is ninety-nine percent his. It's a piece of incriminating evidence, but not the whole pie." He turned off the highway. "We'll be at my mom's in a few minutes."

So the man who smoked those exotic French cigarettes, the suspected arsonist, was named Yuri. Who worked with Marta.

"Why do you think Marta asked me to do the honey trap?"

"They needed a young female who was new at the P.I. game, someone they could manipulate. Yuri probably asked around, learned Jayne Diamond had an inexperienced, brand-new female intern, and they made their offer too good to resist. I bet you've been closing up most days at the agency, right?"

"F'true."

"They knew that. Probably had been watching the agency for a few days. They learned I'd be at Topaz Wednesday night because I said that in a phone message I left my brother, who manages the club. Maybe he mentioned it to an employee, or maybe one of them has access to his voice messages—whoever it was, told Yuri." He looked thoughtful. "At this point, I'm confident they think you and I don't know each other, except for the honey trap."

"How can you be sure?"

"Marta would never have returned to Diamond Investigations if they thought otherwise."

"I guessed the same thing."

"Plus, I know Yuri and his crew. They're greedy and devious, but they have the work ethic of a herd of sloths. They'd rather drink vodka than take the time to dig deeper, see if you and I have other connections. Because of their laziness, we can work this case."

We. She liked how he said it, as though they were a team, fighting shoulder to shoulder in this crusade. Plus it gave her a big, fat thrill that she'd be working a *real* case. One that didn't require her to play garbage collector.

"Tell me about Yuri."

"A low-life slimeball who's sucked my brother into his schemes. I had a problem five years ago, turned to Yuri for a loan." The muscle in his jaw ticked. "You mentioned Marta was wearing a large diamond ring the first time she came into the office."

"I noticed she wasn't wearing it today," Val responded. "I asked why, and she said it was being appraised at a jeweler's." She paused. "May I ask—why are you interested in the ring?"

"Belongs to my family."

For a moment, his hard, stoic features crumbled. Almost imperceptibly, but Val caught it. Then he put his mask on, the one that told the world he had it together, could handle any problem that came his way, didn't need anyone's help.

She ached for his pain, wished she could touch him, offer silent comfort, but knew instinctively he'd view such an overture as an act of pity. God forbid anyone should pity him.

And God forbid she should fall in love with him.

As Drake and Val walked across the yard toward his mom's home, his phone vibrated.

"Let me check this." He recognized the number on caller ID as Tony Cordova's, and debated whether to answer, but Tony would only step up the calls. As he should. A good investigator got the job done through tenacity and persistence.

"Morgan," he answered.

"It's Tony Cordova. How you doin'?"

"Fine."

"How's the tyke?"

"Better. Heard you dropped by the agency."

"Yeah. Wanted to tell you that I've been on-site, did a walk-through of your place. Looks like they broke in through your office window."

They. He wondered who had been with Yuri.

"Got proof an accelerant was used. Missing motive, though." He paused. "How about we meet tomorrow?"

"Busy, sorry."

"Yeah, I try to leave my Sundays for rest, but you know the lives of us investigators. Chasing crime isn't an eight-to-five job. How about Monday around ten?"

"That works."

Drake didn't completely trust Tony, and he didn't want a state fire department vehicle parked in the Diamond Investigations lot. If Yuri or Marta drove by, they'd easily guess it was an arson investigator's.

"Don't park in the front lot," Drake added. "I'm temporarily using a back office in the Diamond Investigations duplex. Go behind the private, fenced-off driveway and you'll see my office door."

"Thank you, my friend. By the way, do you go out your backyard gate much? The one that opens on the alley?"

"Never. Why?"

"Looks like somebody caught their hand on a nail in the gate. Crime scene tech swabbed the blood, got a piece of skin."

Sounded as if Yuri, and maybe his accomplice, had exited by the back gate to the alley. Drake doubted a getaway car had been waiting—an unknown, parked car would have raised neighbors' suspicions. But a person could easily walk undetected down that alley at night. Which raised the possibility Yuri parked nearby, walked to Drake's and set the fire, then exited down the alley and looped back to his car. So where did he leave his car?

The answer hit Drake. *At the strip mall near his house.* Most businesses were closed by six, so the lot was dark and empty in the evenings. He made a mental note to visit the area, see what else he might learn.

After finishing the call, Drake and Val continued walking toward the house. "By the way," he said, dropping his voice, "don't mention my brother. He's persona non grata for my mom."

Val's brown eyes widened. She nodded.

He took a step, stopped, turned to Val. Introducing her to his mother would be like lighting a fuse on a bomb. Certain to explode in his face. But it was too late to retreat now.

"Here's the deal. My mom and Grams took it personally when my fiancée walked a few years ago. I had some bad times after that." He shrugged. "So, when it comes to me and women, they tend to get…"

Val nodded, her features pert with curiosity. "Protective."

He nodded. "Not that we're…"

"Of course not." She glanced at the house then to

him. "All women have that nobody's-gonna-hurt-my-baby gene," she said in a half whisper. "Not to worry. I got it under control."

He wasn't sure if he should be relieved or scared. Guessed he'd find out soon enough. "Let's go."

A few seconds later, his mother answered the door. She wore a peasant top embellished with blue-and-pink flowers, denim shorts and a favorite pair of Teva sandals. She stared at Val, her gaze migrating slowly to her purple-streaked hair.

"Hi, Ma," Drake said, "This is Val. Val, my mom, Dorothy."

"I am so pleased to meet you, ma'am," Val said, extending her hand, which his mother tentatively shook. "Heath, the other intern, forgot he had a class tonight and felt mighty bad because he was going to help you cook dinner. I told him I'd be happy to fill in. Hope that's all right."

"Of course," she murmured.

"Oh, and I love cheese enchiladas. Also love to cook, used to do it all the time in New Orleans."

Drake lightly touched her back. Miraculously, she got the hint to stem the information flow.

His mother raised her eyebrows. "Yes, you'll have to tell me more about your Cajun cooking." She ushered them in.

Val walked in ahead of Drake. As he passed his mother, she gave him a variation of the look. This one said "unusual," which meant she was a little surprised, a little confused, open to possibilities.

He knew the feeling.

In the living room, he set the bag with the cameras on the coffee table. "I'll install these while you're cooking dinner."

"Fine, dear." She looked at Val. "Your internship is in private investigations?"

"Yes, ma'am."

Her lips tightened. "Dangerous business."

"Not always," Val said, oozing Southern charm from every pore. "Some P.I.s, like pet detectives, rarely experience danger."

"Is that what you're going to be? A pet detective?"

"No, ma'am. I like to get into the thick of it, solve crimes, chase down bad guys, go undercover..." She darted a look at Drake. "Although some people don't think I'll be able to do that because of my accent."

From the look on his mother's face, Drake knew her bowling league team was going to hear about this conversation, word for word.

She turned to him. "You didn't mention there were two interns, dear."

"Heath isn't very talkative, probably forgot to mention me to Drake," Val chimed in, "plus I've been working at home. I live with Heath. We're boyfriend-girlfriend. Not sure if we'll get married, but—"

"Any beer in the fridge?" Drake interrupted.

"Six-pack of your favorite," his mom said. "I need

to finish helping your grandmother get ready, so grab a beer and relax. I'll be back in a few minutes."

After she left the room, Drake turned to Val. "Heath?"

"Your alter ego." She shrugged. "It's a better story than your mama learning you fibbed to her."

"Okay. Fine. But starting now, let's put the brakes on the Heath stories. It's getting deep in here."

"I was trying to help."

"You did," he lied. "But those two are like human heat-seeking missiles who love nothing better than to zero in on the truth. Think of them as the Jessica Fletcher twins. They might be older, but they're crafty."

A smile tugged the corner of her mouth.

"What?"

"You."

"Okay, me."

"Underneath that macho exterior, you're a funny guy. Sweet, too, but you probably don't like hearing that."

He didn't. But when Val said it, in that drawl, he'd need to have antifreeze running through his veins to not like it.

He felt that way despite her locking him out of the car and letting him damn near liquefy under the sun. And driving like some kind of hot-rod hoodlum on crack. She got to him. In a good way. At this moment he could imagine nothing better in the world than standing here, studying her face, deflecting her teasing gibes.

"Keep it to yourself," he grumbled, "and let's park ourselves on the couch. I want to show you something."

VAL SAT ON the couch, surveying the room. "This place has a real down-home feel to it. You grow up here?"

"Yes."

"Well, isn't that the berries," she said, looking at the clock on the wall behind the TV. "That clock has dice spots for hours."

"Gave it to my dad for his birthday many years ago."

"He liked to gamble?"

A funny look crossed Drake's face. "Cards with the boys, that's about it."

"Would've thought he liked playing games with dice."

"That would be me," he said, sitting next to her. "But I don't gamble anymore."

"Why not?"

"Let's just say I liked roulette but it didn't like me back."

"You…had a gambling problem?" she asked softly.

"No, I had a stopping problem." He retrieved his phone from his pocket. "We're going to check up on our friend Marta." He handed her the phone.

She accepted it, wondering if his turning to Yuri for a loan meant Drake had gotten into some serious gambling debt. At her former casino job, she'd seen gamblers who sat for hours at a machine or a table, winning sometimes, but losing more often. They rarely looked happy. Her former pit boss had told her there were two kinds of gambling addicts—those who wanted people to view them as victorious, and those suppressing emotional pain.

Drake was too confident to seek anybody's approval. More as if he gambled to push down whatever was hurting him.

Putting aside those thoughts, she glanced at the phone in her hands. "I don't think it's a good idea to call Marta."

"We're not. Find the Tracker app and open it." He stood. "I'm gonna grab a beer. Want anything? Mom usually has some wine around."

"Not a wine fan, but thanks."

She flipped through the screens, found the app labeled Tracker and pressed it. A maplike grid displayed. Enlarging the image, she recognized major street names in Las Vegas. A tiny red square moved slowly along one of those streets.

"It's a real-time GPS software tracking system," Drake said, sitting again. "See the red dot?"

"I do."

"It's Marta's Lexus."

Took a moment for the words to sink in. She raised her head, gave him an incredulous look. "You attached a GPS device to her car?"

He nodded. "When I returned to the agency this

afternoon and saw that black Lexus in the lot, I had a feeling we had a Russian visitor."

"Thought you didn't practice paranormal investigations."

"Every Russian I've met has a thing for black Lexuses and Benzes, so I made a calculated guess. I grabbed a burner—a throwaway cell phone—that I'd loaded with GPS software and hoped she had her car windows open. She had. I tossed it under the driver's seat. Then I took the picture of her license plate."

Looking at the little red dot, she murmured, "Well, aren't you James Bond." Except... "This is illegal."

"If Marta were to find the burner, who's to say it's mine? No registration, no other viable ID."

She gave him a skeptical look, remembering how he'd grilled her about breaking the law as though he never crossed that line. "Thought you always walked the straight and narrow, Drake."

"When it comes to Yuri," he said, conviction tightening his features, "there are no rules."

His chilling tone frightened her. She knew only pieces of his troubles with Yuri, and that parts of it involved his family. But there was no doubt in her mind that Drake Morgan would do whatever it took, even commit barbaric acts, to defend those he loved.

She knew how that felt.

"...tracking is live until the phone's battery runs out of power in two or three days. Tap the history button."

Val pressed the button, and a report displayed.

"See how it lists the date, time and duration of all driving periods and stops?"

"Yes."

"After leaving Diamond Investigations this afternoon, Marta traveled to an address in Summerlin South." He pointed at the entry. "Which is one of the more affluent neighborhoods in the Las Vegas Valley. Notice she only stayed at the address for five minutes before driving again. Memorize that address, then close the app."

She repeated the address to herself, then closed the program.

"Now, open Google and run a reverse on the address."

She opened the browser and entered the address. "It's a jewelry store named Mousseux. Oh! That must be where the ring is being appraised."

"Good thinking." He leaned closer, looked at the screen. "These tracking programs aren't always exact. They pick the *nearest* address, so you usually need to travel to the location and check around, see which business the car is parked in front of. From the photo, I see Mousseux doesn't sit on a block with other businesses. It's by itself, so we nailed that location."

He sat so close, his thigh pressed against hers. She could feel his body heat radiating through her dress, warming her bare skin. His nearness, the roughness in his voice were almost too much to bear.

As he talked about the various ways satellite signals to a GPS device sometimes got blocked, she let the husky timbre of his voice curl around her spine. Easing in a lungful of his manly scent, she held it within her, filling herself with his essence, never wanting to let it go.

As she slowly exhaled, she studied his eyes. She had witnessed different moods and needs through the shadings of those gray eyes. Yet at this moment she observed something new—the silvery-gray looked almost blue, like the sky at dusk or the color of distant mountains. And had she noticed before that he had the tiniest white scar at his hairline?

Staring into his eyes, she had a woozy feeling, as though she were plummeting into their depths, being drawn into a swell of secrets, longings and need.

It seemed as though the summer heat had seeped through the walls and permeated her body. Her blood was on fire, a fever burned within her and any second her entire being would burst into flames.

"Val?" Drake murmured huskily, "you're trembling."

Her heart beat so furiously she could hardly hear above its thundering and pounding. All she could think, imagine, desire was the touch of his lips, the taste of his kiss…. Blame it on the excruciating summer heat, the stress of handling a business in her boss's sudden absence or the plain fact that she hadn't touched or kissed a man in years—not some backseat fumble, but the real, get-down-and-feel-it deal.

She had to accept that she'd never be cool, never be refreshingly uncomplicated. Life was complicated, messy, confusing, but most of all, fun. If you didn't seize the moment, it went away, and she was tired of playing are-we-or-aren't-we with this man. She was going in to take it, now, right here, propriety be damned.

She zeroed in, half-aware of the surprise in his eyes, more aware of the smile on his lips. Those firm, full lips. She grabbed onto his collar and reeled him in the rest of the way, ready to indulge in one big, high-voltage lip-meld.

She caught a movement in the corner of her eye.

Someone gasped loudly.

Val jerked back with a start, her hands still gripping Drake's collar.

There, in a wheelchair, sat a petite elderly woman, swathed in a pink-and-orange satin caftan, a halo of white hair radiating from her head. A Siamese cat lay curled on her lap, its tail coiling lazily in the air.

Next to her stood Drake's mother, her mouth agape, her hand over her heart as though it might fail her any moment, looking shocked and furious at the same time.

After a tense silence during which Val wondered if she'd be asked to leave the house or leave Drake alone or both, his mother said, "Drake, I'm expecting a call any minute. A friend who's going through some difficult times. I just put the meat loaf in the oven because it will take longer to cook than…cheese enchiladas." On *cheese enchiladas,* she cast a stinging look at Val that made her feel like a pile of steaming roadkill, then slid her gaze to her son. "I'll be back shortly."

Her head high, Dorothy walked briskly out of the room and down the hallway.

In the awkward silence that followed, Drake, Val and Grams darted glances at each other.

"My darling," the elderly woman finally said to Val, the rings on her hand sparkling as she gestured, "let me make you a martini."

CHAPTER TWELVE

DRAKE STOOD HASTILY, muttering a soft curse as he bumped his knee on the coffee table. He held out his hand for Val. She grappled to hold on to it as she shakily stood.

They stood there, awkwardly holding hands, looking at his grandmother, who appeared calm and a little amused.

"Grams," he said, "this is Val LeRoy."

She extended her hand to Grams. "I'm delighted to meet you, ma'am."

Grams lifted her hand and they shook.

This evening had been doomed before it even began. Lying to his mom about Val's identity was bad enough, but letting Val fabricate more stories about the mythical Heath was the kiss of death. Maybe he should make an excuse and whisk her out of here to a fast-food joint where they could absolve their guilt with a greasy Quarter Pounder and fries.

But before he could make the suggestion, his grandmother cast a sweet smile at Val.

"Delighted to make your acquaintance, as well. Please call me Grams or Glenda, your choice."

A shy smile curved Val's mouth. "I like Grams."

She tilted her head and looked inquisitively at Val's hair. "Do I see purple in there?"

"Yes, ma'am."

"My," she said, "aren't you fun."

Val smiled. "What's your cat's name?"

"Maxine. She has a bit of the devil in her, but so do I, so we get along fabulously."

"Hello, Maxine," Val cooed, reaching out, "may I pet you?"

Drake put his hand on Val's arm. "I wouldn't—"

He watched, amazed, as cranky spitfire Maxine purred, her eyes glazing over, as Val petted her head. First his dog took a liking to her, now the meanest cat on the planet, and his grandmother's face was creased with smile lines, her eyes sparkling. It was obvious she'd taken a liking to Val.

His mother, different story.

She would dislike Val. Immensely. Of course, she had good reason based on the stories she'd been fed. Val lived with her boyfriend, Heath, whom she was considering marrying, yet she was sneaking around behind his back and putting the moves on Drake, who worked with the two of them. It had all the makings of a bad office-romance soap opera, and Dorothy Morgan wouldn't like it one bit that her son was in the middle of it.

But there was another reason his mother wouldn't be fond of his new intern. Even if Val had lived her entire life in a convent, her bloodline traced back to

British royalty and she was the sole heir to the Rubik's Cube fortune, his mother still wouldn't like her.

Because Val was in the private-investigations business.

He could maybe smooth over the lies and misunderstandings, but he could never fix that.

He peered toward the hallway that led to the bedrooms. His mom was in hers by now, probably talking to her friend, listening to her problems, pretending nothing distressing had just occurred in her life. His mom liked to be strong for others, needed to be needed.

He related to that.

When she came out, he'd talk to her. Maybe after being distracted by someone else's problems, her mood would be better.

He looked at Val and Grams, who were chatting about Maxine. The cat lay in his grandmother's lap, purring and cuddling as though she didn't have one freaky-mean bone in her body.

"She likes you," Grams said to Val.

"And I like her. Where did you get Maxine?"

"A neighbor. Her Siamese cat had a litter, and she was giving away the kittens, except nobody wanted the runt because she was feisty. She was ready to take the kitten to a shelter, because it was terrorizing the other cats in her house, when I said, 'Give her to me.' I know she's a challenge at times, but—" when she looked at Val, the color of her eyes softened to a sea-green "—everybody deserves a chance."

Val stared at her shoes for a moment, then looked up, her eyes moist. "Sometimes my impetuous streak gets the best of me. Grams, I am so mortified, so sorry about…" She bit her lip.

His grandmother sighed. "Impetuous streaks are quite common. I have one of those myself. It's gotten the best *and* the worst of me, but I must say, my life has been more far more interesting thanks to it. Now," she said, putting on a serious face, "I have a confession. I've been rude."

Val blinked. "What? No, you haven't been at all."

"Yes, I have been. I should have first asked if you like martinis."

"Why, yes, I do."

"Gin martinis, I hope?"

Val smiled. "Is there any other kind?"

"Somebody obviously raised you well." Grams pressed a button and the chair slowly pivoted. "Drake, sweetheart, did you find that app for me?"

"Yes."

"Goody. My smartphone is on my dresser. Perhaps you'll download it while Val and I are mixing our drinks." Grams motioned for Val to join her, then she pushed the joystick and the wheelchair moved slowly forward.

"My grandson doesn't like martinis," Grams said. "He's strictly a beer man…or did you already know that?"

"Not really. I mean, I knew he drank beer, just didn't know he never branched out."

Drake took a swig of his brew, watching them as they headed toward the kitchen, Grams's hands gesturing as she talked, the rings glittering, Val walking alongside, head tilted so as to not miss a word of what she was saying.

"Yes," Grams said, "he's definitely not the type to branch out. Once he finds something he likes, he sticks with it."

Standing alone in the living room, Drake frowned. He never branched out? His grandmother made him sound like a stick in the mud. So what if he drove the same pickup he'd had for years? It was a Ford, and it ran like a tank. He swigged again. And when it came to beer, who wanted to drink overpriced craft beers with cutesy names like Hopped Up and Polygamy Porter, the latter's tagline being Why Have Just One? Beer was beer, and he'd be a Bud man till the day he died.

He headed toward the hallway. If that made him a stick in the mud, then more power to the sludge.

A minute later, he stopped outside his grandmother's room, his hand on the knob, and listened to the gentle cadence of his mom's voice behind her closed door at the end of the hall.

Once she found something she liked, she stuck with it, too. Same hairstyle, same style of clothes, and he wouldn't be surprised if one day those Tevas ended up in the Smithsonian for the longest-worn pair of shoes in North America. Not that any of it was negative. She reminded him of one of her favorite actresses, Katharine Hepburn. Tough and self-determined, sticking with styles that were uniquely theirs.

Dorothy Morgan stuck with things she *didn't* like, too. Her anger over Brax's lifestyle. And probably her first bad impression of Val.

He ran a hand over his bristly hair. It wouldn't be easy to talk to her about his lying and Val's made-up stories, but he trusted she'd come around. He and his mom were usually able to work through their misunderstandings.

He doubted, though, that she'd ever be open to talking about Brax again. She would die stuck in that rut of anger, unable to forgive. Not that she was wrong for closing the door on Braxton, but he wondered who got hurt more in the long run—she or his brother, her other son?

He recalled something his father said in his last days. That his life seemed to have passed in the blink of an eye. Maybe everyone felt that way in the end. It pained Drake to think that his mother, in her final moments, might regret that she'd stayed pinned to her anger over Braxton.

He entered Grams's room, headed for the smartphone on her dresser. He set his brew on the dresser, then paused, looked at the bottle.

One of these days, for the hell of it, he might try one of those microbrewed beers.

VAL SAT ON a chair next to Grams at a small table against the kitchen wall. On the table was a small

crystal bucket of ice, which Grams had filled from
the refrigerator's ice maker, a bottle of vermouth, a
box of toothpicks and a jar of olives.

Maxine was noisily eating from a bowl of kibble
on the floor under the table. As Grams had explained,
it was their evening ritual. While Grams mixed her
martini, Maxine ate her dinner. "It's our cocktail
hour."

"Darling, check if the glasses and shaker are frosty."

It was a long, narrow kitchen. The rest of the house
had a comfy, lived-in feeling, but the white, steel and
glass kitchen reminded Val of Jayne's office. It had
a sterile feel about it, as though it had seceded from
the rest of the home.

In New Orleans, the large, messy kitchen had been
her and Nanny's favorite room in the house. Towels
tossed on tables, dirty dishes piled in the sink and
Ball jars everywhere, filled with everything from coffee beans to grits. As Nanny used to say, *Be thankful
if you have food to make a mess with, and people to
make a mess for.*

The Morgan kitchen was the opposite. So spare
and tidy-clean it made Val's teeth squeak. Against
one wall along with the table were cupboards, with
one of the lower cabinets shelving Grams's martini
wares. Against the opposite wall were the sink, counter, stove-oven and refrigerator. A person could tra-
verse the kitchen in a few steps. Took Val three to
reach the freezer.

She checked the glasses. "They're frosty."

"Wonderful. Bring them over."

Val's fingers stuck slightly to the metal shaker, which she brought over first. As she headed back to collect the rest, she sniffed the air. "That meat loaf smells awesome."

"Dorothy Morgan's world-famous meat loaf. Years ago, she won several cooking contests with that recipe. Told her she should market it to restaurants in Vegas, but she said she'd rather lie in the road and be a traffic cone than spend the rest of her days mass-producing meat loaf."

Val had to admire Dorothy's conviction. It was one thing to love creating something, another to be forced to recreate it over and over again, ad nauseam. One reason Val was attracted to private investigations was that no two cases were alike.

"Well, I can't wait to taste this world-famous meat loaf," Val said, sitting. She scanned the layout of glasses, shaker, crystal bowl. "Martinis call for cool jazz playing in the background, don't you think?"

"Yes, that would set the mood, wouldn't it? Drake's father, Benny, loved jazz. There was always music playing in the house. Tony Bennett. Sarah Vaughan. Ella Fitzgerald." She grew thoughtful for a moment. "Dorothy and Benny were good for each other. He taught her about music, she taught him about persistence. And how they loved to laugh! Even when they were arguing." She opened the box of toothpicks. "I'd love to hear her laugh like that again," she said softly.

Val hesitated, wondering if she should share this, but maybe her experience offered hope.

"I...didn't laugh much, either, after I lost my grand-mother."

Although she had shared many of her experiences during and after Katrina with her cousins and best friend Cammie, she had never discussed how it felt to lose Nanny with anyone else.

"She was everything to me," she continued. "My mother, my father, my best friend rolled into one. Guess I'm telling you this because..." She swallowed with difficulty. "I didn't laugh for a long time after losing her. Not that I wasn't mighty grateful to be alive, and appreciated people's kindnesses more than I can ever express...but laughter? I mean *real* laughter. The kind that comes from deep inside, that makes the most unbearable things bearable. I didn't laugh like that again until I moved in with my cousins, here in Vegas."

Grams nodded. "When was that, darling?"

"Two years ago."

"And you lost your beloved nanny in..."

"Two thousand five."

The elderly woman studied Val's face. "Katrina."

Val nodded. She was consumed with emotion, but didn't dare speak. But by Grams saying that one word, *Katrina,* Val knew she understood, knew she cared. No other words were necessary.

The elderly woman put her hand on Val's and gave it a squeeze. "You're a brave girl. You do your nanny proud."

She swallowed the tightness in her throat. "I don't know if it was courage that made me swim in those floodwaters. More like desperation and fear. All I know is I failed. And I should never have left Nanny alone on our roof."

There. She'd said it. The heavy burden on her heart she'd carried all these years, the one thing she had never divulged to anyone, not even Jaz, because it ripped her apart, filled her with shame. She had left her grandmother to die.

Grams slowly nodded her head, as though comprehending the pain and self-recrimination Val carried with her always. Every day, every hour, every minute.

"Darling," she said gently, "it's all right to open your heart."

Maybe it was looking into the older woman's face, soft and lined like her nanny's, or that they were sitting in a kitchen talking the way she and her grandmother used to do, but Val couldn't push down the ache, the remorse, anymore.

"Superdome was a nightmare," she whispered. "Rumors were rampant—names of people found dead or sick traveled person to person, day and night. Thought I heard Nanny's name once—Alva LeRoy—but didn't catch the rest. Wandered through the crowd, repeating her name, but nobody knew anything. All those lost people, all their stories, all that suffering...it was like looking into the face of God." She ran her finger along the edge of the table. "After I got to Houston, I learned she had died."

"It's a lesson of life that all our living leads to death," Grams said gently. "Take it from this eighty-five-year-old—our challenge is not fearing death, but fearing living. I think we need to learn not to be afraid to burn the candle for fear of its end. Feel fortunate, my sweet girl, that you had such a loving experience with your nanny." Sadness flitted across her face. "My other grandson, Braxton, is no longer allowed to visit the house. Perhaps you know about this."

Val nodded.

"When love is imperfect, something else can be learned. Forgiveness. Not only toward others, but to ourselves, too." She leaned forward, her eyes earnest. "When it comes to what happened during Katrina, the only person not forgiving you is yourself, darling. Your nanny loves you, knows you did your very best."

"I hope so," she whispered.

"The great thing about hope, once you choose it, is that anything's possible." She glanced at the gin. "Shall we light that candle?"

Val picked up the bottle and poured it into the shaker.

Grams picked up the vermouth. "A little? A splash?"

"Splash, definitely."

"A girl after my own heart."

After pouring a healthy shot into the shaker, Grams speared olives on two toothpicks while Val shook the canister, then poured the frothy liquid into their glasses.

"One should never take drinking advice from fictional characters," Grams said, plopping olive-laden picks into each glass, "but James Bond was right. Martinis are much better shaken, not stirred."

"James Bond," Val murmured, thinking back to that hot near kiss on the couch.

She had definitely been shaken, not stirred. Even more shaken when she looked up and saw Drake's mother and grandmother there, but at least they hadn't caught them in the middle of their first real kiss. Although at this rate, she was starting to wonder if that would ever happen.

But one thing she knew, she didn't want to be the aggressor again. Twice was enough, thank you. Three times if she threw in the honey-trap mess. Maybe it was the universe sending her a message that three times *wasn't* a charm.

If Drake wanted this sizzle between them to go anywhere, he had to make the next move. She wanted proof that what she sensed between them was real and not some fantasy in her head.

Grams held up her glass. "To the sacred rite that affirms tribal identity."

"You said it," Val said, raising her glass.

After they quietly enjoyed the first few sips of their martinis, Grams set her glass on the table with a soft clink. "How long have you known Drake?"

"Told his mama I met him today," Val said, getting a sinking feeling in her stomach. "To tell you the truth, I lied."

With a scratchy meow, Maxine jumped onto Grams's lap. "I thought so."

Val blinked. "How did you know?"

"Drake has a head for numbers."

Tell me about it. Val took another sip.

"When he told Dorothy earlier that there was one intern, and he shows up with a *second* intern, well…" She picked up her drink, gave Val a knowing look over the rim of the glass. "Also, I don't know too many vegetarians who can't wait to eat meat loaf."

Busted. Val cringed inside. "I'm a moron."

"No," Grams said, "you're just a girl in love."

Stunned, Val opened her mouth to deny it, but all that came out was a strangled, wispy sound.

"That's how it was for me, too," Grams continued, a faraway look in her eyes. "I met Drake's grandfather, Jack Lassiter, in 1944, his first night stateside after piloting a B-17 Flying Fortress named Bolt From the Blue. Falling in love was like that, too. A bolt from the blue. When we eloped ten days later, I wore a powder-blue suit."

"Got the app downloaded, Grams." Drake strolled into the kitchen and set her phone on the table. He took a last draw on his beer, put it on the kitchen counter. "Was waiting to talk to Mom, but she's still on that call. I'll go install the outdoor cameras, then I'll sync up the feeds to your smartphone." He stopped, looked at the two of them. "What?"

"Nothing," Val murmured.

"From the looks on your faces, especially yours," he said, indicating Val, "I'm having a hard time believing that."

With a loud mew, Maxine jerked her head toward the hallway.

"You hear Dorothy leaving her bedroom, don't you?" Grams said gently to the cat. She shifted her gaze to Drake. "As Dorothy will be joining us any moment, I suggest we all have a good, get-it-out-on-the-table truth-telling session about these bogus Heath stories, which has made your mother think this lovely girl is some kind of two-timing harlot."

The lovely girl finished off her martini in one gulp.

DRAKE LOOKED AT his mother as she entered the kitchen. Grams was right. Time to put the truth out there. He would have preferred to talk one-on-one with his mom, but it would be silly to invite her into the other room for a private talk at this point. Plus, his apology was to Grams, too.

"Ma, I'm sorry I said the intern was a guy. There is no Heath."

She dropped her gaze to the black-and-white tiled floor, to the far window still bright with early-evening summer light, her eyes finally returning to Drake's.

"You lied to me." The disappointment in her tone was worse than if she'd yelled at him.

The room was uncomfortably quiet except for a faint ticking from the clock above the stove.

"I'm sorry," Drake said.

Dorothy notched up her chin. "Anybody can say they're sorry after the fact," she said, her voice growing thin. "What I want to know is…why did you lie to me?"

He watched her, hating himself for hurting her. And for letting down the old man. He was breaking his promise to take care of his mother and Grams by lying to them. It deceived them and degraded him.

Some secrets were meant to be kept. In Iraq, the year before he returned home, he had killed a man with his bare hands. Other secrets were commonly known, just not discussed. How in the course of his hotel security job, and later in the investigations business, he had made enemies, suffered bodily punishment, uncovered dirt on people who were sitting in prison at this very instant.

But some secrets turned ugly when forced into hiding, as though they were too sinister to be viewed in the light of day. The act of hiding had worse consequences than the secret, because it crippled the confidence of the person who unearthed the secret, deprived them of the dignity of being trusted.

It pained him to see the hurt in his mother's eyes. Didn't matter if he thought his actions to be insignificant or his deception harmless. If the end result caused his family pain, he had been dead wrong.

"After Liz walked," he said, pacing a few steps, "you and Grams got…overprotective. That dinner with Laura…" He gave his head a shake. "I wasn't sure what was grilled more that night—the steaks or her. I didn't want that to happen again."

His mother darted a questioning look at Val, who was toying with her empty glass, staring at the table.

He could guess what was going through his mom's mind—was Val someone special in Drake's life? After all, she was the first woman he'd brought home since Laura. No, he wanted to say, it wasn't like that between him and Val.

And yet…seeing how Val and Grams clicked, the respect Val showed his mom, the miracle of Maxine taking a liking to her…she fit in here.

More than that, she fit into his life.

The thought jolted him. Crossing to the kitchen window, he looked outside, his back to the others. He needed a moment to digest this without staring into three sets of scrutinizing, curious eyes.

He hadn't wanted to make room in his world for Val, yet she had somehow taken up space in his thoughts, so he spent an inordinate amount of energy wanting to see her, talk to her, be with her. Didn't mean she *fit* into his life, though, right?

Don't be a semantic jackass. If she's that prevalent, she fits.

He looked toward the northwest, saw the gray clouds hovering over Mount Charleston. Hadn't noticed them while driving over here, but he hadn't been paying attention. Just like the truth sharpening in his consciousness. He hadn't paid attention to it before, either, but he had no choice but to acknowledge it now.

His fear wasn't about intimacy, but about failing to achieve with someone the kind of closeness his parents, and his grandparents, had shared.

What he really feared was Val's rejection.

"Drake?" his mother called out softly.

He turned, met her gaze. She was waiting to hear why he'd lied to her. He'd never again put her in this position.

"Before I left yesterday," he said, turning slowly to face her, "you said how much Grams would love to talk about that trip she took to New Orleans, and you were happy that you'd be cooking with someone again…"

He looked at the stove, could almost see a ten-year-old Braxton stirring a bubbling pot, listening attentively to their mother reading directions from a cookbook.

"When you assumed the intern was a man," he said, turning back to his mom, "I went along with it. Figured the less time you two had to ponder who Val was, the smoother the evening would go." He gave a wry smile. "Obviously, I was wrong about that."

All three women spoke at the same time.

"I'm sorry, too," Val said.

"I need to say something," Grams said.

"I want to apologize," his mother whispered.

After a beat of silence, Val said, "Well, that was a gumbo ya-ya!" Seeing the confused looks on their faces, she explained, "Everybody talking at the same time."

"Gumbo ya-ya, indeed." Dorothy turned to Grams. "You first, Mom."

Her face etched with a fierce tenderness, she touched Val's hand. "This darling girl already shared a little about her city with me. As much as I would love to bore everyone again with that trip Jack and I took to New Orleans in eighty-four, I will save it for another time."

Dorothy, her eyes glimmering with emotion, spoke up. "I need to apologize to my son."

"Ma—"

"I do." She rolled back her shoulders. "It's true, I didn't like Laura. That night, son, while you were marinating the steaks, I overheard her talking on her cell to some man…they were obviously more than friends." Catching her breath, she fussed absently with her hair. "I acted badly, I know, but I didn't want to see you hurt again."

His mouth crooked into a half smile. "You didn't act badly, you acted like a mama bear. I had my suspicions she was dating somebody else, but to be fair, we hadn't had the exclusivity talk."

"Even so," Grams piped up, "Maxine didn't like her."

Dorothy huffed. "Like Maxine's preferences are an indicator of human character."

"Oh, you'd be surprised," Grams muttered, handing the shaker to Drake. "Mind filling it with more ice, dear? I think another martini is in order."

Drake crossed to the fridge and filled it, the ice clattering into the container.

"Plus," Grams added, "I was following Laura on Twitter, and she was flirting with Vegas-ace-high."

Dorothy frowned. "What's that?"

"His Twitter handle," Grams explained, swirling the toothpick in her martini glass. "I've since blocked both of them."

Val raised her hand. "May I apologize, too?"

"The more, the merrier," Drake muttered, carrying the shaker to the table.

Nervously readjusting the sash on her dress, Val said to Dorothy, "I said I had a boyfriend named Heath because I thought it was better to have a cover story than for you to find out that Drake lied."

His mother intently studied Val's face. "Is there someone else you're seeing?"

Drake leaned against the stove and watched Val. It was a personal question, but he had to admit, his mom had the right to ask after what they'd put her through.

Plus, he had wondered, too, if there was anyone in Val's life. Not a boyfriend—she wasn't the type to cheat on someone—but she was too damn cute to be spending Friday nights alone.

"No, ma'am."

Good. He didn't have to annihilate the competition.

"But you are from New Orleans," his mother said.

Val grinned wide, flashing that disarming crooked front tooth. "Who Dat Nation, f'sure!"

"Which means," Drake explained to his mom's

confused look, "she's from New Orleans, no question about it."

Dorothy looked back at Val. "Are you also a vegetarian?"

"No, ma'am. Said I was because—"

"Heath was." She made an exasperated sound. "Is there really a Heath? Because if there is, we should invite this poor man over so he can tell *his* side of the story."

Val bit back a smile. "There's no Heath. I made him up."

Dorothy rolled her eyes to Grams. "Did you know all this?"

"One moment, dear, I'm splashing the vermouth." After setting down the bottle, she looked at her daughter. "I figured out there was no Heath, and when she told me she couldn't wait to taste Dorothy's world-famous meat loaf, well…" She motioned to Val. "Let's light that candle again, darling."

Val poured in gin, secured the lid and shook the canister.

As the ice and liquid slushed and rattled, Dorothy leaned against the refrigerator, flicking a look between Val and Drake.

"Are you two dating?"

"Whoops!" Val missed the glass, sloshing some martini onto the table. "Sor-ree!" She righted the shaker.

Drake grabbed a paper towel. "I'll get it."

As he blotted the spill, Val looked sheepishly at his mother. "No, we're not dating."

He took the shaker and finished pouring the drinks. There hadn't been an official date yet, so technically Val was right. "I'm mentoring her."

Dorothy's brow wrinkled. "Is *that* what they call what you two were doing on the couch? *Mentoring?*"

"Dear," Grams murmured, "you've learned that Val is single, she's from the Big Easy and she's a carnivore. But whatever was going on when we walked in is none of our business."

Dorothy gave a grudging nod. "One more question. You and Hearsay are staying at Li'l Bit's, correct?"

"Yes," Drake said, getting the intent of her question. She wanted to know if he was living at Val's place. He'd only accepted a few minutes ago that Val fit into his life, was open to exploring that, but living together? As much as he wanted closeness, he wasn't ready to be that close.

"I've always wondered what Li'l Bit's place looks like," Grams said.

"Probably exactly what you'd imagine," Drake answered, "although there are no lava lamps."

"I'm glad we're not making cheese enchiladas," Dorothy said to Val, "because I have no idea how to make them. Bought the ingredients for my bowling league's Mexican fiesta potluck, but at the last minute, brought chips and salsa instead." She gave a halfhearted shrug. "Sometimes I'm not in the mood to cook alone."

"I know how that feels." Val paused. "Don't know what else you've planned for dinner, but if you've got some lettuce and, as we call 'em in New Orleans, some *vedgetibbles,* I can dress up a salad."

Dorothy's face brightened. "Yes, I have some lettuce and vedgetibbles." She gestured at the shaker. "Is there enough in there for a third martini?"

"Let me do the honors," Drake said. "I'd join you but I'm driving, and one beer is my limit."

As he retrieved another martini glass from Grams's cabinet, his mom asked, "A beer man would drink a martini?"

He set the glass on the table, poured some gin and vermouth into the container. "Not right now, but maybe sometime," he said, securing the lid. "I've decided to branch out."

With a grin, he gave the canister a hearty shake.

CHAPTER THIRTEEN

A LITTLE AFTER eight that night, Drake and Val left his mom's. Before driving off, Drake checked the tracking app on his phone, which flashed an error message that it was unable to locate the GPS device in Marta's car. He explained to Val that the car was likely parked in a garage, which blocked the satellite signals.

Fifteen minutes later, Drake drove the Honda down West Charleston Boulevard. Val sat in the passenger seat, bobbing her head along to Lady Gaga's song "Poker Face," which was playing on the radio.

"At my last job, I was thinking about lipping this song. I think I coulda pulled off one hot ya-ya Lady Gaga." She caught Drake's perplexed look. "I was a celebrity dealer at the Shamrock."

"The Shamrock," he mused. "That place is a Vegas classic. Haven't been there in years."

After several martinis, she felt a buzz. And less inhibited to ask point-blank, "You were a gambling addict?"

"*Am* a gambling addict. I'm in recovery."

She reached over and turned off the radio. Listening to a song about poker and talking about gambling addiction felt hypocritical.

"This money you borrowed from Yuri," she asked, "was it to pay off a gambling debt?"

"Yes."

She strung the pieces of the story together. "Is that why he has your family's ring? As a payment?"

"Yes."

"Must be a very nice ring."

"Five marriages going back to 1854. Grams knows all the stories. One is called the Breckenridge Diamond, named after the Colorado mountain town that my great-great-grandmother and her husband helped found. During the winters, they cross-country skied everywhere. Not long after her husband died, she found an ailing owl on a skiing trip and nursed it back to health. It stayed with her after that. When she died, it was always seen near her gravesite. Family legend claims it was her husband, who promised he'd never leave her side."

"What a touching story. And how horrible that Yuri has it. He'll never know its significance."

He was quiet for a moment. "I would never have given him that ring. Just learned a few weeks ago that my father gave it to him as partial payment, twenty grand, for my debt. After I paid that back to Mom, she handed it all to me in a savings account, which had been Dad's wish. When I heard about the ring, I offered the cash to Yuri. He wouldn't give up the ring. Instead, he jacked up the price to thirty, refused a penny less."

"Jerk."

"Yeah, they broke the mold with him." He took a right at South Jones Boulevard.

"Where are we going?"

"Wanted to drive by my old place—it's not far out of the way. Since I'm meeting the arson investigator on Monday, I want to get an idea of the damage before the monsoons hit."

"Think they're coming that soon?" Craning her neck, she checked out the rear window. "Looks like those clouds are staying in the mountains."

"Looks can be deceiving."

She studied his profile. So strong, so hard. Not a flicker of what he was feeling inside. One thing she'd noticed tonight was how his mother and grandmother, for all their independence and strength, relied on him. Yet he didn't seem to rely on anyone else.

"Can you go inside your house?"

"No. It's still a crime scene. Tony might have an idea when I can get back inside, but…"

"What?"

He shrugged. "Hearsay survived, that's all that really matters. Most everything else is replaceable. I've only really missed two things. Connelly's book *The Lincoln Lawyer*—was halfway through reading it—and my dad's old suits. At least I still got the one I was wearing that night. Jacket's a bit of a mess, but it can be cleaned."

So that retro suit she'd seen him wearing that night had been his dad's. It fit him so well, Val guessed he'd had it altered. She loved vintage clothes, but she had no idea who had owned them before. But to wear something of a loved one's was, in a sense, like an embrace. A quiet, tangible way to remain close.

Drake might keep a tough exterior about life, but his feelings ran deep. Indeed, looks could be deceiving.

"You lost everything in fire," she murmured, "me, in water." She remembered something. "Nanny once told me about some ancient goddess of fire and water. In winter, she's the fire that cracks the ice and brings the frozen world alive again."

She tapped her fingers on the armrest, thinking how, in an oddly similar way, a fire—Grams's warmth—had cracked the ice of Val's long-suppressed shame of leaving her nanny on the roof. She felt some relief from her admission, but it would take time to completely release all the guilt and shame. Just as it took time for a frozen world to come fully alive again.

She didn't know if she'd feel any better admitting this next thing to Drake, but she needed to talk about it.

"I lied to Nanny," she said softly.

He glanced at her, his brow furrowed. "Val, it's been a long night. Maybe this isn't the time."

She almost smiled. There'd been a lot of venting and confessing and forgiving going on this evening—probably enough to last a lifetime for a man who didn't like to discuss feelings.

"It's long past time, actually. I made a promise to Nanny to find my biological mother, who left me when I was two. I broke my promise. I haven't done even one Google search."

After a pause, he said, "Maybe you were *late* acting on your promise, but you didn't break it." His voice gentled. "I'll help you find your mother."

"I wasn't telling you to reel you in—"

"I know. You're helping me with my case, so let me help you with yours. Anyway, keeping promises makes people whole."

She looked out the window at the stream of flashy signs, half-empty parking lots and seedy strip malls. Maybe she'd feel whole, too, after fulfilling the promise to Nanny, but she doubted that finding the mother who'd abandoned her would make her feel much of anything except angry. Granted, she'd given Val life, but a few years later she hadn't cared if her baby daughter lived or died. What was the meaning in finding someone like that?

"After you get home tonight," Drake continued, "send me a message with whatever information you know about your birth mother. Which reminds me— I'd like to see that interview you did with Marta right away. Can you attach it to a text message?"

She tugged her phone out of her purse, glad to be concentrating on something else.

"I've been thinking about that arson investigator. He probably has access to all kinds of government databases unavailable to private investigators. Maybe he can help you dig up some of that dirt on Yuri."

"True. But I'm not telling him about Yuri."

"Wait, I'm finishing sending my interview with Marta…okay, done." She dropped her phone into her purse. "Why not?"

"One phone call or door knock from a government investigator will send Yuri underground."

She thought about what Drake had said earlier. "So that's what you meant when you said things could backfire if you gave too much information, too soon, to Tony."

He nodded.

"Like a game of chess. You want to help Tony, eventually, but he can't move *too* fast because you want to blackmail Yuri by showing him evidence you've found that he committed the arson—"

"Or some other criminal act—"

"Which forces Yuri to sell the ring to you at twenty thousand."

"You got it." He shot her an interested look. "You play chess?"

"Nanny tried to teach me. After a few lessons we agreed we'd both live much happier lives if she played chess with her friends and I took piano lessons."

He half choked a laugh. "I can only imagine how *that* conversation played out." He reflected for a moment. "I know you'll never let me hear the end of this, but I've been thinking how something else might play out. Taking that Riviera case isn't such a bad idea."

She did a double take. "Well, paint me green and call me a cucumber!"

"It's decent money. Established client. And it gives me time to work the kinks out of my life. But this isn't a ghost chase, it's about collecting evidence through established means such as taking video and setting up motion detectors."

"Which is how Miss Doyle views it, too."

"I wonder about that." He turned on South Myrtle Avenue. "My house is up here. By the way, I'll text you Yuri's name and a link later tonight. Want you to check out what he looks like."

"F'sure," she murmured as they approached the house.

The streetlights cast a surreal light on the gutted, burned building. Drake pulled over to the far side of the road and stopped but kept the engine running. He rolled down his window and looked at it.

The silence was eerie, broken only by a dog barking in the distance. The stench of smoke permeated the air. Yellow crime tape and no-trespassing signs circled the charred remains.

The devastation wakened memories of New Orleans in Val. The emptiness. The hope against hope that something had survived. "Do you want to get out and look around?"

"What's the point? Total loss."

"I'm sorry," she said softly.

He rolled up his window, then turned to her and gently put his hand under her chin, tilting her face so he could see it better.

"Fire and water," he murmured.

AFTER LEAVING DRAKE'S old house, they listened to a local soft rock station on the radio. Five songs later, Drake parked in front of Val's house and killed the engine.

"I'm going back to the office, pick up Hearsay. In the morning, Li'l Bit will follow me over in his car, and I'll park yours out in front. Plan to put some time in at the office after that."

"Li'l Bit. Funny name."

"Met him when I subcontracted a process service, but our friendship took off after I helped him out of a jam."

There weren't as many lights on this street, making it darker inside the car. She sensed something in the air—a tension, an expectancy—and wished she could see the look in his eyes. He might be a master at hiding his emotions, but those gray eyes signaled more than he realized.

"Thanks again for inviting me to your family's for dinner."

He chuckled under his breath. "Next time, it'll be a family get-together, not a group therapy session."

She caught his familiar, masculine scent, felt a tingling in the pit of her stomach. The air seemed to thrum with their connection, their energy.

Across the street, the neighbor's porch light went on. A group of people, laughing and talking, exited the front door. A small black dog, tail wagging, scampered outside with them, barking.

The image of Drake's home, reduced to scorched

rubble, rose in her mind. Seeing the horrifying destruction firsthand, knowing how recently it had occurred, jarred her.

Here he sat, looking so calm, so controlled…but she didn't buy the facade. She had experienced such devastation and loss, knew how emotions—exhaustion, anger, confusion—bombarded a person those first days after the trauma. She remembered a social worker walking through the Superdome, asking people what they needed, offering coping tips. Although dazed and frightened, Val had forced herself to memorize three tips that became her mantra over the following days and weeks. Even now, eight years later, she could repeat them in her sleep.

Identify concrete needs.

Don't make important decisions.

Find ways to alleviate stress.

The best thing she could do for Drake right now was help him cope. As much as she'd prefer to go for the gusto, it did a disservice to him, her, too, to behave like some P.I. intern with more hormones than sense. She needed to be his friend and work associate. If they were meant to be more, that would come in time. But not right now.

She put her hand on the door handle. "Need anything else for Monday's interview with Tony?"

"No."

Was there disappointment in his voice?

"Whenever you get the rental car back here is fine.

Anytime Sunday works, I don't have plans." She opened the door.

"Val, wait."

She paused, looking back at his shadowy face.

"Want to…do something tomorrow night?"

"Rain check?"

"That's not an answer."

"No," she said softly.

He blew out a breath. She could feel his withdrawal. Probably had that look of puzzlement on his face. The one that made him look shy and sweet, although based on the way his massive, shadowy form hunched over the steering wheel, more like one of those churlish gargoyles on a French Quarter balcony. Shy and sweet didn't peg his mood at the moment.

This wasn't going well. She needed to explain.

"You need to identify your concrete needs, not make important decisions, alleviate stress."

He snorted with disbelief. "Are you a shrink all of a sudden?"

"No," she said, forcing herself to sound calm, together. "I'm your friend."

He started the car and revved the engine like a race car driver at the start line. "Get out and close the door."

His words stung. "I didn't explain that well. What I meant was—"

"Val, enough."

"I need to get my purse." She grabbed it, then paused. With her other hand, she reached out, offering peacemaking fingertips. "You're going through a difficult—"

He snarled something about crazy who dats and she jumped back, shoving the door shut with a slam.

Standing on the sidewalk, she watched the plumes of smoke from his burning-rubber peel out as he erratically drove her rental Honda down the street. It truly was disheartening when people didn't aspire to be mannerly and communicative, even in times of stress.

Across the street, the neighbors stood still, nobody laughing or talking, staring silently at her. Even the dog had stopped barking.

She plastered a smile on her face and waved. "G'night, y'all!"

Shivering, she walked to the front door, rubbing her arms as though it was chilly out, knowing it had nothing to do with the weather but the absence of the physical and emotional warmth she had desired. Yes, *desired*. Sensations pounded and raged within her, but she had made a choice to do the right thing and put his well-being ahead of her hot, sticky, primal needs.

But damn, he had asked her out.

These past eight years, Val had dated off and on, but she eventually found fault with the guy and ended things. Or she acted like a jerk and to her relief, he ended things. Could it be that until she absolved herself for abandoning Nanny, she wouldn't allow herself to risk a deep attachment with anyone else? Especially risk falling in love, because that meant opening herself to feeling wanted and good and safe?

The realization surprised her. How could she—a woman who could work and fight so hard for a career—also stand in the way of her own personal happiness? It just seemed plain dumb, and yet that's what she had done.

So now what? Call him up and say, "Hey, I know I said no, but how about yes instead?" Considering the way he'd left skid marks on the street tonight, she seriously doubted the man would be receptive to her changing her mind, if he even picked up the call after seeing her caller ID.

Feeling glum, she stepped onto the porch and halted. Opening her purse, she angled it under the porch light. What a mess. Honestly, bag ladies carried around less stuff then she did.

She pawed through the clutter for the house key, mentally flogging herself for cluttering up her relationship with Drake, too.

Just as she found her keys, the front door clicked open.

Jaz stood there, wearing a trench coat, her face slathered with makeup.

"Hey, bay-bee!" She swept back a curl of her raven hair. "I was just on my way out."

Val glanced at her cousin's black seamed stockings and leopard-print stilettos with pointy toes. "Where you fixin' to go?"

"Have an interview with a club manager at ten. He's looking for burlesque dancers."

"You're wearing your burlesque outfit under that coat?"

Jaz flipped it open. "Whattya think?"

Val checked out her barely legal cousin's breasts, damn near spilling out of a leopard corset trimmed in red satin with a black tulle skirt that barely covered her whoozit.

"You look like a hooker."

Jaz vigorously closed her coat. "I cannot believe," she muttered indignantly, cinching the belt, "that you just called me that."

"Well, if it looks like a duck…"

With a haughty toss of her neonoir head, she gave Val a withering drop-dead look.

"Don't be so juvenile," Val muttered, staring into her cousin's eyes, determined to not be the first to blink. "Going on an interview dressed like that, at *ten o'clock at night,* in *Las Vegas,* is asking for trouble."

"Ten p.m. in Las Vegas is like noon anywhere else in the world."

"I see they're also teaching logic at Dottie the Body's burlesque school."

Jaz sniffed. "You're insufferable."

"Yeah, well, you blinked first."

Del and Char's car wasn't parked in the driveway. Probably working late at the Gumbo Stop.

"If you thought what you were doing was acceptable," Val said, "you wouldn't be sneaking out, dressed like some kind of burlesque cat in heat, before your mama and daddy get home."

"Cat in—?" Jaz heaved an affronted gasp and fisted her hand on her hip. "My, listen to Miss Holier-Than-Thou. The other night, as I recall, you came home dressed up like some kind of *putain* after trying to seduce a strange man you'd never laid eyes on before in your life, in the *parking lot* of one of the biggest dive bars in the city."

She had a point.

Nevertheless, it pissed Val off that her cousin would throw out *putain,* French for "prostitute," in the heat of an argument. As though to say, "I might be losing my temper, but I never lose my sophistication."

"That was a *forfait,*" Val said, not above flaunting a little sophistication herself.

Jaz frowned. "What does that mean?"

Val didn't have a clue. She'd overhead it once, and liked how it sounded. "It's French for 'job.'"

"So strumpin' in a parking lot is your *forfait,* sugar? Bein' a burlesque dancer is going to be my *career!*" She paused, then dropped her fist-on-jutted-hip stance and stuck out her slick crimson bottom lip in a pout. "Cuz," she whined, "I don't like it when we argue."

Val released a heavy sigh. "Me, neither. It's just that I feel protective of you, Jaz. I support your burlesque dreams, but…who is this guy you're meeting anyway?

"Manager of the Boom Boom Room."

"The *Boom Boom Room?*" Val looked up at the

heavens, counted five stars, then one more for good measure, before meeting her cousin's eyes again.

"Bless your heart," she said, oozing sweetness, "That's a *bar,* dawlin', not a theater." What she really wanted to say was, *if Dino's is a dive, the Boom Boom Room is one big ol' nasty belly flop.*

"They've built a stage in the back room," Jasmyn said, all bubbly, "where they'll feature monthly burlesque shows."

Val could only imagine what that backroom stage looked like. Somebody's kitchen table in a cleaned-out storage room?

Arguing didn't change her cousin's mind. Neither did being so sweet a frozen cube sugar could've melted in Val's mouth. Time to put her foot down.

She crossed her arms, faced her cousin straight on. "I won't let you go, and that's that. Someday you'll thank me for this."

Arching a shapely eyebrow in profound disdain, Jaz brushed past her. "Excuse me, but I already have a mama."

Val stood on the porch, watching her cousin head down the walk to her car, her heels clicking purposefully.

At least Jaz didn't peel out, burning rubber. But then, she was a sophisticated girl.

DRAKE PICKED UP the eight-track tape case stuck behind the potted plant, opened it and retrieved the spare key. Inserting it into the lock, he gave it a twist and pushed open the door. It slammed against the sliding chain lock.

He reminded himself that Li'l Bit was a good friend, even if he was a space cadet who left a key outside for Drake to let himself in, then locked the door from the inside.

"It's Drake," he called through the slightly open door. "Open up."

Hearsay, who'd been sniffing the plant intensely, looked up, his ears perked.

Seconds later, Li'l Bit's sleepy face peered through the crack. "Dude, sorry. Sliding that chain lock is an autopilot thing."

A moment later, Li'l reopened the door and Drake stepped inside.

Hearsay trotted behind him as he entered the living room, which still smelled like marijuana smoke, but to Li'l Bit's credit, the smell wasn't as bad since he'd been taking his smoke breaks in the bathroom. The room also smelled like popcorn, a large bowl of which sat on the steamer-trunk coffee table next to several bottles of beer.

"Hungry, man? Just made popcorn."

Drake shook his head. "Had dinner at Mom's."

"Going to watch *The Man Who Fell to Earth*," Li'l Bit said. He wore a pair of wrinkled plaid shorts and a T-shirt that read *Is This Your Homework, Larry?* "David Bowie plays a humanoid alien who falls to Earth. He rocks in this film."

"Sounds interesting, but we have a problem."

Li'l Bit, who'd been shuffling toward the couch, froze. Turning, he stared at Drake for a long, drawn-out moment.

"Yuri followed you here," he said in a dead-solemn tone. "This is getting severely unradical."

"No." Drake pointed at the couch. "That's my bed, and you're on it."

He looked at the couch, back to Drake. "Going to bed soon?"

"Yes."

"Want to watch some *Man Who Fell to Earth* first?"

"No. It's too much like my life right now."

"I get your meaning, Aqua Man. You need some space, time to chill and heal." He looked at Hearsay, who had curled up next to the couch. "How's our boy?"

"Like his old self."

"Animals, man…" Li'l Bit's eyes moistened. "They rule the earth."

He decided to step over that conversation. "Got a favor to ask."

"After that parking ticket problem you got me out of, anything. Name it."

"Need to drop off someone's car in the morning. Mind following, giving me a ride to my office afterward?"

"I'm there, my brother."

"Around ten?"

"Word."

The wear and tear of the day suddenly hit him. He

could feel his energy bleed out, and all he wanted was to crash. "I'm bushed. Gotta hit the sack."

"I'll grab my popcorn, do a J in the bathroom. Peace out, Aqua Man."

Drake watched Li'l Bit amble toward the hall, the bowl of popcorn in one hand, a beer in the other. Probably the only person he knew who, for the most part, lived in the here and now. A hippie who truly walked the talk.

He tossed the sheet onto the couch, topped it with a pillow, tugged off his shirt. Hearsay was already up on the couch, waiting for him. He left a bowl of water on the kitchen floor, and gave the dog his pill wrapped in a wad of peanut butter. He'd already given Hearsay his nightly snack of kibble at the office before driving over here, so now he could take off his pants and shoes and snag some z's.

Drake laid his head on the pillow and pulled the thin blanket over him. Hearsay snuggled up against his side and within seconds started snoring lightly.

But Drake couldn't sleep. Kept seeing Val sitting next to him in the car, her features indistinct in the dark, her form a shadow. Yet he could perceive her smile, see those twinkling brown eyes in his mind's eye, but most of all, feel her sassy sexiness, its heat rippling across the space between them like a hot summer breeze.

Then, with no provocation, her soft, lazy drawl morphed into clinical psychobabble, and she said no to a date because she was his friend.

His *friend?*

Whatever happened in the car tonight, and he had a hunch he might never know, she'd rejected him.

He turned, trying to get comfortable on the couch, which was impossible. Place smelled like an overworked popcorn machine at a movie theater. One of his legs was half off the couch to make room for Hearsay, whose snoring was starting to sound like a low-flying drone. In the other room, Li'l Bit was talking to somebody on his phone, most of it unintelligible except for the occasional "man" and "dude."

He stared at the Jimi Hendrix poster, wondering why a rainbow flowed out of his guitar. He shifted his gaze to the ceiling. Boring. He returned to Jimi.

Hell of a thing when a body's bone tired, but the mind keeps sprinting like a racehorse on the inside track. He knew it was going to be a long night alone with his racing thoughts, not dreams. He'd get up and warm himself a glass of milk, but there wasn't any in the fridge. Several boxes of dry, sugary cereal, but no milk. Almost seemed un-American.

So Drake lay there, sharing space and time with Jimi. Somewhere in the dark recesses of his mind, he had the half-aware understanding that just because he had chosen to live his life a certain way, didn't mean others were supposed to understand it, like it or put up with it.

Yet…he vaguely wondered if it was too late to slow down, switch lanes and be a different kind of man.

One who could win Val's heart, not be her friend.

WHEN VAL WOKE up Sunday morning, she was still tired. Although she'd taken a long, hot bath last night before going to bed, she had slept fitfully. She stared groggily at the bedside clock radio. Nine a.m.

Shifting her gaze to her bedroom window, she stared at a chitalpa tree in the backyard, its soft green leaves fluttering with passing breezes, their lazy, undulating movements bringing back a piece of a dream. She'd been swimming in the ocean, the water surprisingly warm and calm. Light sparkled on the surface, like scattered diamonds, and she swam effortlessly with broad, strong strokes.

Then she dived beneath the surface, kicking hard to propel herself downward, the green waters shading to gray, and she realized she was on fire.

Shivering, Val slid out of bed, walked across the smooth hardwood floor to the leather chair she'd bought for a hundred bucks on Craigslist and pulled her robe off its back. Everything else in the room— a nightstand, queen-size bed with a metal frame and dark wood vanity table, had been here when she moved in, courtesy of Char and Del. She kept the room tidy, except for the vanity table, which rivaled her purse for clutter.

Her real stamp on the room was the colors. She'd read that the color purple symbolized peace of mind, good judgment and mystery—she'd always wanted to exude mystery, and figured she needed help with the other two—so after she moved in, she painted one of the walls a soft eggplant. Another she painted a squash yellow because it went well with the purple. Later she read that the color yellow had all kinds of meanings, from causing frustration to sharpening memory and creativity. At that point, she decided colors were like life choices—choose what you want to believe and stick with it.

She found a purple, gold and green bedspread that tied the room together. She hadn't planned it, but those were the Mardi Gras colors. A visual echo from New Orleans.

Toddling into the kitchen, she smelled the rich scent of coffee.

A man and woman were singing a soulful, twangy duet about being tangled up and sideways in love. Char sat at the table, wrapped in her pink chenille robe, reading her iPad.

She looked up at Val and grinned mischievously. "Didn't see your car out front, thought you'd stayed out all night."

Which Val had never done in her two years living here. Not that she wouldn't have if the opportunity had presented itself, but then, she hadn't exactly been open to dating anyone. So Val being invited to dinner at Drake's family's house was big news in the Jackson household.

"Had a few martinis last night, so Drake drove me home. He's dropping the rental car off some time today."

Char glanced out the far window, which provided a

COLLEEN COLLINS 281

partial view of the street and gravel-filled yard. "Not here yet. Will he be comin' to the front door?"

Which Val interpreted to mean, *Shall I invite him in for coffee, have him meet your family?* Oh, wouldn't Del love that.

"No, he's working today."

Which was the truth, although that didn't preclude his coming inside for a few minutes. But unless Drake had lost his short-term memory between last night and this morning, she seriously doubted he wanted to see Val unless it was business related.

Regret twisted in her chest. She really knew how to screw up a good thing.

"Brought some beignets from the store," Char said. "Box is on the counter."

Beignets, fried fritters dusted with powdered sugar, were the Louisiana state doughnut. And the perfect comfort food for Val this morning.

She poured herself a cup of dark-roasted coffee with chicory, whitened it with milk and slid a beignet on a plate. Added a second one. Maybe that's how she'd spend her day, drowning her sorrows in beignets.

She sat at the table next to Char, listening to the woman singer wail about not being able to unlove him.

"What's this song?" she asked.

"'Better in the Long Run.' That's Miranda Lambert and her husband, Blake Shelton, singing. The song's sad, but they aren't. I swear, they are just the cutest, happiest twosome singing country today."

Val took a big bite of beignet and chewed sorrowfully.

"So," Char said, her pale eyes twinkling, "how was it meeting his family?"

Val swallowed, not easy when your heart's in your throat and you're trying to pass food by it at the same time. She forced a shaky smile.

"Few bumps when I first got there because his mother was expecting a man, so I made up a story about a live-in boyfriend…" She waved her hand as though erasing something in the air. "That part gets complicated, so I'll skip it. Then his grandmother and I made martinis and after I told her some things, she told me I should forgive myself, and I'm really taking that to heart."

Her voice sounded strangely airy and high-pitched, so she cleared her throat. "Had a little shakedown in the kitchen before dinner, but after I apologized to his mama for lying, things picked up. Then we ate Dorothy's world-famous meat loaf, and later went by Drake's burned-up house, which tore me up something fierce, then he drove me home and asked me out…" Her chin trembled. "And I said no, and he…" She swiped at her eye. "Tore outta here like Jimmie Johnson on the last lap at Daytona—if Jimmie Johnson were really, really pissed—and would you mind terribly if I just took that box o' beignets into my room and stayed in there all day, eating myself sick?"

Choking back a sob, her vision blurry with tears, she brought the beignet to her mouth. Char gently took it out of her hand and set it back on the plate.

"*Cher,* baby," she said, holding open her arms.

Val fell into them and sobbed, holding on to her cousin's soft, warm body that smelled like flowers and coffee, letting herself be rocked like a baby, finding the comfort no beignet could ever offer.

Minutes later, her tears subsided enough so she could hear Miranda singing another song, this one about killing an ex-boyfriend who'd done her wrong, which wasn't very happy, but at least it didn't make Val want to write her last will and testament.

Her head was on Char's shoulder. Her cousin was humming along with Miranda, stroking Val's hair, occasionally murmuring, "It's gonna be all right, dawlin'."

Jaz, wearing her *Je rêve* jammies, shuffled into the kitchen, pausing to stare blearily at her mother and Val. Without a word, she walked over, her arms open, and wrapped them around Val, too. She obviously didn't have a clue what was going on, but it didn't matter. Taking her mother's lead, she murmured, "It's gonna be okay, cuz."

Maybe it would be okay, and maybe not.

But one thing Val knew at that moment. What really mattered in life came down to one word.

Family.

LATE MORNING ON Sunday, Drake drove his pickup to the strip mall near his old place, and parked in front of Ronald's Donuts, a favorite stop of his when he lived down here. He'd tossed on a white T-shirt, jeans and sneakers this morning, keeping it simple for the work ahead.

A minute later, he walked inside the store. A middle-aged couple sat at one of the small Formica tables, noshing on glazed doughnuts. Behind the glass counter with displays of pastries stood the owner, Henry, wearing a white bib apron over street clothes, his short black hair neatly parted on the side.

He bowed his head slightly as Drake approached the counter.

"Hi, Henry."

"Hello, Drake. So sorry about fire."

When he had first dropped by Ronald's Donuts five years ago, Drake had thought it was another hole-in-the-wall doughnut shop with bad coffee and cheap doughnuts. It took him several visits to catch on that Henry, a devout Buddhist, was somewhat famous in the doughnut world for his vegan specialties, from soy-cream-filled éclairs to vegan-glazed doughnut holes. Drake, a meat-and-potatoes guy, now sometimes jokingly referred to himself as a Doughnut Vegan.

"I appreciate your concern, Henry. It happened late Wednesday night—was wondering if you've seen any new people hanging around the neighborhood lately... or a black Mercedes sedan?"

He looked thoughtful for a moment. "No, Drake, sorry."

"I'm gonna leave my truck parked outside for a bit.

Could I have one of your small paper bags, and a few of those wax tissues?"

Henry walked away for a few moments, returning with two small paper bags. "This one with tissues," he said, handing it to Drake, "and this with your usual."

An apple fritter. Drake reached for his wallet.

"No." Henry shook his head gently. "Gift."

DRAKE MEANT TO toss the bag with the fritter into his truck for later, but couldn't resist the enticing scents of warm dough and sugar. As he walked out of Ronald's Donuts, he took his first bite. By the time he reached the weed-filled lot behind the doughnut shop, the fritter was history.

For the next half hour or so, Drake walked around the dusty patch of ground. Rocks crunched under his shoes. The air pulsed with the high-pitched whine of insects. He stopped and mopped his brow with the back of his hand as he looked at the two-lane street that rounded the lot's far edge. His former home sat another hundred feet or so down that street. An easy fifteen-minute walk from where he stood.

A melancholy swept over him, unsettling as the hot, dusty winds, prickling his memories about all he'd lost. Not the objects that had vanished in the fire—most were replaceable anyway—but what he'd lost of himself. His purpose. His meaning.

Sometimes lately he felt like his own ghost, haunting his own life.

He kept going through the motions, getting up each

day, taking care of Hearsay, wrestling with issues and commitments. If someone took a snapshot of his life, though, he'd be a shadow on the film. A specter in a world he once inhabited.

It'd be easy to say something out there could anchor him again to his life. A great case, a new apartment, Val...

He had a hunch the answer was somehow within him, but he had no idea how to get to that place.

After wandering around the lot some more, he decided to head back. That's when he looked down, and there it was. Under a scraggy bush, nearly blending into the dusty earth.

He pulled a tissue out of the paper bag and used it to pick up the cigarette butt.

LATER THAT AFTERNOON, Drake was working in his back office when Hearsay lifted his head and gave a low woof.

"What is it, boy?" Drake listened, thought he heard a muffled noise.

The dog shot across the floor and down the hallway to the connecting door, which he kept barking at.

Somebody appeared to be in the Diamond Investigations office. Had Val forgotten to lock its front door yesterday when she left? No. She might have been angry when she'd left, but she would have locked up.

Downtown Las Vegas was deserted on Sundays, which gave him an uneasy feeling about who this unexpected visitor might be.

He walked quietly down the hall to Hearsay, still yapping like a maniac at the door. He touched the dog's head. "Shh, boy."

Hearsay emitted a low-throttled growl.

Drake looked at the slide lock, which he'd left unbolted. He drew Hearsay behind him.

Then grabbed the knob and jerked open the door.

CHAPTER FOURTEEN

STARTLED, VAL EMITTED a wispy shriek.

Drake didn't say a word. Heavy, dark eyebrows hovered over narrowed eyes glittering with anger. The sullen slant of his mouth was back with a vengeance. His white T-shirt was rumpled, stained with sweat.

His big, bad self reminded her of Heathcliff, a character she had always found laughable, with a mystique about as hot as a cold, distant star. What she hadn't put together until this moment was that such distance alluded to the depth of the man, and that the closer you got to a distant star, the hotter it burned.

Standing here, she was damn near melting under the dark rays of this Heathcliff's bad-boy sun.

"What the hell are you doing here?" he growled.

Hearsay, his tail wagging, sniffed Jaz's shoes that Val had borrowed. At least somebody in this office was happy to see her.

"I, uh, didn't want to bother you if you had a visitor," she said, her voice barely audible, "so I was listening to see if I heard voices, but this door is so thick, it's hard to hear, and then you opened the door so suddenly it scared me."

Earlier that morning, after her crying spell was

over, Jaz and Char had decided Val's best approach to heal this rift was to go after her man in style. Or as Char said, "You need to air up your tires for this trip, dawlin'."

So Val took a shower, spritzed on Jaz's spicy patchouli perfume, polished her nails and borrowed a brightly flowered summer dress from Jaz, who also helped her create a sleek, one-sided do accessorized with a hot-pink flower hair clip.

Which had all seemed like a great idea until now.

The way he glared at her, she wished she'd just eaten the box of beignets and called it a day.

She'd turn around and leave, but Jasmyn's high-heel platforms were a tad too large, which made it difficult to walk faster than a snail's pace, and besides, her knees were shaking so badly, she didn't trust herself to walk away with any grace whatsoever.

So she decided to stay put and give him the makeup gift she hoped would inspire peace between them.

She held it toward him. "This is for you."

He took it from her, stared at the cover. *"The Lincoln Lawyer."*

"Thought you'd like it."

The fury in his eyes gave way to a perplexed look. "You coulda called, let me know you were coming into the office today."

She bit her tongue to not say, *And you coulda said thank you.* "I wanted to surprise you."

"In our business," he said, his voice taut, "the less surprises the better."

At least he said *our*. "I'll keep that in mind when I plan your next birthday party," she quipped.

He glowered at her. "I don't like birthday parties."

Oh, good Lord. She liked to think of herself as a pretty easygoing person, off and on anyway, who practiced good manners even when her temper got in the way. This man obviously did not share that value.

"Give me the book back, please, because you don't even have the good sense to behave graciously when you receive a gift."

He frowned. "Don't tell me how to behave."

She sucked in a breath. "Forget it! Can't believe I got aired up for this trip. If I didn't want to be a P.I. so damn bad, I'd quit right now. Let some other poor, hardworking intern put up with your badass, know-it-all, ungrateful attitude. Now I'm going to say something I've never said to anyone in my entire life. *Kiss my ass*."

She pivoted slowly and started a glacial slide back down the hallway.

None of this was going according to plan. She was supposed to knock on his door, he'd open it, his anger going by the wayside after he got an eyeful of her. She would flash him a thousand-dollar smile, hand him the gift, apologize and they'd pick up where they left off.

She pressed one hand against the wall for balance as she took another gingerly step. Hearsay trotted up to her, nuzzled her leg. She reached down to pet his head, and her ankle gave way.

With a soft shriek, she tumbled to the floor.

Drake was instantly at her side, leaning over her, a concerned expression on his face. "You okay?"

"These shoes don't fit," she muttered, seeing one had slipped off in the fall.

He touched the ankle on her bare foot. "Does it hurt?"

"No."

He picked up the shoe. "Hold this."

The next thing she knew, he'd scooped her up in his arms and was carrying her into the front office. Leaning her head against his shoulder, she gazed up at his strong, determined and very worried profile.

"How do you feel?" he asked, setting her down carefully in her desk chair.

"Pretty good," she whispered, thinking how the soft gray of his eyes, the color so light, reminded her of moonlight.

He pulled back, dropped to one knee. "How's your foot?"

"Pretty good, too."

"No pain anywhere else?"

"My ego's bruised, but that's it."

His mouth worked into a grin, then he turned serious again. "I owe you an apology. Should've said thank you, and not opened my big mouth."

"I'm sorry I said kiss my ass."

"Am I really the first person you've ever said that to?"

She nodded.

SLEEPLESS IN LAS VEGAS

"I'm honored."

She leaned over and lightly popped the back of her hand on his chest. "Suck-up."

"Is it working?"

"Yes."

This felt good. The two of them being playful, teasing each other. No struggle, no tension, just easy-breezy. The perfect moment to tell him what she came here to say.

"I'm sorry about last night."

He took a deep breath, blew it out. "You spoke your mind. Nothing wrong with that."

"But I shouldn't have said—"

He waved it off. "No, Val. You were honest. I admire that, even if it drives me crazy at times." He held out his hand. "Give me your shoe. I'll put it on for you."

She handed it to him, and he gently lifted her bare foot with one big, warm hand and slid on the shoe with the other.

"Your dress survive that fall?" he asked, holding her foot with both hands.

The roughness of his voice, the heat of his touch and the fact she caught him darting a look at the inside of her exposed white thigh, which made an appearance thanks to the angle of her leg, made her stomach clench.

She glanced down at the filmy, flowery material. "Looks fine."

"Because if it got torn or something, I'd pay for a new one."

"It's not even my dress," she admitted, "but I thank you for the offer."

As they held each other's gaze, she felt a fluttering inside, imagining how it would be to face him like this, look into his eyes, day after day for the rest of her life. Sometimes their personalities clashed like the Hatfields and McCoys, then sometimes she realized how much they had in common. Their love of this profession. Their independent natures. Their loyalty to family. And as much as he tried to hide his, their passionate natures.

She wet her lips and swallowed. The thought of what she was about to say quickened her breath, damn near put her heart into overdrive. She wasn't sure exactly how to say it—although *I like you, Drake, as more than friends*—seemed pretty good. But sometimes it wasn't about finding the exact right words as having the guts to say what was on your heart.

"I—"

"Hear that?" He jerked his head toward his office. "It's the tracking alert I set. Marta's car is on the move again."

After setting her foot back on the floor, he jogged down the hallway. Hearsay followed, yapping. Val heard the connecting door open and click shut.

Lowering her hand, she stared at the space of air where he'd just been. She'd been ready to tell him she liked him. A lot. That she'd been an idiot last night to pull back, make that comment about the two of them being friends. Yes, they were that…but they were so much more.

But suddenly the words didn't fit how she really felt, which was so much deeper.

"I love you," she whispered.

She sat there for a moment, stunned and happy at the revelation. At the freedom, the *relief,* to have expressed the words. A laugh bubbled up from inside and she leaned back in her chair, looking up at the ceiling and grinning like a crazy person.

"I love you, Drake," she whispered again, seeing how the words felt in her mouth. Damn good. Tasted sweet, too.

Could she say it to him when he came back in? No, she might be a girl in love—just like Grams said—but she was also a girl who was learning to harness that impetuous streak.

Wouldn't Jayne be proud of her.

Her gaze slid to the grandfather clock. Nearly three o'clock.

She frowned.

On the very top of the clock sat a small black object with a hole in the center. No, not a hole. A lens.

A surveillance camera.

Hearing the scrabble of Hearsay's nails on the floor and the heavy steps of Drake, she turned to face him.

"She's back at the jewelry store," he said, carrying his smartphone. After she leaves, I'm going to place a pretext call to Mousseux, say I'm her fiancé or husband, ask if she's had a chance to pick up the ring yet. Doesn't mean they'll tell me, but it's worth a shot." He paused. "You started to say something when I left?"

She pointed at the top of the clock. "What's with the surveillance camera?"

He glanced at it, back to her. "Picked up an extra one the other day, figured it'd be handy for me to see the front office while I'm in the back. Plus it's a good security measure."

"Could've told me."

"Just put it up today, Val. We haven't exactly had time to discuss work."

"Is it recording now?"

"Yeah. Haven't set up a feed to my smartphone or computer yet, though."

Her stomach plummeted. He hadn't seen her saying she loved him, but a video of her performance existed on some storage device. "Erase that recording."

He bit back a laugh. "It's only been running for the past hour or so."

"*Please.* I don't want a video of me…being carried to my desk." *And saying* I love you. *Twice.*

"Women and their vanity." He eyed her for a moment. "Okay, I'll erase it."

She released a pent-up breath. "Thank you." She stood, picked up her purse that she'd left on the desk. "For the record, men can be vain, too."

"Duly noted."

It had been a strange day. Too many ups and downs,

but at least the playing field was level again. "I should be leaving—"

The office phone jangled. She glanced at the caller ID. Local number. She picked up the receiver. "Diamond Investigations."

"Miss LeRoy, it's Suzanne Doyle. The Riviera had a last-minute cancellation for the penthouse this Wednesday night, so I reserved it for your investigation. That is, if you and Mr. Morgan are still interested?"

AT TEN ON Monday morning, Hearsay trotted toward the back-entrance door to Drake's office and barked sharply.

"Hold on, buddy, be right there."

He glanced at the tracking app on his smartphone. Red dot hadn't moved in a few hours. Yesterday, he'd called Mousseux, but the girl who answered hadn't known how to check if Marta had picked up the ring yet, and suggested he call back later in the week.

After closing the app, he headed across the room, tucking his polo shirt, this one blue, into the waistband of his jeans. It had seemed a good idea after the fire to simplify things by buying a stack of polo shirts, but wearing the same thing every day was getting monotonous. Wouldn't Grams love to know that Drake was dying to branch out and buy a stack of casual button-down shirts next time.

He opened the door. Tony Cordova stood on the porch. He smiled, his teeth white in his brown face.

"Hi, Drake," he said in his signature rasp, "how you doin'?"

"Fine, Tony. Come on in."

The arson investigator wore a striped short-sleeve shirt, untucked, khaki pants and a pair of scuffed brown leather shoes. His slicked-back hair exposed a broad, lined forehead. At the scene of the fire, it had been difficult to tell his age. Seeing him today, Drake guessed late forties.

As Tony walked to the center of the room, one foot dragged slightly. Drake hadn't noticed the limp the other night, but they'd only talked for a few seconds. Plus his focus had been on Hearsay.

"Parked across the street and walked over," Tony said, pressing the back of his hand against his brow. "This heat's a killer. Nice and cool in here, though. Smells good, too."

"Egg and sausage sandwich."

"I envy you, my friend." Tony patted his stomach. "Ulcer won't let me eat my favorite foods anymore."

Hearsay trotted over to his bed, where he curled up and gnawed eagerly at the big pink ball. Drake had put away the chicken toy so he and Tony wouldn't be trying to talk over nonstop squeaking.

"Tyke's looking good." He scanned the room. "Both of you staying here?"

"No." Drake walked around the desk and sat down in the tufted chair, which creaked softly. Tony settled in one of the guest chairs Drake had brought in earlier from Jayne's office.

He wondered if Tony had parked his fire-department-issued vehicle across the street rather than in the lot outside so as to not draw possible attention to Drake's new office space. He appreciated the courtesy.

Tony glanced at the smartphone. "That your main piece of equipment?"

"Beats carrying a satchel with cameras, recorders, notebooks."

"I hear ya. One of our guys has some new, state-of-the-art wireless recording device the size of a half dollar—when planted on a person, picks up their words even if there's white noise. Me, I like using the digital recorder." He pulled one out of his shirt pocket. "But the old-fashioned way—taking notes—is the best security. Nobody can hack into your notepad and steal information."

"Sorry," Drake said, "but I don't want to be recorded."

A fellow investigator would especially understand that taped interviews weren't always in the best interest of the interviewee. If the person being recorded inadvertently provided an incorrect fact, or came off sounding arrogant, or even used bad grammar, a slick lawyer would be all over that like a fly on trash.

"Old-fashioned note taking?"

When Drake nodded his assent, Tony dropped the recorder back into one pocket, pulled a small notepad from another, then helped himself to a ballpoint pen lying on the desk.

Tony began asking basic questions. Drake's full

name, address, phone numbers. The location of fire alarms inside the home. His location at time of fire. Had he left the house locked, did anyone else have keys, were there any suspicious vehicles or activities recently in the neighborhood?

Drake gave honest, short answers.

Fifteen minutes in, Tony sat back in his chair, his dark brown eyes studying Drake's face. "You're a tough investigator who's made some enemies."

"Everybody has enemies."

"Not like you, my friend." Tony slipped his notepad into one of his shirt pockets, placed the pen back on the desk. "We're off the record."

"There's nothing in the law that puts a fence around off the record."

"True. The only thing that's gonna make our conversation private is the trust we have in each other."

Drake didn't trust most people he met. Even fewer people did he feel he could count on. To trust someone was like hoping for something—vague attributes people bandied about, as though by saying *I trust you* made it so.

Yet a part of him envied Tony that he could talk about trust as though it was a fact.

"Tell me about Yuri," Tony said.

"My brother's work associate, but you already know that."

Tony had undoubtedly run a background check on Drake, a standard investigative procedure, in which he'd learned he had a brother who worked at Topaz.

Tony might have dropped by the club later that night, or called, hoping to interview Braxton. He would have identified himself as an investigator—savvy enough not to say *arson* investigator. If Brax had answered the phone, he wouldn't have said much more than confirming he was Drake's brother. An employee, however, could have let it slip that recently Drake had been in the club, asking about Yuri.

"Hey, got the DNA results on the blood and piece of skin," Tony said, shifting the topic away from Yuri. "Both samples match a very specific population of Caucasian males from Eastern Europe."

They sat in silence for a while...a situation they had both been in many times, waiting for a witness or suspect to open up and talk. The interview might be tense, even confrontational, but as investigators, they would remain cool, watchful, patient as they waited to hear that one piece of information that could crack a case.

The air-conditioning hummed, Hearsay chewed and pawed at his new toy, and Tony and Drake sat across from each other, not saying a word.

Tony leaned forward, searching Drake's face. "You don't have to do this alone. I can help you."

"Let's call it a day. I'll walk you to the door." He felt lousy ignoring the offer, but he didn't know if he was ready to trust Tony. Too much was at stake.

As they crossed the floor, Tony said, "You and me, my friend, we're like foot soldiers in the war for truth, our best weapons being here." He pointed at his head.

"And here." He indicated his heart. "We win our battles only when people surrender their most cherished commodity. Their secrets."

As Drake opened the door, he decided to take a risk. It might be a mistake, but it could also be a win.

"Hold on." He reached into his pants pocket and pulled out two plastic baggies. "They're both sealed. Yuri Glazkov smokes this brand. I wrote where they were found, and the date, on the outside. As you can read, one was found in an empty lot, a fifteen-minute walk to my house. My bet is the DNA on both matches what was found on the gate."

Tony slid the baggies into his shirt pocket. "Thank you, my friend."

"I…want something from Yuri. It belongs to my family."

"I see." He thought for a moment. "I can delay executing the arrest warrant until you've had a chance to chat with him."

After Drake closed the door, he went to the window and peered through the blinds. Tony ambled across Garces Avenue, his limp barely noticeable at this distance. Many arson investigators were former firefighters. He wondered if Tony, after being disabled in the line of duty, had segued his career into arson investigations. And to think he'd called Drake tough.

When Tony reached the other side of the street, he waved once over his shoulder, but not turning back to look, as he headed toward a small business's parking area.

Drake got the message. Tony had just let him know he knew he was being watched, in fact, didn't expect less.

It meant something else, too. They trusted each other.

WEDNESDAY MORNING, VAL showed up at Diamond Investigations at nine. As she and Drake had discussed after the Riviera manager's call, she would take off this afternoon and get some rest, as she and Drake were, as he kept reminding her, *gathering evidence*— not ghost hunting—in the Riviera penthouse tonight.

Today she wore one of her more sedate little black dresses with a pair of black pumps. She kept her hair simple, too. Yesterday Drake had finally set up the feed from the office surveillance camera to his smartphone. Now that her every move was being broadcast back to him in his man cave, she wanted to look her professional best.

As she sprinkled food into the aquarium, the yellow-blue fish glided into his castle. And to her surprise, back out again.

"Glory be, the prince is mingling with the common folk."

Sitting down at her desk, she wondered if Drake was already in his office, watching her. Looking at the camera, she gave a small salute. "Mornin', mentor."

After checking email, she called the car repair shop and confirmed her Toyota was ready for pickup. After ending the call, she looked at the camera.

"I'm going to pick up my car now. The rental car agency will give me a ride to the repair shop."

This felt weird. Like those ghost hunters on that reality show who'd walk around a dark house, asking questions to the spirits, waiting for answers that never came back. Maybe this one-way communication was good practice for tonight, she mused.

"While I'm gone," she said, looking at the surveillance camera, "do you want to sit in Jayne's office? That way, if there are any walk-ins, you can help them. I'd knock on your door and ask you in person, but…"

Her cell phone emitted a soft ping, notifying her she'd just received a text message. She picked it up and read his single-word response.

Fine.

Looking at the camera, she smiled. "Got your text. Thanks."

This didn't just feel weird, it felt out of balance. He got to be the great and all-powerful Oz behind the curtain, or in this case the cam, and she was Dorothy trying to chat him up.

She stood, picked up her purse. "Heading out now to get my car."

Walking to the door, she waited until out of camera range and gave her eyes a big ol' roll. Maybe she'd move that camera so it pointed somewhere else—like the fish tank.

Gripping the doorknob, she paused. *Wait a minute.*

Just as she finally figured out the other night that she had been the one standing in the way of her happiness, she was also the only one who had the authority to take away her power. Unless she broke the law and got caught, of course, but she'd promised Jayne and Drake she'd not do that again.

Strolling back to her desk, she perched herself on the edge of it, facing the camera, although she acted as if it wasn't there. Taking her lipstick out of her purse—the kickass red color called Devil—she took off the top and twisted the base. She'd put on lipstick almost every day of her life since turning fifteen, so she could do this flying solo, no mirror.

Looking directly at the camera, she applied it… slowly, methodically, not missing a single sweet spot on her lips. Then smoothed it on a second time, emitting a few breathy noises. The kind that went with a lipstick named Devil.

With a smile, she tossed the lipstick back into her purse, slid off the desk and strolled to the door.

Take that, Oz.

ON THE DRIVE back to Diamond Investigations in her newly repaired Toyota, Val's phone started playing "When the Saints Go Marching In."

Keeping the phone on her thigh, she pressed the answer button. "Hello?"

"It's Drake."

She smiled to herself. Had she encouraged him to come out from behind the curtain?

"Hi, Drake," she said sweetly.

"Burner phone's out of power," he said, going straight to the point. "No more tracking. But the good news is, did another call to the jewelry store this morning and learned Marta picked up the ring. The employee isn't real happy with her. Seems she argued with him over a gold bracelet she wanted to buy, caused a scene in the store. I'm beginning to think she's Yuri's girlfriend. He likes those in-your-face types." He paused. "Gotta find him before he fences that ring. Or before he and Marta have a blowup and she returns to Russia wearing it. Wish I could figure out where he hangs."

"Maybe visit Topaz again and ask around?"

"Not a good idea. The arson investigator has made his presence known to them."

"What about revisiting some of those addresses Marta stopped at?"

"Exactly. Called to let you know I'll be doing that this afternoon. Just dropped Hearsay off with Li'l Bit, who'll take care of him tonight. You and I can catch up at the Riviera. Weather report says possible storms later today, so be careful."

In the distance, she saw a billowing cloud, but otherwise the skies were blue, the sun bright.

"Besides my smartphone," she said, "I'm bringing notepads, pens, and I read that ghosts can drain equipment energy, so it's a good idea to also bring candles and matches."

"Val."

"Not saying I believe in ghosts," she added quickly, "but I do think we should bring items that ghost hunters would bring. Call it catering to our client's belief system." When he didn't say anything, she continued, "Do you have a compass? They're supposed to be good for picking up electromagnetic forces out of the ordinary."

"Yes," he said grudgingly, "I have had a compass since I was a Boy Scout."

Drake, a former Boy Scout? Made total sense. They were big on honor and duty, which struck at the core of Drake's character.

"What time do I show?" she asked.

"Six. All expenses are paid, so we can order room service."

"Since you're going to be gone this afternoon, I'll go back to the office. Jayne wouldn't want the office closed during the weekdays."

"No. Go home, rest. Even she would tell you to do that."

The thought of her boss brought an ache to her chest.

"Let's compromise," she said quietly. "I'll leave early."

"I understand. One more thing. I, uh…found out some information about your mother."

She'd been having a nice day up until now. "And?"

"It appears she lived in New Orleans until 1999."

Val felt a wave of disgust. "Which means she and

I were in the same town the first ten years of my life, and she never visited me *once*."

"I'm sorry."

She drove in silence for a moment, her insides writhing.

"Val," Drake said gently, "maybe there are reasons why she didn't want you seeing *her*. Have you ever thought about that? She might have been sick…or had other issues…"

If she wasn't driving this car, she would yell and scream her frustration to the heavens about this stupid, meaningless task. Nanny must have been wrought with guilt that her own daughter had abandoned her child, Val, to run away with some man or whatever, so she'd asked Val to find her. This was really about giving her grandmother, bless her soul, peace of mind.

If she could bring Nanny back for even a minute, she'd move heaven and earth to do so. She loved her so much, she'd keep her promise. But the truth was, Val LeRoy didn't give a damn about the answer.

"For dinner," she said, "let's order us some big ol' fancy steaks tonight and fat baked potatoes loaded with sour cream and butter—"

"Val…"

"Let's get something straight," she said tightly. "Just because a woman gave birth to me doesn't mean she's my mother. See you at six."

TWO HOURS LATER, Val sat at her desk, finishing a list of items to bring for the ghost hunting. When the office phone jangled, she jumped a little. Checking the caller ID, she recognized Marta's cell phone number.

"Diamond Investigations," she answered, steeling herself.

"Val, it's Marta. Being twelve-thirty, afraid you might be out to lunch. My fiancé, he be seen at strip club."

"Topaz?" She frowned. Drake had made a point of saying he wasn't going back there.

"No. Different club. Body Double. On Western Avenue."

She'd driven past that place numerous times. Outside was a big sign advertising "neon-illuminated strippers," which had always sounded more frightening than alluring.

"Who saw him there?"

"Friend."

Yuri, she guessed. Had he seen Drake snooping around that address? If so, why have Marta call Val?

"Since you know where he is," Val said, "go and talk to him. You don't need my services anymore."

"He see me, he get mad."

"Then have your friend talk to him."

"Val, please, you know how bad this is for me. You go watch. Call me like before, tell me what he do."

It crossed Val's mind that maybe this was a real request. Yuri had gotten word Drake was at a certain location, and he wanted him watched. Maybe he didn't ask one of his thug buddies to do it because he was afraid Drake might recognize him. Of course, Drake would recognize her, too, but she'd give him a heads-up in a text message.

Goose bumps skittered over her skin as a horrible thought hit her. *What if Drake's in trouble?* Or maybe she was being asked to monitor him as they pulled another monstrous stunt.

She hadn't heard from him since they spoke a few hours ago. Now she was worried.

"What did your friend say Drake was doing there?" she asked, picking up her cell phone.

As Marta babbled something about Drake drinking vodka and tipping strippers, Val sent a text message to Drake.

Text me. Urgent.

She asked a few more questions, keeping Marta on the phone as she waited for a text message back from Drake. None came.

The Body Double was a public place. It was lunchtime. Not like anything could happen to Val by going inside, looking around. If she sensed Drake was in trouble, she could dial nine-one-one on her cell.

She couldn't leave his well-being to chance, the way she had left her nanny.

"I'll be there in twenty minutes."

SHE MADE IT to Body Double in seventeen. Towering gray clouds rose in the distance. On the way over, she'd read the LED display on a local bank: "Monsoon Alert Later Today. Stay High and Stay Dry."

Because Body Double was a "higher-class" strip club, there was valet parking only. So first she drove down Western Avenue and scanned the parking lot that was visible from the street. Didn't see Drake's pickup.

A few minutes later, she pulled her Toyota into the valet parking, grabbed her receipt and headed into the club.

As she approached the doorman, she paused and opened her purse to retrieve her wallet. He shook his head. "Baby, it's always ladies' night at Body Double, even when the sun's out. Put your wallet away, no cover." He handed her a free drink coupon. "Drink up, make new friends."

Like that's what she wanted to do. As he grabbed the brass handle on the carved oak door, she put away her wallet and headed into the gloom.

The air-conditioning smacked her in the face as she stepped inside—like walking into a meat locker. An irony that didn't escape her. She paused, letting her eyes adjust to the darkness. The air reeked of cigarette smoke and cheap cologne. Electronic music pulsed in the air.

She'd passed plenty of strip clubs in the French Quarter, had even been inside a few with pals on a lark, but a Las Vegas strip club was a whole different beast. Powered by more money, driven by more greed, selling broken promises as if they were silver linings.

Walking past displays of sex toys and Body Double T-shirts, Val checked out the stages at the back of the room, where women wriggled and danced around poles under colored lights. On one stage, flashing neon lights splashed red, blue and yellow on a stripper's body.

Ringing the stages were chairs filled with men, and some women, waving bills at the dancers. Behind the chairs were dozens of small, round tables, at least half filled with customers, some getting lap dances.

She scanned the dimly lit room, looking for Drake. Like this was going to be easy. Except for the faces flanking the brightly lit stages, people resembled lumpy shadows. She'd have to get closer.

She walked past a long bar on her left where scantily clad cocktail waitresses lined up with their drink trays. A few customers sat at the bar, hunched over their drinks. No Drake. Moseying around the cocktail tables, she acted as though she was looking for someone.

"Hey, baby," murmured a husky male voice, "I got a bottle of Beaujolais breathing here for you."

I bet you do.

After touring the tables, and receiving several more enticing invitations—*not*—she angled back to the bar just as a door behind it opened, spilling light.

There stood Drake, dressed in a tailored suit, talking to a short, round-faced man with a Nero haircut whom she recognized after seeing his picture on the internet.

Yuri.

Panic seized her. She reached into her purse and snatched her phone, ready to dial nine-one-one.

Yuri slapped Drake on the back as they laughed about something.

Her panic dissolved into confusion. What was Drake doing, acting buddy-buddy with this slime-ball? After another laugh, Yuri walked back into the office and shut the door.

She crossed to Drake, who leaned against the bar, chatting with a bartender.

"Drake, what's going on?" she whispered, "Why didn't you answer my text? I've been worried sick about you. Marta called, told me to come here and watch you—"

His powerful arms tugged her close, and he pressed her body full-length against his.

"Kiss me," he growled, gripping the back of her neck as he lowered his lips to hers.

If she had a moment of lucidity, it shattered when his mouth met hers, the world spinning away, leaving the two of them in their own private world of heat and need.

Kissing him was everything she had imagined and more. He tasted like coffee and something sweetly decadent. His scent—a musky cologne she'd never smelled on him before—shot straight to her brain. As his tongue prodded her mouth, she opened wider for him, taking him in, tangling her tongue with his, wanting more, more…

When he pulled back his head, it was all she could do to lean against him and gaze up into his slitted eyes, glistening in the muted light. He held her in place, his fingers sinking into the flesh of her arms, his chest heaving breaths. Like a beast interrupted from his feasting.

With some effort, she rocked back onto her feet and steadied herself. The sounds of the room returned— the clinking of glasses, buzz of conversations, throbbing beat of music. Patting her hair, she darted a look around. She had never behaved this way in public. At least it was dark at this corner of the bar. The bartender had moved to the far end, making drinks. Nobody sat nearby. And who would care about two people kissing anyway, when women in G-strings were undulating around poles and performing scissor kicks?

"Tell me, Val," he murmured huskily, "do I kiss better than my brother?"

She blinked. "Pardon?"

"I'm Braxton."

It took a moment for the shock to hit.

Drake and Braxton were *identical* twins.

The realization left her numb all over, as though she'd been packed in ice cubes. No wonder he wore a different style of clothes, a different cologne, although it would have been damn helpful if they didn't both wear buzz cuts.

Hot indignation started to thaw the numbness. Would it have been so difficult for Drake to say something, give her a freaking clue that he and his brother were mirror images? Of course, because of the cold war going on at his mother's home, there hadn't been any discussion of Braxton...or photos of the two brothers together. Still, it would have been nice to have been given a heads-up that a carbon copy of him was running around Vegas.

When he chuckled under his breath, giving her a sly, gotcha look, her response was immediate and instinctual.

She slapped him.

As he reared back, his hand on his cheek, she turned to leave.

He grabbed her arm. "Not so fast, Val," he snarled. "Somebody wants to talk to you."

A FEW MINUTES later, she entered a back office, situated behind another office whose door opened into the bar. The room was chilly and smelled like aftershave and cigarettes. Mostly cigarettes.

Unlike the flashy interior of the adjacent strip club, the room was cheap, drab. A folding table sat in the middle of the room with a few unmatched folding chairs clustered around it. In the corner was a dented metal filing cabinet. The dingy yellow walls were marred with dirt marks, their only adornment a taped-up posted of a blonde, silicon-enhanced stripper, signed, *To Yuri, You're the best, Cindy Sparxx.*

The floor safe was the only expensive item in the room. Large, black, with a shiny spin dial and locking wheel. The top surface served as an informal bar with several bottles of Russian vodka and red plastic tumblers.

Yuri and another man, who was counting stacks of bills, sat at the table, a tumbler in front of each of them. A yellowish cigarette burned in an ashtray filled with ash and butts.

Yuri wore a silk shirt, the top button undone. Strands of gold chains hung around his neck. The other man wore a dark blue gym suit, a chunky gold bracelet and a butterfly bandage across the bridge of his nose. In the center of the table was a white device, the size of a paperback novel, with buttons and a speaker.

Yuri looked up and smiled, one of those smiles that had teeth but no warmth.

"Hello, Val, nice to meet you." He extended his hand across the table.

She noticed a jagged cut on the back of his hand. From a nail on Drake's back gate? Her throat was so tight she couldn't speak, so she said nothing and shook his hand, trying not to cringe at the touch of his weak, moist fingers.

"Sit." He gestured to a folding chair across from him. Braxton took the chair next to her. "This my friend Vadim," he said, gesturing to the man next to him.

Vadim shot her a dark look, went back to counting money.

She sat absolutely still, trying to feign calm, but her

insides had constricted to the size of a pea. On the negative side, she was sitting in a back room with the Russian Mafia, who knew she'd lied and conspired against them. On the positive side, the door had been left open, with men and women milling about in the next room, apparently employees, and she still had possession of her purse and phone. And her life.

Yuri gave a lazy wave at her hair. "Blue spots."

Purple highlights, actually, but only a woman with a serious death wish would correct him. "Yes."

He looked at Braxton's head. "And you, today with stubble."

"Told you it was a good idea to cut my hair short like Drake's," Braxton said. "She thought I was my brother, asked why I hadn't returned her messages. Just as we thought, our little P.I. is tight with him."

Our little P.I. What an asshole.

"You try to get tight, too, Brax?" Yuri asked, patting his own cheek. Pointing at Braxton's face, he said something in Russian to the bald man, and the two of them laughed.

She glanced at Braxton's profile. The imprint of her hand could still be seen on his reddened cheek.

"Val, you seem like smart girl," Yuri said, zeroing in on her with his beady dark eyes. The kind you looked into, but nothing looked back. "But…how you say…green as snoop."

"Inexperienced," Braxton offered.

"Yes," Yuri said, nodding vigorously, "inexperienced. Which very good for me. You do honey trap.

And you visit me today." He tapped his stubby fingers on the tabletop. "I have very excellent offer for you. But before discussion, you want something to say?"

She was so scared, the back of her legs were sweating. For the girl who used to not think twice about charging into the mist, she wanted nothing more than to stand at these crossroads, center herself and not do anything foolish. If there was ever a time to stop and smell the reality, this was it.

She eased in a slow breath, ready to say what any rational woman would under these circumstances.

"I'd like a shot of vodka."

CHAPTER FIFTEEN

AFTER A THIRD shot, and repeating an enthusiastic *"Kährs!"* which Val hoped meant "cheers!" in Russian, and not "to your short life," it was fast becoming like old home week in the Russian mafia back office.

Yuri told stories about living in Russia, how his gold jewelry was worth "Zouzands of Ue-Es dolarz" and how Americans ruined chicken Kiev. "It too dry," he bellowed, gesturing broadly with a cigarette in his hand. "Butter must splatter shirt when you stick in knife!"

She smiled and nodded, thinking it sounded more like a crime scene than a dish.

All the while the other Russian, his bald head shiny under the fluorescent lights, never stopped counting money, occasionally pausing to jot down a number. Braxton sat quietly next to her, passed on the vodka, suggesting American words when Yuri got stumped. In the next room, a staticky radio played "Waking Up in Vegas" by Katy Perry.

Yuri sloshed more vodka into his tumbler, then pressed a button on the white device, which emitted a sound like rushing air.

How handy, a white-noise machine. Its frequencies masked sounds in its vicinity, so apparently Yuri turned it on when he didn't want people outside the office listening in on his conversations.

"Now, my Val, we get serious." He lit another cigarette.

A jolt of horror surged through her. She clutched her trembling hands together in her lap, out of Yuri's sight. Katy Perry wailed about putting your money where your mouth is.

"Where is Drake?" he asked, blowing out a stream of smoke.

She could lie, but what if he already knew the answer and this was a trick question? Then she remembered Drake's comment. *He likes those in-your-face types.*

She gave him her best tough-girl look. "What's it worth to you?"

After an uncomfortable stare-down, during which Val decided she was on her way to being the next splattering chicken Kiev, he thumped his hand hard on the table, threw back his head and let go with a guffaw.

Braxton quietly sat next to her, fussing with a gold cuff link. The money counter kept flipping bills and taking notes. Katy Perry was almost finished waking up in Vegas.

Yuri, his face flushed, gave her an approving look. "I like your style."

"Thank you."

"Why spend months, years being snoop intern with

bad pay, bad hours?" He gave a dramatic shrug, as though it was incomprehensible that anyone could be so dumb as to pursue such a dead-end career. "When instead, you work for me and I pay…" He held up three fingers. "*Three* times your salary."

"But Yuri, it is advantageous for me to remain a private eye because I have access to databases and court records, which you don't."

Picking up the vodka bottle, he looked at Braxton. "Advan…"

"Advantageous. Helpful."

"And instead of a salary," she continued, "I'd like Drake's family ring and first choice on other loot you gather from tourists vacationing in Las Vegas."

His eyes narrowing, he set down the bottle hard. "How you know about ring?"

"Jayne Diamond, my boss, told me," she lied. "She and Drake have been friends for years."

Yuri took a sip, swallowed, a thoughtful look on his face. "Yes, Jayne Diamond. Big casinos use her as gatekeeper for granting big-dollar credit lines." He stubbed out his cigarette. "My first job for you. Give me some of her big-money clients' information."

Jayne sometimes conducted exhaustive asset checks on high rollers for casino credit departments, in the course of which she accrued wealthy people's confidential data—Social Security numbers, bank account information, stock and real-estate holdings. Confidential financial information that a criminal could use to electronically steal their wealth. Looked like Yuri was keen to commit some white-collar electronic fraud.

Exactly the kind of dirt Drake wanted on the Russian.

If only if there was a way to surreptitiously turn on the recorder app on her phone. She listened to the continuous sound of rushing air from the device that Yuri had turned on. Wouldn't matter if she tried to record their conversation, the white noise would block out their voices.

If she wanted to help Drake, she had only one option.

"Yes," she said, trying to sound delighted with the prospect, "I would love to work for you, Yuri."

AFTER THE MEETING, she headed to the valet and waited for her car. She'd quaffed two shots of vodka with Yuri but had faked indulging in the third, so she had a light buzz, nothing more.

The temperatures were cooling and the air thickening with humidity thanks to the incoming storm clouds. While waiting for the valet to deliver her car, she texted and called Drake. No response.

If Yuri was inside Body Double, Drake had to be safe. That's all that mattered. Probably busy checking out places Marta had visited. If he was interviewing someone, he couldn't stop to answer her call.

But she'd feel so much better hearing his voice.

Cranking up the air-conditioning, she drove through Theo's Burgers, got a diet cola and chili-cheese fries. Driving home, she tried calling Drake again. No answer.

Okay, now she was concerned. The guy lived and died by his smartphone, so he should have called or texted her back by now. Something was wrong. She needed to find him.

Turning around, she headed back to Diamond Investigations.

There, she drove around the back lot, checked if his pickup was in the fenced-off parking space. It wasn't. She parked in the front lot, went inside and headed to the connecting door and knocked. Knocked again. Even though his pickup wasn't here, didn't hurt to check if he was inside his office. She retrieved the spare back office key from her desk and checked out his man cave. No Drake.

Before leaving Diamond Investigations, she called Dorothy Morgan. Not wanting to alarm her, she said Drake had asked Val to call and check how the new surveillance cameras were working. Fine? Good. Had he already called to ask? Val's spirits plunged when Dorothy said she'd last talked to him yesterday evening.

There was only one more place she knew to check: Li'l Bit's. Even if Drake wasn't there, she could ask his friend if he'd heard from him lately.

She didn't know Li'l Bit's real name, so she ran an online search on the nickname, found a comment Li'l Bit had left at a Marijuana for the People website that included his email address, nathan@boss_services.

She ran that through a property database and learned Li'l Bit, aka Nathan Davidovitch, lived in apartment 3B at the Willow Creek Apartments.

As she walked across the lot to her Toyota, the clouds began spitting rain.

At FOUR-THIRTY, she knocked on the door marked 3B. Fat gray clouds now hovered over the city, obliterating the sun. The air had cooled to an almost comfortable temperature, which in Vegas meant it was no longer three-digit heat. After her adrenaline-pumping meeting with Yuri and the hyperanxiety of looking for Drake, her energy had taken a sharp spiral downward. Maybe she should've skipped the chili-cheese fries.

She heard Hearsay bark on the other side of the door.

"Who is it?" asked a sleepy-sounding male voice.

"I'm looking for Drake."

Hearsay barked again. "Don't know a Drake, man."

She reread the number on the door—3B. Definitely the right place. "Are you Li'l Bit?"

"No."

She thought back to the email address. "Nathan Davidovitch? Of Boss Services?"

"You need a process server?"

Oh, for heaven's sake. This was Li'l, or Nathan, who owned Boss Services. That was Hearsay barking behind the door. Why was he lying about not knowing Drake? Took her all of a second to understand the reason. Being a good friend to Drake, Li'l Bit was protecting him from Yuri's Mafia types.

"Nathan, I'm Drake's friend. We work together. I need to find him. I'm worried. He could be in danger. Please, open up."

Another pause. "What's his nickname?"

She frowned. "He never told me his nickname. But I know his mother's name is Dorothy, and his grandmother's is…" Shit, she forgot. "Well, she's Grams. And his dog's name is Hearsay."

Who woofed. Followed by a "Dude, chill." Then, "You know Yuri?"

"Yes! Not that I want to know him, but unfortunately I do."

Silence. "Drake doesn't live here, man."

She glared at the door. Her adrenaline slump was on the rebound, spiking high and fast.

She was beginning to wonder if Drake was inside and in trouble. Maybe Hearsay's barks were alerting her that something was wrong.

"If you don't open up *right now*…" She looked around, spied the potted plant. "I'm going to pick up this plant in its heavy-lookin' clay pot and throw it through your damn window."

"Lady, you and your negative energy need to leave, man."

One more *man* and she'd lose it. Hell, why wait. She was ready to lose it now. In fact, she *deserved* to lose it. As her beloved Saints said, and if they hadn't, they should've, *Go big or go home.*

"No, me and my *negative energy* have had one hell of an extremely *trying* day, and we've decided nobody, and I do mean *nobody,* is gonna stand in our way, so I suggest you step back from your window 'cause, *man,* the glass is gonna fly!"

As she bent over to lift the clay pot, which in fact was extraordinarily heavy, too heavy to back up her glass-flying speech, she heard a click and the slithery slide of a lock.

The door opened, and a paunchy guy wearing a pair of cutoff jeans and a T-shirt with the word Abide in big red letters about the color of his eyes, stared at her. He reeked of buttered popcorn and beer.

Hearsay scampered onto the porch, his tail wagging. She reached down, petted his head, then pushed past Li'l Bit into the living room. On the TV, a young David Bowie with bright orange hair was walking through some kind of space-age desert.

Li'l Bit followed her, dragging his hand through a mass of tangled hair. "This is a private residence, man."

She heard a loud clunk, followed by an expletive, from down the hallway. A not-so-subtle panic crossed Li'l Bit's face.

"What's back there?" She glanced down at Hearsay, who looked overly alert, as though saying, "You need to check it out, *now.*" Or maybe she was projecting her thoughts onto the dog, but it was a good idea anyway.

Drake was missing, nobody seemed to know where he was, he obviously lived in this very apartment and

Li'l Bit was one odd, zoned-out strangeoid who was definitely hiding something.

No guts, no glory.

She speed walked toward the hall. Hearsay yapped, scampering along with her.

"Dude," he yelled, "I'm going to call the police!"

She broke into a jog, catching scents of incense and marijuana. Passing the bathroom, she glanced inside. A bag of weed in the sink, towels all over the floor, tapestry-print shower curtain. She headed for the closed door at the end of the hall.

Li'l Bit, heaving breaths, passed her, blocking the door with his body. "Look, man…" He waved his hands in the air as though dispersing her angry aura. "You need to go away now."

"Is Drake in there?"

"Not really. The cops…they'll arrest you on…first-degree trespass."

Not really? What, just some of his body parts were in there? Although her heart was doing its best to rip free from her chest, and her brain was preparing to burn graphic images into her cortex that would haunt her the rest of her life, there was no way she wasn't going in.

"If you don't open that door," she snarled, "they're also going to arrest me for attempted homicide."

Mumbling something about Mercury in retrograde, he opened the door and quickly stepped out of her way.

But she didn't enter. Instead, she looked inside the room, frozen at the sight.

Drake, reading a magazine, lounged on a bed covered in a fluffy, purple-paisley bedspread. He wore earbuds whose wire connected to the smartphone he held, his head bobbing to whatever he was listening to. The room was a hodgepodge of tie-dye, books, an orange vinyl bean bag chair, a poster of a clipper ship titled "Where's Our Wooden Ships?" and macramé curtains threaded with feathers and beads. Except for the bed, it looked like the inside of a hippie van following a Grateful Dead tour.

Hearsay plopped down on the floor at the foot of the bed, and chewed on a rawhide bone lying there.

As she stepped into the room, Drake looked up, a surprised look on his face. Setting aside the magazine, he pulled out the earbuds and flashed a lazy, sexy smile, his eyes grazing her body. He wore a polo shirt and jeans she'd seen him wear before, but his hair was longer and stylishly textured.

She stopped at the foot of the bed, stupefied. "What happened to your hair?"

One side of his mouth lifted in a cocky grin. "What's wrong, doll, did I put on too much gel?"

He sounded like Drake, but the smarmy come-on wasn't him. Plus, Drake had never called her *doll*. And she seriously doubted Drake had ever touched a bottle of gel, much less used it.

Li'l Bit wandered into the room, clutching the bowl of popcorn to his chest. "Dude, I wasn't sure if she was Marta or not. That accent, hard to tell. And she didn't know Aqua Man's nickname. Tried to get her to leave, man, but she threatened to break my window and kill me." He shoved a handful of popcorn into his mouth.

"S'okay, Li'l Bit," he said, "she's not one of Yuri's people."

Val walked closer, checked out the magazine. *Men's World.* The articles on its cover sounded like *Cosmo* for guys: "How to Dress Like Tom Cruise," "Summer Muscle Foods," "Double Your Endurance."

She shifted her gaze to his face. Same gray eyes, arrogant nose, but totally different hair and no tiny white scar on his hairline. She caught a whiff of his musky cologne. A scent she'd smelled today…on somebody pretending to be him.

"You're Braxton," she murmured.

For a moment, she felt no emotion, no nothing, just numb, as though somebody had shot her with a tranquilizer gun. Except she wasn't going to fall over, unconscious any moment. Instead, she was stuck in this alternate universe, trying to make sense of it.

"We needed to swap him out with Drake," Li'l Bit said around a mouthful of popcorn, "so he could psych out that nihilistic dipshit Yuri, man, who torched his place…"

Letting Li'l Bit's voice roll over her, she stared at Braxton. Her insides twisted. So that had been Drake back at Body Double. He couldn't have given her a hint it was him? Maybe not while sitting at the table with Yuri staring her down, but before? Like outside at the bar when he'd kissed her?

"…wanted to help Drake out, man," Li'l Bit continued, holding on to the bowl as if it was a life preserver, "because he's been good to me, once got me out of an unfortunate incident involving some unpaid parking tickets and a shipment of guns…"

A spark of anger flickered to life inside her. She deserved better than to be the last to know. Maybe she was an intern, and had mishandled a few situations lately, but hadn't Drake said the two of them were a team? Yet he'd entrusted his confidences and welfare to a lounging rake and a popcorn-eating weed dude, leaving her completely out of the loop.

She was insulted.

"What's your name, doll?" Braxton asked.

"For starters," she said tightly, "it's not *doll.*"

"Feisty," he murmured, "I like that. Also like that strict little librarian dress you're wearing. Have I been bad and forgotten to pay my late-book fines?"

"Her name is Val," said a familiar voice. "She's a top-notch P.I. in the making, and if you say one more disrespectful thing to her, Brax, my fist is going to be visiting your face."

Drake stood in the doorway, still wearing the blue suit he'd worn at Body Double. Hearsay bounded over to him, sniffing the suit, licking his hand, wagging his tail.

Braxton held up his hands in surrender. "Sorry, bro."

"Here's something else you should know," Drake said, his black eyebrows snapping together as he drilled a look at his brother. "She put herself on the line today for our family, did some gutsy brokering, better than I've seen some professional negotiators carry off, with Yuri for the possible return of our family's heirloom ring."

Val stared at Drake, her anger taking a backseat to her ego, which wallowed in his glowing appraisal like a pig in mud. Top-notch P.I. Better than some professional negotiators. Almost made up for not being included in today's twin-swap shenanigans.

He turned his head, those gray eyes gleaming as they met hers. "I cannot believe what you did today. Jayne said you had been heroic…and today I witnessed it firsthand."

"I wasn't…" She gave her head a small shake. Maybe survivors never felt like heroes, and one day she'd finally accept that. As for today, she hadn't felt courageous at the time. But in retrospect, hell, yeah.

For the next few moments, it was all Drake could do to stare at her, marvel at her. Admiration ballooned in his chest. Her face was drained of color, mascara had smudged below one eye and her purple-black hair had taken on a wild, free-to-be-me look.

And she looked more beautiful than ever to him.

She crossed her arms and gave him a look. "Would've been nice, don't you think, if you'd told me you and Braxton are identical twins?"

He glanced over at Brax, who was suddenly engrossed in some magazine article. Li'l Bit sat on the edge of the bed, eating popcorn and watching them as though they were characters in a movie.

He looked back at Val and the emotions crowding her face. A little displeasure. Some lingering irritation. But from that sly, three-cornered smile on her face, he could tell she was secretly pleased he'd lauded her with those compliments. She knew him well enough to know he didn't give praise lightly.

He knew her well, too. Funny to think he'd been engaged a year to Liz and could never read her the way he could read Val after a few days.

"I told you about my brother on our way to Mom's for dinner," he said gently, "but we started talking about something else and…it never came up again, that's all. I wasn't trying to hide anything from you."

"I called and texted you today," she said. "Multiple times."

"Couldn't carry my own phone. I had Braxton's on me. And he still has mine."

She looked at his brother, who raised his hands in an I'm-innocent gesture. "Hey, I don't read his messages or take his calls."

"Why the swap?" she asked, turning back to Drake.

"It's a complicated story."

"One I'll never know because the subject doesn't come up again?"

He deserved that one. "Tonight, during our investigation, I'll explain everything. Promise."

Whatever lingering smile she'd had on her face

dissolved. "Being isolated like that…left me vulnerable to Yuri…"

He moved forward and wrapped her in his arms. "Val," he murmured, "I didn't know he had lured you to the club until I was already there. I want you to know—*need* you to know—that if he'd made one wrong move…" His voice dropped to a harsh whisper. "I would have killed the bastard with my bare hands."

Outside, thunder rumbled. Gusts of wind rattled the window. Fat drops of rain splattered against the glass. Li'l Bit was at the window, eating popcorn, watching the show. Hearsay looked at the window, his ears perked, then went back to gnawing the bone. Braxton had his earbuds back in, his head bobbing while he read *Men's World*.

"Sorry I slapped you," she whispered.

"I'll live."

She pressed her face closer. "Why'd you kiss me?"

He smiled. "Guess I have an impetuous streak."

AN HOUR LATER, a rain-drenched Drake and Val opened the door with a brass plaque engraved with "The Frank Sinatra Suite."

"Why, it's Ol' Blue Eyes himself," Val said, shivering as she stopped at a large framed portrait of Frank Sinatra in the entryway. "And look at the candelabras and textured wallpaper!"

Drake, carrying a duffel bag, headed down the hallway. He frowned as he passed a marble statue of a cherub, thinking it didn't fit a suite named after tough-guy Frank.

He flipped a switch in the bathroom the size of his old bedroom, and looked around. Matching sinks in a black marble counter. Gold-plated fixtures. Mood lighting.

Val walked in and gasped. "Is that a Jacuzzi tub or a swimming pool? And look at all those mirrors behind it!"

Her hair hung in wet clumps, her face and arms were slick with rain, yet she carried her purse, its handle delicately draped over her arm, as though ready to attend a society event.

"You need to get out of those wet clothes," he said, zipping open the bag he'd purchased earlier. He'd tossed in the video camera and compass he kept in his truck, some more clothes he'd picked up at Target. "Gotta T-shirt in here you can wear. Couple of pairs of new boxers—not pretty, I know, but maybe one of 'em will fit. Looks like there's face-washing stuff on the counter." He glanced at her soggy shoes. "Want me to go downstairs and buy you some sandals or something at the gift shop?"

"They'll dry out. Probably ruined, but I can still wear them home."

He pulled out a pair of jeans and a T-shirt for himself. "I'll call room service. Steak and baked potato?"

She shook her head. "It's gonna be a long night, and heavy food will make me sleepy. I'll have a strawberry shake. Salad. No dressing, just lemon. If they ask if I want whipped cream on the shake, say yes."

Deciding not to ponder the conflicting logic in that order, he headed down the hall to a bedroom, turned on the light. The room boasted a king-size bed with an ornate wooden headboard, lush carpeting, a max-size flat-panel TV screen and a sitting area with a small bar. Hell, *he'd* haunt this place.

Through the sliding glass doors on the far side of the room, he watched the storm clouds unleash tor-rents of rain. Lightning zigzagged blue across the sky, followed seconds later by bellowing thunder.

After changing into dry clothes, he called room service. As he hung up the phone, Val walked into the room.

She'd blow-dried her hair, which hung loose. The white T-shirt and roomy white cotton boxers hinted at her curves. Her freshly scrubbed face was shiny and pink. He doubted many women could be this pared down and still look sexy.

He'd been distracted by the storm and flooding streets while driving over, but now that they were alone, in a bedroom, his libido came back full force. He craved her, wanted to make love to her so badly it hurt. He'd damn near lost it earlier today watching her on the surveillance cam applying that red lipstick over her luscious lips. And the way she'd kissed him back at the club he knew she desired him, too, but... she'd still pulled away the other night.

She wouldn't have done that unless she had con-

flicted feelings about him. Even he knew that being
hot over someone could be a world apart from caring
deeply about them.

Never thought he'd be in this position: ready to
give his heart to someone who seemed to be holding back hers.

Val ruffled her hands through her hair. "When will
supper be here?"

"They said forty minutes."

Outside, lightning crackled and hissed.

"Oh, my, reminds me of hurricane season back
home," she said, crossing to the glass doors. "Did
you see that big ol' porch? You could hold a party
out there!"

"I imagine Frank did. It wraps all the way around
the penthouse."

As thunder boomed, her eyes widened and she
turned back to the window. "Glory be," she said, "it's
like one of those scary movies where people are stuck
in a haunted mansion and there's a wild storm outside."

"Except they didn't have room service."

"Or a gift shop, tattoo parlor, casino and theater
downstairs. Did you see the Four Franks is playing
in the theater here?"

"Saw the poster in the lobby. Hard to imagine four
Frank Sinatra impersonators on the same stage."

"And one's a woman!"

"Sure Frank would've loved that."

"F'true." She laughed. "Especially as he was all macho like you."

Was that what was holding her back? Was he too tough, too hell-bent to prove his manhood?

"Except I hate parties," he said.

"And you don't play the ladies." Obviously seeing his perplexed look, she added, "I mean, that's my impression, but it's none of my business." She blew out a breath, dug her toes into the rug. "'Fraid my mouth left the station before my brain took a seat."

"I'm a one-woman man, Val."

He'd never said that before to a woman. Hadn't even thought that way with anyone else. But now that she'd heard it, he hoped she took it to heart. He couldn't make his intentions plainer.

She held his gaze for a moment, then started ambling away from the window.

"Before the food gets here," she said, "I suggest we set up the equipment, go over some ghost-hunting strategy. I know you prefer to say evidence gathering, not ghost hunting, but tonight I'd sure find it easier to just say both, not worry about—"

"Ghost hunting is fine," he said brusquely.

She nodded. "Good. I made notes on equipment, ghost-hunting tips, other stuff...maybe we can meet in the living room, go over our plan?"

"How about we make *you* the lead investigator on this case," he said, standing. "You call the shots, I'll take directions."

She gave him a look of utter incredulity. "Me, the lead investigator?"

"Why not? You've done the research, compiled most of the equipment."

"*I'm* to tell *you* what to do?"

"Think I can't take instructions from a woman?"

She backed up a step, a funny look on her face. "I'd prefer not to answer that."

"It might surprise you, *woman,* but I happen to believe that no person, no matter what their gender, has a greater right to power. Now if you'll excuse me, I'm going out to the living room to *help* strategize this *ghost-hunting* case."

As he headed toward the hall, he heard Val mutter, "Well, slap me with bread and call me a sandwich."

CHAPTER SIXTEEN

A SHORT WHILE later, they sat in the living room, adjacent to a separate dining room and bar area, both rooms decorated with sumptuous carpeting, sparkling chandeliers, high-end furniture. Off the living room was a second bedroom and a black-marbled bathroom with another oversize whirlpool tub.

Two sides of the living room were sliding-glass doors that opened onto the wraparound patio. Through the gray clouds and lashing rains, the bright lights of the Strip were reduced to hazy smudges of color.

They sat next to each other on a leather couch, their equipment laid out on the walnut coffee table.

"These are my notes about ghost hunting," Val said, picking up a piece of paper. "The most important tip is that we stay together at all times, to validate any witnessed activity and ensure team members' safety. Also, many researchers believe ghosts communicate on wavelengths outside of human hearing, but digital recorders can pick up those wavelengths. Because they also recommend motion detectors, I thought I'd leave my smartphone, with the motion detector app running, in this room where people have reported hearing and seeing Frank's cocktail parties."

"All right if I keep my phone with me?"

Surging winds rattled the glass. A bright flash of lightning popped, turning the sky neon-blue.

"F'sure," she whispered, glancing outside. She looked back at her list. "Let's see…where's your compass?"

He patted his T-shirt pocket. "Here."

"It's supposed to be good for picking up any magnetic or electrical stimulus out of the ordinary. And here's another tip. Do not take chances with things you don't understand."

"Or maybe what a person *assumes* they understand is actually wrong."

"Yes, that could be true, too, but what they mean is if you're confused about a situation, don't take a risk."

"But sometimes, Val, taking a risk is worth it. You need to trust your instincts."

She stared at him for a moment. "For a man who just said he was ready to take instruction from a woman, you sure seem to be fighting it."

"Not fighting it, just making observations. Go ahead."

"Not quite sure what this means, but several ghost hunters mentioned it. If you need to calm spirits, pour lots of water."

"I'd think Frank would want us to pour him a big whiskey on the rocks."

"If I were to actually see a ghost, I'd want a big ol' triple whiskey on the rocks!"

A crack of lightning streaked through the atmosphere, illuminating the ominous clouds, before the sky closed up again.

She raised her eyebrows. "Although a few more of those well-timed responses could make me a believer." After a beat, she said softly, "Actually, I believe in heaven, but to tell you the truth, I'm afraid not to. I need to trust that Nanny's watching over me, waiting for me." She gave a small shrug. "But what I'd give for a sign."

With a sigh, she returned to their task. "Okay, let's review our equipment. Which we're keeping to bare bones as this will be our only ghost-hunting investigation." She ran her finger down the page. "Got notepads and pens. Flashlights. I brought that big ol' candle and matches. You brought your video camera. Oh, here's a suggestion. We should walk around with the video camera and ask questions like, 'Is anybody here? Would you like to tell us anything?'" She wrinkled her nose. "I dunno. Seems kinda corny."

"Two thousand, five hundred dollars."

"You hold the camera, I'll ask the questions."

A loud creaking sound from the other room made her jump. "What was that?" She looked anxiously toward the second bedroom.

He stared at her hand gripping his arm, liked the feel of her skin against his. Maybe they should take on more ghost-hunting cases.

"Just the wind," he said, putting a protective hand on hers. "Don't forget this hotel is over fifty years old.

In this kind of weather, we'll hear all kinds of noises. I'll go check, though."

"I'm going with you. Remember, we can't be apart."

He smiled to himself. Yeah, they should definitely accept more of these cases.

She picked up the video camera. "Let's take footage."

When they got to the room, he turned on the lights.

"Looks like that far window is cracked open. I'll take video of it." As he pointed the camera and began filming, he documented the situation. "At approximately seven p.m., we heard a noise, like a thud, from this room. Entering, we saw the far window slightly open." He moved forward, zooming in on the window. "Apparently a light gust of wind blew over this silk flower arrangement." He turned and filmed the artificial flowers.

He turned off the camera. "I think we solved this mystery."

As he closed the window, she set the arrangement back on the dresser.

Hearing a loud knocking, Val jumped. "Did you hear that?"

"Unless it's a ghost we accidentally locked outside the suite, I believe it's room service."

"Very funny." She hesitated. "I don't want the delivery person to see me dressed like this."

"But we're supposed to never be apart," he said, putting on his best straight face.

"We'll start doing that after supper."

"You're the boss," he said, heading to the door.

As they laid out their meals on the polished wood dining table underneath a large, sparkling chandelier, Val thought how different Drake had been tonight. Sometimes she was certain she'd angered him, then other times it seemed as though he was trying desperately to please her. And insisting she be the lead investigator, well, would wonders never cease.

At first, they ate quietly, watching the storm outside the windows. Halfway through his burrito, Drake began explaining the twin swap this afternoon. She listened, occasionally asking questions.

"Let me get this straight," she said, setting down her fork. "After figuring out one of Marta's stops was at Body Double, you checked the online state business records and learned Yuri was a new shareholder at the strip club. Checking further, you found documents showing he'd also recently eliminated Braxton's shares in Topaz."

"Correct."

"And after calling Body Double and learning Yuri was there most afternoons, you called Braxton and told him about his now zero shares."

"Right." Drake took a drink of his soda, swallowed. "That's when he confided that he was sick of Yuri's dirty tricks and he was ready to walk. Said he'd stayed at Topaz these past few years because Yuri had blackmailed him. Something about a photo showing Brax talking to a guy who was later found murdered, and 'witnesses'—more like Yuri's buddies—who would testify that Braxton had threatened him. He didn't want to be railroaded into prison, so he stayed put."

"But after hearing Yuri wiped out his shares, he's ready to face the accusations."

"If the DNA from the fence and cigarettes are a match, he has nothing to face." He thought for a moment. "My mother is still angry about Braxton's past problems, but I believe he sincerely wants to clean up his life. Then the two of them can have a relationship again."

She studied the rugged lines in Drake's face, thought how he'd struggled with gambling, finally turning to his family for help. Thought how Braxton, too, had struggled alone, and now he needed his family's help.

"Everybody deserves a chance," Val said, repeating Grams's words.

"Absolutely. I've asked him to stay put at Topaz, carry on with business as usual, until we hear the results of the DNA tests. Don't want to make Yuri suspicious that we're closing in. Brax is on board, although he's not happy about getting a buzz cut. But Yuri last saw 'Braxton' with one, so my brother's getting shorn before going to work tomorrow."

She sipped her strawberry shake, thinking about that for a moment.

"But…didn't you risk raising his suspicions when you pretended to be Braxton?"

"Did it all the time as kids, figured I could pull it off. I wanted access to Yuri's inner office, was hoping for a chance to look through his files. Because of my research, I've learned a lot about Yuri's corporate holdings, knew what information to look for. Things Brax doesn't know. Got a few minutes alone in that office, but didn't find anything. Although I picked up more cigarette butts and the cup Yuri drank from." He grinned. "Just in case Tony has a yen to run more DNA tests."

Outside the winds and rains lashed at the windows. Thunder growled across the darkening skies.

She stared for a moment out the window before meeting his eyes again. "I still don't understand…you could have told me it was you."

He put down his fork. "Val, I was afraid if I told you it was me, you might accidentally let it slip. Not necessarily saying it in words, but maybe with a look. A gesture. I regret hurting you more than you'll ever know, but I couldn't chance Yuri picking up on a stray signal and figuring out who I was. He would have destroyed us. Brax, too." He stared at her for a long moment. "You're my partner. I'll never let you down again."

In the following seconds, Val inspected the worry on his face. His lips were compressed into a tight line, the muscle in his jaw clenched. His eyes were shiny, like glassy volcanic rock.

The knot of hurt she'd been holding inside unraveled as a seeping warmth filled her every cell.

"Your intention was to protect us," she said softly, "That's what matters."

Hearing her words, she realized they were to herself, too. She'd blamed herself for years about abandoning Nanny, leaving her to die, but her intention had been to save her grandmother. She'd let self-blame stand like a wall between herself and the world all these years.

It was time to let it go. Time to finally forgive herself.

She smiled at Drake, ready to be his partner again. "I know you and Tony are working the DNA angle, but I have another idea how to nab Yuri."

He raised a questioning eyebrow.

"What if I call him tomorrow, tell him I have those documents he wanted, which he can pick up at Diamond Investigations. When he's there, I talk about the data he asked for, ask questions…and that handy-dandy surveillance camera records everything he says, including accepting the papers."

He gave her an approving nod. "Very good. However, considering the illegal activity he's asking you do for him, he probably won't come inside the agency. Private investigators and surveillance equipment go together like vodka and Russians. Let's brainstorm a backup plan."

AFTER DISCUSSING AN alternative plan, they set up their equipment for the evening's investigations. Afterward, they walked around the suite, Drake taking video while Val asked if anybody was there and would they like to talk. They continually checked the compass for signs of electromagnetic activity. There were none.

At one point, they both heard a distant tune, a man singing. So faint they had to strain to hear it.

"The Four Franks," Val said.

"But we're on the twenty-ninth floor. Theater's at ground level."

"Did you see the ceiling speakers in the hallway? The hotel occasionally broadcasts songs from the show throughout the casino and hotel. Read about it online."

From nine to ten, the hours the ghostly cocktail party was supposed to take place, Val and Drake sat on the living room couch, monitoring their equipment. No ghostly clinking glasses, no phantom party laughter. Just the outside winds howling and rain battering the windows.

Val suddenly stilled, her eyes wide. "Did you hear that?"

"Beep means I got a voice message." He retrieved his phone from his pocket, punched a button and listened.

"It's Mom," he said, concerned. "Somebody kept ringing the doorbell, so she checked the surveillance monitor, saw a strange man." He punched the keypad. "I'm calling her back."

Val's insides chilled. "Yuri?"

"He'd be crazy to drive in this weather, but then, he's crazy."

Lightning popped, igniting the sky an eerie white-blue.

"Ma, Drake. He still there?" He listened intently. "How long has this been going on?" Pause. "We're on surveillance. Yes, I will." He ended the call.

"What?" Val asked.

A smile teased his lips. "Seems Grams has a boyfriend. Lives down the block. Got worried about her during the storm, dropped by to check on her."

"Why hasn't she mentioned him?"

"She told Mom they just started dating." He slapped the back of his hand on his forehead. "*That's* why Li'l Bit said, 'It's about love, man.' He knew she had a boyfriend."

"Sounds like she hasn't been visiting the senior center at night."

"Got that right. By the way, Mom says hi, asked if next Saturday is good to make gumbo."

"It's a date."

They sat in silence for a while, listening to the splattering rain. Occasionally the room creaked, or a window clattered softly.

Slam.

With a shriek, Val fell against Drake.

"Door shut," he murmured.

"No shit, Sherlock."

"Wind."

"Down the hallway?"

"Let's investigate."

"Can't wait," she muttered. "I'm also bringing the candle and matches." She could sense his question. "Ghosts can drain equipment energy. The lead investigator has spoken."

As they walked down the hall, Val whispered, "Bedroom door is open."

"But the bathroom door is closed."

"Maybe we closed it?"

"It was open when we walked past it earlier." He put his hand on the knob. "Let's go inside."

They turned on the lights and looked around the bathroom.

"Everything's as we left it," said Drake.

Val crossed to the tub and turned on the water. Catching his questioning look, she explained, "I'm calming the spirits."

"It's an old building. Could be the building settling, or the air-conditioning unit might have kicked in…"

"Or it really could be…ghosts…" She wheezed in a breath. "I don't think…I'm coping…all that well."

He moved forward, grabbed her by the shoulders. "Val, you okay?"

With a half nod, she sank against him. He wrapped his arms around her, pulled her close. His chin nestled against her soft, coconut-scented hair.

"It's been a long day," he murmured. "You need to rest."

He felt more than heard the single-word response—

no—muffled against his chest. He had to smile. Die-hard Val, trouper to the end.

"A short break, then." He looked at the filling tub. "Maybe a hot bath."

She pulled back her head and looked up at him with big, moist brown eyes. "Only if you take it with me," she whispered.

He cupped her chin. Her skin felt like satin. "Are you sure?"

She blinked. "About wanting this?"

"More than that."

"Respecting you afterward?"

He half smiled. "Are you…over your conflicted feelings about me?"

"Like you're Mr. Uncomplicated."

He sighed, tracing the delicate curve of her cheek, his fingers threading into her silky hair. "I want…" The ache inside was almost debilitating. "More than… one night."

She pressed closer and whispered, "Me, too."

"Hold that thought. Let me check our bath." As he adjusted the water temperature, the lights went off.

"I did that." Val set the lighted candle on the far edge of the tub. "Also locked the door. Just made me feel better."

He straightened and faced her. The flickering light cast a golden haze in the room. His chest filled with an unbearable ache as he watched how the light played with her hair, shimmered down the graceful sweep of her neck, glossed her elegant bare arms.

Val's hair, eyes, skin had stolen every fragment of light in the room. What she hadn't robbed seemed to linger around her, hovering like an aura.

"C'mere, beautiful."

With a slow smile, she moved closer.

He cupped her face in his hands, feeling as though he stood on the edge of a hundred-foot cliff with the ground crumbling beneath his feet.

He had never been more eager to fall.

"You're like the air I breathe," he murmured, "with me all the time, tormenting my thoughts, stealing my sleep."

Just before his mouth met hers, he felt her sigh release on his lips. Before, his kiss had been rough, demanding. This time he wanted to do it right. Savor the sensation of his lips on hers, explore this sweet mouth made for love.

He nuzzled her cheek, trailing his lips across her silky skin to the corner of her mouth. Brushing a light kiss there, he murmured, "Let me inside, Val."

She opened her mouth, and he played his tongue along the sensitive inside of her lip, tasting strawberries and lemon. Anchoring her head with his hands, he tangled his tongue with hers in erotic play, then slowly probed deeper into the moist warmth until he filled her mouth, his groin tightening when she responded with a soft, needy groan.

When he pulled back, she stood there, gulping air.

"We have on…" She heaved a breath. "Way too many clothes."

It was as if a starting gun went off.

As she reached for the waistband of his pants, he grappled for the hem of her T-shirt. When she popped the button of his jeans, he bunched the thin cotton material in his fist, only to lose his grip when he felt her hands on the outside of his groin, wrestling with the zipper. Managing the intricacies of what went where required too much thinking.

Driven by hunger, impatient with need, he grabbed fistfuls of the T-shirt, and with a guttural cry, ripped it off her.

"Lord have mercy," she whispered shakily, her arms dangling at her sides.

He yanked off his shirt, tugged down his zipper and hauled off his jeans, shoving them aside. "Turn around," he growled.

VAL FACED HER reflection in the mirror behind the sinks. In the soft candlelight, she eyed her pink satin bra and the white cotton boxers that hung low on her hips. Not exactly the sexy outfit she would have liked to wear their first time, but it would soon be off anyway.

He muttered a curse as he fumbled with the back of her bra. "Where's the…"

"In front." As she undid the fastening between the cups, he slid his hands around to her mounds and kneaded them. The clasp released and he gently peeled off the bra. His eyes glinted like a cat's as he stood behind her, admiring her naked breasts.

"Beautiful," he whispered huskily, his fingers slowly circling her puckering nipples.

She leaned her head against him, lost in the sensations of his masculine scent, the roughened pads of his fingertips, the cushion of his hairy chest against her back.

Through the haze of her arousal, she became aware of a ceaseless, rushing sound. Water.

"Hot tub," she rasped.

"Got it under control, baby," he murmured in the curve of her neck, his low-throttled tone sending goose bumps skittering across her skin. "Not even half-full."

Unlike how she felt, full nearly to bursting with white-heat desire and a frustration so painfully exquisite it'd be a miracle if she didn't liquefy. Aching, greedy, she tugged blindly on the boxers as a needy moan escaped her throat.

"Let me help," he murmured, snaking his fingers into the waistband, yanking them down. Crouching before her, he pressed a kiss on her triangle before pulling the boxers the rest of the way down and helping her step out of them.

He stood, giving her body a once-over. "I've died and gone to heaven."

"I wouldn't say that here," she teased, "just in case."

He grinned. "Don't move."

She watched his reflection in the mirrors behind the tub as he spread a soft towel on the marble counter. Behind it he stacked several more towels. Then he stepped in front of her, and in one smooth movement, he lifted her effortlessly, setting her gently on the flattened towel.

Crossing back to the tub, he turned off the faucets, then reached down to his discarded jeans. A moment later, he removed his boxers and kicked them aside.

In the hazy light, she admired the dark carpet of hair on his chest, the lines of his strong, muscled body. Dropping her gaze, she paused *there*. This was one girl who wouldn't have to lie and say size didn't matter.

He ripped open the wrapper and rolled a condom down his shaft. "I could say I always carry one," he murmured, "but the truth is, only for the past few days."

His gaze dropped to her breasts. Fondling and kneading one, he lowered his head and suckled its sister. She clung to his sweat-slicked shoulders, whimpering as sensations ripped through her, howling for completion.

Standing upright, he cupped her buttocks and pulled her closer, wrapping her legs around his hips. Leaning forward, he bunched the fluffy towels behind her for support.

"Comfortable?" he murmured.

"Yes…yes…"

His eyes boring into hers, he drew his hand slowly down her stomach, over her abdomen, down to her cleft. He slid a finger gently through her folds.

"Show me," he murmured.

She tilted her pelvis slightly, guiding his touch. "There," she murmured. His touch tormented her, drove her higher, until it was almost more than she could stand.

"Please," she begged, reaching for him, "now."

Raw need shuddered in her throat as he entered her, her fingers sinking into his flesh, holding on as he rocked her, every thrust pushing her closer to the edge, tightening every wanton, pent-up, throbbing need into a white-hot ball of lust…

Arching her back, a moan escaped her throat, escalating into a cry as wave after wave of release convulsed her body.

Fighting for breath, he gripped her buttocks as he continued thrusting, gently, rhythmically…his gray eyes dazed with passion until, with one last deliberate deep thrust, her name emerged from his throat in a low, guttural growl.

Drake sank onto the cool marble floor into a cross-legged sit, easing Val's body into his arms, where he cradled her, occasionally planting light kisses on her face, her shoulder, her hair. They sat that way for a while, not speaking, their bodies meshed together as one.

Two people who had finally found their refuge.

A SHORT WHILE later, they were in the water, Val cradled in Drake's arms.

"So, Aqua Man," she murmured, having just heard the story of his nickname, "did you fulfill your promise to your dad and learn how to swim?"

"Took some lessons, but I've never put my skills to the test."

"I used to love to swim, but after that day in Katrina, I never swam again. Sometimes I still dream I'm standing in front of dark waves, too paralyzed to move." She shuddered. "Onto better thoughts. You said you made two other promises to your father."

"To take care of the family. To stop gambling. Hasn't always been easy trying to watch out for Braxton, but never gambling again is rock solid. Keeps me whole." He listened for a moment. "Hear that?"

Faint strains of music played. A man warbled a tune.

"The Four Franks again," Val said.

As they watched the flickering candle, they listened to a man sing about stealing a love song from the birds to express his feelings to a woman.

Drake thought how, not so long ago, he'd fought the first signs of his vulnerability to Val. But his fate had been sealed at the first barrage of fire. There was no way he could have withstood the bombardment.

"Dollar for your thoughts?" Val asked.

"Sometimes," Drake murmured, tugging her closer, "surrender is unavoidable."

BY LATE MORNING the following day, the storms had broken and the sun was shining again. After Drake dropped Val off at her Toyota, she headed home, showered, put on her makeup and changed into a light gray halter dress.

By one that afternoon, she was back at Diamond In-vestigations, where she and Drake reviewed the video footage they had taken at the Sinatra suite, burned it onto a CD and wrote their investigation report. Next, they compiled a set of bogus documents that detailed asset resources for five of Jayne's wealthy, and very fake, clients.

Afterward, Val called Suzanne Doyle and left a message that she'd drop off the report and CD later in the day. Her second call was to Yuri, informing him she had the documents he requested. He said he'd be by around four. After she hung up, she looked up at the surveillance camera.

"It's on."

AT QUARTER TO four, the agency phone jangled. For a change, the irritating ring didn't give Val a start.

"Diamond Investigations," she answered.

"This is Jayne."

"Jayne…how are you?"

"Holding my own." Pause. "A former client dropped by the agency this morning, said the front door was locked, no lights on inside. Is everything all right?"

She didn't sound as tired as the last time they spoke, which was a good sign. Nevertheless, Val decided to not share everything that was going on, just to keep it simple. The last thing her boss needed right now was more stress and worry.

"I came in late after working an all-night surveil-lance with Drake."

"Sounds like you two are getting along."

"Yes."

"Excellent." Pause. "I also called to tell you that…" Her voice softened. "You remind me of myself when I was younger. Ambitious, eager, a risk taker. I have counseled you many times that you cannot always do things your way, but I wanted you to know before…" She paused. "Wanted you to know," she repeated, her voice turning solemn, "if you trust your choice, even if others disagree, taking a risk is sometimes the only way to win."

CLOSE TO FOUR, Val's cell phone rang. Yuri's number displayed on the caller ID.

She took a calming breath. "Hello?"

"I am outside, parked at the curb. Bring papers to me."

"I thought you would come inside," she said pleasantly.

"I like outside."

Just as Drake had guessed, Yuri did not want to conduct business inside the agency.

"I'll be right there," she said, looking at the surveillance camera.

She picked up the manila envelope on her desk, filled with the phony documents she and Drake had prepared, slipped on her sunglasses and headed outside.

As she approached the Mercedes, the tinted driver's window rolled down.

"Hello, Yuri," she said in her best cheerful voice, stopping at the side of the car.

He wore an embroidered blue short-sleeve shirt, the corner of a white handkerchief sticking out of the pocket, and slacks. Vadim sat in the passenger seat, wearing another leisure suit, typing on an iPad. The car was running, air-conditioning on high, and the radio played.

He accepted the envelope. Saying something in Russian, he handed it to Vadim, who nodded.

Yuri turned back to Val, giving her a smile that reminded her of a lizard. When he reached down, she froze, wondering if he had a gun. Instead, he handed her a bottle of Russian vodka.

"Kährs."

"Kährs," she said, forcing a smile.

The tinted window rolled back up.

Moments later, she sat at her desk. "Everything went as planned," she said to the surveillance camera.

She pulled off her sunglasses and removed one of its temple arms with the built-in video-recording device. "Except I couldn't record the conversation because not only did he keep the air conditioner running the whole time, he played music on the radio."

The connecting door clicked open. She heard Hearsay's skittering claws and Drake's footsteps heading down the hall. A moment later, he stood next to her desk. She had the fleeting thought that a man dressed in jeans and a simple white T-shirt didn't have a right to look so good.

Hearsay curled up at her feet and slipped his nose beneath a foreleg.

"All that work for nothing," she murmured.

Drake gave a half shrug. "Next time, we'll try something different."

"Like?"

"We'll brainstorm options."

"Want to do that now?"

"No," he said, his brow creasing with worry. He opened his arms. "C'mere."

She stood, sank into his embrace, her heart thudding, steeling herself for bad news. Was he going to say last night was a mistake?

"I pulled some records," he said gently, stroking her back, "your biological mother…died twelve years ago, a few years after she left New Orleans. Seems she had been sick for a long time." He hugged her tight. "I'm sorry, Val."

It was as though someone turned a valve and her life force leaked out of her. She felt hollow, and in a strange way, lonelier than she'd ever been. Even after losing her nanny. For all the times she'd told herself she felt nothing for the woman who'd abandoned her as a child, the news saddened her.

"Didn't think I'd care," she whispered hoarsely, "but I do. How selfish of me to not think there were other reasons she stayed away…what did she die of? No, I'm not ready to hear. Did she…have a husband?"

"It appears there was a boyfriend."

"He was with her when she…?"

"Don't know."

"Now I'm nobody's child," she murmured.

He tightened his arms around her, cradling her head against his chest. "Maybe I'm rushing things, but you'll always have my family. You'll always have me."

She listened to his heartbeat, breathed in his familiar scent, remembering how last night after they'd made love she had felt refuge in their embrace. At this moment, she sensed something more profound in his arms.

The promise of a future.

CHAPTER SEVENTEEN

AFTER LOCKING THE front door to Diamond Investigations, Val joined Drake in his back office. He was tossing the pink ball to Hearsay, who would catch it in his mouth, then stand there and stare at Drake as though to say, "Now what?"

"You're supposed to return it to me!" Drake gave Val an exasperated look. "*I'm* the one fetching it back from him every time. Obviously I'm failing as a dog trainer."

Val smiled. "Or maybe he's training you."

"C'mon, buddy," Drake said, heading to his office door, "you've trained me enough for today.

He opened the door and Hearsay trotted outside, then stopped. Dropping the ball, he began barking loudly.

"Buddy," Drake said, stepping outside with Val, "what's up?"

They froze.

Yuri leaned against the pickup truck, pressing a folded white handkerchief on his shiny forehead. The black Mercedes blocked the parking space entrance, the sun glinting off its tinted windows.

"Vadim check information on his iPad and learn it

all *bullshit*." He jammed the handkerchief into a shirt pocket. "Bad names. Closed bank accounts. You think Yuri stupid?"

Hearsay growled.

Yuri glanced at him. "Hello, missing link. I remember Marta say dog at Diamond Investigations. I call her few minutes ago, ask to describe. Funny," he said, mocking great surprise, "it look *exactly* like dog I see at Drake's house! So Vadim and I visit Diamond Investigations, look around...and look where I find Drake's pickup."

"What do you want, Yuri?" Drake asked.

He pulled a sparkling diamond ring out of his pocket. "Very pretty family ring, Drake. Worth *zouzands*."

"I offered you twenty," Drake said calmly, holding tightly onto Val's hand.

"With interest, thirty."

"I don't have thirty."

Yuri shrugged, dropped the ring back into his pocket. "I have other deal for twenty thousand. Protection money for your girlfriend. Would be shame for pretty intern to get hurt."

"Don't threaten her," Drake snarled.

"Or what?"

"I'll kill you."

Yuri laughed. "For that, protection now cost twenty-*five* thousand. Tonight I host private party at Mandalay Bay wave pool. Bring money there, eight o'clock."

He started to walk away, stopped and turned. "One more thing. If you not show up with money at eight, Val no longer under protection."

As the Mercedes drove away, Val said, "Let's call the police."

Drake expelled a sharp breath, hating himself for bringing this danger into Val's life. "Police can't do anything. There's no evidence of his threat, just our word against his."

She gave him a wary look. "You can't give in to his demands, you know that, right?"

"This is between me and Yuri."

"Bull. I'm involved, too." She searched his face, her expression growing grim. "You're going to cash out the twenty thousand in your savings account, and somehow tag on another five, aren't you?"

What he really wanted to do was show up at Mandalay Bay, beat Yuri to a pulp and stuff him on a flight back to his mother country. But Yuri had friends, like Vadim, who'd only pick up where Yuri left off. So, yes, Drake's real plan was to cash out his savings and figure out how to get the rest, but he didn't want to discuss it with her.

"Let's go," he said, swiping his brow. "It's hot out here."

"No," she said, shaking her head vehemently, "let's go back inside the office where it's cool and call Tony. Maybe he has the rest of those DNA results by now, which you seem certain will point to Yuri, and you two can alert the authorities to arrest Yuri."

His taut nerves snapped. "Drop it, Val, it's none of your business."

VAL STARED INTO Drake's dark, foreboding eyes, not believing that this was happening. "This involves *both* of us, but it's none of my business? We're a team, remember? Partners. There has to be another way to handle Yuri!"

"I said *drop it.*"

She met his defiance with an unflinching gaze. "You're retreating into your I'll-handle-this-by-myself cave again. As though nobody has the right to stand with you. But I won't let you do this alone. I love you, damn it." She blinked back angry tears. "Let's go away. Move to another state, another country, where Yuri can never find us."

"That's implausible and you know it. My family's here. So is yours. As are our careers."

She threw her hands up into the air. "Then I'll move away. If I'm gone, there's no need to pay protection money."

He snorted something rude under his breath. "Be a refugee again? Haven't you been exiled enough for one lifetime?"

The words cut deep. But more than the words, his harsh, cold tone. As though they'd never shared a single intimate moment, never opened their hearts to each other.

Giving a low whistle to Hearsay, he yanked the handle on the passenger side of his pickup. The door creaked as he swung it open. "C'mon, buddy, get inside."

Hearsay scrambled into the truck, then sat on the seat, watching her as though saying, "You coming with us?"

Drake jerked his head, motioning for her to get inside the pickup.

She didn't move. Hot breezes rustled through the leaves.

"Val." He pointed at the front seat, "Get in."

"I'm not your dog," she said quietly.

The words had left her mouth before she'd realized it, but hearing them, it's exactly how she felt. He was treating her as though she were something he owned, who obeyed his dictates. She accepted his being her mentor, her temporary boss, but out here, at this moment, they were acting out their *personal* relationship.

Was this how a future with him would be? Had she been so blinded by her feelings for him, or by her intent to have her career, that she lost sight of who they really were?

He studied her, scathingly. "I'm a better man than that, and you know it."

"Maybe I don't know it."

A long silence drew out between them. She held herself in place, her insides roiling with fury and hurt. At the same time, a part of her wanted to coax him out of his mood, make him laugh at their silliness, admit how they needed to be a team and brainstorm a way out of this.

He slammed shut the passenger door and turned his body, the one that only last night had been pressed against hers, and strode around the pickup and got inside.

She watched as the engine growled to life and he backed out of the parking lot.

For a moment she just stood there, alone, thinking how quickly life could change. How people and homes and friends were there one moment, gone the next. How loved ones disappeared or died. The lesson for survivors was to learn how to redo their lives and hopefully find another welcoming home.

Fishing her keys from her pocket, she headed to Drake's back office door. She'd do a last check of the offices, then head out to her car and go home, figure out what to do next.

She spied the ball, bright and pink in the sun, and remembered Jayne saying it had been her ritual to always buy one to welcome her dog back home. She walked over and picked it up, wondering if Drake had ever guessed Val had bought it, not Jayne.

Inside Drake's office, she set the ball where Hearsay would see it the moment he bounded in the door.

At seven-thirty that night, Drake stood near the roulette table at the Mandalay Bay casino. He still wore his jeans and T-shirt, having spent the afternoon running around, calling people, trying to raise five grand.

Eddie, who'd hit it big at the horse races, loaned him seven hundred, Li'l Bit donated a hundred and Braxton left an envelope with five hundred in it with a note: "I got your back."

He'd called Tony, who didn't answer. When it rolled over to voice mail, Drake left a message asking Tony to call him when he got the DNA test results.

He watched the players scatter their bets among the numbers and colors. He could sense their excitement as the dealer closed the bids and the ball clattered around and around until it lost momentum, falling into the winning slot.

Two of the players whooped loudly, raising their fists.

It was like old times, being surrounded by the smell of cigarettes, the bustling crowds and the beeps, whirs and clicks of slot machines. Like old times wrestling with the tangled feelings of excitement and despair before he gambled.

He also wrestled with the miserable, tortured feelings he'd had since leaving Val this afternoon. He hadn't known how to defuse her anger. Hadn't had the sense to keep his mouth shut. So he'd closed off and split.

He missed her. Missed that lax drawl, the way emotions paraded across her face, even missed those funny purple streaks in her hair. Her idea to uproot their lives wasn't a solution—it was running away from a problem—but he hadn't taken the time to discuss it with her. Truth was, he'd been scared for her life, wanted to get moving, find the money, but in his urgency, he'd lost what mattered the most. Val.

Maybe he'd blown their relationship, but he wasn't going to fail at protecting her. He peeled off six one-hundred-dollar bills, shoved his wallet back into his jeans pocket. He needed three thousand, seven hundred dollars more to make twenty-five thousand. He hoped the old man forgave him for what he was about to do.

As he stepped toward the roulette table, someone gripped his arm. He stopped, looked down at the small hand, up the slender arm to the face that haunted his every thought.

Val wore a simple black dress, her sleek hair framing her face. It was all he could do to stare into those glistening brown eyes, amazed how his heart pounded just at the sight of her.

"Don't," she said, choking on the word.

"Bets are closing," called out the dealer.

He flinched. She held on.

"We can get through this," she said, sliding her hand into her pocket. She pulled out a wad of bills, put them into his hand. "A thousand cash from Marta's last visit, four hundred left over from her first." She shrugged. "If I hadn't bought that minifridge, nearly five."

He smiled. Couldn't help himself. "After what I raised, we have two thousand, three hundred to go."

"We," she repeated, her heart in her eyes, "that's

what this is about. The two of us. Let's go to Yuri, together, negotiate how to pay the rest."

"He doesn't make deals," Drake said coldly, "only enforces them."

"Eighteen red," called out the dealer at the roulette table.

"Yee-haw!" yelled a fiftysomething man wearing a Hawaiian shirt and a cowboy hat. "I just made me a mortgage payment!"

Drake lifted her hand off his arm, held it for a moment.

"If you go to that table," she said, her face hardening, "it's really over. For good."

He peered at her, so beautiful and strong, the ultimatum flashing in her eyes, but this was bigger than his problems. This was about saving her life. He released her hand.

"Maybe someday you'll realize how much I loved you."

He turned and headed to the gambling table.

ANGRY AND BROKEN, Val walked away, her legs carrying her as far as an empty seat in front of a slot machine before she let herself crumble.

Slumping into the chair, she smothered back the sob in her throat. Her nerves were raw, her heart torn and the man she loved was falling, falling into an abyss that would be his undoing. How insane, how crazy, that both of them were willing to lose dignity, their love, for a worthless, conniving lowlife.

She missed Drake already, ached with regret that after spending long days together, overcoming problems and baring their souls to each other, their final parting was tense and chilly. What a waste of their time together for them to return to being the same two people who'd met that first night at Dino's, caught up in self-justifications and personal agendas. But obviously they weren't those two people anymore, otherwise she wouldn't feel the misery of words left unsaid, the pain of two hearts ripped apart before their time.

For the next few minutes, she looked out at the crowd of people, thinking back to the Superdome. All those souls packed in a large room, all those stories of loss and pain. Yet she, and thousands of others, hadn't let the devastation prescribe the rest of their lives. If she simply gave in to Yuri's threat—and for that matter, Drake's foolhardy risk to save her—everything she'd overcome, all the lessons she'd learned, lost their meaning.

She straightened, swiped the tears off her cheeks, knowing there was only one thing to do.

EXITING THE CASINO, Drake walked into the stifling-hot summer night. In the hazy sky, the thin smile of the waxing crescent moon seemed to jeer at him.

He headed to the gated entrance to the wave pool, which had closed several hours ago to the public. Yuri had connections to throw a "private party" here. He gave his name to the stocky shadow, who insisted Drake hand over his phone before opening the gate.

In the flickering light from several tiki torches, a dozen or so people mingled. Over the buzz of conversations and clinking of glasses, he recognized a local radio station's jingle. Far in the background, dark waves rose and crashed on a sandy shore, as real as any Vegas magician's illusion.

Major hotels like the Mandalay had surveillance cameras installed on their property, but with only the torches for light, it was too dark for any cameras to capture footage of the party. And with the bouncer taking his phone, Drake was shit out of luck recording Yuri.

He heard a familiar laugh. Braxton with his new buzz cut stood next to Vadim and Yuri, the three of them laughing, drinks in their hands.

A slim woman in tight black jeans, heels and a sparkly top walked up to Yuri and handed him a drink. He took it, kissed her on the lips. She laughed, nuzzled his cheek, then patted his ass before sashaying away.

Drake's insides curdled. Sally. An item with *Yuri?*

Scenes flashed in his mind. Sally, telling him the hours she'd seen Yuri's car at Topaz. Of course, bogus information Yuri wanted her to feed to Drake. Sally asking Drake if he was going home, then picking up her phone. It sickened him to realize she must have called Yuri, who was probably also on his way to Drake's house, ready to torch it.

He'd once thought he hadn't picked up Sally's signals. Now he realized he'd been picking them up all along. She was a fraud, a snake, and deep down he had known to back off.

Unlike Val, whom he'd met and immediately distrusted. But his gut instincts had known better. She was the real deal, and deep down in his heart he had known to keep chasing her.

He didn't need a gut instinct to help him handle this next relationship, though.

Drake walked up to Yuri, Vadim and Braxton. Standing in front of his brother, he stared him square in the face. "You two-faced bastard."

Clapping Drake on the back, Yuri laughed. He smelled of booze, cigarette smoke and too much cologne. He shooed away Brax and Vadim.

"Hello, Drake," Yuri said, "care for drink?"

"No. Let's get this over with."

Even in the flickering light, Drake could see the greed on Yuri's face. "Straight to business. I like that."

"I have twenty-two thousand, seven hundred dollars."

"I tell you twenty-*five*." He belched.

"And I'm telling you twenty-two seven."

He swayed forward, snarling, "Nobody cheat Yuri Glazkov."

"I'll pay you the rest over the next month."

"No! You pay me *tonight!*" After fumbling in his shirt pocket, he held up the ring. "So sad, your father," he said, dripping false concern, "very sick when he give to me. Tell me ring have much family history."

"I'll pay the thirty in six months." He didn't know how, but somehow he'd do it.

"I give you *two* hours to pay twenty-five thousand protection money," he said darkly, "or girlfriend have unfortunate accident. As to ring…I teach you lesson for late payment."

He staggered away, lumbering toward the crashing surf of the wave pool, yelling in Russian.

Drake, balling his hands into fists, followed Yuri into the shadows beyond the torch flares. The Russian lurched to the edge of the dark swelling waters, and stopped. Screaming a curse, he drew back his arm and threw the ring far into the waves.

"Damn you!" Drake ran forward, staring at another looming dark wave. "It will be sucked into the wave-making machinery within minutes!"

"That's for being late with money." Yuri laughed.

Drake strode over to the Russian and slammed a fist into his gut. "And that's for Hearsay, you scumbag."

As the Russian doubled over, coughing, a woman cried out.

"No!" Val yelled, "We can't lose the ring!"

VAL HAD WALKED into the private party in time to see Yuri waving the ring at Drake, yelling threats. Terrified, she had followed the two of them to the wave pool. It had been too dark to see Yuri throw the ring, but after hearing Drake's shout, she didn't think twice about what to do.

"He won't destroy your family history," she cried, kicking off her shoes and tossing off her dress.

In her panties and bra, she ran across gritty sand, stumbling to a stop at the first jolt of cold water. For an instant she froze, watching a dark wall of water surge forward and crash, its icy spray burning her skin.

She'd chanced dark waters before, and she'd failed. *Taking a risk is sometimes the only way to win.*

A jolt of adrenaline shot through her, spurring her forward. She ran, stumbling as a wave slammed into her. Catching her balance, she lurched forward and dived into the wet gloom.

She'd swum in a wave pool years before, remembered the suction being strongest at the bottom. Kicking and stroking, she propelled herself downward in the black water, which pulsed with the muffled thumping of the wave-making pump. Touching the concrete bottom, she skimmed the surface with her fingertips, feeling, searching.

Long seconds passed as she felt along the floor, her lungs burning, eyes stinging from the chlorine. She couldn't stay down here…she'd failed…

Her fingers touched something small and hard.

Kicking her feet, she thrust forward her hand, grappling for a hold.

Just as she plucked it, strong arms yanked her up, up. As she soared through the black water, images filled her mind. A couple smiling. A bolt of blue. An owl circling a grave. Joy resonated through her.

Bursting through the surface of the water, she

gasped for air, clutching the ring. Drake held her tight as he slogged through the water, waves crashing around them.

"I...have the..."

Her happiness turned to terror as she saw the shadowy shapes moving toward the pool.

HEAVING BREATHS, DRAKE, wearing his boxers and T-shirt, trudged out of the water with Val in his arms, staring at the people heading their way. Too dark to see more than their forms. Several carried flashlights. He lowered Val to her feet, picked up her dress and tossed it to her, then started tugging on his jeans.

"I have three things to say to you," Drake murmured. "One, I didn't gamble. Two, I was an asshole today and I'm sorry. Three, if we get out of this alive, will you marry me?"

"Las Vegas Police," a man yelled.

Followed by Braxton yelling, "Way to go, Aqua Man!"

"And I have three things to say to you," she muttered, adjusting her dress. "One, I think we're getting out of this alive. Two, yes! Three..."

"Aqua Man," Braxton said, walking up. He wrapped a towel around Val's shoulders.

"Couldn't you have found a reason for there to be more lights at the party?" Drake groused. "The hotel surveillance cameras are a bust."

"No need," rasped a familiar voice. Tony moved forward, holding a flashlight. "I gave Braxton that wireless recorder I told you about. He slipped it in Yuri's shirt pocket. Recorded him clear as a bell. Oh, and the rest of the DNA test results came back. I think Yuri needs to start saying his goodbyes, because he's going to prison for a long time."

Sputtering a laugh, Drake tugged Val close to him. "We did it, baby." He looked at Tony. "When did you become part of the sting?"

"Yuri's my suspect, too, my friend. Had a nice chat with the police today, learned about Braxton's call to them, told them to get me a seat at the table."

A police officer walked up. "Mr. Morgan, I have a few questions to ask."

"One minute, Officer," Tony cut in. "I'm starting my interview with him. Miss LeRoy is next." After the cop walked away, he said under his breath to Drake, "Figured you two needed a moment together." He glanced at Braxton. "Let's take a walk, homeboy."

Drake turned to Val, hugged her close. "Three?"

She took his hand and placed the ring in it.

"Unbelievable," he murmured. He cupped her face in his hands, planting a soft kiss on her lips.

"We'll give it to Grams for her birthday."

He picked up her hand and slid the ring on a finger. "She already told me she wants her future grand-daughter-in-law to wear it."

"And one day, we'll add our diamond, too." She paused. "Hear that? It's Frank Sinatra singing."

"Must be the radio station they were playing at the party. Nobody's turned it off yet."

"He's singing that she's too *marvelous for words*. It's that song! Hear that part about stealing a love song from the birds? That's the song we heard him singing in the penthouse. Do you think it was…?"

Holding her close, he looked up at the distant stars. "I think just because you can't touch something doesn't mean it's not real."

EPILOGUE

November, Las Vegas

VAL, DRAKE AND assorted others congregated in the plush office of lawyer Eddie "Bingo" Huttner, who sat behind his mahogany desk perusing a document with a gold seal. Tan and fit in a three-piece pin-striped suit, Eddie looked just like his picture on countless billboards across Vegas advertising the busy Kaufman & Huttner Law Firm.

Ten people sat on folding chairs in the office, Drake and Val at the back, holding hands.

"As you all are aware," Eddie explained, "Jayne Diamond revised her will in the weeks before her death, and I will now announce the bequests." Slipping on a pair of glasses, he began reading. "To her brother, Bradford Diamond, her Las Vegas home, her IRA and numerous family heirlooms. To the Clark County Humane Society, a cash gift of ten thousand dollars, contributed in Hearsay's name. To her protégée, Val LeRoy, she posthumously grants the Diamond Grade along with the Diamond Investigations office and attached living space on the condition that Miss LeRoy continues her mentorship with Drake Morgan, who may share and enjoy this space, as well. On the day of their marriage, which Miss LeRoy had informed Ms. Diamond will be this coming month, Drake will receive an equal interest as a joint tenant in the office and residential space." He paused, looked at Val. "There is a message directed to Val LeRoy solely, which I will only share with others, if given Miss LeRoy's permission."

Her chin trembling, Val nodded.

"Val, my wedding gift to you is the crystal figurine. Just as the birds symbolized my and Margaret's love for many years, may it represent your and Drake's love for the rest of your days."

TWENTY MINUTES LATER, Drake and Val walked hand in hand to their car in the law-firm parking lot. It was typical Las Vegas winter weather, warm and breezy.

"Ma invited us over for dinner tomorrow," Drake said. "She and Brax are cooking."

"Great. And don't forget Saturday is the grand opening of Jasmyn's new dance studio, *Je Rêve*. I was thinking of buying her a beret and an Edith Piaf CD to go with the Parisian decor of the studio."

Three months earlier, Dottie the Body had retired and invited Jaz, her star pupil, to take over her burlesque school. Jaz, using her background in dance, added tap and ballet lessons to the class schedule.

Val paused, watching a hearse as it drove down the street.

"Goodbye, Jayne," she whispered.

"Goodbye, old friend," Drake murmured.

Turning to Drake, Val lightly touched her tummy. "If it's a girl, I'd like her middle name to be Jayne. What do you think?"

He cupped her face in his hands and kissed her. "I think that sounds too marvelous for words."

* * * * *

REQUEST YOUR FREE BOOKS!
2 FREE WHOLESOME ROMANCE NOVELS IN LARGER PRINT
PLUS 2
FREE
MYSTERY GIFTS